John Buchan

THE COMPLETE SHORT STORIES

◆

Volume Three

John Buchan

THE COMPLETE SHORT STORIES

◆

Volume Three

Edited by

ANDREW LOWNIE

THISTLE PUBLISHING

First published in Great Britain in 1997 by
Thistle Publishing
122 Bedford Court Mansions
London WC1B 3AH

A CIP catalogue record for this book is available from the British Library

ISBN 0-9526756-1-7

Designed by Wendy Bann

Typeset by DP Photosetting, Aylesbury, Bucks

Printed and bound in England by Clays Limited, St Ives plc

Contents

Introduction by Andrew Lownie

A profile of John Buchan in the December 1912 issue of *The Bookman* described him as 'probably the best modern exponent of the short story' and noted how he had made 'the short story what a cameo might be when it is cut by the hand of a master', but it continued: 'Mr John Buchan has now attained his literary majority; we still wait for the great work; the more ambitious flight of his matured imagination.' That great work was about to come, but its publication, and then those of a series of sequels, meant the eclipse of his reputation as a short story writer, a position from which he has never completely recovered.

Buchan's first attempt at a thriller, *The Power House* (1916), was serialised in *Blackwood's Magazine* in December 1913 and nine months later he finished his best-known book, *The Thirty-Nine Steps* (1915), in which Richard Hannay attempts to outwit a German spy-ring by fleeing across the Scottish moors. It was followed by *The Power House*, *Greenmantle* (1916) and *Mr Standfast* (1919). Buchan called *The Thirty-Nine Steps* a 'romance where the incidents defy the probabilities and march just inside the borders of the possible'. It is a description which might equally well be applied to the stories in this third and final volume of his stories, which cover the period from just before the outbreak of the First World War to Buchan's death in 1940.

At the outbreak of war Buchan had attempted to enlist but was rejected on grounds of his age and health. Instead he became a war correspondent, one of only five journalists to be attached to the British army on the Western Front. His reporting of the Battle of Ypres directly inspired the story 'The King of Ypres', while his further experiences as a staff officer at Haig's GHQ and then running a propaganda organisation, the Department of Information, provided material for four further stories – 'The Shut Door', 'The Loathly Opposite', *'Tendebant Manus'* and 'Dr Lartius'. Indeed the shadow of the war hangs over several other stories as the returning soldiers attempt to come to terms with civilian life.

Physically and mentally drained by his time as a wartime civil servant, and with a young family to bring up, Buchan decided to move to the country. It was one of these house-hunting trips which supposedly inspired the story 'Fullcircle'. In 1920 he bought Elsfield Manor, a seventeenth-century house with associations with Dr Johnson situated four miles outside Oxford; he was to live there until his departure to Canada as Governor-General in 1935, and it was there he would write the succession of thrillers, historical novels and biographies that would establish his reputation as one of the most successful British writers of the inter-war period.

It may appear surprising, given that success, that nine of the stories in this volume were never included in the English editions of any of Buchan's own short story collections and therefore remain largely unknown, even to Buchan enthusiasts. They are 'Basilissa', 'The King of Ypres', 'Watches of the Night', 'The Shut Door', 'Nemesis', 'The Post', 'The Magic Walking Stick', 'The Strange Adventure of Mr Andrew Hawthorn' and 'Ho! The Merry Masons'; the other twelve come from Buchan's 1928 short story collection, *The Runagates Club*. This was his only post-First World War volume of stories and differs from the earlier collections in not being based on a single theme. Indeed one of their strengths, as the reviewer in *The Times Literary Supplement* noted, is that they 'are pleasingly diverse in subject, incident and treatment'. They range from Richard Hannay's eerie tale set in the Transvaal and the Duke of Burminster's comic adventure in the Scottish Borders to Edward Leithen's tangle with South American revolutionaries in central London and Oliver Pugh's journey of discovery in 'the Sachischen Sweitz'.

Buchan attempted to impose a structure on the collection by creating a dining club, The Thursday Club, at which one of the fifteen members told a story each month. It was these stories that were brought together in book form. According to Buchan, The Thursday Club had been 'founded just after the close of the War by a few people who had been leading queer lives and wanted to keep together ... The War had flattened out groves and set every man adventuring so the lawyer and the financier were also soldiers; the Greek scholar had captained a Bedawin tribe; the traveller had dabbled in secret service; the journalist had commanded a battalion; the historian had been mate on a novel kind of tramp; the ornithologist had watched more perilous things than birds; the politician had handled a rougher humanity than an English electorate.'

The Thursday Club may have been based on The Club, a dining society founded by Dr Johnson and still active today, which in Buchan's time met fortnightly on Tuesday evenings while Parliament was in session, at the Café Royal. Buchan had been elected in 1918 and other influential members included the Archbishop of Canterbury, King George V's Private Secretary Lord Stamfordham, Lord Curzon, Stanley Baldwin, G.M. Trevelyan, Lord Haldane, Henry Newbolt, H.A.L. Fisher and Rudyard Kipling.

While some of the characters who tell their stories, such as Francis Martendale, only feature once in the Buchan oeuvre, others were already Buchan favourites; these include Richard Hannay, Edward Leithen and Sir Arthur Warcliff, whose son had been one of the kidnap victims in *The Three Hostages* (1924). Indeed, The Thursday Club had itself figured in *The Three Hostages*, where membership had been confined to twenty members, including Sandy Arbuthnot and the villain of the book, Dominick Medina.

In the past Buchan had tended to publish stories in magazines and then collect them in book form. After the First World War the reverse seems to have happened. He wrote stories which were then collected in book form, and sold as magazine extract rights to coincide with book publication. Many of them first appeared in this form in *Pall Mall Magazine*, a monthly founded in 1893 and absorbed by *Nash's* in September 1914, which had serialised R.L. Stevenson's posthumous *St Ives* and whose contributors included Conan Doyle, Rudyard Kipling, Ford Madox Ford, G.K. Chesterton, P.G. Wodehouse and George Bernard Shaw. Another regular outlet was *Argosy*, a magazine with equally distinguished writers. For example, Buchan's 'Sing a Song of Sixpence' appeared in a September 1933 issue alongside stories from Hugh Walpole, Luigi Pirandello, Emile Zola and Alphonse Daudet. Given that many of his stories were sold several times over both in this country and abroad and subsequently included in anthologies, his income from his short stories alone must have been quite considerable.

Certain, rather obvious, criteria have been followed in making the selection for this volume, one of which is that only original short stories should be included. Buchan was constantly being asked to contribute stories to magazines, and one solution, when a story was not ready, was to draw on a novel currently in production. For example, his story 'Other Gods', which appeared in the Eton College magazine *Masquerade* for the Fourth of June 1933, alongside contributions from Noël Coward, Harold Nicolson and J.M. Barrie, is in fact the first chapter of *The Island of Sheep* (1936), while 'The Kingmaker', an extract from *The House of Four Winds* (1935), appeared in *Chamber's Journal* and several other magazines the autumn before book publication.

Nothing has been chosen from his novel *The Path of the King* (1921), a series of linked stories about the transmission of royal blood through various generations, although parts of it have often been anthologised. Two stories, for example, appeared in *A Century of Historical Stories* (1936), another in Dennis Wheatley's *A Century of Spy Stories* (1938) and yet another in the 1927 *Nelson Annual*. Parts of *The Gap in the Curtain* (1932), a novel about the nature of time which consists of several self-contained stories, have sometimes been extracted, but no part of it has been included here. Likewise I decided not to include Buchan's version of *Coriolanus*, one of six versions of Shakespeare stories published in book form in 1934 – another was written by Winston Churchill – because it was not a story from his own imagination. 'The Lusitania Waits' in Alfred Noyes' *Mystery Ships* (1916) is supposed to be by Buchan, but I could find no evidence of this and have not included it. A lyrical piece of travel writing from *The African Colony* (1903), 'Evening on the Veld', was included in a Blackwood anthology of *Travellers' Tales* but this is not reprinted here as it is non-fiction. The stories selected have appeared in different forms in magazines and books, and I have generally used the earliest and rarest versions.

As in the two previous collections of stories, part of the interest lies in the links between the full-length fiction and the short stories. 'Basilissa' is an early version of *The Dancing Floor* (1926), 'The Frying-pan and the Fire' looks to *John Macnab* (1925) and the short story 'The Magic Walking Stick' is expanded to make the children's book of the same name (published in 1932). Names reappear, so that Vernon in 'Basilissa' is related to the Karolides family, the name Buchan gives to the Greek premier in *The Thirty-Nine Steps*; the Applebys are mentioned in both 'Basilissa' and 'Fullcircle'; while Machray, an important Buchan place, is referred to in 'Fullcircle'.

There is the same fascination with the mystical. It may be the power exerted by place, especially a house, as in 'Fullcircle', 'Ho! The Merry Masons' and 'Basilissa'; part of a house, as in 'The Wind in the Portico'; or an island, as in 'Skule Skerry'. Or it may be a spell that only affects certain people and can pass through several generations. Throughout his life, Buchan was intrigued by the idea that certain qualities or susceptibilities could be passed from one person to another. His novel *The Path of the King* (1921) is about the idea that kingship can be passed through different quite ordinary people. Just as Lawson in 'The Grove of Ashtaroth' is drawn to worship an ancient goddess because of his Jewish blood, so too Andrew du Preez in 'The Green Wildebeest', with his mixed blood, is caught in an ancient spell. After his death Reggie Souldern energises his brother George, while in contrast Reinmar's death in 'The Post' diminishes his father Christoph's powers.

At the same time appearances may be deceptive. Reinmar in 'The Loathly Opposite' is not what Channell or Pugh envisage, and the lowly Peter Galbraith in 'The King of Ypres' achieves a momentary greatness before reverting to type. There is still the sense, as in the previous volumes, that many of the characters feel they are outsiders and unsettled in Britain. For example, Vernon in 'Basilissa' 'had a thousand acquaintances and a hundred friends, but no comrade.' They feel a need to be tested to prove their worth, and part of that redemption can only be found in the wild or abroad. Vernon goes to Greece to face up to his life, while Jim Hallward in 'The Last Crusade' attempts to prove himself by going to Canada.

Although few of the stories are actually set in the Empire, its presence, like that of the First World War, infuses these stories. Vernon spends his twenty-third birthday 'somewhere between the sources of the Congo and the Nile, in the trans-African expedition when Waldemar found the new variety of okapi', which is presumably the same expedition in which Hyde in 'The Shut Door' once took part. Captain Thomson in ' "Divus" Johnston' was 'principally engaged in the China trade, but made odd trips into the Malay Archipelago and once or twice to Australia' and was shipwrecked near the Philippines; in *'Tendebant Manus'* Sir Arthur Warcliff had been a colonial governor and 'was seriously spoken of for India', while George Souldern had written a book on colonial nationalism.

In *The Three Hostages*, Dr Greenslade describes the recipe for writing a thriller: 'I begin by fixing on one or two facts which have no sort of obvious connection – an old blind woman spinning in the Western Highlands, a barn in a Norwegian saeter, and a little curiosity shop in North London kept by a Jew with a dyed beard. Not much connection between the three? You invent a connection ... The reader ... is pleased with the ingenuity of the solution, for he doesn't realise that the author fixed upon the solution first, and then invented a problem to suit it.'

This approach is also evident in the stories, most notably in 'The Frying-pan and the Fire' which begins with an after-dinner game where 'You invented a preposterous situation and the point was to explain naturally how it came about. Drink, lunacy and practical joking were barred as explanations.' In the story, the Duke of Burminster has to explain just how he came to appear on the station at Langshiels with a muddy face, a scratched nose, dressed in a strange assortment of torn clothes and was then escorted by a band to a political meeting at the Town Hall.

'The Frying-pan and the Fire' is interesting because of its similarities with *John Macnab*. There is the same theme of 'degenerate patrician youth', it revolves around a sporting bet, and it shows Buchan's strong sense of irony and ability to describe the Scottish countryside, but it is raddled with coincidences, such as Burminster suddenly coming across his Aunt Letitia in a lunatic asylum, which is the necessity of this sort of literary device. One of the criticisms often made of Buchan in his novels is that he relies on coincidence, and the same is true of many of these stories. For example, in ' "Divus" Johnston' the ship's captain who finds Johnston realises he 'used to bide in the same close as me in Glasgow' while in 'Sing a Song of Sixpence' Leithen recognises Pelem because both played in the same Eton/Harrow cricket match.

If the weaknesses of Buchan's novels are to be found in these stories, concomitantly so too are the strengths. Reviewing *Sick Heart River* Graham Greene drew attention to Buchan's being one of 'the first to realize the enormous dramatic value of adventure in familiar surroundings happening to unadventurous men ... murder in the atmosphere of breeding and simplicity and stability.' Leithen discovers in 'Sing a Song of Sixpence' that political assassination of foreign leaders is a real possibility in the streets of Mayfair, and Burminster finds comic adventure in the Scottish Borders in 'The Frying-pan and the Fire', while the narrator in 'Nemesis' has similar adventures while fishing in the Highlands.

Over fifty stories have been collected over the three volumes that constitute this first attempt to bring together all of John Buchan's shorter fiction in chronological order of either writing or publication. It is an impressive body of work, in terms of quantity if not always of quality, and gives a particularly good insight into the versatility of his literary styles and the peculiar cast of his imagination. Many stories were clearly written to a deadline; others are highly repetitive or imitative; but some have that mark of greatness: the ability to stay in the mind long after the piece has been read.

'Divus' Johnston

' "Divus" Johnston' made its first appearance in December 1913 in the first issue of *The Golden Hynde*, a small magazine edited by the daughter of Buchan's close friend F.S. Oliver. *The Golden Hynde*'s profits were to be devoted to sending poor London children away for holidays in the country but, in spite of its good intentions, it was not a commercial success and closed in June 1914, having numbered among its contributors Hilaire Belloc and E.M. Forster. The story also appeared in a wartime charity anthology, *The Queen's Gift Book* (1918), in the American edition of *The Watcher by the Threshold* (1918), and as Lord Lamancha's story in Buchan's last short story collection, *The Runagates Club* (1928).

'Divus' means Divine and, according to Buchan in a lecture he gave in 1921, it was inspired by the story of a German expedition to Medina where they found the governor was a Scot called Thomas Keith.

In deorum numerum relatus est non ore modo decernentium sed et persuasione vulgi.

SUETONIUS

WE WERE DISCUSSING the vagaries of ambition, and decided that most of the old prizes that humanity contended for had had their gilt rubbed off. Kingdoms, for example, which younger sons used to set out to conquer. It was agreed that nowadays there was a great deal of drudgery and very little fun in being a king.

'Besides, it can't be done,' Leithen put in. 'The Sarawak case. Sovereignty over territory can only be acquired by a British subject on behalf of His Majesty.'

There was far more real power, someone argued, in the profession of prophet. Mass-persuasion was never such a force as today. Sandy

Arbuthnot, who had known Gandhi and admired him, gave us a picture of that strange popular leader – ascetic, genius, dreamer, child. 'For a little,' he said, 'Gandhi had more absolute sway over a bigger lump of humanity than anybody except Lenin.'

'I once knew Lenin,' said Fulleylove, the traveller, and we all turned to him.

'It must have been more than twenty years ago,' he explained. 'I was working at the British Museum and lived in lodgings in Bloomsbury, and he had a room at the top of the house. Ilyitch was the name we knew him by. He was a little, beetle-browed chap, with a pale face and the most amazing sleepy black eyes, which would suddenly twinkle and blaze as some thought passed through his mind. He was very pleasant and good-humoured, and would spend hours playing with the landlady's children. I remember I once took him down with me for a day into the country, and he was the merriest little grig . . . Did I realise how big he was? No, I cannot say I did. He was the ordinary Marxist, and he wanted to resurrect Russia by hydraulics and electrification. He seemed to be a funny compound of visionary and *terre-à-terre* scientist. But I realised that he could lay a spell on his countrymen. I have been to Russian meetings with him – I talk Russian, you know – and it was astounding the way he could make his audience look at him like hungry sheep. He gave me the impression of utter courage and candour, and a king of demoniac simplicity. . . No, I never met him again, but oddly enough I was in Moscow during his funeral. Russian geographers were interesting themselves in the line of the old silk-route to Cathay, and I was there by request to advise them. I had not a very comfortable time, but everybody was very civil to me. So I saw Lenin's funeral, and unless you saw that you can have no notion of his power. A great black bier like an altar, and hundreds and thousands of people weeping and worshipping – yes, worshipping.'

'The successful prophet becomes a kind of god,' said Lamancha. 'Have you ever known a god, Sandy? . . . No more have I. But there is one living today somewhere in Scotland. Johnston is his name. I once met a very particular friend of his. I will tell you the story, and you can believe it or not as you like.'

I had this narrative – he said – from my friend Mr Peter Thomson of 'Jessieville', Maxwell Avenue, Strathbungo, whom I believe to be a man incapable of mendacity, or, indeed, of imagination. He is a prosperous and retired ship's captain, dwelling in the suburbs of Glasgow, who plays two rounds of golf every day of the week, and goes twice every Sunday to a pink, new church. You may often see his ample figure, splendidly habited in broadcloth and finished off with one of those square felt hats which are the Scottish emblem of respectability, moving sedately by Mrs Thomson's side down the avenue of 'Balmorals' and 'Bellevues' where dwell the aristocracy of Strathbungo. It was not there that I met him, however, but in a Clyde steamboat going round the Mull, where I spent a comfortless night on my way to a Highland fishing. It was blowing what he called 'wee bit o' wind', and I could not face the odorous bunks which opened on the dining-room. Seated abaft the funnel, in an atmosphere of ham-and-eggs, bilge and fresh western breezes, he revealed his heart to me, and this I found in it.

'About the age of forty' – said Mr Thomson – 'I was captain of the steamer *Archibald McKelvie*, 1,700 tons burthen, belonging to Brock, Rattray, and Linklater of Greenock. We were principally engaged in the China trade, but made odd trips into the Malay Archipelago and once or twice to Australia. She was a handy bit boat, and I'll not deny that I had many mercies vouchsafed to me when I was her skipper. I raked in a bit of salvage now and then, and my trading commission, paid regularly into the British Linen Bank at Maryhill, was mounting up to a fairish sum. I had no objection to Eastern parts, for I had a good constitution and had outgrown the daftnesses of youth. The berth suited me well, I had a decent lot for ship's company, and I would gladly have looked forward to spending the rest of my days by the *Archibald McKelvie*.

'Providence, however, thought otherwise, for He was preparing a judgment against that ship like the kind you read about in books. We were five days out from Singapore, shaping our course for the Philippines, where the Americans were then fighting, when we ran into a queer lown sea. Not a breath of air came out of the sky; if you kindled a match the flame wouldna leap, but smouldered like touchwood; and every man's body ran with sweat like a mill-lade. I kenned fine we were in for the terrors of hell, but I hadna any kind of notion how terrible hell could be. First came a wind that whipped away my funnel, like a potato-peeling. We ran before it, and it was like the swee-gee we used to play at when we were laddies. One moment the muckle sea would get up on its hinder end and look at you, and the next you were looking at it as if you were on top of Ben Lomond looking down on Luss. Presently I saw land in a gap of the waters, a land with great blood-red mountains, and, thinks I to myself, if we keep up the pace this boat of mine will not be hindered from ending two or three miles inland in somebody's kail-yard. I was just wondering how we would get the *Archibald McKelvie* back to her native element when she saved me the trouble; for she ran dunt on some kind of a rock, and went straight to the bottom.

'I was the only man saved alive, and if you ask me how it happened I don't know. I felt myself choking in a whirlpool; then I was flung through the air and brought down with a smack into deep waters; then I was in the air again, and this time I landed amongst sand and tree-trunks and got a bash on the head which dozened my senses.

'When I came to it was morning, and the storm had abated. I was lying about half-way up a beach of fine white sand, for the wave that had carried me landwards in its flow had brought me some of the road back in its ebb. All round me was a sort of free-coup – trees knocked to matchwood, dead fish, and birds and beasts, and some boards which I jaloused came from the *Archibald McKelvie*. I had a big bump on my head, but otherwise I was well and clear in my wits, though empty in the stomach and very dowie in the heart. For I knew something about the islands, of which I supposed this to be one. They were either barren wastes, with neither food nor water, or else they were inhabited by the bloodiest cannibals of the archipelago. It looked as if my choice lay between having nothing to eat and being eaten myself.

'I got up, and, after returning thanks to my Maker, went for a walk in the woods. They were full of queer painted birds, and it was an awful job climbing in and out of the fallen trees. By and by I came into an open bit with a burn where I slockened my thirst. It cheered me up, and I was just beginning to think that this was not such a bad island, and looking to see if I could find anything in the nature of coconuts, when I heard a whistle like a steam-siren. It was some sort of signal, for the next I knew I was in the grip of a dozen savages, my arms and feet were lashed together, and I was being carried swiftly through the forest.

'It was a rough journey, and the discomfort of that heathen handling kept me from reflecting upon my desperate position. After nearly three hours we stopped, and I saw that we had come to a city.

The streets were not much to look at, and the houses were mud and thatch, but on a hillock in the middle stood a muckle temple not unlike a Chinese pagoda. There was a man blowing a horn, and a lot of folk shouting, but I paid no attention, for I was sore troubled with the cramp in my left leg. They took me into one of the huts and made signs that I was to have it for my lodging. They brought me water to wash, and a very respectable dinner, which included a hen and a vegetable not unlike greens. Then they left me to myself, and I lay down and slept for a round of the clock.

'I was three days in that hut. I had plenty to eat and the folk were very civil, but they wouldn't let me outbye and there was no window to look out of. I couldna make up my mind what they wanted with me. I was a prisoner, but they did not behave as if they bore any malice, and I might have thought I was an honoured guest, but for the guards at the door. Time hung heavy on my hands, for I had nothing to read and no light to read by. I said over all the chapters of the Bible and all the Scots songs I could remember, and I tried to make a poem about my adventures, but I stuck at the fifth line, for I couldna find a rhyme to McKelvie.

'On the fourth morning I was awakened by the most deafening din. I saw through the door that the streets were full of folk in holiday clothes, most of them with flowers in their hair and carrying palm branches in their hands. It was like something out of a Bible picture book. After I had my breakfast four lads in long white gowns arrived, and in spite of all my protests they made a bonny spectacle of me. They took off my clothes, me blushing with shame, and rubbed me with a kind of oil that smelt of cinnamon. Then they shaved my chin, and painted on my forehead a mark like a freemason's. Then they put on me a kind of white nightgown with a red sash round the middle, and they wouldna be hindered from clapping on my head a great wreath of hothouse flowers, as if I was a funeral.

'And then like a thunder-clap I realised my horrible position. *I was a funeral.* I was to be offered up as a sacrifice to some heathen god – an awful fate for a Free-kirk elder in the prime of life.

'I was so paralytic with terror I never tried to resist. Indeed, it would have done me little good, for outside there were, maybe, two hundred savages, armed and drilled like soldiers. I was put into a sort of palanquin, and my bearers started at a trot with me up the hill to the temple, the whole population of the city running alongside, and singing songs about their god. I was sick with fear, and I durstna look up, for I did not know what awesome sight awaited me.

'At last I got my courage back. "Peter," I says to myself, "be a man. Remember your sainted Covenanting forefathers. You have been chosen to testify for your religion, though it's no likely that yon savages will understand what you say." So I shut my jaw and resolved before I died to make a declaration of my religious principles, and to loosen some of the heathen's teeth with my fists.

'We stopped at the temple door and I was led through a court and into a muckle great place like a barn, with bats flying about the ceiling. Here there were nearly three thousand heathens sitting on their hunkers. They sang a hymn when they saw me, and I was just getting ready for action when my bearers carried me into another place, which I took to be the Holy of Holies. It was about half the size of the first, and at the end of it was a great curtain of leopards' skins hanging from roof to floor. My bearers set me in the middle of the room, and then rolled about on their stomachs in adoration before the curtain. After a bit they finished their prayers and crawled out backwards, and I was left alone in that fearsome place.

'It was the worst experience of my life. I believed that behind the skins there was a horrible idol, and that at any moment a priest with a knife would slip in to cut my throat. You may crack about courage, but I tell you that a man who can wait without a quiver on his murderers in the middle of a gloomy kirk is more than human. I am not ashamed to confess that the sweat ran over my brow, and my teeth were knocking in my head.

'But nothing happened. Nothing, except that as I sat there I began to notice a most remarkable smell. At first I thought the place was on fire. Then I thought it was the kind of stink called incense that they make in Popish kirks, for I once wandered into a cathedral in Santiago. But neither guess was right, and then I put my thumb on the proper description. It was nothing but the smell of the third-class carriages on the Coatbridge train on a Saturday night after a football match – the smell of plug tobacco smoked in clay pipes that were no just very clean. My eyes were getting accustomed to the light, and I found the place no that dark; and as I looked round to see what caused the smell, I spied something like smoke coming from beyond the top of the curtain.

'I noticed another thing. There was a hole in the curtain, about six feet from the floor, and at that hole as I watched I saw an eye. My heart stood still, for, thinks I, that'll be the priest of Baal who presently will stick a knife into me. It was long ere I could screw up courage to look again, but I did it. And then I saw that the eye was not that of a savage, which would be black and blood-shot. It was a blue eye, and, as I looked, it winked at me.

'And then a voice spoke out from behind the curtain, and this was what it said. It said, "God-sake, Peter, is that you? And how did ye leave them a' at Maryhill?"

'And from behind the curtain walked a muckle man, dressed in a pink blanket, a great red-headed man, with a clay pipe in his mouth. It was the god of the savages, and who do ye think it was? A man Johnston, who used to bide in the same close as me in Glasgow . . .'

Mr Thomson's emotion overcame him, and he accepted a stiff drink from my flask. Wiping away a tear, which may have been of sentiment or of mirth, he continued:

'You may imagine that I was joyful and surprised to see him, and he, so to speak, fell on my neck like the father of the Prodigal Son. He hadna seen a Scotch face for four years. He raked up one or two high priests and gave instructions, and soon I was comfortably lodged in a part of the temple close to his own rooms. Eh, man, it was a noble sight to see Johnston and the priests. He was a big, red-haired fellow, six feet four, and as strong as a stot, with a voice like a north-easter, and yon natives fair crawled like caterpillars in his presence. I never saw a man with such a natural talent for being a god. You would have thought he had been bred to the job all his days, and yet I minded him keeping a grocer's shop in the Dalmarnock Road.

'That night he told me his story. It seemed that he had got a post in Shanghai in a trading house, and was coming out to it in one of those God-forgotten German tramps that defile the China seas. Like me, he fell in with a hurricane, and, like me, his ship was doomed. He was a powerful swimmer, and managed to keep afloat until he found some drifting wreckage, and after the wind had gone down he paddled ashore. There he was captured by the savages, and taken, like me, to their city. They were going to sacrifice him, but one chief, wiser than the rest, called attention to his size and strength, and pointed out that they were at war with their neighbours, and that a big man would be of more use in the fighting line than on an altar in the temple.

'So off went Johnston to the wars. He was a bonny fighter, and very soon they made him captain of the royal bodyguard, and a fortnight later the general commanding-in-chief over the whole army. He said he had never enjoyed himself so much in his life, and when he got back from his battles the whole population of the city used to meet him with songs and flowers. Then an old priest found an ancient prophecy about a Red God who would come out of the sea and lead the people to victory. Very soon there was a strong party for making Johnston a god, and when, with the help of a few sticks of trade dynamite, he had blown up the capital of the other side and brought back his army in triumph with a prisoner apiece, popular feeling could not be restrained. Johnston was hailed as divine. He hadna much grip of the language, and couldna explain the situation, so he thought it best to submit.

' "Mind you," he said to me, "I've been a good god to these poor blind ignorant folk." He had stopped the worst of their habits and put down human sacrifices, and got a sort of town council appointed to keep the city clean, and he had made the army the most efficient thing ever heard of in the islands. And now he was preparing to leave. This was what they expected, for the prophecy had said that the Red God, after being the saviour of his people, would depart as he had come across the sea. So, under his directions, they had built him a kind of boat with which he hoped to reach Singapore. He had got together a considerable fortune, too, chiefly in rubies, for as a god he had plenty of opportunities of acquiring wealth honestly. He said there was a sort of greengrocer's and butcher's shop before his altar every morning, and he got one of the priests, who had some business notions, to sell off the goods for him.

'There was just one thing that bothered Mr Johnston. He was a good Christian man and had been an elder in a kirk in the Cow-caddens, and he was much in doubt whether he had not committed a mortal sin in accepting the worship of these heathen islanders. Often I argued it out with him, but I did not seem able to comfort him rightly. "Ye see," he used to say to me, "if I have broken anything, it's the spirit and no the letter of the commandment. I havena set up a graven image, for ye canna call me a graven image."

'I mind that I quoted to him the conduct of Naaman, who was allowed to bow in the house of Rimmon, but he would not have it. "No, no," he cried, "that has nothing to do with the point. It's no a question of my bowing in the house of Rimmon. I'm auld Rimmon himself." '

'That's a strange story, Mr Thomson,' I said. 'Is it true?'

'True as death. But you havena heard the end of it. We got away, and by-and-by we reached Singapore, and in course of time our native land. Johnston, he was a very rich man now, and I didna go without my portion; so the loss of the *Archibald McKelvie* turned out the best piece of luck in my life. I bought a share in Brock's Line, but nothing would content Johnston but that he must be a gentleman. He got a big estate in Annandale, where all the Johnstons came from long ago, and one way and another he has spent an awful siller on it. Land will swallow up money quicker than the sea.'

'And what about his conscience?' I asked.

'It's keeping quieter,' said Mr Thomson. 'He takes a great interest in Foreign Missions, to which he subscribes largely, and they tell me that he has given the funds to build several new kirks. Oh yes, and he's just been adopted as a prospective Liberal candidate. I had a letter from him no further back than yesterday. It's about his political career, as he calls it. He told me, what didna need telling, that I must never mention a word about his past. "If discretion was necessary before," he says, "it's far more necessary now, for how could the Party of Progress have any confidence in a man if they heard he had once been a god?"'

Basilissa

'Basilissa' was published in *Blackwood's Magazine* in April 1914 and was included in the American edition of *The Watcher by the Threshold* (1918). It was inspired by a house on one of the Petali Islands seen during a month's cruise in the Aegean in the spring of 1910.

WHEN VERNON WAS a very little boy he was the sleepiest of mortals, but in the spring he had seasons of bad dreams, and breakfast became an idle meal. Mrs Ganthony, greatly concerned, sent for Dr Moreton from Axby, and homely remedies were prescribed.

'It is the spring fever,' said the old man. 'It gives the gout to me and nightmares to this baby; it brings lads and lasses together, and scatters young men about the world. An antique complaint, Mrs Ganthony. But it will right itself, never fear. *Ver non semper viret.*' Chuckling at his ancient joke, the doctor mounted his horse, leaving the nurse only half comforted. 'What fidgets me,' she told the housekeeper, 'is the way his lordship holds his tongue. For usual he'll shout as lusty as a whelp. But now I finds him in the morning with his eyes like moons and his skin white and shiny, and never a cheep has he given the whole blessed night, with me laying next door, and it open, and a light sleeper at all times, Mrs Wace, ma'am.'

Every year the dreams came, generally – for his springs were spent at Severns – in the big new night-nursery at the top of the west wing, which his parents had built not long before their death. It had three windows looking over the moorish flats which run up to the Lancashire fells, and from one window, by craning your neck, you could catch a glimpse of the sea. It was all hung, too, with a Chinese paper whereon pink and green parrots squatted in wonderful blue trees, and there seemed generally to be a wood fire burning. Vernon's recollections of his childish nightmare are hazy. He always found himself in a room different from the nursery and bigger, but with the same smell of wood smoke. People came and went, such as his nurse, the butler, Simon the head-keeper, Uncle Appleby his guardian, Cousin Jennifer, the old woman who sold oranges in Axby, and a host of others. Nobody hindered them from going away, and they seemed to be pleading with him to come too. There was danger in the place; something was going to happen in that big room, and if by that time he was not gone there would be mischief. But it was quite clear to him that he could not go. He must stop there, with the wood smoke in his nostrils, and await the advent of a terrible Something. But he was never quite sure of the nature of the compulsion. He had a notion that if he made a rush for the door at Uncle Appleby's heels he would be allowed to escape, but that somehow he would be behaving badly. Anyhow, the place put him into a sweat of fright, and Mrs Ganthony looked darkly at him in the morning.

Vernon was nine before this odd spring dream began to take definite shape — at least he thinks he must have been about that age. The dream-stage was emptying. There was nobody in the room now but himself, and he saw its details a little more clearly. It was not any apartment in the modern magnificence of Severns. Rather it looked like one of the big old panelled chambers which the boy remembered from visits to Midland country-houses, where he had arrived after dark and had been put to sleep in a great bed in a place lit with dancing firelight. In the morning it had looked only an ordinary big room, but at that hour of the evening it had seemed an enchanted citadel. The dream-room was not unlike these, for there was the scent of a wood fire and there were dancing shadows, but he could not see clearly the walls or the ceiling, and there was no bed. In one corner was a door which led to the outer world, and through this he knew that he might on no account pass. Another door faced him, and he knew that he had only to turn the handle and enter it. But he did not want to, for he understood quite clearly what was beyond. There was another room like the first one, but he knew nothing about it, except that opposite the entrance another door led out of it. Beyond was a third chamber, and so on interminably. There seemed to the boy no end to this fantastic suite. He thought of it as a great snake of masonry, winding up hill and down dale away to the fells or the sea. Yes, but there was an end. Somewhere far away in one of the rooms was a terror waiting on him, or, as he feared, coming towards him. Even now it might be flitting from room to room, every minute bringing its soft tread nearer to the chamber of the wood fire.

About this time of life the dream was an unmitigated horror. Once it came while he was ill with a childish fever, and it sent his temperature up to a point which brought Dr Moreton galloping from Axby. In his waking hours he did not, as a rule, remember it clearly; but during the fever, asleep and awake, that sinuous building, one room thick, with each room opening from the other, was never away from his thoughts. It fretted him to think that outside were the cheerful moors where he hunted for plovers' eggs, and that only a thin wall of stone kept him from pleasant homely things. The thought used to comfort him for a moment when he was awake, but in the dream it never came near him. Asleep, the whole world seemed one suite of rooms, and he, a forlorn little prisoner, doomed to wait grimly on the slow coming through the many doors of a Fear which transcended word and thought.

He was a silent, self-absorbed boy, and though the fact of his nightmares was patent to the little household, the details remained locked in his heart. Not even to Uncle Appleby would he tell them when that gentleman, hurriedly kind, came down to visit his convalescent ward. His illness made Vernon grow, and he shot up into a lanky, leggy boy – weakly, too, till the hills tautened his sinews again. His Greek blood – his grandmother had been a Karolides – had given him a face curiously like the young Byron, with a finely-cut brow and nostrils, and hauteur in the full lips. But Vernon had no Byronic pallor, for his upland home kept him sunburnt and weather-beaten, and below his straight Greek brows shone a pair of grey and steadfast and very English eyes.

He was about fifteen – so he thinks – when he made the great discovery. The dream had become almost a custom now. It came in April at Severns during the Easter holidays – a night's discomfort (it was now scarcely more) in the rush and glory of the spring fishing. There was a moment of the old wild heart-fluttering; but a boy's fancy is quickly dulled, and the endless corridors were now more of a prison than a witch's ante-chamber. By this time, with the help of his diary, he had fixed the date of the dream: it came regularly on the night of the first Monday of April. Now the year I speak of he had been on a long expedition into the hills, and had stridden homewards at a steady four miles an hour among the gleams and shadows of an April twilight. He was alone at Severns, so he had his supper in the big library, where afterwards he sat watching the leaping flames in the open stone hearth. He was very weary, and sleep fell upon him in his chair. He found himself in the wood-smoke chamber, and before him the door leading to the unknown. But it was no indefinite fear that lay beyond. He knew clearly – though how he knew he could not tell – that each year the Something came one room nearer, and was even now but ten rooms off. In ten years his own door would open, and then—

He woke in the small hours, chilled and mazed, but with a curious new assurance in his heart. Hitherto the nightmare had left him in gross terror, unable to endure the prospect of its recurrence, till the kindly forgetfulness of youth had soothed him. But now, though his nerves were tense with fright, he perceived that there was a limit to the mystery. Some day it must declare itself, and fight on equal terms. As he thought over the matter in the next few days he had the sense of being forewarned and prepared for some great test of courage. The notion exhilarated as much as it frightened him. Late at night, or on soft dripping days, or at any moment of lessened vitality, he would bitterly wish that he had been born an ordinary mortal. But on a keen morning of frost, when he rubbed himself warm after a cold tub, or at high noon of summer, the adventure of the dream almost pleased him. Unconsciously he braced himself to a harder discipline. His fitness, moral and physical, became his chief interest, for reasons which would have been unintelligible to his friends and more so to his masters. He passed through school an aloof and splendid figure, magnificently athletic, with a brain as well as a perfect body – a good fellow in everybody's opinion, but a grave one. He had no intimates, and never shared the secret of the spring dream. For some reason which he could not tell, he would have burned his hand off rather than breathe a hint of it. Pure terror absolves from all conventions and demands a confidant, so terror, I think, must have largely departed from the nightmare as he grew older. Fear, indeed, remained, and awe and disquiet, but these are human things, whereas terror is of hell.

Had he told any one, he would no doubt have become self-conscious and felt acutely his difference from other people. As it was, he was an ordinary schoolboy, much beloved, and, except at odd moments, unaware of any brooding destiny. As he grew up and his ambition awoke, the moments when he remembered the dream were apt to be disagreeable, for a boy's ambitions are strictly conventional and his soul revolts at the abnormal. By the time he was ready for the University he wanted above all things to run the mile a second faster than any one else, and had vague hopes of exploring wild countries. For most of the year he lived with these hopes and was happy; then came April, and for a short season he was groping in dark places. Before and after each dream he was in a mood of exasperation; but when it came he plunged into a different atmosphere, and felt the quiver of fear and the quick thrill of expectation. One year, in the unsettled moods of nineteen, he made an attempt to avoid it. He and three others were on a walking tour in Brittany in gusty spring weather, and came late one evening to an inn by an estuary where seagulls clattered about the windows. Youth-like they ordered a great and foolish feast, and sat all night round a bowl of punch, while school songs and 'John Peel' contended with the dirling of the gale. At daylight they took the road again, without having closed an eye, and Vernon told himself that he was rid of his incubus. He wondered at the time why he was not more cheerful. Next April he was at Severns, reading hard, and on the first Monday of the month he went to bed with scarcely a thought of what that night used to mean. The dream did not fail him. Once more he was in the chamber with the wood fire; once again he was peering at the door and wondering with tremulous heart what lay beyond. For the Something had come nearer by two rooms, and was now only five doors away. He wrote in his diary at that time some lines from Keats' 'Indian Maid's Song':

> I would deceive her,
> And so leave her,
> But ah! she is so constant and so kind.

And there is a mark of exclamation against the 'she,' as if he found some irony in it.

From that day the boy in him died. The dream would not suffer itself to be forgotten. It moulded his character and determined his plans like the vow of the young Hannibal at the altar. He had forgotten now either to fear or to hope; the thing was part of him, like his vigorous young body, his slow kindliness, his patient courage. He left Oxford at twenty-two with a prodigious reputation which his remarkable athletic record by no means explained. All men liked him, but no one knew him; he had a thousand acquaintances and a hundred friends, but no comrade. There was a sense of brooding power about him which attracted and repelled his little world. No one forecast any special career for him; indeed, it seemed almost disrespectful to condescend upon such details. It was not what Vernon would do that fired the imagination of his fellows, but what they dimly conceived that he already was. I remember my first sight of him about that time, a tall young man in his corner of a club smoking-room, with a head like Apollo's and eyes which received much but gave nothing. I guessed at once that he had foreign blood in him, not from any oddness of colouring or feature but from his silken reserve. We of the North are angular in our silences; we have not learned the art of gracious reticence.

His twenty-third April was spent in a hut on the Line, somewhere between the sources of the Congo and the Nile, in the trans-African expedition when Waldemar found the new variety of okapi. The following April I was in his company in a tent far up on the shoulder of a Kashmir mountain. On the first Monday of the month we had had a heavy day after ovis, and that night I was asleep almost before my weary limbs were tucked into my kaross. I knew nothing of Vernon's dream, but next morning I remember that I remarked a certain heaviness of eye, and wondered idly if the frame of this Greek divinity was as tough as it was shapely.

Next year Vernon left England early in March. He had resolved to visit again his grandmother's country and to indulge his passion for cruising in new waters.

His 20-ton yawl was sent as deck cargo to Patras, while he followed by way of Venice. He brought one man with him from Wyvenhoe, a lean gypsy lad called Martell, and for his other hand he found an Epirote at Corfu, who bore a string of names that began with Constantine. From Patras with a west wind they made good sailing up the Gulf of Corinth, and, passing through the Canal, came in the last days of March to the Piraeus. In that place of polyglot speech, whistling engines, and the odour of gas-works, they delayed only for water and supplies, and presently had rounded Sunium, and were beating up the Euripus with the Attic hills rising sharp and clear in the spring sunlight. Vernon had no plan. It was a joy to him to be alone with the racing seas and the dancing winds, to scud past little headlands, pink and white with blossom, or to lie of a night in some hidden bay beneath the thymy crags. It was his habit on his journeys to discard the clothes of civilisation. In a blue jersey and old corduroy trousers, bare-headed and barefooted, he steered his craft and waited on the passing of the hours. Like an acolyte before the temple gate, he believed himself to be on the threshold of a new life.

Trouble began under the snows of Pelion as they turned the north end of Euboea. On the morning of the first Monday in April the light west winds died away, and scirocco blew harshly from the south. By midday it was half a gale, and in those yeasty shallow seas with an iron coast on the port the prospect looked doubtful. The nearest harbour was twenty miles distant, and as no one of the crew had been there before it was a question if they could make it by nightfall. With the evening the gale increased, and Constantine advised a retreat from the maze of rocky islands to the safer deeps of the Ægean. It was a hard night for the three, and there was no chance of sleep. More by luck than skill they escaped the butt of Skiathos, and the first light found them far to the east among the long seas of the North Ægean, well on the way to Lemnos. By eight o'clock the gale had blown itself out, and three soaked and chilly mortals relaxed their vigil. Soon bacon was frizzling on the cuddy-stove, and hot coffee and dry clothes restored them to comfort.

The sky cleared, and in bright sunlight, with the dregs of the gale behind him, Vernon stood in for the mainland, where the white crest of Olympus hung in the northern heavens. In the late afternoon they came into a little bay carved from the side of a high mountain. The slopes were gay with flowers, yellow and white and scarlet, and the young green of crops showed in the clearings. Among the thyme a flock of goats was browsing, shepherded by a little girl in a saffron skirt, who sang shrilly in snatches. Midway in the bay and just above the anchorage rose a great white building, which showed to seaward a blank white wall pierced with a few narrow windows. At first sight Vernon took it for a monastery, but a look through the glasses convinced him that its purpose was not religious. Once it had been fortified, and even now a broad causeway ran between it and the sea, which looked as if it had once held guns. The architecture was a jumble, showing here the enriched Gothic of Venice and there the straight lines and round arches of the East. It had once, he conjectured, been the hold of some Venetian sea-king, then the palace of a Turkish conqueror, and now was, perhaps, the homely manor-house of this pleasant domain.

A fishing-boat was putting out from the shore. He hailed its occupant and asked who owned the castle.

The man crossed himself and spat overboard. 'Basilissa,' he said, and turned his eyes seaward.

Vernon called Constantine from the bows and asked him what the word might mean. The Epirote crossed himself also before he spoke. 'It is the Lady of the Land,' he said, in a hushed voice. 'It is the great witch who is the Devil's bride. In old days in spring they made sacrifice to her, but they say her power is dying now. In my country we do not speak her name, but elsewhere they call her "Queen".' The man's bluff sailorly assurance had disappeared, and as Vernon stared at him in bewilderment he stammered and averted his eyes.

By supper-time he had recovered himself, and the weather-beaten three made such a meal as befits those who have faced danger together. Afterwards Vernon, as was his custom, sat alone in the stern, smoking and thinking his thoughts. He wrote up his diary with a ship's lantern beside him, while overhead the starless velvet sky seemed to hang low and soft like an awning. Little fires burned on the shore at which folk were cooking food – he could hear their voices, and from the keep one single lit window made an eye in the night.

He had leisure now for the thought which had all day been at the back of his mind. The night had passed and there had been no dream. The adventure for which he had prepared himself had vanished into the Ægean tides. He told himself that it was a relief, that an old folly was over, but he knew in his heart that he was bitterly disappointed. The fates had prepared the stage and rung up the curtain without providing the play. He had been fooled, and somehow the zest and savour of life had gone from him. No man can be strung high and then find his preparation idle without suffering a cruel recoil.

As he scribbled idly in his diary he found some trouble about dates. Down in his bunk was a sheaf of Greek papers bought at the Piraeus and still unlooked at. He fetched them up and turned them over with a growing mystification. There was something very odd about the business. One gets hazy about dates at sea, but he could have sworn that he had made no mistake. Yet here it was down in black and white, for there was no question about the number of days since he left the Piraeus. The day was not Tuesday, as he had believed, but Monday, the first Monday of April.

He stood up with a beating heart and that sense of unseen hands which comes to all men once or twice in their lives. The night was yet to come, and with it the end of the dream. Suddenly he was glad, absurdly glad, he could almost have wept with the joy of it. And then he was conscious for the first time of the strangeness of the place in which he had anchored. The night was dark over him like a shell, enclosing the half-moon of bay and its one lit dwelling. The great hills, unseen but felt, ran up to snows, warding it off from a profane world. His nerves tingled with a joyful anticipation. Something, some wonderful thing, was coming to him out of the darkness.

Under an impulse for which he could give no reason, he called Constantine and gave his orders. Let him be ready to sail at any moment – a possible thing, for there was a light breeze off shore. Also let the yacht's dinghy be ready in case he wanted it. Then Vernon sat himself down again in the stern beside the lantern, and waited . . .

He was dreaming, and did not hear the sound of oars or the grating of a boat alongside. Suddenly he found a face looking at him in the ring of lamplight – an old bearded face curiously wrinkled. The eyes, which were grave and penetrating, scanned him for a second or two, and then a voice spoke—

'Will the Signor come with me? There is work for him to do this night.'

Vernon rose obediently. He had waited for this call these many years, and he was there to answer it. He went below and put a loaded revolver in his trouser-pocket, and then dropped over the yacht's side into a cockleshell of a boat. The messenger took the oars and rowed for the point of light on shore.

A middle-aged woman stood on a rock above the tide, holding a small lantern. In its thin flicker he made out a person with the air and dress of a French maid. She cast one glance at Vernon, and then turned wearily to the other. 'Fool, Mitri!' she said. 'You have brought a peasant.'

'Nay,' said the old man, 'he is no peasant. He is a Signor, and as I judge, a man of his hands.'

The woman passed the light of her lantern over Vernon's form and face. 'His dress is a peasant's, but such clothes may be a nobleman's whim. I have heard it of the English.'

'I am English,' said Vernon in French.

She turned on him with a quick movement of relief.

'You are English and a gentleman? But I know nothing of you, only that you have come out of the sea. Up in the House we women are alone, and my mistress has death to face, or a worse than death. We have no claim on you, and if you give us your service it means danger – ah, what danger! The boat is waiting. You have time to go back and go away and forget that you have seen this accursed place. But, O Monsieur, if you hope for Heaven and have pity on a defenceless angel, you will not leave us.'

'I am ready,' said Vernon.

'God's mercy,' she sighed, and, seizing his arm, drew him up the steep causeway, while the old man went ahead with the lantern. Now and then she cast anxious glances to the right where the little fires of the fishers twinkled along the shore. Then came a point when the three entered a narrow uphill road, where rocky steps had been cut in a tamarisk thicket. She spoke low in French to Vernon's ear—

'My mistress is the last of her line, you figure; a girl with a wild estate and a father long dead. She is good and gracious, as I who have tended her can witness, but she is young and cannot govern the wolves who are the men of these parts. They have a long hatred of her house, and now they have rumoured it that she is a witch and blights the crops and slays the children. No one will look at her; the priest – for they are all in the plot – signs himself and crosses the road; the little ones run screaming to their mothers. Once, twice, they have cursed our threshold and made the blood mark on the door. For two years we have been prisoners in the House, and only Mitri is true. They name her Basilissa, meaning the Queen of Hell, whom the ancients called Proserpine. There is no babe but will faint with fright if it casts eyes on her, and she as mild and innocent as Mother Mary . . .'

The woman stopped at a little door and in a high wall of masonry. 'Nay, wait and hear me out. It is better that you hear the tale from me than from her. Mitri has the gossip of the place through his daughter's husband, and the word has gone round to burn the witch out. The winter in the hills has been cruel, and they blame their sorrow on her. The dark of the moon in April is the time fixed, for they say that a witch has power only in moonlight. This is the night, and down on the shore the fishers are gathered. The men from the hills are in the higher woods.'

'Have they a leader?' Vernon asked.

'A leader?' her voice echoed shrilly. 'But that is the worst of our terrors. There is one Vlastos, a lord in the mountains, who saw my mistress a year ago as she looked from the balcony at the Swallow-singing, and was filled with a passion for her. He has persecuted her since with his desires. He is a king among these savages, being himself a very wolf in man's flesh. We have denied him, but he persists, and this night he announces that he comes for an answer. He offers to save her if she will trust him, but what is the honour of his kind? He is like a brute out of a cave. It were better for my lady to go to God in the fire than to meet all Hell in his arms. But this night we must choose, unless you prove a saviour.'

'Did you see my boat anchor in the bay?' Vernon asked, though he already knew the answer.

'But no,' she said. 'We live only to the landward side of the House. My lady told me that God would send a man to our aid. And I bade Mitri fetch him.'

The door was unlocked and the three climbed a staircase which seemed to follow the wall of a round tower. Presently they came into a stone hall with curious hangings like the old banners in a church. From the open flame of the lantern another was kindled, and the light showed a desolate place with crumbling mosaics on the floor and plaster dropping from the cornices. Through another corridor they went, where the air blew warmer and there was that indefinable scent which comes from human habitation. Then came a door which the woman held open for Vernon to enter. 'Wait there, Monsieur,' she said. 'My mistress will come to you.'

It was his own room, where annually he had waited with a flut-tering heart since he was a child at Severns. A fire of wood – some resinous thing like juniper – burned on the hearth, and spirals of blue smoke escaped the stone chimney and filled the air with their pungent fragrance. On a Spanish cabinet stood an antique silver lamp, and there was a great blue Chinese vase filled with spring flowers. Soft Turcoman rugs covered the wooden floor – Vernon noted every detail for never before had he been able to see his room clearly. A woman had lived here, for an embroidery frame lay on a table and there were silken cushions on the low divans. And facing him in the other wall there was a door.

In the old days he had regarded it with vague terror in his soul. Now he looked at it with the hungry gladness with which a traveller sees again the familiar objects of home. The hour of his destiny had struck. The thing for which he had trained himself in body and spirit was about to reveal itself in that doorway ...

It opened, and a girl entered. She was tall and very slim, and moved with the free grace of a boy. She trod the floor like one walking in spring meadows. Her little head on the flower-like neck was bent sideways as if she were listening, and her eyes had the strange disquieting innocence of a child's. Yet she was a grown woman, nobly made, and lithe and supple as Artemis herself when she ranged with her maidens through the moonlit gades. Her face had the delicate pallor of pure health, and above it the masses of dark hair were bound with a thin gold circlet. She wore a gown of some soft white stuff, and had thrown over it a cloak of russet furs.

For a second – or so it seemed to Vernon – she looked at him as he stood tense and expectant like a runner at the start. Then the hesitation fled from her face. She ran to him with the confidence of a child who has waited long for the coming of a friend and has grown lonely and fearful. She gave him both her hands and in her tall pride looked him full in the eyes. 'You have come,' she sighed happily. 'I did not doubt it. They told me there was no help, but, you see, they did not know about you. That was my own secret. The Monster had nearly gobbled me, Perseus, but of course you could not come quicker. And now you will take me away with you? See, I am ready. And Elise will come too, and old Mitri, for they could not live without me. We must hurry, for the Monster is very near.'

In that high moment of romance, when young love had burst upon him like spring, Vernon retained his odd discipline of soul. The adventure of the dream could not be satisfied by flight, even though his companion was a goddess.

'We will go, Andromeda, but not yet. I have something to say to the Monster.'

She broke into a ripple of laughter. 'Yes, that is the better way. Mitri will admit him alone, and he will think to find us women. But you will be here and you will speak to him.' Then her eyes grew solemn. 'He is very cruel, Perseus, and he is full of evil. He may devour us both. Let us begone before he comes.'

It was Vernon's turn to laugh. At the moment no enterprise seemed too formidable, and a price must be paid for this far-away princess. And even as he laughed the noise of a great bell clanged through the house.

[29]

Mitri stole in with a scared face, and it was from Vernon that he took his orders. 'Speak them fair, but let one man enter and no more. Bring him here, and see that the gate is barred behind him. After that make ready for the road.' Then to the girl: 'Take off your cloak and wait here as if you were expecting him. I will stand behind the screen. Have no fear, for I will have him covered, and I will shoot him like a dog if he lays a finger on you.'

From the shelter of the screen Vernon saw the door open and a man enter. He was a big fellow of the common mountain type, gorgeously dressed in a uniform of white and crimson, with boots of yellow untanned leather, and a beltful of weapons. He was handsome in a coarse way, but his slanting eyes and the heavy lips scarcely hidden by the curling moustaches were ugly and sinister. He smiled, showing his white teeth, and spoke hurriedly in the guttural Greek of the north. The girl shivered at the sound of his voice, and to the watcher it seemed like Pan pursuing one of Dian's nymphs.

'You have no choice, my Queen,' he was saying. 'I have a hundred men at the gate who will do my bidding, and protect you against these fools of villagers till you are safe with me at Louko. But if you refuse me I cannot hold the people. They will burn the place over your head, and by to-morrow's morn these walls will be smouldering ashes with your fair body in the midst of them.'

Then his wooing became rougher. The satyr awoke in his passionate eyes. 'Nay, you are mine, whether you will it or not. I and my folk will carry you off when the trouble begins. Take your choice, my girl, whether you will go with a good grace, or trussed up behind a servant. We have rough ways in the hills with ungracious wenches.'

'I am going away,' she whispered, 'but not with you!'

The man laughed. 'Have you fetched down friend Michael and his angels to help you? By Saint John the Hunter, I would I had a rival. I would carve him prettily for the sake of your sweet flesh.'

Vernon kicked aside the screen. 'You will have your chance,' he said. 'I am ready.'

Vlastos stepped back with his hand at his belt. 'Who in the devil's name are you?' he asked.

'One who would dispute the lady with you,' said Vernon.

The man had recovered his confidence. 'I know nothing of you or whence you come, but to-night I am merciful. I give you ten seconds to disappear. If not, I will spit you, my fine cock, and you will roast in this oven.'

'Nevertheless the lady goes with me,' said Vernon, smiling.

Vlastos plucked a whistle from his belt, but before it reached his mouth he was looking into the barrel of Vernon's revolver. 'Pitch that thing on the floor,' came the command. 'Not there! Behind me! Off with that belt and give it to the lady. Quick, my friend.'

The dancing grey eyes dominated the sombre black ones. Vlastos flung down the whistle, and slowly removed the belt with its silver-mounted pistols and its brace of knives.

'Put up your weapon,' he muttered, 'and fight me for her, as a man should.'

'I ask nothing better,' said Vernon, and he laid his revolver in the girl's lap.

He had expected a fight with fists, and was not prepared for what followed. Vlastos sprang at him like a wild beast and clasped him round the waist. He was swung off his feet in a grip that seemed more than human. For a second or two he swayed to and fro, recovered himself, and by a back-heel stroke forced his assailant to relax a little. Then, locked together in the middle of the room, the struggle began. Dimly out of a corner of his eye he saw the girl pick up the silver lamp and stand by the door holding it high.

Vernon had learned the rudiments of wrestling among the dalesmen of the North, but now he was dealing with one who followed no ordinary methods. It was a contest of sheer physical power. Vlastos was a stone or two heavier, and had an uncommon length of arm; but he was clumsily made, and flabby from gross living. Vernon was spare and hard and clean, but he lacked one advantage – he had never striven with a man save in friendly games, and the other was bred to kill. For a minute or two they swayed and stumbled, while Vernon strove for the old Westmorland 'inside click'. Every second brought him nearer to it, while the other's face was pressed close to his shoulder.

Suddenly he felt a sharp pain. Teeth met in his flesh, and there was the jar and shiver of a torn muscle. The thing sickened him, and his grip slackened. In a moment Vlastos had swung him over in a strangle-hold, and had his neck bent almost to breaking.

On the sickness followed a revulsion of fierce anger. He was contending not with a man, but with some shaggy beast from the thicket.

The passion brought out the extra power which is dormant in us all against the last extremity. Two years before he had been mauled by a leopard on the Congo, and had clutched its throat with his hand and torn the life out. Such and no other was his antagonist. He was fighting with one who knew no code, and would gouge his eyes if he got the chance. The fear which had sickened him was driven out by fury. This wolf should go the way of other wolves who dared to strive with man.

By a mighty effort he got his right arm free, and though his own neck was in torture, he forced Vlastos' chin upward. It was a struggle of sheer endurance, till with a snarl the other slackened his pressure. Vernon slipped from his grasp, gave back a step, and then leaped for the under-grip. He seemed possessed with unholy strength, for the barrel of the man gave in his embrace. A rib cracked, and as they swayed to the breast-stroke, he felt the breath of his opponent coming in harsh gasps. It was the end, for with a twist which unlocked his arms he swung him high, and hurled him towards the fireplace. The head crashed on the stone hearth, and the man lay stunned among the blue jets of wood-smoke.

Vernon turned dizzily to the girl. She stood, statue-like, with the lamp in her hand, and beside her huddled Mitri and Elise.

'Bring ropes,' he cried to the servants. 'We will truss up this beast. The other wolves will find him and learn a lesson.' He bound his legs and arms and laid him on a divan.

The fire of battle was still in his eyes, but it faded when they fell upon the pale girl. A great pity and tenderness filled him. She swayed to his arms, and her head dropped on his shoulder. He picked her up like a child, and followed the servants to the sea-stair.

But first he found Vlastos' whistle, and blew it shrilly. The answer was a furious hammering at the castle door ...

Far out at sea, in the small hours, the yacht sped eastward with a favouring wind. Behind in the vault of night at a great distance shone a point of brightness, which flickered and fell as if from some mighty fire.

The two sat in the stern in that first rapture of comradeship which has no words to fit it. Her head lay in the crook of his arm, and she sighed happily, like one awakened to a summer's dawn from a night of ill dreams. At last he spoke.

'Do you know that I have been looking for you for twenty years?'
She nestled closer to him.

'And I,' she said, 'have been waiting on you from the beginning of
the world.'

The King of Ypres

'The King of Ypres' first appeared in *Allied News*, most probably during the First World War, and then in January 1930 in the *Manchester Evening Chronicle*, as part of a series of war stories, followed a few months later by publication in the *South African Cape Argus*. Its only appearances in book form, until now, were in the American edition of *The Watcher by the Threshold* (1918) and in Volume 20 of *The Masterpiece Library of Short Stories: The War* (1923), alongside stories from Edgar Wallace, Alec Waugh, Sapper and Arthur Machen.

It has certain similarities, in its theme of the ordinary man transformed by a wartime experience, to two First World War novels, R.W. Campbell's *Private Spud Tamson* and John Oxenham's *All's Well*.

PRIVATE PETER GALBRAITH, of the 3rd Lennox Highlanders, awoke with a splitting headache and the consciousness of an intolerable din. At first he thought it was the whistle from the forge, which a year ago had pulled him from his bed when he was a puddler in Motherwell. He scrambled to his feet, and nearly cracked his skull against a low roof. That, and a sound which suggested that the heavens were made of canvas which a giant hand was rending, cleared his wits and recalled him to the disagreeable present. He lit the dottle in his pipe, and began to piece out his whereabouts.

Late the night before, the remnants of his battalion had been brought in from the Gheluvelt trenches to billets in Ypres. That last week he had gone clean off his sleep. He had not been dry for a fortnight, his puttees had rotted away, his greatcoat had disappeared in a mud-hole, and he had had no stomach for what food could be got. He had seen half his battalion die before his eyes, and day and night the shells had burst round him till the place looked like the ironworks at Motherwell on a foggy night. The worst of it was that he had never come to grips with the Boches, which he had long decided was the one pleasure left to him in life. He had got far beyond cursing, though he had once had a talent that way. His mind was as sodden as his body, and his thoughts had been focussed on the penetrating power of a bayonet when directed against a plump Teutonic chest. There had been a German barber in Motherwell called Schultz, and he imagined the enemy as a million Schultzes – large, round men who talked with the back of their throat.

In billets he had scraped off the worst part of the mud, and drunk half a bottle of wine which a woman had given him. It tasted like red ink, but anything liquid was better than food. Sleep was what he longed for, but he could not get it. The Boches were shelling the town, and the room he shared with six others seemed as noisy as the Gallowgate on a Saturday night. He wanted to get deep down into the earth where there was no sound; so, while the others snored, he started out to look for a cellar. In the black darkness, while the house rocked to the shell reverberations, he had groped his way down the stairs, found a door which led to another flight, and, slipping and stumbling, had come to a narrow, stuffy chamber which smelt of potatoes. There he had lain down on some sacks and fallen into a frowsty slumber.

His head was spinning, but the hours of sleep had done him good. He felt a slight appetite for breakfast, as well as an intolerable thirst. He groped his way up the stairs, and came out in a dilapidated hall lit by a dim November morning.

There was no sign of the packs which had been stacked there the night before. He looked for a Boche's helmet which he had brought in as a souvenir, but that was gone. Then he found the room where he had been billeted. It was empty, and only the stale smell of tobacco told of its occupants.

Lonely, disconsolate, and oppressed with thoughts of future punishment, he moved towards the street door. Suddenly the door of a side room opened and a man came out, a furtive figure, with a large, pasty face. His pockets bulged, and in one hand was a silver candlestick. At the sight of Galbraith he jumped back and held up a pistol.

'Pit it down, man, and tell's what's come ower this place?' said the soldier. For answer, a bullet sang past his ear and shivered a plaster Venus.

Galbraith gave his enemy the butt of his rifle and laid him out. From his pockets he shook out a mixed collection of loot. He took possession of his pistol, and kicked him with some vehemence into a cupboard.

'That yin's a thief,' was his spoken reflection. 'There's something michty wrong wi' Wipers the day.'

His head was clearing, and he was getting very wroth. His battalion had gone off and left him in a cellar, and miscreants were abroad. It was time for a respectable man to be up and doing. Besides, he wanted his breakfast. He fixed his bayonet, put the pistol in his pocket, and emerged into the November drizzle.

The streets suddenly were curiously still. The occasional shell-fire came to his ears as if through layers of cotton-wool. He put this down to dizziness from lack of food, and made his way to what looked like an *estaminet*. The place was full of riotous people who were helping themselves to drinks, while a distracted landlord wrung his hands. He flew to Galbraith, the tears running down his cheeks, and implored him in broken words.

'Vere ze Engleesh?' he cried. 'Ze méchants rob me. Zere is une émeute. Vere ze officers?'

'That's what I'm wantin' to ken mysel',' said Galbraith.

'Zey are gone,' wailed the innkeeper. 'Zere is no gendarme or anyzing, and I am rob.'

'Where's the polis? Get the Provost, man. D'ye tell me there's no polis left?'

'I am rob,' the wail continued. 'Ze méchants rob ze magasins and ve vill be assassinés.'

Light was dawning upon Private Galbraith. The British troops had left Ypres for some reason which he could not fathom, and there was no law or order in the little city. At other times he had hated the law as much as any man, and his relations with the police had often been strained. Now he realised that he had done them an injustice. Disorder suddenly seemed to him the one thing intolerable. Here had he been undergoing a stiff discipline for weeks, and if that was his fate no civilian should be allowed on the loose. He was a British soldier – marooned here by no fault of his own – and it was his business to keep up the end of the British Army and impose the King's peace upon the unruly. His temper was getting hot, but he was curiously happy. He marched into the *estaminet*. 'Oot o' here, ye scum!' he bellowed. 'Sortez, ye cochons!'

The revellers were silent before the apparition. Then one, drunker than the rest, flung a bottle which grazed his right ear. That put the finishing touch to his temper. Roaring like a bull, he was among them, prodding their hinder parts with his bayonet, and now and then reversing his rifle to crack a head. He had not played centre-forward in the old days at Celtic Park for nothing. The place emptied in a twinkling – all but one man whose legs could not support him. Him Private Galbraith seized by the scruff and the slack of his trousers, and tossed into the street.

'Now I'll hae my breakfast,' he said to the trembling landlord.

Private Galbraith, much the better for his exercise, made a hearty meal of bread and cold ham, and quenched his thirst with two bottles of Hazebrouck beer. He had also a little brandy, and pocketed the flask, for which the landlord refused all payment. Then, feeling a giant refreshed, he sallied into the street.

'I'm off to look for your Provost,' he said. 'If ye have ony mair trouble, ye'll find me at the Toun Hall.'

A shell had plumped into the middle of the causeway, and the place was empty. Private Galbraith, despising shells, swaggered up the open, his disreputable kilt swinging about his putteeless legs, the remnant of a bonnet set well on the side of his shaggy red head, and the light of battle in his eyes. For once he was arrayed on the side of the angels, and the thought encouraged him mightily. The brandy had fired his imagination.

Adventure faced him at the next corner. A woman was struggling with two men – a slim pale girl with dark hair. No sound came from her lips, but her eyes were bright with terror. Galbraith started to run, shouting sound British oaths. The men let the woman go, and turned to face him. One had a pistol, and for the second time that day a bullet just missed its mark. An instant later a clean bayonet thrust had ended the mortal career of the marksman, and the other had taken to his heels.

'I'll learn thae lads to be sae free wi' their popguns,' said the irate soldier. 'Haud up, Mem. It's a' by wi' noo. Losh! The wumman's fentit!'

Private Galbraith was as shy of women as of his Commanding Officer, and he had not bargained for this duty. She was clearly a lady from her dress and appearance, and this did not make it easier. He supported her manfully, addressing to her the kind of encouragements which a groom gives to a horse. 'Canny now, Mem. Haud up! Ye've no cause to be feared.'

[37]

Then he remembered the brandy in his pocket, and with much awkwardness managed to force some drops between her lips. To his vast relief she began to come to. Her eyes opened and stared uncomprehendingly at her preserver. Then she found her voice.

'Thank God, the British have come back!' she said in excellent English.

'No, Mem; not yet. It's just me, Private Galbraith, "C" Company, 3rd Battalion, Lennox Highlanders. Ye keep some bad lots in this toun.'

'Alas! what can we do? The place is full of spies, and they will stir up the dregs of the people and make Ypres a hell. Oh, why did the British go? Our good men are all with the army, and there are only old folk and wastrels left.'

'Rely upon me, Mem,' said Galbraith stoutly. 'I was just settin' off to find your Provost.'

She puzzled at the word, and then understood.

'He has gone!' she cried. 'The Maire went to Dunkirk a week ago, and there is no authority in Ypres.'

'Then we'll make yin. Here's the minister. We'll speir at him.'

An old priest, with a lean, grave face, had come up.

'Ah, Mam'selle Omèrine,' he cried, 'the devil in our city is unchained. Who is this soldier?'

The two talked in French, while Galbraith whistled and looked at the sky. A shrapnel shell was bursting behind the cathedral, making a splash of colour in the November fog. Then the priest spoke in careful and constrained English.

'There is yet a chance for a strong man. But he must be very strong. Mam'selle will summon her father, Monsieur le Procureur, and we will meet at the Mairie. I will guide you there, *mon brave*.'

The Grande Place was deserted, and in the middle there was a new gaping shell-hole. At the door of a great building, which Galbraith assumed to be the Town Hall, a feeble old porter was struggling with a man. Galbraith scragged the latter and pitched him into the shell-hole. There was a riot going on in a café on the far side which he itched to have a hand in, but he postponed that pleasure to a more convenient season.

Twenty minutes later, in a noble room with frescoed and tapestried walls, there was a strange conference. The priest was there, and Galbraith, and Mam'selle Omèrine, and her father, M. St Marais.

There was a doctor too, and three elderly citizens, and an old warrior who had left an arm on the Yser. Galbraith took charge, with Mam'selle as his interpreter, and in half an hour had constituted a Committee of Public Safety. He had nervous folk to deal with.

'The Germans may enter at any moment, and then we will all be hanged,' said one.

'Nae doot,' said Galbraith; 'but ye needna get your throats cut afore they come.'

'The city is full of the ill-disposed,' said another. 'The Boches have their spies in every alley. We who are so few cannot control them.'

'If it's spies,' said Galbraith firmly, 'I'll take on the job my lone. D'ye think a terrier dowg's feared of a wheen rottens?'

In the end he had his way, with Mam'selle's help, and had put some confidence into civic breasts. It took him the best part of the afternoon to collect his posse. He got every wounded Belgian that had the use of his legs, some well-grown boys, one or two ancients, and several dozen robust women. There was no lack of weapons, and he armed the lot with a strange collection of French and English rifles, giving pistols to the section leaders. With the help of the Procureur, he divided the city into beats and gave his followers instructions. They were drastic orders, for the situation craved for violence.

He spent the evening of his life. So far as he remembered afterwards, he was in seventeen different scraps. Strayed revellers were leniently dealt with – the canal was a cooling experience. Looters were rounded up, and, if they showed fight, summarily disposed of. One band of bullies made a stout resistance, killed two of his guards, and lost half-a-dozen dead. He got a black eye, a pistol-bullet through his sleeve, a wipe on the cheek from a carving-knife, and he lost the remnants of his bonnet. Fifty-two prisoners spent the night in the cellars of the Mairie.

About midnight he found himself in the tapestried chamber. 'We'll hae to get a Proclamation,' he had announced; 'a gude strong yin, for we maun conduct this job according to the rules.' So the Procureur had a document drawn up bidding all inhabitants of Ypres keep indoors except between the hours of 10 A.M. and noon, and 3 and 5 P.M.; forbidding the sale of alcohol in all forms; and making theft and violence and the carrying of arms punishable by death. There was a host of other provisions which Galbraith imperfectly understood, but when the thing was translated to him he approved its spirit. He signed the document in his large sprawling hand – 'Peter Galbraith, 1473, Pte., 3rd Lennox Highlanders, Acting Provost of Wipers.'

'Get that prentit,' he said, 'and pit up copies at every street corner and on a' the public-hooses. And see that the doors o' the publics are boardit up. That'll do for the day. I'm feelin' verra like my bed.'

Mam'selle Omèrine watched him with a smile. She caught his eye and dropped him a curtsey.

'Monsieur le Roi d'Ypres,' she said.

He blushed hotly.

For the next few days Private Galbraith worked harder than ever before in his existence. For the first time he knew responsibility, and that toil which brings honour with it. He tasted the sweets of office; and he, whose aim in life had been to scrape through with the minimum of exertion, now found himself the inspirer of the maximum in others.

At first he scorned advice, being shy and nervous. Gradually, as he felt his feet, he became glad of other people's wisdom. Especially he leaned on two, Mam'selle Omèrine and her father. Likewise the priest, whom he called the minister.

By the second day the order in Ypres was remarkable. By the third day it was phenomenal; and by the fourth a tyranny. The little city for the first time for seven hundred years fell under the sway of a despot. A citizen had to be on his best behaviour, for the Acting Provost's eye was on him. Never was seen so sober a place. Three permits for alcohol and no more were issued, and then only on the plea of medical necessity. Peter handed over to the doctor the flask of brandy he had carried off from the *estaminet* – Provosts must set an example.

The Draconian code promulgated the first night was not adhered to. Looters and violent fellows went to gaol instead of the gallows. But three spies were taken and shot after a full trial. That trial was the master effort of Private Galbraith – based on his own regimental experience and memories of a Sheriff Court in Lanarkshire, where he had twice appeared for poaching. He was extraordinarily punctilious about forms, and the three criminals – their guilt was clear, and they were the scum of creation – had something more than justice. The Acting Provost pronounced sentence, which the priest translated, and a file of *mutilés* in the yard did the rest.

'If the Boches get in here we'll pay for this day's work,' said the judge cheerfully; 'but I'll gang easier to the grave for havin' got rid o' thae swine.'

On the fourth day he had a sudden sense of dignity. He examined his apparel, and found it very bad. He needed a new bonnet, a new kilt, and puttees, and he would be the better of a new shirt. Being aware that commandeering for personal use ill suited with his office, he put the case before the Procureur, and a *Commission de Ravitaillement* was appointed. Shirts and puttees were easily got, but the kilt and bonnet were difficulties. But next morning Mam'selle Omèrine brought a gift. It was a bonnet with such a dicing round the rim as no Jock ever wore, and a skirt — it is the truest word — of that pattern which graces the persons of small girls in France. It was not the Lennox tartan, it was not any kind of tartan, but Private Galbraith did not laugh. He accepted the garments with a stammer of thanks — 'They're awfu' braw, and I'm much obliged, Mem' — and, what is more, he put them on. The Ypriotes saw his splendour with approval. It was a proof of his new frame of mind that he did not even trouble to reflect what his comrades would think of his costume, and that he kissed the bonnet affectionately before he went to bed.

That night he had evil dreams. He suddenly saw the upshot of it all — himself degraded and shot as a deserter, and his brief glory pricked like a bubble. Grim forebodings of court-martials assailed him. What would Mam'selle think of him when he was led away in disgrace — he who for a little had been a king? He walked about the floor in a frenzy of disquiet, and stood long at the window peering over the Place, lit by a sudden blink of moonlight. It could never be, he decided. Something desperate would happen first. The crash of a shell a quarter of a mile off reminded him that he was in the midst of war — war with all its chances of cutting knots.

Next morning no Procureur appeared. Then came the priest with a sad face and a sadder tale. Mam'selle had been out late the night before on an errand of mercy, and a shell, crashing through a gable, had sent an avalanche of masonry into the street. She was dead, without pain, said the priest, and in the sure hope of Heaven.

The others wept, but Private Galbraith strode from the room, and in a very little time was at the house of the Procureur. He saw his little colleague laid out for death after the fashion of her Church, and his head suddenly grew very clear and his heart hotter than fire.

'I maun resign this job,' he told the Committee of Public Safety.

'I've been forgettin' that I'm a sodger and no a Provost. It's my duty to get a nick at thae Boches.'

They tried to dissuade him, but he was adamant. His rule was over, and he was going back to serve.

But he was not allowed to resign. For that afternoon, after a week's absence, the British troops came again into Ypres.

They found a decorous little city, and many people who spoke of 'le Roi' – which they assumed to signify the good King Albert. Also, in a corner of the cathedral yard, sitting disconsolately on the edge of a fallen monument, Company Sergeant-Major Macvittie of the 3rd Lennox Highlanders found Private Peter Galbraith.

'Ma God, Galbraith, ye've done it this time! *You'll* catch it in the neck! Absent for a week wi'out leave, and gettin' yoursel' up to look like Harry Lauder! You come along wi' me!'

'I'll come quiet,' said Galbraith with strange meekness. He was wondering how to spell Omèrine St Marais in case he wanted to write it in his Bible.

The events of the next week were confusing to a plain man. Galbraith was very silent, and made no reply to the chaff with which at first he was greeted. Soon his fellows forbore to chaff him, regarding him as a doomed man who had come well within the pale of the ultimate penalties.

He was examined by his Commanding Officer, and interviewed by still more exalted personages. The story he told was so bare as to be unintelligible. He asked for no mercy, and gave no explanations. But there were other witnesses besides him – the priest, for example, and Monsieur St Marais, in a sober suit of black and very dark under the eyes.

By and by the Court gave its verdict. Private Peter Galbraith was found guilty of riding roughshod over the King's Regulations; he had absented himself from his battalion without permission; he had neglected his own duties and usurped without authority a number of superior functions; he had been the cause of the death or maltreatment of various persons who, whatever their moral deficiencies, must be regarded for the purposes of the case as civilian Allies. The Court, however, taking into consideration the exceptional circumstances in which Private Galbraith had been placed, inflicted no penalty and summarily discharged the prisoner.

Privately, his Commanding Officer and the still more exalted personages shook hands with him, and told him that he was a devilish good fellow and a credit to the British Army.

But Peter Galbraith cared for none of these things. As he sat again in the trenches at St Eloi in six inches of water and a foot of mud, he asked his neighbour how many Germans were opposite them.

'I was hearin' that there was maybe fifty thoosand,' was the answer.

Private Galbraith was content. He thought that the whole fifty thousand would scarcely atone for the death of one slim, dark-eyed girl.

Fullcircle

'Fullcircle' was first published in the January 1920 editions of *Blackwood's Magazine* and *The Atlantic Monthly* in a slightly shorter form than was used in *The Runagates Club* (1928), and with a narrator called Jardine; it is this first version which is reprinted here. It was included as Martin Peckwether's tale in *The Runagates Club* and appeared in the magazine *Argosy* in 1935.

In September 1917 Buchan and his wife spent four days in the Cotswolds house-hunting and he returned to the area the following year with a friend, Hugh Macmillan, Lord Chancellor in the first Labour Government, on the same task. On one of those trips he came across Weald Manor at Bampton, reputedly the inspiration for this story. The Giffens bear a certain resemblance to Sidney and Beatrice Webb.

> Between the Windrush and the Colne
> I found a little house of stone –
> A little wicked house of stone.

THE OCTOBER DAY was brightening toward late afternoon when Leithen and I climbed the hill above the stream and came in sight of the house. All morning a haze with the sheen of pearl in it had lain on the folds of downland, and the vision of far horizons, which is the glory of Cotswold, had been veiled, so that every valley seemed as a place inclosed and set apart. But now a glow had come into the air, and for a little the autumn lawns stole the tints of summer. The gold of sunshine was warm on the grasses, and only the riot of colour in the berry-laden edges of the fields and the slender woodlands told of the failing year.

We were looking into a green cup of the hills, and it was all a garden. A little place, bounded by slopes that defined its graciousness

[44]

with no hint of barrier, so that a dweller there, though his view was but half a mile on any side, would yet have the sense of dwelling on uplands and commanding the world. Round the top edge ran an old wall of stones, beyond which the October bracken flamed to the skyline. Inside were folds of ancient pasture, with here and there a thorn-bush, falling to rose gardens and, on one side, to the smooth sward of a terrace above a tiny lake.

At the heart of it stood the house like a jewel well-set. It was a miniature, but by the hand of a master. The style was late seventeenth century, when an agreeable classic convention had opened up to sunlight and comfort the dark magnificence of the Tudor fashion. The place had the spacious air of a great mansion, and was furnished in every detail with a fine scrupulousness. Only when the eye measured its proportions with the woods and the hillside did the mind perceive that it was a small dwelling.

The stone of Cotswold takes curiously the colour of the weather. Under thunderclouds it will be as dark as basalt; on a grey day it will be grey like lava but in sunshine it absorbs the sun. At the moment the little house was pale gold, like honey.

Leithen swung a long leg across the stile.

'Pretty good, isn't it?' he said. 'It's pure, authentic Sir Christopher Wren. The name is worthy of it, too. It is called Fullcircle.'

He told me its story. It had been built after the Restoration by the Carteron family, whose wide domains ran into these hills. The Lord Carteron of the day was a friend of the Merry Monarch; but it was not as a sanctuary for orgies that he built the house. Perhaps he was tired of the gloomy splendour of Minster Carteron, and wanted a home of his own and not of his ancestors' choosing. He had an elegant taste in letters, as we can learn from his neat imitations of Martial, his pretty *Bucolics* and the more than respectable Latin hexameters of his *Ars Vivendi*. Being a great nobleman, he had the best skill of the day to construct his hermitage, and thither he would retire for months at a time, with like-minded friends, to a world of books and gardens. He seems to have had no ill-wishers; contemporary memoirs speak of him charitably and Dryden spared him four lines of encomium. 'A selfish old dog,' Leithen called him. 'He had the good sense to eschew politics and enjoy life. His soul is in that little house. He only did one rash thing in his career – he anticipated the King, his master, by some years in turning Papist.'

I asked about its later history.

'After his death it passed to a younger branch of the Carterons. It left them in the eighteenth century, and the Applebys got it. They were a jovial lot of hunting squires and let the library go to the dogs. Old Colonel Appleby was still alive when I came to Borrowby. Something went wrong in his inside when he was nearly seventy, and the doctors knocked him off liquor. Not that he drank too much, though he did himself well. That finished the poor old boy. He told me that it revealed to him the amazing truth that during a long and, as he hoped, publicly useful life he had never been quite sober. He was a good fellow and I missed him when he died. The place went to a remote cousin called Giffen.'

Leithen's eyes as they scanned the prospect, seemed amused.

'Julian and Ursula Giffen – I dare say you know the names. They always hunt in couples, and write books about sociology and advanced ethics and psychics – books called either "The New This or That" or "The Truth about Something or Other". You know the sort of thing. They're deep in all the pseudo-sciences. They're decent souls, but you can guess the type. I came across them in a case I had at the Old Bailey – defending a ruffian who was charged with murder. I hadn't a doubt he deserved hanging on twenty counts, but there wasn't enough evidence to convict him on this one. Dodderidge was at his worst – it was just before they induced him to retire – and his handling of the jury was a masterpiece of misdirection. Of course, there was a shindy. The thing was a scandal, and it stirred up all the humanitarians till the murderer was almost forgotten in the iniquities of old Dodderidge. You must remember the case. It filled the papers for weeks. Well, it was in that connection that I fell in with the Giffens. I got rather to like them, and I've been to see them at their house in Hampstead. Golly, what a place! Not a chair fit to sit down on, and colours that made you want to howl. I never met people whose heads were so full of feathers.'

I said something about that being an odd *milieu* for him.

'Oh, I like human beings, all kinds. It's my profession to study them, for without that the practice of the law would be a dismal affair. There are hordes of people like the Giffens – only not so good, for they really have hearts of gold. They are the rootless stuff in the world to-day. In revolt against everything and everybody with any ancestry. A kind of innocent self-righteousness – wanting to be the people with whom wisdom begins and ends. They are mostly sensitive and tender-hearted, but they wear themselves out in an eternal dissidence. Can't build, you know, for they object to all tools, but very ready to crab. They scorn any form of Christianity, but they'll walk miles to patronise some wretched sect that has the merit of being brand-new. "Pioneers" they call themselves – funny little unclad people adventuring into the cold desert with no maps. Giffen once described himself and his friends to me as "forward-looking", but that, of course, is just what they are not. To tackle the future you must have a firm grip of the past, and for them, the past is only a pathological curiosity. They're up to their necks in the mud of the present – but good, after a fashion; and innocent – sordidly innocent. Fate was in an ironical mood when she saddled them with that wicked little house.'

'Wicked' did not seem to me to be a fair word. It sat honey-coloured among its gardens with the meekness of a dove.

The sound of a bicycle on the road behind made us turn round, and Leithen advanced to meet a dismounting rider.

He was a tallish fellow, some forty years old, perhaps, with one of those fluffy blond beards that have never been shaved. Short-sighted, of course, and wore glasses. Biscuit-coloured knickerbockers and stockings clad his lean limbs.

Leithen introduced me. 'We are walking to Borrowby and stopped to admire your house. Could we have just a glimpse inside? I want Jardine to see the staircase.'

Mr Giffen was very willing. 'I've been over to Clyston to send a telegram. We have some friends for the week-end who might interest you. Won't you stay to tea?'

He had a gentle, formal courtesy about him, and his voice had the facile intonations of one who loves to talk. He led us through a little gate, and along a shorn green walk among the bracken, to a postern which gave entrance to the garden. Here, though it was October, there was still a bright show of roses, and the jet of water from the leaden Cupid dripped noiselessly among fallen petals. And then we stood before the doorway above which the old Carteron had inscribed a line of Horace.

I have never seen anything quite like the little hall. There were two, indeed, separated by a staircase of a wood that looked like olive. Both were paved with black-and-white marble, and the inner was oval in shape, with a gallery supported on slender walnut pillars. It was all in miniature, but it had a spaciousness which no mere size could give. Also it seemed to be permeated by the quintessence of sunlight. Its air was of long-descended, confident, equable happiness.

There were voices on the terrace beyond the hall. Giffen led us into a little room on the left. 'You remember the house in Colonel Appleby's time, Leithen. This was the chapel. It had always been the chapel. You see the change we have made. – I beg your pardon, Mr Jardine. You're not by any chance a Roman Catholic?'

The room had a white panelling and, on two sides, deep windows. At one end was a fine Italian shrine of marble, and the floor was mosaic, blue and white, in a quaint Byzantine pattern. There was the same air of sunny cheerfulness as in the rest of the house. No mystery could find a lodgement here. It might have been a chapel for three centuries, but the place was pagan. The Giffens' changes were no sort of desecration. A green baize table filled most of the floor, surrounded by chairs like a committee room. On new raw-wood shelves were files of papers and stacks of blue-books and those desiccated works into which reformers of society torture the English tongue. Two type-writers stood on a side table.

'It is our workroom,' Giffen explained. 'We hold our Sunday moots here. Ursula thinks that a week-end is wasted unless it produces some piece of real work. Often a quite valuable committee has its beginning here. We try to make our home a refuge for busy workers, where they need not idle but can work under happy conditions.'

' "A college situate in a clearer air," ' Leithen quoted.

But Giffen did not respond except with a smile; he had probably never heard of Lord Falkland.

A woman entered the room, a woman who might have been pretty if she had taken a little pains. Her reddish hair was drawn tightly back and dressed in a hard knot, and her clothes were horribly incongruous in a remote manor-house. She had bright eager eyes, like a bird, and hands that fluttered nervously. She greeted Leithen with warmth.

'We have settled down marvellously,' she told him. 'Julian and I feel as if we had always lived here, and our life has arranged itself so perfectly. My mothers' cottages in the village will soon be ready, and the Club is to be opened next week. Julian and I will carry on the classes ourselves for the first winter. Next year we hope to have a really fine programme. And then it is so pleasant to be able to entertain one's friends. Won't you stay to tea? Dr Swope is here, and Mary Elliston, and Mr Percy Blaker – you know, the Member of Parliament. Must you hurry off? I'm so sorry. – What do you think of our workroom? It was utterly terrible when we first came here – a sort of decayed chapel, like a withered tuberose. We have let the air of heaven into it.'

I observed that I had never seen a house so full of space and light.

'Ah, you notice that? It is a curiously happy place to live in. Sometimes I'm almost afraid to feel so light-hearted. But we look on ourselves as only trustees. It is a trust we have to administer for the common good. You know, it's a house on which you can lay your own impress. I can imagine places which dominate the dwellers, but Fullcircle is plastic, and we can make it our own as much as if we had planned and built it. That's our chief piece of good fortune.'

We took our leave, for we had no desire for the company of Dr Swope and Mr Percy Blaker. When we reached the highway we halted and looked back on the little jewel. Shafts of the westering sun now caught the stone and turned the honey to ripe gold. Thin spires of amethyst smoke rose into the still air. I thought of the well-meaning, restless couple inside its walls, and somehow they seemed out of the picture. They simply did not matter. The house was the thing, for I had never met in inanimate stone such an air of gentle masterfulness. It had a personality of its own, clean-cut and secure, like a high-born old dame among the females of profiteers. And Mrs Giffen claimed to have given it her impress!

That night, in the library at Borrowby, Leithen discoursed of the Restoration. Borrowby, of which, by the expenditure of much care and a good deal of money, he had made a civilised dwelling, is a Tudor manor of the Cotswold type, with its high-pitched narrow roofs and tall stone chimneys, rising sheer from the meadows with something of the massiveness of a Border keep.

He nodded toward the linen-fold panelling and the great carved chimney-piece.

'In this kind of house you have the mystery of the elder England. What was Raleigh's phrase? "High thoughts and divine contemplations." The people who built this sort of thing lived close to another world, and thought bravely of death. It doesn't matter who they were – Crusaders or Elizabethans or Puritans – they all had poetry in them and the heroic and a great unworldliness. They had marvellous spirits, and plenty of joys and triumphs; but they had also their hours of black gloom. Their lives were like our weather – storm and sun. One thing

[49]

they never feared – death. He walked too near them all their days to be a bogey.

'But the Restoration was a sharp break. It brought paganism into England; paganism and the art of life. No people have ever known better the secret of bland happiness. Look at Fullcircle. There are no dark corners there. The man that built it knew all there was to be known about how to live. The trouble was that they did not know how to die. That was the one shadow on the glass. So they provided for it in a pagan way. They tried magic. They never become true Catholics – they were always pagan to the end, but they smuggled a priest into their lives. He was a kind of insurance premium against unwelcome mystery.'

It was not till nearly two years later that I saw the Giffens again. The May-fly season was about at its close, and I had snatched a day on a certain limpid Cotswold river. There was another man on the same beat, fishing from the opposite bank, and I watched him with some anxiety, for a duffer would have spoiled my day. To my relief I recognised Giffen. With him it was easy to come to terms, and presently the water was parcelled out between us.

We foregathered for luncheon, and I stood watching while he neatly stalked, rose, and landed a trout. I confessed to some surprise – first that Giffen should be a fisherman at all, for it was not in keeping with my old notion of him; and second, that he should cast such a workmanlike line. As we lunched together, I observed several changes. He had shaved his fluffy beard, and his face was notably less lean, and had the clear even sunburn of the countryman. His clothes, too, were different. They also were workmanlike, and looked as if they belonged to him – he no longer wore the uneasy knickerbockers of the Sunday golfer.

'I'm desperately keen,' he told me. 'You see it's only my second May-fly season, and last year I was no better than a beginner. I wish I had known long ago what good fun fishing was. Isn't this a blessed place?' And he looked up through the canopy of flowering chestnuts to the June sky.

'I'm glad you've taken to sport,' I said, 'even if you only come here for the week-ends. Sport lets you into the secrets of the countryside.'

'Oh, we don't go much to London now,' was his answer. 'We sold our Hampstead house a year ago. I can't think how I ever could stick that place. Ursula takes the same view. I wouldn't leave Oxfordshire just now for a thousand pounds. Do you smell the hawthorn? Last week this meadow was scented like Paradise. – D'you know, Leithen's a queer fellow?'

I asked why.

'He once told me that this countryside in June made him sad. He said it was too perfect a thing for fallen humanity. I call that morbid. Do you see any sense in it?'

I knew what Leithen meant, but it would have taken too long to explain.

'I feel warm and good and happy here,' he went on. 'I used to talk about living close to nature. Rot! I didn't know what nature meant. Now—' He broke off. 'By Jove, there's a kingfisher. That is only the second I've seen this year. They're getting uncommon with us.'

'With us.' I liked the phrase. He was becoming a true countryman.

We had a good day, – not extravagantly successful, but satisfactory, – and he persuaded me to come home with him to Fullcircle for the night, explaining that I could catch an early train next morning at the junction. So we extricated a little two-seater from the midst of a clump of lilacs, and drove through four miles of sweet-scented dusk, with nightingales shouting in every thicket.

I changed into a suit of his flannels in a room looking out on the little lake where trout were rising, and I remember that I whistled from pure light-heartedness. In that adorable house one seemed to be still breathing the air of the spring meadows.

Dinner was my first big surprise. It was admirable – plain, but perfectly cooked, and with that excellence of basic material which is the glory of a well-appointed country house. There was wine, too, which I am certain was a new thing. Giffen gave me a bottle of sound claret, and afterwards some more than decent port. My second surprise was my hostess. Her clothes, like her husband's, must have changed, for I did not notice what she was wearing, and I had noticed it only too clearly the last time we met. More remarkable still was the difference in her face. For the first time I realised that she was a pretty woman. The contours had softened and rounded, and there was a charming well-being in her eyes, very different from the old restlessness. She looked content, infinitely content.

I asked about her mothers' cottages. She laughed cheerfully.

'I gave them up after the first year. They didn't mix well with the village people. I'm quite ready to admit my mistake, and it was the wrong kind of charity. The Londoners didn't like it – felt lonesome and sighed for the fried-fish shop; and the village women were shy of them – afraid of infectious complaints, you know. Julian and I have decided that our business is to look after our own people.'

It may have been malicious, but I said something about the wonderful scheme of village education.

'Another relic of Cockneyism,' laughed the lady, but Giffen looked a trifle shy.

'I gave it up because it didn't seem worth while. What is the use of spoiling a perfectly wholesome scheme of life by introducing unnecessary complications? Medicine is no good unless a man is sick, and these people are not sick. Education is the only cure for certain diseases the modern world has engendered, but if you don't find the disease, the remedy is superfluous. The fact is, I hadn't the face to go on with the thing. I wanted to be taught rather than to teach. There's a whole world round me of which I know very little, and my first business is to get to understand it. Any village poacher can teach me more of the things that matter than I have to tell him.'

'Besides, we have so much to do,' his wife added. 'There's the house and the garden and the home farm and the property. It isn't large, but it takes a lot of looking after.'

The dining-room was long and low-ceilinged, and had a white panelling in bold relief. Through the deep windows came odours of the garden and a faint tinkle of water. The dusk was deepening and the engravings in their rosewood frames were dim, but sufficient light remained to reveal the picture above the fireplace. It showed a middle-aged man in the clothes of the later Stuarts. The plump tapering fingers of one hand held a book; the other was hidden in the folds of a flowered waistcoat. The long curled wig framed a delicate face with something of the grace of youth left to it. There were quizzical lines about the mouth, and the eyes smiled pleasantly yet very wisely. It was the face of a man I should have liked to dine with. He must have been the best of company.

Giffen answered my question.

'That's the Lord Carteron who built the house. No – no relation. Our people were the Applebys, who came in 1753. We've both fallen so deep in love with Fullcircle that we wanted to see the man who conceived it. I had some trouble getting it. It came out of the Minster

Carteron sale, and I had to give a Jew dealer twice what he paid for it. It's a jolly thing to live with.'

It was indeed a curiously charming picture. I found my eyes straying to it till the dusk obscured the features. It was the face of one wholly at home in a suave world, learned in all the urbanities. A good friend, I thought, the old lord must have been, and a superlative companion. I could imagine neat Horatian tags coming ripely from his lips. Not a strong face, but somehow a dominating one. The portrait of the long-dead gentleman had still the atmosphere of life. Giffen raised his glass of port to him as we rose from table, as if to salute a comrade.

We moved to the room across the hall which had once been the Giffens' workroom, the cradle of earnest committees and weighty memoranda. This was my third surprise. Baize-covered table and raw-wood shelves had disappeared. The place was now half smoking-room, half library. On the walls hung a fine collection of coloured sporting prints, and below them were ranged low Hepplewhite bookcases. The lamplight glowed on the ivory walls, and the room, like everything else in the house, was radiant.

Above the mantelpiece was a stag's head – a fair eleven-pointer.

Giffen nodded proudly toward it. 'I got that last year at Machray. My first stag.'

There was a little table with an array of magazines and weekly papers. Some amusement must have been visible in my face, as I caught sight of various light-hearted sporting journals, for he laughed apologetically. 'You mustn't think that Ursula and I take in that stuff for ourselves. It amuses our guests, you know.'

I dared say it did, but I was convinced that the guests were no longer Dr Swope and Mr Percy Blaker.

One of my many failings is that I can never enter a room containing books without scanning the titles. Giffen's collection won my hearty approval. There were the very few novelists I can read myself – Miss Austen and Sir Walter and the admirable Marryat; there was a shelf full of memoirs, and a good deal of seventeenth- and eighteenth-century poetry; there was a set of the classics in fine editions. Bodonis and Baskervilles and such like; there was much county history and one or two valuable old Herbals and Itineraries. I was certain that two years earlier Giffen would have had no use for literature except some muddy Russian oddments, and I am positive that he would not have known the name of Surtees. Yet there stood the tall octavos recording the unedifying careers of Mr Jorrocks, Mr Facey Romford, and Mr Soapy Sponge.

I was a little bewildered as I stretched my legs in a very deep armchair. Suddenly I had a strong impression of looking on at a play. My hosts seemed to be automata, moving docilely at the orders of a masterful stage manager, and yet with no sense of bondage. And as I looked on, they faded off the scene, and there was only one personality – that house so serene and secure, smiling at our modern antics, but weaving all the while an iron spell around its lovers.

For a second I felt an oppression as of something to be resisted. But no. There was no oppression. The house was too well-bred and disdainful to seek to captivate. Only those who fell in love with it could know its mastery, for all love exacts a price. It was far more than a thing of stone and lime: it was a creed, an art, a scheme of life – older than any Carteron, older than England. Somewhere far back in time, in Rome, in Attica, or in an Ægean island, there must have been such places; and then they called them temples, and gods dwelt in them.

I was roused by Giffen's voice discoursing of his books. 'I've been rubbing up my classics again,' he was saying. 'Queer thing, but ever since I left Cambridge I have been out of the mood for them. And I'm shockingly ill-read in English literature. I wish I had more time for reading, for it means a lot to me.'

'There is such an embarrassment of riches here,' said his wife. 'The days are far too short for all there is to do. Even when there is nobody staying in the house I find every hour occupied. It's delicious to be busy over things one really cares for.'

'All the same I wish I could do more reading,' said Giffen. 'I've never wanted to so much before.'

'But you come in tired from shooting and sleep sound till dinner,' said the lady, laying an affectionate hand on his shoulder.

They were happy people, and I like happiness. Self-absorbed, perhaps, but I prefer selfishness in the ordinary way of things. We are most of us selfish dogs, and altruism makes us uncomfortable. But I had somehow in my mind a shade of uneasiness, for I was the witness of a transformation too swift and violent to be wholly natural. Years, no doubt, turn our eyes inward and abate our heroics, but not a trifle of two or three. Some agency had been at work here, some agency other and more potent than the process of time. The thing fascinated

[54]

and partly frightened me. For the Giffens – though I scarcely dared to admit it – had deteriorated. They were far pleasanter people, I liked them infinitely better, I hoped to see them often again. I detested the type they used to represent, and shunned it like the plague. They were wise now, and mellow, and most agreeable human beings. But some virtue had gone out of them. An uncomfortable virtue, no doubt, but still a virtue; something generous and adventurous. In the earlier time, their faces had had a sort of wistful kindness. Now they had geniality – which is not the same thing.

What was the agency of this miracle? It was all around me: the ivory panelling, the olive-wood staircase, the lovely pillared hall.

I got up to go to bed with a kind of awe on me. As Mrs Giffen lit my candle, she saw my eyes wandering among the gracious shadows.

'Isn't it wonderful,' she said, 'to have found a house which fits us like a glove? No! Closer. Fits us as a bearskin fits the bear. It has taken our impress like wax.'

Somehow I didn't think that impress had come from the Giffens' side.

A November afternoon found Leithen and myself jogging homeward from a run with the Heythrop. It had been a wretched day. Twice we had found and lost, and then a deluge had set in which scattered the field. I had taken a hearty toss into a swamp, and got as wet as a man may be, but the steady downpour soon reduced everyone to a like condition. When we turned toward Borrowby the rain ceased, and an icy wind blew out of the east which partially dried our sopping clothes. All the grace had faded from the Cotswold valleys. The streams were brown torrents, the meadows lagoons, the ridges bleak and grey, and a sky of scurrying clouds cast leaden shadows. It was a matter of ten miles to Borrowby; we had long ago emptied our flasks, and I longed for something hot to take the chill out of my bones.

'Let's look in at Fullcircle,' said Leithen, as we came out on the highroad from a muddy lane. 'We'll make the Giffens give us tea. You'll find changes there.'

I asked what changes, but he only smiled and told me to wait and see.

My mind was busy with surmises as we rode up the avenue. I thought of drink or drugs, and promptly discarded the notion. Full-circle was, above all things, decorous and wholesome. Leithen could not mean the change in the Giffens' ways which had so impressed me a year before, for he and I had long ago discussed that. I was still puzzling over his words when we found ourselves in the inner hall, with the Giffens making a hospitable fuss over us.

The place was more delectable than ever. Outside was a dark November day, yet the little house seemed to be transfused with sunshine. I do not know by what art the old builders had planned it; but the airy pilasters, the perfect lines of the ceiling, the soft colouring of the wood seemed to lay open the house to a clear sky. Logs burned brightly on the massive steel andirons, and the scent and the fine blue smoke of them strengthened the illusion of summer.

Mrs Giffen would have us change into dry things, but Leithen pleaded a waiting dinner at Borrowby. The two of us stood by the fireplace, drinking tea, the warmth drawing out a cloud of vapour from our clothes to mingle with the wood-smoke. Giffen lounged in an armchair and his wife sat by the tea-table. I was looking for the changes of which Leithen had spoken.

I did not find them in Giffen. He was much as I remembered him on the June night when I had slept here – a trifle fuller in the face, perhaps, a little more placid about the mouth and eyes. He looked a man completely content with life. His smile came readily, and his easy laugh. Was it my fancy, or had he acquired a look of the picture in the dining-room? I nearly made an errand to go and see it. It seemed to me that his mouth had now something of the portrait's delicate complacence. Lely would have found him a fit subject, though he might have boggled at his lean hands.

But his wife! Ah, there the changes were unmistakable. She was comely now rather than pretty, and the contours of her face had grown heavier. The eagerness had gone from her eyes and left only comfort and good humour. There was a suspicion, ever so slight, of rouge and powder. She had a string of good pearls – the first time I had seen her wear jewels. The hand that poured out the tea was plump, shapely, and well cared for. I was looking at a most satisfactory mistress of a country house, who would see that nothing was lacking to the part.

She talked more and laughed oftener. Her voice had an airy lightness which would have made the silliest prattle charming.

'We are going to fill the house with young people and give a ball at Christmas,' she announced. 'This hall is simply clamouring to be

danced in. You must come, both of you. Promise me. And, Mr Leithen, it would be very nice if you brought a party from Borrowby.
Young men, please. We are overstocked with girls in these parts. We
must do something to make the country cheerful in winter-time.'

I observed that no season could make Fullcircle other than cheerful.

'How nice of you!' she cried. 'To praise a house is to praise the
householders, for a dwelling is just what its inmates make it. Borrowby is you, Mr Leithen, and Fullcircle us.'

'Shall we exchange?' Leithen asked.

She made a mouth. 'Borrowby would crush me, but it suits a
Gothic survival like you. Do you think you would be happy here?'

'Happy?' said Leithen thoughtfully. 'Happy? Yes, undoubtedly.
But it might be bad for my soul. – There's just time for a pipe, Giffen,
and then we must be off.'

I was filling my pipe as we crossed the outer hall, and was about to
enter the smoking-room that I so well remembered, when Giffen laid
a hand on my arm.

'We don't smoke there now,' he said hastily.

He opened the door and I looked in. The place had suffered its third
metamorphosis. The marble shrine which I had noticed on my first
visit had been brought back, and the blue mosaic pavement and the
ivory walls were bare. At the eastern end stood a little altar, with,
above it, a copy of a Correggio Madonna.

A faint smell of incense hung in the air, and the fragrance of hothouse flowers. It was a chapel, but, I swear, it was a more pagan place
than when it had been workroom or smoking-room.

Giffen gently shut the door. 'Perhaps you may not have heard, but
some months ago my wife became a Catholic. It is a good thing for
women, I think. It gives them a regular ritual for their lives. So we
restored the chapel, which had always been there in the days of the
Carterons and the Applebys.'

'And you?' I asked.

He shrugged his shoulders.

'I don't bother much about that sort of thing. But I propose to
follow suit. It will please Ursula and do no harm to anybody.'

We halted on the brow of the hill and looked back on the garden
valley. Leithen's laugh, as he gazed, had more awe than mirth in it.

'That wicked little house! I'm going to hunt up every scrap I can find about old Tom Carteron. He must have been an uncommon clever fellow. He's still alive down there and making people do as he did. In that kind of place you may expel the priest and sweep it and garnish it, but he always returns.'

The wrack was lifting before the wind, and a shaft of late watery sun fell on the grey walls. It seemed to me that the little house wore an air of gentle triumph.

Watches of the Night

This story has only appeared in *The Scottish Mountaineering Club Journal* (1921–3), under the pseudonym Beta Minus.

9.30 P.M. – THE 'GARDIEN' HAS just put out the light and bumped noisily into his cubby-hole. The hut is as dark as the pit; an uneasy quiet reigns, and I compose myself to sleep.

This (my reason tells me) is the precious hour of rest; the storehouse of the body's strength against the toil and tribulation of the morning; not a moment must be lost! Come, now, let me concentrate upon oblivion: I will speak softly – perhaps I shall catch it unawares – Sleep ... Sleep ... (It would be easier, all the same, if there were fewer lumps in this mattress, and if the straw were less prickly within the pillow.)

Sleep ...

It is a grim business. Half an hour has gone already. I have tried all manner of ways; on the right side, and on the left; I have passed in hot pursuit down all the byways of my mind; I have lain in wait among the shadows of idle thought – and sleep eludes me still! It has been deaf to my prayers; it has scorned my little scientific ruses; it has treated my mathematical contrivances with contempt. As usual, it has played the woman with my over-anxious wooing, and taken a delight in denying the too assiduous lover. Fool that I am! To conquer, my wooing should, of course, be the wooing of the Apache: I must be careless and brutal, seemingly indifferent, lazily sure of my success. Men of genius have always done this. Napoleon, for instance, found sleep the moment he desired it, even on the eve of a critical battle. Wonderful!

I fear in this respect I do not resemble Napoleon. It is unfortunate.

Raymond does though; he is off already – the lucky devil. So does the Gardien. *Nom d'un nom!* How the man snores! It is like a double-bass played by clockwork: in spasms it is like the thunder of the Atlantic on a rock-bound shore.

Why don't they make men wear silencers? They have to have them on motor bicycles and things. Compulsory silencers – for use in all SAC huts – a brilliant idea! (I am often exceptionally brilliant on these occasions.) It will be defended not to use them when requested to do so by other Clubists – another excellent precept for voyagers! And why not? After all, they climb Everest in gas-masks; at least, they do on the posters. Why not have some similar sort of apparatus, instruments of silence for the cabane? Surely Mr Unna could invent an ingenious device?

I wonder if it would matter very much if I murdered the Gardien quite quietly? He is probably insured. Not that it would be of much use, for another in all respects like unto him would take his place in the morning.

Hang it all! I MUST get to sleep! It is getting on for eleven o'clock by now: only two hours more, and then – breakfast and that infernal moraine. Perhaps if I try the counting game again ...

One ... Two ... Three ... Yes; we shall take quite three hours to reach the ridge. And then – how many hours? I wonder! Old Dübi is nearly lyrical about it: the stern decorum of topographical science is quite overcome; it has even compassed the majestic word 'anfractuosities' in its service; these are, apparently, numerous, and many of them are difficult (*varappe scabreuse*). Finally there will be an *arête de neige tranchante*, not seldom *garnie d'une corniche* – however, that part looked all right, as far as we could see. But, in any case, we shall have our work cut out; there will be more than one tense moment before we find the summit under foot and are at liberty to descend that glorious sweep of ridge which leads to the broad slopes beyond.

We shall ... we shall ...

What did you say, Raymond?

This valley, into which we are so unaccountably descending, seems strange to you? My good sir! Why – of course – it's the ... it's the ... Well – funny thing – now you come to mention it, it DOES seem a bit unfamiliar, even to me ... It must be ... But – never mind – we shall soon come upon things we recognise – when we get a little lower.

The curious part about it is that the Swiss map seems wrong somehow. I've never known it happen before. It's really quite extraordinary! We shall have to put a pithy little note about it in the next *A.J.*: 'Alpine topography still incomplete – lingering defects in Swiss maps – theory of "wet" drinks among (dry) Federal surveyors.' It'll cause a minor sensation! Theory questioned by Prof. X, angrily pooh-poohed by the Rev. Y, supported by General Z, and so on, to another merry controversy!

It is a very beautiful valley, Raymond! Those pastures – what an exquisite shade of green! How deliciously cool will be those woods after this furnace of a moraine...

We are going down – down – down the pathway under the pines. The sunlight creeps stealthily in through the leaves and spreads a quivering trellis-work of light at our feet. Here and there little streams play hide-and-seek with great moss-clad boulders, and gurgle happily under bushes of alpen rose: we drink as we pass downward and are well content. Anything may happen in these woods. We may wander on for ever...

Hullo – what is this?

We have come to a clearing in the forest, a grassy glade among the pines, and in the middle of it stands a large chalet, many windowed, generously roofed, and richly carved about the corners and under the eaves. The very sight of the place is an invitation. The perfect valley must possess a perfect inn. We approach and enter as a matter of course. We have scarcely crossed the threshold before a stately old man, clad in flowing robes of purple edged with gold, comes forward to meet us with a smile of welcome. Strange ... but it is almost certainly the concierge. We murmur the usual phrases about food and beds. 'But yes, Messieurs, everything is prepared! The Messieurs will surely bathe before they sit down to eat? All is in readiness. Excusez.' With the utmost deference he relieves us of our axes and sacks. If we will be so good as to follow him. He leads the way down several passages, and then, opening a door suddenly, ushers us into a darkened chamber. As soon as our eyes grow accustomed to the gloom, we see that it is a beautifully appointed *chambre de bain*, floored with black marble, and in the centre is a circular pool of clear water from which the steam is rising softly to fill the chamber with a delicious perfume, as of a garden of roses on summer's morning. 'Messieurs will take an *apéritif* while they prepare for the bath ... and a cigarette, perhaps?' 'Certainly we will, mon ami!' Silent-footed attendants appear from out the shadows, bearing stimulating drinks. Hastily we shed our clothing and leap into the pool. The temperature is perfect; we abandon ourselves to an ecstasy of physical well-being and delight.

Dimly I am aware of Raymond's sun-burnt visage, like a great blood-orange, floating in a cloud of steam.

'Ah!' says he, in a deep languorous voice, 'this is wonderful! Amazingly . . . incredibly . . . wonderful.'

The bath is over. The attendants bring us clean raiment, soft and very pleasant to the touch. I dress myself at leisure. Then I wander out into a spacious hall. Through a curtained doorway I get a peep into an inner room which is full of light. A magnificent banquet is being prepared within! The table groans under great bowls of silver filled with flowers and luscious fruits: melons, grapes, figs, peaches, and pomegranates. Numberless little dishes are there also, laden with the trifles which toy with the palate at unimportant intervals. From somewhere underground there comes the inviting aroma of savoury meat well cooked. Comely maidens pass with beakers of sparkling wine.

'This,' I find myself murmuring, 'is a fit reward of toil. This must be the climber's Valhalla.'

Hark!

That will be the dinner gong! The feast is about to begin. I feel I possess a hunger worthy of the occasion. We will go in. The sound of the gong is faint at first; it has a deep note, soft and seemingly distant. How sweetly it rouses the echoes of that sombre hall! Then it grows louder and more shrill; louder yet – until now it is drumming in my ears.

Ding-dong – ding-dong – ding-dong – ding-ding-ding-ding-ding . . .

DAMN!!

Where are my matches? Stop that infernal din, will you? I'm awake. One o'clock.

Through the window of the hut I can see a cold, triangular wedge of stars. It is a perfect night.

I tumble out of bed and start to light the fire. There is a stir among Raymond's blankets; he sits up and rubs his eyes. Has he, too, I wonder, been piped out of Elysium on the note of the alarm?

The Shut Door

A First World War story published in two Nelson Annuals –
The Boys' All-Round Book (1926) and *The Splendid Adventure
Book for Boys* (1930) – 'The Shut Door' appears for the first
time in a Buchan collection. Cecil Rawlings, with whom
Buchan had planned to explore the northern side of Everest in
1913, was one of those killed in the war.

WE WERE TALKING – said the Fusilier Captain – in our dugout near
Gouzeaucourt, the night before the Boche made his counter-attack at
Cambrai. There seemed no reason to anticipate bad trouble in the near
future, but all the same there was a queer feeling in the air as if
something ugly was about to happen, and we were all a bit edgy. You
know how on these occasions men talk and smoke cigarette after
cigarette to keep their nerves quiet? Well, that night we had the most
interesting yarns I ever heard on the Western Front. You see, our
Division had been right through the whole of Gallipoli before we were
hoicked back to the West, and we had every stamp of fellow in our
mess. But that night we didn't talk about the war, but about the
things we were going to do when the beastly show was over.

I, as you know, was before 1914 a peaceful Fellow of a Cambridge
College, and my only journeys had been to look at manuscripts in
Berlin or Rome. But there were three of us who between them had
pretty well covered the globe. Peachey, who commanded 'B' Company, was a rich man's son, who had spent his time since he came
down from Oxford in trying to beat height records in the Himalayas.
Our M.O., Hyde, had been with three big exploring expeditions – one
in the Northern Congo, when a special kind of okapi was discovered,
one in Eastern Tibet after new species of flowers, and one, five months
before the War broke out, in South-eastern Arabia. There were some
people who said he had been to Mecca in disguise, and I can well
believe it, for he spoke a dozen Oriental tongues, and had written a big

book on the religion of Islam. The third was a very dark horse called Lacon, and the name suited him, for he rarely opened his mouth. He had been in the engineering business somewhere in South America, and his work had taken him into odd places and odder company. You could see that from the way he would drop a quiet word now and then. He would suddenly cut in and explain some point in one of our arguments with a story, and his stories were always those of an eye-witness. It was not, 'I have heard,' but 'I have seen'; and though we all pulled each other's legs a bit, there was something about Lacon which made you believe him implicitly.

That night the talk drifted, I remember, to the things that would be left worth doing in the world. We were all fed up with our particular job of beating the Boche, and because we were young we all wanted – after we had had a rest and a drink, so to speak – to get busy with something really amusing. There was a good deal of nonsense, you know, talked about the utter weariness of the men at the front. Most of us were not weary, only bored, and wanted not peace so much as real excitement.

The Boche was extraordinarily well-behaved that night. Now and then there would be a sputter of fire, chiefly from our own outposts, but most of the time it was so quiet in that dugout that you could hear the rats scurrying and the drip of grease from the candle in the bottle-mouths. It made us all feel a little eerie, and I think Peachey talked mainly to break the spell.

He had planned, as soon as the war was over, to have a try for Everest. He drew a map on the back of a picture from *L'Illustration* to show us how, from Tibet, it was a comparatively simple business, starting at a high elevation up slopes set at a reasonable angle. The events of two summers ago were to disprove Peachey's optimism.

'It beats me what pleasure you find in climbing mountains,' put in Hyde, who had the scientific Cambridge mind. 'If I am going to risk my life and have the deuce of a bad time, I want to get some profit out of it – for myself or the world.'

'What about this old war?' somebody asked.

'Well, I fancy there is some profit to the world in it, or we wouldn't be here. But about Everest. What on earth's the use of getting to the top of it?'

'Thank God, there is no earthly use,' said Peachey. 'That's just where the fun comes in.'

'I don't see it,' said Hyde stubbornly. 'There is no profit to science; at least nothing you couldn't get from laboratory experiments with the pressure of air on a guinea pig's lungs. You leave geology and zoology several thousand feet below you. It is simply a gymnastic feat. All right for boys, but not for grown men.'

I thought Peachey would get nettled, but he didn't. He only smiled his slow, superior smile. 'I couldn't explain to a chap like you what mountaineers are after if I tried till Doomsday. It is like great poetry – you feel it or you don't. It is our own private secret. – By the way, if we come out of this show, how are *you* going to employ your scientific mind?'

'I'm off again with Mallison. There is just one big geographical riddle left unsolved, and that is the Desert of Southern Arabia. It is 800 miles by 500, and nobody has crossed it for at least 300 years. I want to put that bit of *terra incognita* on the map.'

'But if you cross it,' I said, 'that will be just another feat – same as Peachey's Everest.'

'Not a bit of it. We know there was a famous trade route across it till well on in the Middle Ages, and along that route at one time there were great cities. Sand is a good preservative, as Aurel Stein found. There is a chance of writing several new chapters in history, and of adorning a dozen more chapters with footnotes. God knows what relics of the past we might find – the lost books of Aristotle, perhaps, or some masterpiece of the Greek drama. It is a more hopeful business by a long chalk than digging bits of papyri out of Egyptian rubbish heaps. I tell you, the chances are two to one that if we do not leave our bones in the desert we will add more to human knowledge than Schliemann did at Mycenæ or Evans in Crete. We are going in from the east coast, of course. South-west Arabia is always a bit too unhealthy.'

It was then that Lacon spoke. He had a habit of sitting with his chin on his breast, puffing slowly at an old pipe, and looking at the company from under his brows. He was a hard-bitten fellow, with the sallow tint in his skin which comes from much malaria. The men liked him, for he was very considerate of their comfort, but he was never what you could call companionable. We respected him, for as a machine-gun officer he was incomparable, but he was too silent to be popular.

'You're only relic-hunting like the rest,' he told Hyde.

'I am a man of science,' said Hyde hotly. 'I don't want junk for a museum, but something which may enable the world to understand its origins.'

'All the same you are looking for relics. When you have got them you will proceed to use your imagination and make a picture of the life of the past which people will accept. I want to find a living past – the world as it was centuries ago still intact.'

'What do you mean?' asked Hyde.

'I mean that I want to step into an ancient society like the man in Wells's *Time Machine*, and see the thing functioning, and not have to reconstruct it.'

'You don't want much!'

'I want a good deal. But you see I happen to have found it. Also, I am like Peachey, and want to perform a feat – to do something very difficult and dangerous which nobody has ever done before.'

'Anything more?' Hyde asked satirically.

'No, that's all. I am not talking through my hat. I believe I am going to do both.'

I suppose it was that funny tension caused by the imminence of a battle we did not expect that made the taciturn Lacon talk freely. We all opened our eyes, for we felt that this was not any kind of bluff.

'You can't leave it at that,' I said, when Lacon seemed to be relapsing into taciturnity. 'We have got to hear more. I suppose your hunting-ground is South America.'

He nodded. 'I have spent twelve years there – first of all in a frontier delimitation job, and then on my own account. You talk about Southern Arabia. But the big blank place on the map is not there, but in the Amazon valley. There are hundreds of thousands of square miles there of which we know nothing. No maps, no reports, except Indian rumours and the babble of scared rubber-hunters. It is a part of the world that is not specially safe for democracy.'

I asked him where the place lay exactly, and he mentioned names which meant nothing to me. He took up Peachey's blue pencil and drew a rough map on the *L'Illustration* picture. I gathered that his hunting-ground was in the south-west corner of the Amazon area.

Peachey, who was on the Council of the Royal Geographical, observed that that country might be unexplored, but that its nature was pretty well known – nothing but swampy forests lying between the main tributaries of the great river.

'Not known,' said Lacon, 'only guessed at, and the guesses happen to be wrong. There are points where even our vaguest knowledge stops clean and does not begin again for a thousand miles. How could it be otherwise? The place is far more strongly fenced than Tibet was a hundred years ago. It is a poison land – poison everywhere, in the flowers, in the insects, in the sap of the trees, and on every Indian arrow – deadly poison that makes a man die crazy with pain in three minutes.'

'Have you been there?' some one asked.

'I have been through the defences. I was lost, you see, for four years. There is a way through. I found it, and I know how to go back again.'

A young second-lieutenant shrugged his shoulders. 'I don't fancy that poison idea. Any other attractions for the tourist?'

'Many. It is an unhallowed country, and things become cannibal there which are harmless anywhere else. Not only the men.'

'I know about the cannibal fish that Roosevelt found,' said Peachey. 'Horrid little blighters about the size of a sea-trout, who get mad on blood. Anything beyond that?'

'Yes,' said Lacon, 'there are foxes.'

I don't think any of us believed him. Peachey laughed out loud. 'That's a good idea. I wish we could introduce the strain at home. It would add to the excitement of hunting if the fox turned and rent the hounds and took a leg off the first whip!'

Lacon was deadly serious, and if you looked at him you somehow couldn't laugh. 'That is the horror of it. There is nothing alarming in a lion or a tiger who wants your blood, but when a thing which we think of as a fugitive becomes aggressive and venomous it puts the fear of God into a man. Think of our little English fox with his sharp nozzle, snarling lips, and bright, wicked eyes. Think of him as big as a wolf-hound, and cunning – well, as a fox, and as bloodthirsty as a stoat! I still dream of the brutes at night.'

There was something about Lacon's tone and his eyes which compelled conviction. Peachey reached for the whisky. 'I want a drink,' he said, 'after that nightmare. You say this cheerful land of yours is a hedge or a belt or something. That means there must be something inside it. What did you find when you got there?'

'I didn't get there,' said Lacon. 'I only squeezed a shut door a little way ajar. I am going back to open it, but I know a little of what is on the other side.'

We all waited on Lacon's next words with something of the tenseness which one feels before going over the top. He spoke very slowly, as if he were overburdened with long-suppressed memories.

'There is a people – a great people.' Then he stopped.

'White?' somebody asked. 'The old Rider Haggard business?'

'I don't know. White, after all, is a relative word. They are not Indians. They are pale, but that may be from their mode of life. I have only seen one of them. I think they are hardly human, but all the same they must be marvellous.'

'You saw one of them?' I put in.

'Yes; but he came to me. I never got into their country. I only heard of it. I was raving with fever at the time, so my memory is not very good. Also, I was in a hurry, for he wanted to have me murdered, and my Indian friends had a job to hustle me away.'

Lacon's pale eyes had a funny, fixed look, almost of pain.

'He was a dwarf. They are all dwarfs, so the Indians told me. That may be the in-breeding, for they are the oldest human society on earth.'

'You mean they are the Inca people?' Hyde asked sharply.

'Lord, no! Centuries, millenniums before the Incas. They were there before the Caribs came from the North – before the Indians. They are far older than the Phœnicians, or the Egyptians, or the Minoans. They were a great people when there was a land bridge to Asia, and before the towers of Atlantis had fallen.'

Hyde tried to look sceptical, but completely failed. There was something about Lacon's quiet staccato sentences which held us spellbound. He, at any rate, believed every word he said, and he was no fool.

'I never crossed their borders,' he went on; 'but I built up bit by bit a pretty complete knowledge of what was inside. Oddly enough, two Portuguese in the eighteenth century must have preceded me and heard the same tales. Perhaps they got a little further than I did. Anyhow, they left a record which no one believed, and you will find it to-day in the Lisbon archives. What impressed them most was that this people lived not in cities, but in gigantic towers – things as big as a Pyramid – and that these towers had no windows.'

'How on earth—' I began.

'They are earth-dwellers,' Lacon went on, 'but their burrows are above the ground. They spend most of their life inside their great blank walls, and they have some form of artificial light, which goes on day and night. The Indians said it was fire from heaven, and for all I know it may be electricity. They are evidently advanced scientists.'

'How do they defend themselves,' I asked, 'if they are surrounded by murderous cannibals? I gather they are not a race of warriors.'

'Oh, they are a race of warriors all right, but they do not fight with steel. They are the greatest adepts in poison that the world has ever known. I expect they could teach the Boche something about poison gas. They could blot out a tribe which annoyed them, and the terror of them was like a mist on the countryside. It was even taboo to mention them. That was why it took me four years to find out anything.'

'I should give that lot a miss, if I were you, old man,' said Peachey.

Lacon shook his head. 'No; I'm going back. The place draws me, for it is the biggest thing undiscovered on the globe. Think of them, these pale dwarfish slugs, masters of every kind of hellish device, lairing in their great blank castles. Hoar-ancient, you know – so old that the Sphinx is young beside them. Something out of the "dark backward and abysm of time", left untouched by the centuries. My God! how's that for a discovery?'

Hyde had ceased to be critical. Very solemnly he asked Lacon if he had written it all down. 'For you know,' he said, 'our life here is pretty chancy. Any day you may stop something heavy.'

Lacon laughed – a laugh of complete confidence. 'Oh no. I have written nothing down. It is all in my head. Nobody's going to poach on my preserve. I am quite certain about my destiny. The Boche can't harm me till I have got that shut door open.'

There fell a sudden silence among us. The words grated somehow, like an impiety. In those days, whatever our faults, the Greek *aidos* was a virtue which flourished among us.

Early next morning, as all the world knows, the Boche broke into our front. The first we knew of it was that he was behind our Battalion Headquarters, and after that for twenty-four hours my old lot had a remarkably cheap time. I got knocked out early in the day, and heard nothing more till Peachey was tucked into a bed beside me in the Base Hospital. I asked him the question which had been on my lips ever since I recovered consciousness.

'Poor devil,' he said. 'He and half his squad were wiped out by some heavy stuff. There wasn't much of him left. Extraordinarily gallant chap he was, too. I saw him when we first counter-attacked, with that funny crooked smile of his, as cool as if he were walking up partridges. It's a big loss to the battalion.'

I couldn't say anything, for I felt, more acutely than I had ever felt it before, the preposterous waste of war. It was more than the loss of a fine soldier to the British Army. I thought that a door leading to amazing mysteries had now been shut and bolted.

Nemesis

Another little-known Buchan story which has appeared only in Nelson's *The Boys' All-Round Book* (1928) and *Budget Book for Boys* (1935). It has certain resemblances to *Castle Gay* (1930) and 'The Frying-pan and the Fire' (*see* p. 199).

[We were talking in the smoking-room about the vicissitudes of fortune. Some one said that in the war he never shaved of a morning without wondering where he would shave next, or whether he would ever use a razor again. Scanlan observed that he never put on his clothes now, when he got up, without wondering where he would take them off, since an event which befell him last autumn. Then he told us this story.]

I HAD BEEN staying in Yorkshire – for a cricket week – and was due on a Scots salmon river, which I shall call the Clee. It was blisteringly hot weather, but I looked forward with hope to my fishing, for I had read in *The Times* that there had been a good deal of rain in the North. I had a stuffy journey before me, so I came down to breakfast, on the morning I was to leave, in a suit of thin grey flannels. Being on the main line, it was possible to leave Revelsham comfortably about ten o'clock, and get to my destination in good time for dinner.

Old Alderson was leaving at the same hour, and was going to Scotland by a different route – a business journey, to take part in an arbitration in the city of Glasgow. He nodded with approval when he saw my clothes, which were much the same as his own. 'It is going to be hideously hot,' he said; 'but you, lucky chap, will be undressing to-night in a cool Highland glen, while I shall be turning to my stuffy couch in a Glasgow hotel.'

I agreed, with a certain amount of complacency. Revelsham spoils one for work. I rejoiced that I had still some weeks of holiday before me, and I had that selfish satisfaction which one feels when the misfortunes of others by contrast heighten one's own luck. I am afraid I gloated a little. 'Yes,' I said, 'there will be a river outside my window, and a wind in the pine trees, and I will wake to hear the salmon plopping, and in the morning . . .' I said a good deal more till he threatened me with a toast rack.

'You are guilty of *Hubris*,' he said, 'which, if you have not forgotten your classics, was, according to the Greeks, the worst vice a man could have. "Hot-foot upon pride follows Nemesis the Avenger!" I shall be interested to hear what happens to you, my lad.'

For a long summer day I dozed and read in the express, which took me through coal-fields and smoky towns, and among Border glens, and through the champaign of the Lowlands, and into a country where lochs shimmered beside the track, and the heather grew up to the edge of the wayside stations. About six o'clock I reached my destination, from which it was a short three-mile drive to Inverclee.

When I reached that hospitable house I found it empty, for the whole party were on the moor at a grouse drive, and not expected back for another hour. It was a divine evening, blue and windless, and I saw that the Clee in the haugh below was in fine trim; so when the butler suggested that I might try a cast before dinner, I readily agreed. I selected a twelve-foot greenheart from the great rod box in the hall, to save time, borrowed tackle and a fly book, and soon I was crossing the lawn in the delightful mood of trepidation which attends the angler who has not been on a salmon river for a twelvemonth.

There had been rain in the hills, and the river was in perfect condition, the pools the colour of cairngorms, and the streams swirling nobly in great arcs round the beds of shingle. The Clee is an easy water to fish, for there is no need to wade, and very little undergrowth to circumvent. I put up a small Blue Doctor and fished the first pool with care. There were too many salmon topping and tailing, but it is always pleasant to see signs of life, and I was very well content with my job. I rose a fish in the tail of that first pool, but he would not come again. So I walked over half a mile of meadow to the next. There I had no better luck, though I changed the fly twice.

On and on I wandered, oblivious of the fact that the light was failing, and then I came to the pool which is the most famous on the whole Inverclee beat, the Red Scour by name, where I had often killed fish. The sight of the place intoxicated me, the more so as the salmon in it were not skylarking as elsewhere. I saw one great brute come up in a most business-like manner, and I thirsted for his blood. I changed my fly to a large-size Silver Doctor, and put all my skill into covering the swirl under the rocks on the far side. I was rewarded, for at my third cast I was fast in a good fish.

I glanced at my wrist watch after I hooked him, and saw to my consternation that it was a quarter past eight. I was at least a couple of miles from the house, and dinner could not conceivably be later than 8.30, and it would take me twenty minutes to dress. But I dismissed these considerations. A tight line is the most important thing in the world, while it remains tight.

I had brought neither net nor gaff, and to kill the fish I had to get him pretty well beat. He behaved abominably. If he had stuck to the stream I could have worn him out in ten minutes, but after a rush or two he went to the bottom and sulked. He must have sulked for at least twenty minutes. When he changed his mind he took me to the tail of the pool, where the water ran very fast and deep between edges of rock before tumbling over a considerable fall. For a moment I thought he was going to attempt the fall, but he thought better of it. He ran up to the head, where I got my thin shoes badly cut in following him, dived to the bottom for five minutes, and then came to the surface near the tail again, showing considerable signs of distress.

By this time it was almost dark, that clear, lucent, amber darkness which you get in the Highlands in fine weather. I had forgotten all about dinner, and my whole soul was concentrated on that wretched fish. It was my business to tail him, and I debated the best tactics. The proper way would have been to bring him in at right angles to the bank and get his head up on the shore. But that was impossible, since the current ran swift between two steep edges of rock. There was nothing for it but to bring him parallel to the bank and do the best I could. I had the rod in my left hand, with the butt well forward, and knelt down to get a grip of his tail. He was a bigger fish than I had thought — at least twenty pounds. As I reached for him he walloped outward, and I missed my clutch. In bending forward for a second try I overbalanced, and the next I knew I was in the water.

The current in these narrows was like a mill race. Before I knew, I was swirled over the fall, and then I seemed to be drawn a mile down into the deeps of a great pool. I had swallowed pints of water before I came to the surface. I struck out for the nearest bank, got hold of an alder root, and with a good deal of trouble dragged myself up on dry land. What had become of the rod and the fish I had no notion. I could see nothing but a black chasm of water, flecked with foam, and purple ghosts beyond, which were trees and boulders.

I had come out on the wrong side of the river, and the next thing to be done was to get back to Inverclee. But I did not fancy trying to jump the narrows where I had fallen in. I shook the water out of my eyes and hair, wrung my trousers and jacket, and, sopping and shaken, began to make my way down the stream to look for a crossing. Then I heard a voice. I knew I was no longer on Inverclee land, but I hoped for some river keeper who would show me the best way home, so I shouted a reply.

I got a startling answer. Suddenly two powerful arms clutched me round the middle, and two massive hands were clapped on my mouth. Before I could utter a sound I was swung into the air and felt myself being carried rapidly up the bank away from the river.

I was too much startled to be able to think, and the next thing that happened confused me still further. I found myself on the edge of a road – a subsidiary highway, I remembered, ran on the other side of the Clee – and before me stood a girl and a young man, who, with my two assailants, made a party of four. Also there was a large closed car with the headlights blazing.

I was given no chance to speak. One of the men neatly and expedi- tiously gagged me – let me add painlessly, for he was evidently an adept at the job. My mouth and jaw were enveloped, but my ears were free. Also my arms were bound to my side with a cord which was tied behind me. Then a large ulster was put over my shoulders and but- toned up in front. All this while the young woman looked on with eyes which, in the glare of the car's lights, seemed profoundly concerned.

'Oh, Bawby,' she wailed, in a voice which I recognised as belonging to the other side of the Atlantic. 'Can't you learn to behave. I told you you would get popped in the river if you riled Charlie any more. You can't say you didn't deserve it. And there is Aunt Anne coming to- morrow, and you just poison to everybody in the house. You've got to go away right now, and then nobody will know.'

'Sure, he has got to go away,' said the other young man. 'Cis and I are going to see him off. Do you hear, Bawby? You have made us all tired, and if you stay on here the Lord knows what will happen. You are not house-broke, and you've got to keep away from Glenclee till you learn manners.'

'He won't take cold?' the girl asked anxiously. 'Aunt Anne used to say he had a weak chest.'

'Not on your life,' said one of my assailants. 'He's as strong as a jack rabbit. You take the flask, Miss Cis, and give him a drink before you cut loose. He will be as warm as a woodchuck under that big coat, and his being wet won't signify. Guess you'd better hurry if you are to be back in time.'

I sat, or rather reclined, on the step of the car, utterly unable to speak a word. My mind was just beginning to work, and I realised that I must be on Glenclee ground, and that these must be some of the Glenclee party. I had heard that Americans had taken the place. Apparently they took me for one of themselves, who had become justly unpopular and had got chucked into the river, and now they wanted to get me away to prevent further unpleasantness. One dripping figure in the darkness is very like another, and probably I was about Master Bobby's height. I made a tremendous effort to explain, but your explanatory style is cramped if your arms are tied to your side and you have a large-sized gag between your teeth. Then I struggled, but all that happened was that I was bundled inside the car, and the next moment it had started.

I could see dimly that the young man was driving and that the girl sat beside him. It was masterly driving, for as soon as we got out of the narrow riverside roads on to a decent highway we fairly ate up the miles. It was a clear night, and presently there was a moon, and through the windows I could see the hills fall back, and the glen open to a strath, and the strath to a plain. We raced in the open, slowed down at the villages, and twice crawled through the streets of little towns, and all the while I sat in my sopping clothes, kept fairly warm by the enveloping ulster, and tried to collect my disordered wits.

Bewilderment had been succeeded by wrath, and wrath by annoyance, and this in the end by amusement. I had certainly been landed in a preposterous comedy... I wondered how I should tell the story at Inverclee. To be taken for an unpleasant young American, who had got to be kidnapped and removed in the public interest, is not exactly flattering... And then the salmon! If I had only got that fish I might have faced my destiny with comfort. My captors seemed rather nice young people. I saw the girl's slim figure silhouetted against the glow of the headlights, and I remembered how kind her eyes had been, and how tragic her face. Was she Bobby's sister? I felt very angry with Bobby, and hoped the worst for him.

Then, wet and all, I think I must have become drowsy, for I know that when we stopped I wakened with a start. We seemed to be in the environs of a city, for there were lamps on the sidewalk. The door opened and the girl came in beside me.

'Oh, Bawby, you've been such a worry,' she said. 'Promise me you will be good now. You have got to go to an hotel and have a hot bath and go to bed. There's a trolley-car at the end of this street. I am going to send a wire to Mr Jephcote that you have been called away on important business. Charlie won't say anything, and Sid and John will back me up. I will see that your baggage is sent to Jermyn Street, and you have got to go back to London to-morrow, and not stir till I see you again. We are serious, Bawby! We have got the credit of the family to think about. I am putting this wad of bills in your pocket, so you won't be short of money.'

She cut the cord which tied my hands, and then with her delicate fingers she unloosed the gag. I noticed that the young man who drove had come to the door to see that Bobby behaved himself. It was pretty dark there, but I had the impression of an extraordinarily pretty girl.

'I am not Bobby,' I said, as soon as my lips would work. 'You've carried off the wrong man. I am a guest at Inverclee, and I fell into the river when I was trying to tail a salmon. You've removed me about fifty miles from my dinner!'

There was utter silence, and then the girl found her voice. 'Where is Bobby?' she cried.

'I don't know,' I said, 'but I hope he is in the river! I expect he is safe at home dining. You must hurry back if you want to prevent him making further mischief.'

Then she began to laugh – a delightful performance, beginning with a melodious chuckle and ending with streaming eyes.

'We can't apologise,' she stammered. 'It is too big and too bad. But we will come over to Inverclee to-morrow covered with sackcloth and ashes!'

'I wish you would ring up my hostess when you get back,' I said, 'and tell her I have missed my train and will arrive to-morrow.'

'What are you going to do now?' she asked. 'Won't you come back with us?'

'Not for worlds,' I said; 'I am very tired and very hungry. Here's your wad of notes for Bobby. I am going to the Western Hotel, where I know the manager, and I am going to bath, and sup in my bedroom, and sleep. . . No, I have plenty of money. If you like you can give me a drink from that flask of yours to keep off chills, and perhaps you could find me a cigarette. My pouch is soaking.'

We parted very good friends, the girl still laughing. I think the fiasco had taken for her the edge off Bobby's misdeeds. I found a tramcar, and then a taxi, and was presently set down at the Western Hotel. I had once acted for the company in a big lawsuit, and I knew the manager, so when I interviewed him in his office the path was made smooth for me. He lent me pyjamas and things, and himself conducted me to my room.

As he had his key in the lock the adjacent door opened, and out of it popped the head and arms of old Alderson, who was depositing his boots on the mat. As his eye fell on me, even his stalwart equanimity was shaken. I must have looked a figure of fun – my neat flannel suit soaked and shapeless, my hair on end, my face scratched and haggard. He stared at me in a kind of ecstasy.

'Nemesis,' he murmured, in a quotation which I recognised. 'Hot-foot upon pride follows Nemesis the Avenger!'

The Green Wildebeest

'The Green Wildebeest' was written in 1912 and marks the first appearance of Richard Hannay, but was only published in *Pall Mall Magazine* in September 1927. It was Hannay's story in *The Runagates Club* (1928) and draws on Buchan's travels while in South Africa at the turn of the century.

We carry with us the wonders we seek without us; there is all Africa and her prodigies in us.

SIR THOMAS BROWNE: *Religio Medici*

JUST AFTER THE Boer War I was on a prospecting job in the north-eastern Transvaal. I was a mining engineer, with copper as my speciality, and I had always a notion that copper might be found in big quantities in the Zoutpansberg foothills. There was of course Messina at the west end, but my thoughts turned rather to the north-east corner, where the berg breaks down to the crook of the Limpopo. I was a young man then, fresh from two years' campaigning with the Imperial Light Horse, and I was thirsty for better jobs than trying to drive elusive burghers up against barbed wire and blockhouses. When I started out with my mules from Pietersburg on the dusty road to the hills, I think I felt happier than ever before in my life.

I had only one white companion, a boy of twenty-two called Andrew Du Preez. Andrew, not Andries, for he was named after the Reverend Andrew Murray, who had been a great Pope among the devout Afrikanders. He came of a rich Free State farming family, but his particular branch had been settled for two generations in the Wakkerstroom region along the upper Pongola. The father was a splendid old fellow with a head like Moses, and he and all the uncles had been on commando, and most of them had had a spell in Bermuda or Ceylon. The boy was a bit of a freak in that stock. He had been precociously intelligent, and had gone to a good school in the Cape and afterwards to a technical college in Johannesburg. He was as modern a product as the others were survivals, with none of the family religion or family politics, very keen on science, determined to push his way on the Rand – which was the Mecca of all enterprising Afri-kanders – and not very sorry that the war should have found him in a place from which it was manifestly impossible to join the family banner. In October '99 he was on his first job in a new mining area in Rhodesia, and as he hadn't much health he was wise enough to stick there till peace came.

I had known him before, and when I ran across him on the Rand I asked him to come with me, and he jumped at the offer. He had just returned from the Wakkerstroom farm, to which the rest of his clan had been repatriated, and didn't relish the prospect of living in a tin-roofed shanty with a father who read the Bible most of the day to find out why exactly he had merited such misfortunes. Andrew was a hard young sceptic, in whom the family piety produced acute exasperation ... He was a good-looking boy, always rather smartly dressed, and at first sight you would have taken him for a young American, because of his heavy hairless chin, his dull complexion, and the way he peppered his ordinary speech with technical and business phrases. There was a touch of the Mongol in his face, which was broad, with high cheek-bones, eyes slightly slanted, short thick nose and rather full lips. I remembered that I had seen the same thing before in young Boers, and I thought I knew the reason. The Du Preez family had lived for generations close up to the Kaffir borders, and somewhere had got a dash of the tar-brush.

We had a light wagon with a team of eight mules, and a Cape-cart drawn by four others; five boys went with us, two of them Shangaans, and three Basutos from Malietsie's location north of Pietersburg. Our road was over the Wood Bush, and then north-east across the two Letabas to the Pufuri river. The countryside was amazingly empty. Beyer's commandos had skirmished among the hills, but the war had never reached the plains; at the same time it had put a stop to all hunting and prospecting and had scattered most of the native tribes. The place had become in effect a sanctuary, and I saw more varieties of game than I had ever seen before south of the Zambesi, so that I wished I were on a hunting trip instead of on a business job. Lions were plentiful, and every night we had to build a *scherm* for our mules and light great fires, beside which we listened to their eerie serenades.

It was early December, and in the Wood Bush it was the weather of an English June. Even in the foothills, among the wormwood and wild bananas, it was pleasant enough, but when we got out into the plains it was as hot as Tophet. As far as the eye could reach the bushveld rolled its scrub like the scrawled foliage a child draws on a slate, with here and there a baobab swimming unsteadily in the glare. For long stretches we were away from water, and ceased to see big game – only Kaffir queens and tick-birds, and now and then a wild ostrich. Then on the sixth day out from Pietersburg we raised a blue line of mountains on the north, which I knew to be the eastern extension of the Zoutpansberg. I had never travelled this country before, and had never met a man who had, so we steered by compass, and by one of the old bad maps of the Transvaal Government. That night we crossed the Pufuri, and next day the landscape began to change. The ground rose, so that we had a sight of the distant Lebombo hills to the east, and mopani bushes began to appear – a sure sign of a healthier country.

That afternoon we were only a mile or two from the hills. They were the usual type of berg which you find everywhere from Natal to the Zambesi – cut sheer, with an overhang in many places, but much broken up by kloofs and fissures. What puzzled me was the absence of streams. The ground was as baked as the plains, all covered with aloe and cactus and thorn, with never a sign of water. But for my purpose the place looked promising. There was that unpleasant metallic green that you find in a copper country, so that everything seemed to have been steeped in a mineral dye – even the brace of doves which I shot for luncheon.

We turned east along the foot of the cliffs, and presently saw a curious feature. A promontory ran out from the berg, connected by a narrow isthmus with the main *massif*. I suppose the superficial area of the top might have been a square mile or so; the little peninsula was deeply cut into by ravines, and in the ravines tall timber was growing. Also we came to well-grassed slopes, dotted with mimosa and syringa bushes. This must mean water at last, for I had never found yellow-woods and stinkwoods growing far from a stream. Here was our outspan for the night, and when presently we rounded a corner and looked down into a green cup I thought I had rarely seen a more habitable place. The sight of fresh green herbage always intoxicated me, after the dust and heat and the ugly greys and umbers of the bushveld. There was a biggish kraal in the bottom, and a lot of goats and leggy Kaffir sheep on the slopes. Children were bringing in the cows for the milking, smoke was going up from the cooking fires, and there was a cheerful evening hum in the air. I expected a stream, but could see no sign of one: the cup seemed to be as dry as a hollow of the Sussex Downs. Also, though there were patches of mealies and Kaffir corn, I could see no irrigated land. But water must be there, and after we had fixed a spot for our outspan beside a clump of olivewoods, I took Andrew and one of our boys and strolled down to make inquiries.

I daresay many of the inhabitants of that kraal had never seen a white man before, for our arrival made a bit of a sensation. I noticed that there were very few young men about the place, but an inordinate number of old women. The first sight of us scattered them like plovers, and we had to wait for half an hour, smoking patiently in the evening sun, before we could get into talk with them. Once the ice was broken, however, things went well. They were a decent peaceable folk, very shy and scared and hesitating, but with no guile in them. Our presents of brass and copper wire and a few tins of preserved meat made a tremendous impression. We bought a sheep from them at a ridiculously small price, and they threw in a basket of green mealies. But when we raised the water question we struck a snag.

There was water, good water, they said, but it was not in any pan or stream. They got it morning and evening from up there – and they pointed to the fringe of a wood under the cliffs where I thought I saw the roof of a biggish *rondavel*. They got it from their Father; they were Shangaans, and the word they used was not the ordinary word for chief, but the name for a great priest and medicine-man.

I wanted my dinner, so I forbore to inquire further. I produced some more Kaffir track, and begged them to present it with my compliments to their Father, and to ask for water for two white strangers, five of their own race, and twelve mules. They seemed to welcome the proposition, and a string of them promptly set off uphill with their big calabashes. As we walked back I said something foolish to Andrew about having struck a Kaffir Moses who could draw water from the rock. The lad was in a bad temper. 'We have struck an infernal rascal who has made a corner in the water supply and bleeds these poor devils. He's the kind of grafter I would like to interview with a sjambok.'

In an hour we had all the water we wanted. It stood in a row of calabashes, and beside it the presents I had sent to the provider. The villagers had deposited it and then vanished, and our boys who had helped them to carry it were curiously quiet and solemnised. I was informed that the Father sent the water as a gift to the strangers without payment. I tried to cross-examine one of our Shangaans, but he would tell me nothing except that the water had come from a sacred place into which no man could penetrate. He also muttered something about a wildebeest which I couldn't understand. Now the Kaffir is the most superstitious of God's creatures. All the way from Pietersburg we had been troubled by the vivid imaginations of our outfit. They wouldn't sleep in one place because of a woman without a head who haunted it; they dared not go a yard along a particular road after dark because of a spook that travelled it in the shape of a rolling ball of fire. Usually their memories were as short as their fancies were quick, and five minutes after their protest they would be laughing like baboons. But that night they seemed to have been really impressed by something. They did not chatter or sing over their supper, but gossiped in undertones, and slept as near Andrew and myself as they dared.

Next morning the same array of gourds stood before our outspan, and there was enough water for me to have a tub in my collapsible bath. I don't think I ever felt anything colder.

I had decided to take a holiday and go shooting. Andrew would stay in camp and tinker up one of the wheels of the mule-wagon which had suffered from the bush roads. He announced his intention of taking a walk later and interviewing the water-merchant.

'For Heaven's sake, be careful,' I said. 'Most likely he's a priest of sorts, and if you're not civil to him we'll have to quit this country. I make a point of respecting the gods of the heathen.'

'All you English do,' he replied tartly. 'That's why you make such a damned mess of handling Kaffirs ... But this fellow is a business man with a pretty notion of cornering public utilities. I'm going to make his acquaintance.'

I had a pleasant day in that hot scented wilderness. First I tried the low ground, but found nothing there but some old spoor of kudu, and a paauw which I shot. Then I tried the skirts of the berg to the east of the village, and found that the kloofs, which from below looked climbable, had all somewhere a confounded overhang which checked me. I saw no way of getting to the top of the plateau, so I spent the afternoon in exploring the tumbled glacis. There was no trace of copper here, for the rock was a reddish granite, but it was a jolly flowery place, with green dells among the crags, and an amazing variety of birds. But I was glad that I had brought a water-bottle, for I found no water; it was there all right, but it was underground. I stalked a bushbuck ram and missed him, but I got one of the little buck like chamois which the Dutch call *klipspringer*. With it and the paauw strung round my neck I sauntered back leisurely to supper.

As soon as I came in sight of the village I saw that something had played the deuce with it. There was a great hubbub going on, and all the folk were collected at the end farthest away from our camp. The camp itself looked very silent. I could see the hobbled mules, but I could see nothing of any of our outfit. I thought it best in these circumstances to make an inconspicuous arrival, so I bore away to my left, crossed the hollow lower down where it was thick with scrub, and came in on the outspan from the south. It was very silent. The cooking fires had been allowed to go out, though the boys should have been getting ready the evening meal, and there seemed to be not a single black face on the premises. Very uneasy, I made for our sleeping tent, and found Andrew lying on his bed, smoking.

'What on earth has happened?' I demanded. 'Where are Coos and Klemboy and...'

'Quit,' he said shortly. 'They've all quit.'

He looked sulky and tired and rather white in the face, and there seemed to be more the matter with him than ill temper. He would lay down his pipe, and press his hand on his forehead like a man with a bad headache. Also he never lifted his eyes to mine. I daresay I was a bit harsh, for I was hungry, and there were moments when I thought he was going to cry. However at last I got a sort of story out of him.

He had finished his job on the wagon wheel in the morning, and after luncheon had gone for a walk to the wood above the village at the foot of the cliffs. He wanted to see where the water came from and to have a word with the man who controlled it. Andrew, as I have told you, was a hard young realist and, by way of reaction from his family, a determined foe of superstition, and he disliked the notion of this priest and his mumbo-jumbo. Well, it seemed that he reached the priest's headquarters – it was the big *rondavel* we had seen from below, and there was a kind of stockade stretching on both sides, very

[83]

strongly fenced, so that the only entrance was through the *rondavel*.
He had found the priest at home, and had, according to his account,
spoken to him civilly and had tried to investigate the water problem.
But the old man would have nothing to say to him and peremptorily
refused his request to be allowed to enter the enclosure. By and by
Andrew lost his temper, and forced his way in. The priest resisted and
there was a scuffle; I daresay Andrew used his sjambok, for a backveld
Dutchman can never keep his hands off a Kaffir.

I didn't like the story, but it was no use being angry with a lad who
looked like a sick dog.

'What is inside? Did you find the water?' I asked.

'I hadn't time. It's a thick wood and full of beasts. I tell you I was
scared out of my senses and had to run for my life.'

'Leopards?' I asked. I had heard of native chiefs keeping tame
leopards.

'Leopards be damned. I'd have faced leopards. I saw a wildebeest as
big as a house – an old brute, grey in the nozzle and the rest of it green
– green, I tell you. I took a pot shot at it and ran ... When I came out
the whole blasted kraal was howling. The old devil must have roused
them. I legged it for home ... No, they didn't follow, but in half an
hour all our outfit had cut their stick ... didn't wait to pick up their
duds ... Oh, hell, I can't talk. Leave me alone.'

I had laughed in spite of myself. A wildebeest is not ornamental at
the best, but a green one must be a good recipe for the horrors. All the
same I felt very little like laughing. Andrew had offended the village
and its priest, played havoc with the brittle nerves of our own boys,
and generally made the place too hot to hold us. He had struck some
kind of native magic, which had frightened him to the bone for all his
scepticism. The best thing I could do seemed to be to try and patch up
a peace with the water merchant. So I made a fire and put on a kettle
to boil, stayed my hunger with a handful of biscuits, and started out
for the *rondavel*. But first I saw that my revolver was loaded, for I
fancied that there might be trouble. It was a calm bright evening, but
up from the hollow where the kraal lay there rose a buzz like angry
wasps.

No one interfered with me; indeed, I met no one till I presented
myself at the *rondavel* door. It was a big empty place, joined to the
stockades on both sides, and opposite the door was another which
opened on to a dull green shade. I never saw a *scherm* so stoutly built.

There was a palisade of tall pointed poles, and between them a thick wall of wait-a-bit thorns interlaced with a scarlet-flowered creeper. It would have taken a man with an axe half a day to cut a road through. The only feasible entrance was by the *rondavel*.

An old man was squatted on an earthern floor, which had been so pounded and beaten that it looked like dark polished stone. His age might have been anything above seventy from the whiteness of his beard, but there seemed a good deal of bodily strength left in him, for the long arms which rested on his knees were muscular. His face was not the squat face of the ordinary Kaffir, both high-boned and regular, like some types of well-bred Zulu. Now that I think of it, there was probably Arab blood in him. He lifted his head at the sound of my steps, and by the way he looked at me I knew that he was blind.

There he sat without a word, every line of his body full of dejection and tragedy. I had suddenly a horrible feeling of sacrilege. That that young fool Andrew should have lifted his hand upon an old man and a blind man and outraged some harmless *tabu* seemed to me an abominable thing. I felt that some holiness had been violated, something ancient and innocent cruelly insulted. At that moment there was nothing in the world I wanted so much as to make restitution.

I spoke to him, using the Shangaan word which means both priest and king. I told him that I had been away hunting and had returned to find that my companion had made bad mischief. I said that Andrew was very young, and that his error had been only the foolishness and hotheadedness of youth. I said – and my voice must have shown him that I meant it – that I was cut to the heart by what had happened, that I bowed my head in the dust in contrition, and that I asked nothing better than to be allowed to make atonement ... Of course I didn't offer money. I would as soon have thought of offering a tip to the Pope.

He never lifted his head, so I said it all over again, and the second time it was genuine pleading. I had never spoken like that to a Kaffir before, but I could not think of that old figure as a Kaffir, but as the keeper of some ancient mystery which a rude hand had outraged.

He spoke at last. 'There can be no atonement,' he said. 'Wrong has been done, and on the wrong-doer must fall the penalty.'

The words were wholly without menace; rather he spoke as if he were an unwilling prophet of evil. He was there to declare the law, which he could not alter if he wanted.

I apologised, I protested, I pled, I fairly grovelled; I implored him to tell me if there was no way in which the trouble could be mended; but if I had offered him a million pounds I don't believe that that old fellow would have changed his tone. He seemed to feel, and he made me feel it too, that a crime had been committed against the law of nature, and that it was nature, not man, that would avenge it. He wasn't in the least unfriendly; indeed, I think he rather liked the serious way I took the business and realised how sorry I was; his slow sentences came out without a trace of bitterness. It was this that impressed me so horribly – he was like an old stone oracle repeating the commands of the God he served.

I could make nothing of him, though I kept at it till the shadows had lengthened outside, and it was almost dark within the *rondavel*. I wanted to ask him at least to help me to get back my boys, and to make our peace with the village, but I simply could not get the words out. The atmosphere was too solemn to put a practical question like that . . .

I was turning to go away, when I looked at the door on the far side. Owing to the curious formation of the cliffs the sinking sun had only now caught the high tree-tops, and some ricochet of light made the enclosure brighter than when I first arrived. I felt suddenly an overwhelming desire to go inside.

'Is it permitted, Father,' I said, 'to pass through that door?'

To my surprise he waved me on. 'It is permitted,' he said, 'for you have a clean heart.' Then he added a curious thing. 'What was there is there no more. It has gone to the fulfilling of the law.'

It was with a good deal of trepidation that I entered that uncanny *enceinte*. I remembered Andrew's terror, and I kept my hand on my revolver, for I had a notion that there might be some queer fauna inside. There was light in the upper air, but below it was a kind of olive-green dusk. I was afraid of snakes, also of tiger-cats, and there was Andrew's green wildebeest!

The place was only a couple of acres in extent, and though I walked very cautiously I soon had made the circuit of it. The *scherm* continued in a half-moon on each side till it met the sheer wall of the cliffs. The undergrowth was not very thick, and out of it grew tall straight trees, so that the wood seemed like some old pagan grove. When one looked up the mulberrry sunset sky showed in patches between the feathery tops, but where I walked it was very dark.

There was not a sign of life in it, not a bird or beast, not the crack of a twig or a stir in the bushes; all was as quiet and dead as a crypt. Having made the circuit I struck diagonally across, and presently came on what I had been looking for – a pool of water. The spring was nearly circular, with a diameter of perhaps six yards, and what amazed me was that it was surrounded by a parapet of hewn stone. In the centre of the grove there was a little more light, and I could see that that stonework had never been made by Kaffir hands. Evening is the time when water comes to its own; it sleeps in the day but it has its own strange life in the darkness. I dipped my hand in it and it was as cold as ice. There was no bubbling in it, but there seemed to be a slow rhythmical movement, as if fresh currents were always welling out of the deeps and always returning. I have no doubt that it would have been crystal clear if there had been any light, but, as I saw it, it was a surface of darkest jade, opaque, impenetrable, swaying to some magic impulse from the heart of the earth.

It is difficult to explain just the effect it had on me. I had been solemnised before, but this grove and fountain gave me the abject shapeless fear of a child. I felt that somehow I had strayed beyond the reasonable world. The place was clean against nature. It was early summer, so these dark aisles should have been alive with moths and flying ants and all the thousand noises of night. Instead it was utterly silent and lifeless, dead as a stone except for the secret pulsing of the cold waters.

I had had quite enough. It is an absurd thing to confess, but I bolted – shuffled through the undergrowth and back into the *rondavel*, where the old man still sat like Buddha on the floor.

'You have seen?' he asked.

'I have seen,' I said – 'but I do not know what I have seen. Father, be merciful to foolish youth.'

He repeated again the words, that had chilled me before. 'What was there has gone to fulfil the law.'

I ran all the way back to our outspan, and took some unholy tosses on the road, for I had got it into my head that Andrew was in danger. I don't think I ever believed in his green wildebeest, but he had been positive that the place was full of animals, and I knew for a fact that it was empty. Had some fearsome brute been unloosed on the world?

I found Andrew in our tent, and the kettle I had put on to boil empty and the fire out. The boy was sleeping heavily with a flushed face, and I saw what had happened. He was practically a teetotaller, but he had chosen to swallow a good third of one of our four bottles of whisky. The compulsion must have been pretty strong which drove him to drink.

After that our expedition went from bad to worse. In the morning there was no water to be had, and I didn't see myself shouldering a calabash and going back to the grove. Also our boys did not return, and not a soul in the kraal would come near us. Indeed, all night they had kept up a most distressing racket, wailing and beating little drums. It was no use staying on, and, for myself, I had a strong desire to get out of the neighbourhood. The experience of the night before had left an aftertaste of disquiet in my mind, and I wanted to flee from I knew not what. Andrew was obviously a sick man. We did not carry clinical thermometers in those days, but he certainly had fever on him.

So we inspanned after breakfast, and a heavy job trekking is when you have to do all the work yourself. I drove the wagon and Andrew the Cape-cart, and I wondered how long he would be able to sit on his seat. My notion was that by going east we might be able to hire fresh boys, and start prospecting in the hill-country above the bend of the Limpopo.

But the word had gone out against us. You know the way in which Kaffirs send news for a hundred miles as quick as the telegraph – by drum-taps or telepathy – explain it any way you like. Well, we struck a big kraal that afternoon, but not a word would they say to us. Indeed, they were actually threatening, and I had to show my revolver and speak pretty stiffly before we got off. It was the same next day, and I grew nervous about our provisions, for we couldn't buy anything – not a chicken or an egg or a mealie-cob. Andrew was a jolly companion. He had relapsed into the primeval lout, and his manners were those of a cave-man. If he had not been patently suffering, I would have found it hard to keep my temper.

Altogether it was a bright look-out, and to crown all on the third morning Andrew went down like a log with the worst bout of malaria I have ever seen. That fairly put the lid on it. I thought it was going to be black-water, and all my irritation at the boy vanished in my anxiety. There was nothing for it but to give up the expedition and make the best speed possible to the coast. I made for Portuguese territory, and that evening got to the Limpopo. Happily we struck a more civil brand of native, who had not heard of our performances, and I was able to make a bargain with the headman of the village, who undertook to take charge of our outfit till it was sent for, and sold us a big native boat. I hired four lusty fellows as rowers and next morning we started down the river.

We spent a giddy five days before I planted Andrew in hospital at Lourenço Marques. The sickness was not black-water, thank God, but it was a good deal more than ordinary malaria; indeed, I think there was a touch of brain fever in it. Curiously enough I was rather relieved when it came. I had been scared by the boy's behaviour the first two days. I thought that the old priest had actually laid some curse on him; I remembered how the glade and the well had solemnised even me, and I considered that Andrew, with a Kaffir strain somewhere in his ancestry, was probably susceptible to something which left me cold. I had knocked too much about Africa to be a dogmatic sceptic about the mysteries of the heathen. But this fever seemed to explain it. He had been sickening for it; that was why he had behaved so badly to the old man, and had come back babbling about a green wildebeest. I knew that the beginnings of fever often make a man light-headed so that he loses all self-control and gets odd fancies ... All the same I didn't quite convince myself. I couldn't get out of my head the picture of the old man and his ominous words, or that empty grove under the sunset.

I did my best for the boy, and before we reached the coast the worst had passed. A bed was made for him in the stern, and I had to watch him by night and day to prevent him going overboard among the crocodiles. He was apt to be violent, for in his madness he thought he was being chased, and sometimes I had all I could do to keep him in the boat. He would scream like a thing demented, and plead, and curse, and I noticed as a queer thing that his ravings were never in Dutch but always in Kaffir – mostly the Sesutu which he had learnt in his childhood. I expected to hear him mention the green wildebeest, but to my comfort he never uttered the name. He gave no clue to what frightened him, but it must have been a full-sized terror, for every nerve in his body seemed to be quivering, and I didn't care to look at his eyes.

The upshot was that I left him in bed in hospital, as weak as a kitten, but with the fever gone and restored to his right mind. He was again the good fellow I had known, very apologetic and grateful. So with an easy conscience I arranged for the retrieving of my outfit and returned to the Rand.

Well, for six months I lost sight of Andrew. I had to go to Nama-qualand, and then up to the copper country of Barotseland, which wasn't as easy a trek as it is to-day. I had one letter from him, written from Johannesburg – not a very satisfactory epistle, for I gathered that the boy was very unsettled. He had quarrelled with his family, and he didn't seem to be contented with the job he had got in the goldfields. As I had known him he had been a sort of school-book industrious apprentice, determined to get on in the world, and not in the least afraid of a dull job and uncongenial company. But this letter was full of small grouses. He wanted badly to have a talk with me – thought of chucking his work and making a trip north to see me; and he ended with an underlined request that I should telegraph when I was coming down-country. As it happened I had no chance just then of sending a telegram, and later I forgot about it.

By and by I finished my tour and was at the Falls, where I got a local Rhodesian paper. From it I had news of Andrew with a ven-geance. There were columns about a murder in the bushveld – two men had gone out to look for Kruger's treasure and one had shot the other, and to my horror I found that the one who was now lying in Pretoria gaol under sentence of death was my unhappy friend.

You remember the wild yarns after the Boer War about a treasure of gold which Kruger in his flight to the coast had buried somewhere in the Selati country. That, of course, was all nonsense: the wily ex-President had long before seen the main funds safe in a European bank. But I daresay some of the officials had got away with Treasury balances, and there may have been bullion cached in the bushveld. Anyhow every scallywag south of the Zambesi was agog about the business, and there were no end of expeditions which never found a single Transvaal sovereign. Well, it seemed that two months before Andrew and a Dutchman called Smit had started out to try their luck, and somewhere on the Olifants the two had gone out one evening and only one had returned. Smit was found by the native boys with a hole in his head, and it was proved that the bullet came from Andrew's rifle, which he had been carrying when the two set out. After that the story became obscure. Andrew had been very excited when he returned and declared that he had 'done it at last', but when Smit's body was found he denied that he had shot him. But it was clear that Smit had been killed by Andrew's sporting .303, and the natives swore that the men had been constantly quarrelling and that Andrew had always shown a very odd temper. The Crown prosecutor argued that the two believed they had found treasure, and that Andrew had murdered Smit in cold blood to prevent his sharing. The defence seemed to be chiefly the impossibility of a guilty man behaving as Andrew had behaved, and the likelihood of his having fired at a beast in the dark and killed his companion. It sounded to me very thin, and the jury did not believe it, for their verdict was wilful murder.

I knew that it was simply incredible that Andrew could have committed the crime. Men are queer cattle, and I wouldn't have put even murder past certain fairly decent fellows I knew, but this boy was emphatically not one of them. Unless he had gone stark mad I was positive that he could never have taken human life. I knew him intimately, in the way you know a fellow you have lived alone with for months, and that was one of the things I could bank on. All the same it seemed clear that he had shot Smit . . . I sent the longest telegram I ever sent in my life to a Scotch lawyer in Johannesburg called Dalgleish whom I believed in, telling him to move heaven and earth to get a reprieve. He was to see Andrew and wire me details about his state of mind. I thought then that temporary madness was probably our best line, and I believed myself that that was the explanation. I longed to take the train forthwith to Pretoria, but I was tied by the heels till the rest of my outfit came in. I was tortured by the thought that the hanging might have already taken place, for that wretched newspaper was a week old.

In two days I got Dalgleish's reply. He had seen the condemned man, and had told him that he came from me. He reported that Andrew was curiously peaceful and apathetic, and not very willing to talk about the business except to declare his innocence. Dalgleish thought him not quite right in his mind, but he had been already examined, and the court had rejected the plea of insanity. He sent his love to me and told me not to worry.

I stirred up Dalgleish again, and got a further reply. Andrew admitted that he had fired the rifle, but not at Smit. He had killed something, but what it was he would not say. He did not seem to be in the least keen to save his neck.

When I reached Bulawayo, on my way south, I had a brain-wave, but the thing seemed so preposterous that I could hardly take it seriously. Still I daren't neglect any chance, so I wired again to Dalgleish to try to have the execution postponed, until he got hold of the priest who lived in the berg above the Pufuri. I gave him full directions how to find him. I said that the old man had laid some curse on Andrew, and that that might explain his state of mind. After all demoniacal possession must be equivalent in law to insanity. But by this time I had become rather hopeless. It seemed a futile thing to be wiring this rigmarole when every hour was bringing the gallows nearer.

I left the railroad at Mafeking, for I thought I could save the long circuit by De Aar by trekking across country. I would have done better to stick to the train, for everything went wrong with me. I had a breakdown at the drift of the Selous river and had to wait a day in Rustenburg, and I had trouble again at Commando Nek, so that it was the evening of the third day before I reached Pretoria ... As I feared, it was all over. They told me in the hotel that Andrew had been hanged that morning.

I went back to Johannesburg to see Dalgleish with a cold horror at my heart and complete mystification in my head. The Devil had taken an active hand in things and caused a hideous miscarriage of justice. If there had been anybody I could blame I would have felt better, but the fault seemed to lie only with the crookedness of fate. Dalgleish could tell me little. Smit had been the ordinary scallywag, not much of a fellow and no great loss to the world; the puzzle was why Andrew wanted to go with him. The boy in his last days had been utterly apathetic – bore no grudge against anybody – appeared at peace with the world, but didn't seem to want to live. The predikant who visited him daily could make nothing of him. He appeared to be sane enough, but, beyond declaring his innocence, was not inclined to talk, and gave no assistance to those who were trying to get a reprieve ... scarcely took any interest in it ... He had asked repeatedly for me, and had occupied his last days in writing me a long letter, which was to be delivered unopened into my hand. Dalgleish gave me the thing, seven pages in Andrew's neat caligraphy, and in the evening on his stoep I read it.

It was like a voice speaking to me out of the grave, but it was not the voice I knew. Gone was the enlightened commercially-minded young man, who had shed all superstition, and had a dapper explanation for everything in heaven and earth. It was a crude boy who had written those pages, a boy in whose soul old Calvinistic terrors had been awakened, and terrors older still out of primordial African shadows.

He had committed a great sin – that was the point he insisted upon, and by this sin he had set free something awful to prey on the world... At first it seemed sheer raving mania to me, but as I mused on it I remembered my own feelings in that empty grove. I had been solemnised, and this boy, with that in his blood which was not in mine, had suffered a cataclysmic spiritual experience. He did not dwell on it, but his few sentences were eloquent in their harsh intensity. He had struggled, he had tried to make light of it, to forget it, to despise it; but it rode him like a nightmare. He thought he was going mad. I had been right about that touch of brain fever.

As far as I could make it out, he believed that from that outraged sanctuary something real and living had gone forth, something at any rate of flesh and blood. But this idea may not have come to him till later, when his mind had been for several months in torture, and he had lost the power of sleep. At first, I think, his trouble was only an indefinite haunting, a sense of sin and impending retribution. But in Johannesburg the *malaise* had taken concrete form. He believed that through his act something awful was at large, with infinite power for evil – evil not only against the wrongdoer himself but against the world. And he believed that it might still be stopped, that it was still in the eastern bush. So crude a fancy showed how his normal intelligence had gone to bits. He had tumbled again into the blackveld world of his childhood.

He decided to go and look for it. That was where the tough white strain in him came out. He might have a Kaffir's blind terrors, but he had the frontier Boer's cast-iron courage. If you think of it, it needed a pretty stout heart to set out to find a thing the thought of which set every nerve quivering. I confess I didn't like to contemplate that lonely, white-faced, tormented boy. I think he knew that tragedy must be the end of it, but he had to face up to that and take the consequences.

He heard of Smit's expedition, and took a half share in it. Perhaps the fact that Smit had a baddish reputation was part of the attraction. He didn't want as companion a man with whom he had anything in common, for he had to think his own thoughts and follow his own course.

Well, you know the end of it. In his letter he said nothing about the journey, except that he had found what he sought. I can readily believe that the two did not agree very well – the one hungry for mythical treasure, the other with a problem which all the gold in Africa could not solve ... Somewhere, somehow, down in the Selati bushveld his incubus took bodily form, and he met – or thought he met – the thing which his impiety had released. I suppose we must call it madness. He shot his comrade, and thought he had killed an animal. 'If they had looked next morning they would have found the spoor,' he wrote. Smit's death didn't seem to trouble him at all – I don't think he quite realised it. The thing that mattered for him was that he had put an end to a terror and in some way made atonement. 'Good-bye, and don't worry about me,' were the last words, 'I am quite content.'

I sat a long time thinking, while the sun went down over the Magaliesberg. A gramophone was grinding away on an adjacent stoep, and the noise of the stamps on the Rand came like far-away drums. People at that time used to quote some Latin phrase about a new thing always coming out of Africa. I thought that it was not the new things in Africa that mattered so much as the old things.

I proposed to revisit that berg above the Pufuri and have a word with the priest, but I did not get a chance till the following summer, when I trekked down the Limpopo from Main Drift. I didn't like the job, but I felt bound to have it out with that old man for Andrew's sake. You see, I wanted something more to convince the Wakkerstroom household that the boy had not been guilty, as his father thought, of the sin of Cain.

I came round the corner of the berg one January evening after a day of blistering heat, and looked down on the cup of green pasture. One glance showed me that there was not going to be any explanation with the priest ... A bit of the cliff had broken away, and the rock fall had simply blotted out the grove and the *rondavel*. A huge mass of debris sloped down from half-way up the hill, and buried under it were the tall trees through which I had peered up at the sky. Already it was feathered with thorn-bush and grasses. There were no patches of crops on the sides of the cup, and crumbling mud walls were all that remained of the kraal. The jungle had flowed over the village, and, when I entered it, great moon flowers sprawled on the rubble, looking in the dusk like ghosts of a vanished race.

There was one new feature in the place. The landslip must have released the underground water, for a stream now flowed down the hollow. Beside it, in a meadow full of agapanthus and arum lilies, I found two Australian prospectors. One of them – he had been a Melbourne bank-clerk – had a poetic soul. 'Nice little place,' he said. 'Not littered up with black fellows. If I were on a homesteading job, I reckon I'd squat here.'

The Post

'The Post' was found amongst Buchan's Papers in Queen's University and is clearly an early draft version of 'The Loathly Opposite' (*see* p. 109).

Major Oliver Pugh's Story

IT WAS THE day after the Lincolnshire, where there had been a close finish, and the talk at dinner wandered to historic neck-and-neck races of the past. It presently degenerated into a highly technical discussion between Burminster and Collatt, till Sandy Arbuthnot declared that it was like a Newmarket public-house.

'If close finishes are common in racing,' he said, 'it only shows what a bad parallel the Turf makes with human life. I don't know anything about the silly subject, but we English draw most of our ordinary metaphors from it and I believe it has a malign effect on our character. It gives us a false romanticism. The great contests of the world were all won with a wide margin. The true and lasting victories came triumphantly. You remember what Nietzsche said: "The divine always walks on light feet." For your information, Tommy, I may say that Nietzsche was not a trainer.'

It was Sandy's agreeable habit to fling an occasional paradox at the table with a view to starting an argument. He was the genuine sophist. This time he stirred up Pugh, who had come to the War Office from the Indian Staff Corps. Pugh had been a great figure in Secret Service work in the East, but he did not look the part, for he had the air of a polo-playing cavalry subaltern. The skin was stretched as tight over his cheek-bones as over the knuckles of a clenched fist, and was so dark that it had the appearance of beaten bronze. He had black hair, rather beady black eyes, and the hooky nose which in the Celt often goes with that colouring. He looked as if he had spent his life in tents, but as a matter of fact he had made his name in the office rather than in the field. Sandy, who knew his work, used to say Pugh had a positive genius for organising means of getting difficult knowledge, but that he himself could not discover why a child was crying. He could make the scheme: a very different type of man carried it out.

'I don't agree,' Pugh said. 'I think most victories are won by a short head – at any rate the victories worth having. When luck has come my way I've generally won on the post.'

'That's because you think of luck and not of form,' said Sandy.

'Nine times out of ten you need luck for form to win. The real value of form is that it can use the luck when it comes.'

Then he told us this story.

'When I was brought to Europe in March 1918 and given a "hush" department on three floors of an eighteenth-century house in a back street, I had a good deal to learn about my business. That I learned it in reasonable time was due to the extraordinary fine staff that I found provided for me. Not one of them was a regular soldier. They were all gentlemen and educated men – they had to be in that job – but they came out of every sort of environment. One of the best was a Shetland laird, another was a Chancery K.C., and I had besides a metallurgical chemist, a golf champion, a leader-writer, a popular dramatist, several actuaries, and a curate. None of them thought of anything but his job, and at the end of the war, when some ass proposed to make them OBE's, there was a very fair imitation of a riot. A more loyal crowd never existed, and they accepted me as their chief as unquestioningly as if I had been with them since 1914. All they asked was to be allowed to get on with their work.

'The one who most interested me was my second-in-command, Philip Channell. He was a man of forty-three, about five foot four in height, weighing, I fancy, under nine stone, and almost as blind as an owl. He was good enough at papers with his double glasses, but he could hardly recognise you three yards off. I never met anybody quite like him. He had been a professor at some Midland college – mathematics or physics, I think – and as soon as the war began he had tried to enlist. Of course they wouldn't have him – he was about E5 in any physical classification, besides being well over age – but he would take no refusal, and presently he worried his way into the Government service. Fortunately he found the very job he could do superlatively well, for I do not believe there was a man alive with more natural genius for cryptography.

'I don't know if any of you have ever given your mind to that heartbreaking subject. Anyhow you know that secret writing falls under two heads – codes and cyphers; and that codes are combinations of words and cyphers of numerals. I remember how one used to be told that no code or cypher which was practically useful was really undiscoverable, and in a sense that is true, especially of codes. A system of communication which is in constant use must obviously not be too intricate, and a working code, if you get long enough for the job, can generally be read. That is why a code is periodically changed by the users. There are rules in worrying out the permutations and combinations of letters in most codes, for human ingenuity seems to run in certain channels, and a man who has been a long time at the business gets surprisingly clever at it. You begin by finding out a little bit, and then empirically building up the rules of decoding, till in a week or two you get the whole thing. Then, when you are happily engaged in reading enemy messages, the code is changed suddenly, and you have to start again from the beginning . . . You can make a code, of course, that it is simply impossible to read except by accident – the key to which is a page of some book, for example – but fortunately that kind is not of much general use.

'Well, we got on pretty well with the codes, and read the intercepted enemy messages, cables and wireless, with considerable ease and precision. It was mostly diplomatic stuff, and not very important. The more valuable stuff was in cypher, and that was another pair of shoes. With a code you can build up the interpretation by degrees, but with a cypher you either know it or you don't – there are no half-way houses. A cypher, since it deals with numbers, is a horrible field for mathematical ingenuity. Once you have written out the letters of a message in numerals there are many means by which you can lock it and double-lock it. The two main devices, as you know, are transposition and substitution, and there is no limit to the ways one or other or both can be used. There is nothing to prevent a cypher having a double meaning, produced by two different methods, and, as a practical question, you have to decide which meaning is intended. By way of an extra complication, too, the message, when decyphered, may turn out to be itself in a difficult code. I can tell you our job wasn't exactly a rest cure . . .'

Burminster, looking puzzled, inquired as to the locking of cyphers, and Pugh explained.

'You take a message and write it out in numerals – a group of two say, representing each letter – $a = 21$, $b = 39$ and so on. When you have got it written out horizontally, you draw, say, five vertical columns, and choose a word of five letters, which you write above them. Say the word is "Sandy". You divide the numerical groups in your message by five, and the result is, say, 15. Then you take the groups and pour them into the vertical columns, following the alphabetical order of the letters in the key word – the first 15 into the second column headed by A, the second fifteen into the fourth column which is headed D, the last fifteen into the last column which is Y. That means that you have put your first cypher into a frame composed of five vertical columns. Then you lock it. – You write out the contents of the columns *horizontally*, following the lines across. That is a locked message. To unlock it you have to have the key word, so as to put it back into the vertical columns, and then into the original horizontal form.'

'He wasn't quite like the others,' said Pugh. 'Most of my fellows were intent on their job for its own sake, and scarcely gave a thought to the war. You found the same thing in a lot of other behind-the-lines departments, and I daresay it was a good thing – it kept their nerves quiet and their minds undisturbed. After all our business was only to decode and decypher German messages – we had nothing to do with what use was made of them. When the Armistice came some of my people were flabbergasted – they hadn't realised that their job was bound up with the war.

'But Channell was different. He had started out by wanting to fight, and he always regarded himself as an active belligerent. He was there to beat the Boche, and he would have vastly preferred doing it with a machine-gun. Every phase of the campaign in every area was anxiously followed by him, and he used to pester me with questions and schemes. There was something very boyish, almost childlike, about the little man. He had a great brain packed in ice, but his heart was always on the flutter. I think he dreamed of doing something himself, something big, to help on victory, bringing off some great sensational *coup* which would matter tremendously. It was not that he wanted glory, for he was as shy as a woodcock, but he had cherished a picture of his duty and he wanted to live up to it. He was the kind of chap that leads forlorn hopes, for he simply pined to sacrifice himself. He was romantic, too. He used to listen to my yarns with wistful eyes and get terribly excited about things like the Canadians at Passchendaele and the tanks at Cambrai. I used to try and cheer him by telling him that he was doing priceless work, far better than if he were a second-lieutenant in the line, but I could see that he wasn't convinced. He wanted something with more colour in it than puzzling through double spectacles over a mess of figures.

'Well, the war dragged on, and 1918 came and the March retreat, and Channell was a miserable being. The way he behaved he might have been Commander-in-Chief with the whole responsibility on his shoulders. He did his work as well as ever, but he grew as thin as a cock-sparrow and his eyes looked as if he slept badly. All the summer when we were being hammered on the Aisne and the Marne he moved about like a ghost, growing leaner every day, till he was only skin and bone and a pair of owlish eyes. But he perked up after the 18th of July, and when Haig started his advance in August he became a new man. He had read so much and thought so much about military affairs that his judgment was surprisingly sound – a good deal sounder than that of some of my War Office colleagues. He saw that victory before the end of the year was necessary if the world was not to be bankrupted, and he knew about the end of August that, if the game was rightly played, victory was mathematically certain.

'I never saw anybody in such a continuous state of excitement. Our departmental work had rather slacked off, especially the codes, for German diplomatic activity was ebbing, so he had more leisure to think about what was happening in the field. I could see that behind all his keenness there was disappointment; the war was ending and he had never had a chance of the *coup* of which he had dreamed. He was only a spectator now, and he would have given his right hand to be a participant.

'Nevertheless in the last lap his chance came.

'There was one cypher which had always defeated us – the one used in the wireless messages between the German General Staff and Liman in the East. It was a locked cypher, and I fancy that Channell had given more time to it than to any dozen of the others, for it put him on his mettle. But he confessed himself absolutely beaten. He wouldn't admit that it was insoluble, but he declared that he would need a bit of real luck to solve it. I asked what kind of luck, and he said a mistake and a repetition. That, he said, might give him a chance of establishing equations.

'Now about the beginning of September things began to be hectic in the Near East. The great attack of the EEF was fixed for the 19th, and if it succeeded Turkey would be out of the war and the reaction in Europe would be tremendous. To succeed we had to go all out, and to go all out we wanted to be perfectly sure of our ground. The great question was just how much Germany's difficulties in France had already affected Liman's command. We knew that German troops were being brought back, and we had heard of guns on their way home, but we could get no certain information about the latter. Obviously it was of the utmost importance to be sure, for if we knew that the German batteries were no longer against us we could behave like Wellington at Waterloo – send everything in and not worry about reserves. To bring off the *coup* on the grand scale on which it had been conceived needed every atom of strength we possessed, and unless we won on the grand scale victory wouldn't affect the main issue.

'So I was prodded by my chiefs and in turn I prodded Channell. I explained the situation to him, and he saw its gravity. I thought I would cheer him by telling him that now at last he and his cyphers were in the centre of the picture. I didn't cheer him – I only solemnised him.

'I remember that he got as white as a sheet, and sat down plump in a chair. 'P.Y.' he groaned – that was the pet name he had for the Liman cypher. 'It must be all in that damned P.Y. How long have I got?'

' "A week," I said.

' "A week," he cried. "And in eighteen months I've made nothing of it. It's hopeless, I tell you."

' "We must pray for a bit of luck. The Boche is getting pretty well rattled now and may make the mistake you hoped for."

' "Things don't happen that way," he lamented. "Only in books – not in real life."

' "Well, we can only do our best," I said. "Chuck everything but P.Y., for at this moment it's the most important gibberish in the world."

'I looked in on him next day, and found him sitting with a pile of intercepted wireless, and sheets of foolscap covered with figures. His face was puckered in concentration, but when he lifted his eyes they were as plaintive as a sick dog's. I saw that he was not getting on, and I forebore to pass on to him the goading I had had that day from M.I. He didn't need any spur.

'The following afternoon I looked in on him again. There were the same piles of wireless and scribbled foolscap, and a tray with about fifty cigarette ends. He must have broken the record these days for the consumption of gaspers. He simply shook his head and did not look at me. I remember casting my eyes round the little cubby-hole – the air acrid with cheap tobacco, dust on the shelves and floor, for no one was allowed to clean it, a photograph of Foch tacked on the wall, large-scale maps of the Western Front stuck on a frame, the plaster dropping from the dingy ceiling, and the September sun struggling through the dirty window – and thinking that it was an odd place for important things to happen in. Yet on that table was information worth a king's ransom, if the head that bent over it could find the key. I was stale as ditch-water myself and badly needed a holiday, but Channell was simply grizzled and shrunken with fatigue.

'I took him out to dinner that night, but it was like entertaining a mummy. He ate scarcely anything, and was too limp for conversation, and sometimes his eyes would become vacant as his mind went off on some private inquiry. I didn't think that anything would happen about P.Y. but I feared that something serious would happen to Channell's brain, and that presently he would be a casualty. These days both he and I had beds in the office, and before I turned in I tried to make him take a sleeping draught. He refused, for the previous day's wireless was usually delivered about 5 A.M. and he said he couldn't afford to have a muzzy head then, for first impressions were often valuable.

'Next morning I was awoke by a weird figure in a yellow dressing-gown at my bedside. It was Channell, and his scanty hair seemed to be all on end.

' "Get up," he croaked. "I believe the miracle has happened."

'I was as rattled as he when we stood together in his room. He showed me a long message, which was dated *en clair*. Then he produced a very short message, and then a third message about as long as the first.

' "Do you realise what that means?" he cried, his voice cracked with excitement. "They have made a mistake in P.Y. The third message is almost the same as the first. The second can only mean 'Your message of to-day's date unintelligible. Please repeat.' We know the regular German formula for that ... Don't you see what we've got? First the translation of a piece of the cypher! Second, an alteration in a message which may help us to an equation!"

'I dragged him out to breakfast at my club, for I was as much in the air as he was. Indeed I was more, for I knew less about cyphers. "The thing is perfectly simple now," I told him. But he damped my ardour by reminding me that a locked cypher was a subtler thing than I thought, and that he had still to find the key. The short intermediate message would help, and still more would the small difference between the two long messages. I didn't follow that, but it had something to do with the position of the numerals in the vertical framework to which they had to be restored. It might help to give him the key-word – or, as he called it, the wave-length. I don't profess to have understood him, and he was in no mood for long explanations, for he was panting to be back at his desk.

'All morning, as I worked in my office, I expected every minute to have Channell breaking in on me with the translation in his hand. But he never came, and I had a luncheon engagement and after that a conference, so I didn't see him till close on dinner-time. I went softly in-to his room, so as not to disturb him, and for a little watched him as he sat with his head on one hand peering at figures and every now and then making a correction. Then he realised my presence, for he pushed the papers away from him, and stood up.

' "I can't get it," he said, his voice flat with weariness. "My God, this is awful! I seem to be trembling on the edge of it, and then something shoves me back ... I haven't enough yet – I want more – just a fraction more ... I'm going to be beaten – beaten by a hair's breadth, but that's just as bad as if I were beaten by the width of the world."

'He refused to come out to dinner, and when I got back about eleven he was drinking strong tea and still at work. I don't suppose he went to bed, but next morning when I woke I heard him having a bath. I daren't exercise my authority over him and make him come out to breakfast, for I realised the kind of ordeal he was going through. His chance had come and he couldn't take it. He was put-ting every atom of brain power he possessed into the thing, and it kept eluding him. It was like the worst kind of nightmare, when you have only a step to take to reach safety, but your feet are too feeble to take it.

'That morning I did not expect him to appear in my room with news of success. I had lost hope. I felt that if he couldn't do the trick at the first go-off he would never do it, that no amount of brain-cudgelling would achieve the impossible. He wanted just a little more help, and I didn't see where he was to get it from, for P.Y. was not likely to be so accommodating a second time. I was desperately sorry for him, and as the day wore on I began to get alarmed. This kind of strain might put him into brain fever or addle his wits for good.

'I looked in on him after luncheon and was really scared by what I saw. He was sitting idly at his desk, staring before him. At first he didn't seem to know I was there, and then he suddenly asked over his shoulder: "How long have I still got?"

' "Till to-morrow afternoon," I said.

' "But you said two days. This must be the last day."

' "The orders won't go out till to-morrow," I explained. "We should be in time up till the afternoon."

'He shook his head dismally. "No good," he said. "No good. A month would make no difference."

'Then he turned on me a face so drawn and tormented and eyes so abysmally hopeless that I decided that something must be done.

' "This hell is going to stop," I said briskly. "You'll be a lunatic if you have another hour of it. You're going to come straight away with me and sleep to-night in the country. I order you. You're staler than a ship's biscuit and no earthly use to anybody at present. You're coming down with me to Hampshire, and you're starting in half an hour."

'He made objections of course – he had less than a day left – he was bound to work every minute of it – the country air would make him worse. As his superior officer I over-ruled him. I told him that he was stuck in the meshes of his puzzle and needed to get a bit away from it and look round it. But I didn't believe in my heart that anything mattered about that: all I wanted was to prevent his going crazy. I was assured by the limp resistance he made that he too had lost hope.

'We went down to a fishing cottage on the Itchen in which I had a share. We had supper in the bare little parlour and then I took him for a walk through a water-meadow and up to the downs, which under a great harvest moon were the colour of ripe barley. I fancy we walked about five miles, and came to anchor in a field of wheat above the valley. The crop had been cut but not yet carried, and we sat and smoked behind a group of sheaves. There was a pleasant chill in the air, and fresh cold little breezes blew up the river. The place was full of good smells – sunburnt grain, sunburnt earth, distant bracken, wafts of mint and water-weeds from the meadows below; owls were hooting in the woods, and a cart rumbled on a farm road, while above was a misty blue sky and the round moon.

'It did me good, and I think it soothed Channell too. He slipped down till he was on his back, staring at the sky, so quiet that at one moment I thought he was asleep. I daresay he would have stayed there all night if I had let him, and in the end I had some difficulty in persuading him to get up. I remember that, as he shook the straws out of his clothes, he murmured something which sounded like *'securus judicat orbis'* – a tag which, as I remembered, meant that nothing would very much matter in a hundred years. That has always seemed to me to be a sound philosophy, and I was cheered by what seemed to be a further statement of it as we entered the garden wicket. "I am a fool," he said. "So are you – so is all mankind. Lord, what innocent funny fools!" From this I gathered that Channell had accepted defeat and was taking it in the right spirit. He had failed after doing his damnedest, and like a sensible man saw the comedy of it all. I hoped that he might sleep that night.

'I never dared at that time to be out of reach of the telegraph, and early next morning I got a batch of messages which I had to answer. They were the ordinary routine stuff, for we had people all over the shop, and the replies usually went *en clair* without a signature. Channell, who looked rather less like a dead fish, took them from me to deal with, and scribbled the answers in the little telegraph office at the wayside station. "Better stick my name at the end of the one to Mavro," I told him. "That will show that I think it important and want him to hustle."

'We got newspapers at the junction, and I flung a couple to Channell. But he didn't open them, and all the way to town sat in a day-dream. I stole a glance at him now and then and felt greatly relieved by the sight of him. The night in the country seemed to have worked wonders, for his face looked smoothed out in spite of its pallor, and he was actually smiling to himself. There he sat like Buddha, his hands folded on his apron of newspapers, until we reached Vauxhall. Then he suddenly became restless, moved into the corridor and opened the window, and at Waterloo, long before the train had come to a standstill, he was out on the platform and racing for a taxi.

'This looked unpleasantly like craziness, but I couldn't follow him, for I had an important appointment to keep. I sent his kit and mine back to the office by my servant, and spent the morning at the War Office where the coming movement in the East was our chief business. I was told that at three o'clock that afternoon I might shut down my efforts; the orders must go out, and after that couldn't be changed; nothing had come through from spies or air reconnaissance to settle the problem of the batteries, so it was impossible to go forward bald-headed without reserves.

'"You can get nothing out of the wireless?" one man asked me. "We scarcely thought you would. If you couldn't hit off the cypher at leisure it wasn't likely you would do the trick under pressure. You want luck for that, and luck doesn't come at the eleventh hour."

'But it did. I got back to the office before luncheon, and I hadn't been in my chair five minutes before Channell appeared. He said nothing, just put a paper before me, and I saw that his hand trembled. I looked at him, and his mouth was tight shut, as if to keep back tears or laughter.

'"What is it?" I asked.

'"It's P.Y.," he stuttered, "the message they asked to have repeated."

'"Great God," I shouted. "You have got it out?"

'He nodded, and then flopped limply into a chair. I devoured the thing, and saw that it was what we had been hoping for, an order for every German battery to return at once to the West. After that I had no time to consider Channell. I got on the private wire to the War Office, and read the thing to a man who could scarcely take it down from excitement. Then I put the paper in my pocket and five minutes later was presenting it to my chief. It was the most sensational *coup* my show had ever brought off, and I wasn't going to miss any of the melodrama. "It has just about cost a good man his reason," I said. "Channell deserves the Victoria Cross. He risked something quite as important as his life."

'When I sent for him that afternoon I was nervous as to the state I should find him in. Success can be as devastating as failure, and I was afraid that something might have given in his strained nerves. To my relief he was perfectly normal and composed; only there was a kind of glow in his eyes, not so much of pride as of peace. Channell had done what he had wanted to do in the war, and his mind was at rest.

'"I am not going to congratulate you," I said. "It's too big for compliments. You have won on the post – absolutely on the post. Do you mind telling me how it happened?"

'"It was the night in the country," he said. "You were right, sir – I had been living in the undergrowth and needed to take a look round... Well, as soon as I could laugh at myself, I was able to get a longer prospect. When I woke this morning I found that my thoughts were busy not with the message but with its antecedents. I asked myself just how the mistake happened to be made. We never had one before – in codes often, but never in a cypher. The German system is different from ours, as you know. No staff officer encyphers his own messages. They are all sent to a special department, which is so efficient as to be beyond the reach of error – their method of checking makes their work practically fool-proof. So I wondered why in this case it had broken down."

'"Yes," I said, "I never thought of that."

'"Then at the station you said something which made me think. You told me to sign the telegram to Mavro with your own name, that he might see that you considered it important. That occupied my mind on the journey up – you may have noticed that I was rather abstracted."

'"Go on," I said, for I began to see light.

'"Well, it seemed to me that our message might have been encyphered not by the special department but by the staff officer concerned, and that this was the reason for the mistake... That was interesting, and I cast about to see how it could help us... And then I thought that that staff officer might have done as you did, and put his own name to it. That was why I left Waterloo in rather a hurry."

'Channell sat blinking happily at me through his double glasses.

'"We know, of course, the name of the *Generalstabsoffizier* in charge of this business. If I was right, his name would be the last word in the message when decyphered... Well, my guess worked. It gave me just the little more help I needed, and in two hours I had the thing complete... That is all there is to it."

'That was all. I didn't say anything, for I felt awed. The margin of victory had been so narrow, the chain of causes so fantastic. A casual word, a sudden fancy, a fortunate guess had, positively at the last moment, given us the key to the most crabbed cypher of the war. About three weeks later they helped to give us Damascus.'

The Loathly Opposite

'The Loathly Opposite' appeared in *Pall Mall Magazine* in October 1927 and then as Oliver Pugh's story in *The Runa-gates Club* (1928). It was selected by Eric Ambler for his anthology *To Catch a Spy* (1964).

Buchan gives Pugh his own duodenal complaint and may well have written the story when he spent a week at a *kurhaus* in the Black Forest in November 1926. Christoph, possibly based on Buchan's doctor Marten, and the *kurhaus* reappear in *The House of the Four Winds* (1935). The story has certain similarities to Maynard Keynes' account of meeting a defeated enemy at the Versailles Peace Conference in *Two Memoirs: A Defeated Enemy and My Early Beliefs* (1949). The story was one of the first to deal accurately with wartime cypher activities, but Buchan gives it a fresh twist by drawing parallels between the struggle to decode wartime messages and the psychological probings of madness.

How loathly opposite I stood
To his unnatural purpose.
King Lear

BURMINSTER HAD BEEN to a Guildhall dinner the night before, which had been attended by many – to him – unfamiliar celebrities. He had seen for the first time in the flesh people whom he had long known by reputation, and he declared that in every case the picture he had formed of them had been cruelly shattered. An eminent poet, he said, had looked like a starting-price bookmaker, and a financier of world-wide fame had been exactly like the music-master at his preparatory school. Wherefore Burminster made the profound deduction that things were never what they seemed.

'That's only because you have a feeble imagination,' said Sandy Arbuthnot. 'If you had really understood Timson's poetry you would have realised that it went with close-cropped red hair and a fat body, and you should have known that Macintyre (this was the financier) had the music-and-metaphysics type of mind. That's why he puzzles the City so. If you understand a man's work well enough you can guess pretty accurately what he'll look like. I don't mean the colour of his eyes and his hair, but the general atmosphere of him.'

It was Sandy's agreeable habit to fling an occasional paradox at the table with the view of starting an argument. This time he stirred up Pugh, who had come to the War Office from the Indian Staff Corps. Pugh had been a great figure in Secret Service work in the East, but he did not look the part, for he had the air of a polo-playing cavalry subaltern. The skin was stretched as tight over his cheek-bones as over the knuckles of a clenched fist, and was so dark that it had the appearance of beaten bronze. He had black hair, rather beady black eyes, and the hooky nose which in the Celt often goes with that colouring. He was himself a very good refutation of Sandy's theory.

'I don't agree,' Pugh said. 'At least not as a general principle. One piece of humanity whose work I studied with the microscope for two aching years upset all my notions when I came to meet it.'

Then he told us this story.

'When I was brought to England in November '17 and given a "hush" department on three floors of an eighteenth-century house in a back street, I had a good deal to learn about my business. That I learned it in reasonable time was due to the extraordinarily fine staff that I found provided for me. Not one of them was a regular soldier. They were all educated men – they had to be in that job – but they came out of every sort of environment. One of the best was a Shetland laird, another was an Admiralty Court K.C., and I had besides a metallurgical chemist, a golf champion, a leader-writer, a popular dramatist, several actuaries, and an East-end curate. None of them thought of anything but his job, and at the end of the war, when some ass proposed to make them OBEs, there was a very fair imitation of a riot. A more loyal crowd never existed, and they accepted me as their chief as unquestioningly as if I had been with them since 1914.

'To the war in the ordinary sense they scarcely gave a thought. You found the same thing in a lot of other behind-the-lines departments, and I daresay it was a good thing – it kept their nerves quiet and their minds concentrated. After all our business was only to decode and decypher German messages; we had nothing to do with the use which was made of them. It was a curious little nest, and when the Armistice came my people were flabbergasted – they hadn't realised that their job was bound up with the war.

'The one who most interested me was my second-in-command, Philip Channell. He was a man of forty-three, about five-foot-four in height, weighing, I fancy, under nine stone, and almost as blind as an owl. He was good enough at papers with his double glasses, but he could hardly recognise you three yards off. He had been a professor at some Midland college – mathematics or physics, I think – and as soon as the war began he had tried to enlist. Of course they wouldn't have him – he was about E5 in any physical classification, besides being well over age – but he would take no refusal, and presently he worried his way into the Government service. Fortunately he found a job which he could do superlatively well, for I do not believe there was a man alive with more natural genius for cryptography.

'I don't know if any of you have ever given your mind to that heart-breaking subject. Anyhow you know that secret writing falls under two heads – codes and cyphers, and that codes are combinations of words and cyphers of numerals. I remember how one used to be told that no code or cypher which was practically useful was really undiscoverable, and in a sense that is true, especially of codes. A system of communication which is in constant use must obviously not be too intricate, and a working code, if you get long enough for the job, can generally be read. That is why a code is periodically changed by the users. There are rules in worrying out the permutations and combinations of letters in most codes, for human ingenuity seems to run in certain channels, and a man who has been a long time at the business gets surprisingly clever at it. You begin by finding out a little bit, and then empirically building up the rules of decoding, till in a week or two you get the whole thing. Then, when you are happily engaged in reading enemy messages, the code is changed suddenly, and you have to start again from the beginning ... You can make a code, of course, that it is simply impossible to read except by accident – the key to which is a page of some book, for example – but fortunately that kind is not of much general use.

'Well, we got on pretty well with the codes, and read the intercepted enemy messages, cables and wireless, with considerable ease and precision. It was mostly diplomatic stuff, and not very important. The more valuable stuff was in cypher, and that was another pair of shoes. With a code you can build up the interpretation by degrees, but with a cypher you either know it or you don't – there are no half-way houses. A cypher, since it deals with numbers, is a horrible field for mathematical ingenuity. Once you have written out the letters of a message in numerals there are many means by which you can lock it and double-lock it. The two main devices, as you know, are trans-position and substitution, and there is no limit to the ways one or other or both can be used. There is nothing to prevent a cypher having a double meaning, produced by two different methods, and, as a practical question, you have to decide which meaning is intended. By way of an extra complication, too, the message, when decyphered, may turn out to be itself in a difficult code. I can tell you our job wasn't exactly a rest cure.'

Burminster, looking puzzled, inquired as to the locking of cyphers.

'It would take too long to explain. Roughly, you write out a message horizontally in numerals; then you pour it into vertical col-umns, the number and order of which are determined by a key word; then you write out the contents of the columns horizontally, following the lines across. To unlock it you have to have the key word, so as to put it back into the vertical columns, and then into the original horizontal form.'

Burminster cried out like one in pain. 'It can't be done. Don't tell me that any human brain could solve such an acrostic.'

'It was frequently done,' said Pugh.

'By you?'

'Lord bless you, not by me. I can't do a simple crossword puzzle. By my people.'

'Give me the trenches,' said Burminster in a hollow voice. 'Give me the trenches any day. Do you seriously mean to tell me that you could sit down before a muddle of numbers and travel back the way they had been muddled to an original that made sense?'

'I couldn't, but Channell could – in most cases. You see, we didn't begin entirely in the dark. We already knew the kind of intricacies that the enemy favoured, and the way we worked was by trying a variety of clues till we hit on the right one.'

'Well, I'm blessed! Go on about your man Channell.'

'This isn't Channell's story,' said Pugh. 'He only comes into it accidentally... There was one cypher which always defeated us, a cypher used between the German General Staff and their forces in the East. It was a locked cypher, and Channell had given more time to it than to any dozen of the others, for it put him on his mettle. But he confessed himself absolutely beaten. He wouldn't admit that it was insoluble, but he declared that he would need a bit of real luck to solve it. I asked him what kind of luck, and he said a mistake and a repetition. That, he said, might give him a chance of establishing equations.

'We called this particular cypher "PY", and we hated it poisonously. We felt like pygmies battering at the base of a high stone tower. Dislike of the thing soon became dislike of the man who had conceived it. Channell and I used to − I won't say amuse, for it was too dashed serious − but torment ourselves by trying to picture the fellow who owned the brain that was responsible for PY. We had a pretty complete dossier of the German Intelligence Staff, but of course we couldn't know who was responsible for this particular cypher. We knew no more than his code name, Reinmar, with which he signed the simpler messages to the East, and Channell, who was a romantic little chap for all his science, had got it into his head that it was a woman. He used to describe her to me as if he had seen her − a she-devil, young, beautiful, with a much-painted white face, and eyes like a cobra's. I fancy he read a rather low class of novel in his off-time.

'My picture was different. At first I thought of the histrionic type of scientist, the "ruthless brain" type, with a high forehead and a jaw puckered like a chimpanzee. But that didn't seem to work, and I settled on a picture of a first-class *Generalstabsoffizier*, as handsome as Falkenhayn, trained to the last decimal, absolutely passionless, with a mind that worked with the relentless precision of a fine machine. We all of us at the time suffered from the bogy of this kind of German, and, when things were going badly, as in March '18, I couldn't sleep for hating him. The infernal fellow was so water-tight and armourplated, a Goliath who scorned the pebbles from our feeble slings.

'Well, to make a long story short, there came a moment in September '18 when PY was about the most important thing in the world. It mattered enormously what Germany was doing in Syria, and we knew that it was all in PY. Every morning a pile of the intercepted German wireless messages lay on Channell's table, which were as meaningless to him as a child's scrawl. I was prodded by my chiefs and in turn I prodded Channell. We had a week to find the key to the cypher, after which things must go on without us, and if we had failed to make anything of it in eighteen months of quiet work, it didn't seem likely that we would succeed in seven feverish days. Channell nearly went off his head with overwork and anxiety. I used to visit his dingy little room and find him fairly grizzled and shrunken with fatigue.

'This isn't a story about him, though there is a good story which I may tell you another time. As a matter of fact we won on the post. PY made a mistake. One morning we got a long message dated *en clair*, then a very short message, and then a third message almost the same as the first. The second must mean "Your message of today's date unintelligible, please repeat," the regular formula. This gave us a translation of a bit of the cypher. Even that would not have brought it out, and for twelve hours Channell was on the verge of lunacy, till it occurred to him that Reinmar might have signed the long message with his name, as we used to do sometimes in cases of extreme urgency. He was right, and, within three hours of the last moment Operations could give us, we had the whole thing pat. As I have said, that is a story worth telling, but it is not this one.

'We both finished the war too tired to think of much except that the darned thing was over. But Reinmar had been so long our unseen but constantly pictured opponent that we kept up a certain interest in him. We would like to have seen how he took the licking, for he must have known that we had licked him. Mostly when you lick a man at a game you rather like him, but I didn't like Reinmar. In fact I made him a sort of compost of everything I had ever disliked in a German. Channell stuck to his she-devil theory, but I was pretty certain that he was a youngish man with an intellectual arrogance which his country's débâcle would in no way lessen. He would never acknowledge defeat. It was highly improbable that I should ever find out who he was, but I felt that if I did, and met him face to face, my dislike would be abundantly justified.

'As you know, for a year or two after the Armistice I was a pretty sick man. Most of us were. We hadn't the fillip of getting back to civilised comforts, like the men in the trenches. We had always been comfortable enough in body, but our minds were fagged out, and there is no easy cure for that. My digestion went nobly to pieces, and I endured a miserable space of lying in bed and living on milk and olive-oil. After that I went back to work, but the darned thing always returned, and every leech had a different regime to advise. I tried them all – dry meals, a snack every two hours, lemon juice, sour milk, starvation, knocking off tobacco – but nothing got me more than half-way out of the trough. I was a burden to myself and a nuisance to others, dragging my wing through life, with a constant pain in my tummy.

'More than one doctor advised an operation, but I was chary about that, for I had seen several of my friends operated on for the same mischief and left as sick as before. Then a man told me about a German fellow called Christoph, who was said to be very good at handling my trouble. The best hand at diagnosis in the world, my informant said – no fads – treated every case on its merits – a really original mind. Dr Christoph had a modest Kurhaus at a place called Rosensee in the Sächischen Sweitz. By this time I was getting pretty desperate, so I packed a bag and set off for Rosensee.

'It was a quiet little town at the mouth of a narrow valley, tucked in under wooded hills, a clean fresh place with open channels of running water in the streets. There was a big church with an onion spire, a Catholic seminary, and a small tanning industry. The Kurhaus was half-way up a hill, and I felt better as soon as I saw my bedroom, with its bare scrubbed floors and its wide verandah looking up into a forest glade. I felt still better when I saw Dr Christoph. He was a small man with a grizzled beard, a high forehead, and a limp, rather like what I imagine the Apostle Paul must have been. He looked wise, as wise as an old owl. His English was atrocious, but even when he found that I talked German fairly well he didn't expand in speech. He would deliver no opinion of any kind until he had had me at least a week under observation; but somehow I felt comforted, for I concluded that a first-class brain had got to work on me.

'The other patients were mostly Germans with a sprinkling of Spaniards, but to my delight I found Channell. He also had been having a thin time since we parted. Nerves were his trouble – general nervous debility and perpetual insomnia, and his college had given him six months' leave of absence to try to get well. The poor chap was as lean as a sparrow, and he had the large dull eyes and the dry lips of the sleepless. He had arrived a week before me, and like me was under observation. But his vetting was different from mine, for he was a mental case, and Dr Christoph used to devote hours to trying to unriddle his nervous tangles. "He is a good man for a German," said Channell, "but he is on the wrong tack. There's nothing wrong with my mind. I wish he'd stick to violet rays and massage, instead of asking me silly questions about my great-grandmother."

'Channell and I used to go for invalidish walks in the woods, and we naturally talked about the years we had worked together. He was living mainly in the past, for the war had been the great thing in his life, and his professorial duties seemed trivial by comparison. As we tramped among the withered bracken and heather his mind was always harking back to the dingy little room where he had smoked cheap cigarettes and worked fourteen hours out of the twenty-four. In particular he was as eagerly curious about our old antagonist, Reinmar, as he had been in 1918. He was more positive than ever that she was a woman, and I believe that one of the reasons that had induced him to try a cure in Germany was a vague hope that he might get on her track. I had almost forgotten about the thing, and I was amused by Channell in the part of the untiring sleuth-hound.

'"You won't find her in the Kurhaus," I said. "Perhaps she is in some old Schloss in the neighbourhood, waiting for you like the Sleeping Beauty."

'"I'm serious," he said plaintively. "It is purely a matter of intellectual curiosity, but I confess I would give a great deal to see her face to face. After I leave here, I thought of going to Berlin to make some inquiries. But I'm handicapped for I know nobody and I have no credentials. Why don't you, who have a large acquaintance and far more authority, take the thing up?"

'I told him that my interest in the matter had flagged and that I wasn't keen on digging into the past, but I promised to give him a line to our Military Attaché if he thought of going to Berlin. I rather discouraged him from letting his mind dwell too much on events in the war. I said that he ought to try to bolt the door on all that had contributed to his present breakdown.

'"That is not Dr Christoph's opinion," he said emphatically. "He encourages me to talk about it. You see, with me it is a purely intellectual interest. I have no emotion in the matter. I feel quite friendly towards Reinmar, whoever she may be. It is, if you like, a piece of romance. I haven't had so many romantic events in my life that I want to forget this."

' "Have you told Dr Christoph about Reinmar?" I asked.

' "Yes," he said, "and he was mildly interested. You know the way he looks at you with his solemn grey eyes. I doubt if he quite understood what I meant, for a little provincial doctor, even though he is a genius in his own line, is not likely to know much about the ways of the Great General Staff . . . I had to tell him, for I have to tell him all my dreams, and lately I have taken to dreaming about Reinmar."

' "What's she like?" I asked.

' "Oh, a most remarkable figure. Very beautiful, but uncanny. She has long fair hair down to her knees."

'Of course I laughed. "You're mixing her up with the Valkyries," I said. "Lord, it would be an awkward business if you met that she-dragon in the flesh."

'But he was quite solemn about it, and declared that his waking picture of her was not in the least like his dreams. He rather agreed with my nonsense about the old Schloss. He thought that she was probably some penniless grandee, living solitary in a moated grange, with nothing now to exercise her marvellous brain on, and eating her heart out with regret and shame. He drew so attractive a character of her that I began to think that Channell was in love with a being of his own creation, till he ended with, "But all the same she's utterly damnable. She must be, you know."

'After a fortnight I began to feel a different man. Dr Christoph thought that he had got on the track of the mischief, and certainly, with his deep massage and a few simple drugs, I had more internal comfort than I had known for three years. He was so pleased with my progress that he refused to treat me as an invalid. He encouraged me to take long walks into the hills, and presently he arranged for me to go out roebuck-shooting with some of the local junkers.

'I used to start before daybreak on the chilly November mornings and drive to the top of one of the ridges, where I would meet a collection of sportsmen and beaters, shepherded by a fellow in a green uniform. We lined out along the ridge, and the beaters, assisted by a marvellous collection of dogs, including the sporting dachshund, drove the roe towards us. It wasn't very cleverly managed, for the deer generally broke back, and it was chilly waiting in the first hours with a powdering of snow on the ground and the fir boughs heavy with frost crystals. But later, when the sun grew stronger, it was a very pleasant mode of spending a day. There was not much of a bag, but whenever a roe or a capercailzie fell all the guns would assemble and drink little glasses of *Kirschwasser*. I had been lent a rifle, one of those appalling contraptions which are double-barrelled shot-guns and rifles in one, and to transpose from one form to the other requires a mathematical calculation. The rifle had a hair trigger too, and when I first used it I was nearly the death of a respectable Saxon peasant.

'We all ate our midday meal together and in the evening, before going home, we had coffee and cakes in one or other of the farms. The party was an odd mixture, big farmers and small squires, an hotel-keeper or two, a local doctor, and a couple of lawyers from the town. At first they were a little shy of me, but presently they thawed, and after the first day we were good friends. They spoke quite frankly about the war, in which every one of them had had a share, and with a great deal of dignity and good sense.

'I learned to walk in Sikkim, and the little Saxon hills seemed to me inconsiderable. But they were too much for most of the guns, and instead of going straight up or down a slope they always chose a circuit, which gave them an easy gradient. One evening, when we were separating as usual, the beaters taking a short cut and the guns a circuit, I felt that I wanted exercise, so I raced the beaters downhill, beat them soundly, and had the better part of an hour to wait for my companions, before we adjourned to the farm for refreshment. The beaters must have talked about my pace, for as we walked away one of the guns, a lawyer called Meissen, asked me why I was visiting Rosensee at a time of year when few foreigners came. I said I was staying with Dr Christoph.

' "Is he then a private friend of yours?" he asked.

'I told him No, that I had come to his Kurhaus for treatment, being sick. His eyes expressed polite scepticism. He was not prepared to regard as an invalid a man who went down a hill like an avalanche.

'But, as we walked in the frosty dusk, he was led to speak of Dr Christoph, of whom he had no personal knowledge, and I learned how little honour a prophet may have in his own country. Rosensee scarcely knew him, except as a doctor who had an inexplicable attraction for foreign patients. Meissen was curious about his methods and the exact diseases in which he specialised. "Perhaps he may yet save me a journey to Homburg?" he laughed. "It is well to have a skilled physician at one's doorstep. The doctor is something of a hermit, and except for his patients does not appear to welcome his kind. Yet he is a good man, beyond doubt, and there are those who say that in the war he was a hero."

'This surprised me, for I could not imagine Dr Christoph in any fighting capacity, apart from the fact that he must have been too old. I thought that Meissen might refer to work in the base hospitals. But he was positive; Dr Christoph had been in the trenches; the limping leg was a war wound.

'I had had very little talk with the doctor, owing to my case being free from nervous complications. He would say a word to me morning and evening about my diet, and pass the time of day when we met, but it was not till the very eve of my departure that we had anything like a real conversation. He sent a message that he wanted to see me for not less than one hour, and he arrived with a batch of notes from which he delivered a kind of lecture on my case. Then I realised what an immense amount of care and solid thought he had expended on me. He had decided that his diagnosis was right – my rapid improvement suggested that – but it was necessary for some time to observe a simple regime, and to keep an eye on certain symptoms. So he took a sheet of notepaper from the table and in his small precise hand wrote down for me a few plain commandments.

'There was something about him, the honest eyes, the mouth which looked as if it had been often compressed in suffering, the air of grave goodwill, which I found curiously attractive. I wished that I had been a mental case like Channell, and had had more of his society. I detained him in talk, and he seemed not unwilling. By and by we drifted to the war and it turned out that Meissen was right.

'Dr Christoph had gone as medical officer in November '14 to the Ypres Salient with a Saxon regiment, and had spent the winter there. In '15 he had been in Champagne, and in the early months of '16 at Verdun, till he was invalided with rheumatic fever. That is to say, he had had about seventeen months of consecutive fighting in the worst areas with scarcely a holiday. A pretty good record for a frail little middle-aged man!

'His family was then at Stuttgart, his wife and one little boy. He took a long time to recover from the fever, and after that was put on home duty. "Till the war was almost over," he said, "almost over, but not quite. There was just time for me to go back to the front and get my foolish leg hurt." I must tell you that whenever he mentioned his war experience it was with a comical deprecating smile, as if he agreed with anyone who might think that gravity like this should have remained in bed.

'I assumed that this home duty was medical, until he said something about getting rusty in his professional work. Then it appeared that it had been some job connected with Intelligence. "I am reputed to have a little talent for mathematics," he said. "No. I am no mathematical scholar, but, if you understand me, I have a certain mathematical aptitude. My mind has always moved happily among numbers. Therefore I was set to construct and to interpret cyphers, a strange interlude in the noise of war. I sat in a little room and excluded the world, and for a little I was happy."

'He went on to speak of the enclave of peace in which he had found himself, and as I listened to his gentle monotonous voice, I had a sudden inspiration.

'I took a sheet of notepaper from the stand, scribbled the word *Reinmar* on it, and shoved it towards him. I had a notion, you see, that I might surprise him into helping Channell's researches.

'But it was I who got the big surprise. He stopped thunder-struck, as soon as his eye caught the word, blushed scarlet over every inch of face and bald forehead, seemed to have difficulty in swallowing, and then gasped. "How did you know?"

'I hadn't known, and now that I did, the knowledge left me speechless. This was the loathly opposite for which Channell and I had nursed our hatred. When I came out of my stupefaction I found that he had recovered his balance and was speaking slowly and distinctly, as if he were making a formal confession.

' "You were among my opponents . . . that interests me deeply . . . I often wondered . . . You beat me in the end. You are aware of that?"

'I nodded. "Only because you made a slip," I said.

' "Yes, I made a slip. I was to blame – very gravely to blame, for I let my private grief cloud my mind."

'He seemed to hesitate, as if he were loath to stir something very tragic in his memory.

' "I think I will tell you," he said at last. "I have often wished – it is a childish wish – to justify my failure to those who profited by it. My chiefs understood, of course, but my opponents could not. In that month when I failed I was in deep sorrow. I had a little son – his name was Reinmar – you remember that I took that name for my code signature?"

'His eyes were looking beyond me into some vision of the past.

' "He was, as you say, my mascot. He was all my family, and I adored him. But in those days food was not plentiful. We were no worse off than many million Germans, but the child was frail. In the last summer of the war he developed phthisis due to malnutrition, and in September he died. Then I failed my country, for with him some virtue seemed to depart from my mind. You see, my work was, so to speak, his also, as my name was his, and when he left me he took my power with him . . . So I stumbled. The rest is known to you."

'He sat staring beyond me, so small and lonely, that I could have howled. I remember putting my hand on his shoulder, and stammering some platitude about being sorry. We sat quite still for a minute or two, and then I remembered Channell. Channell must have poured his views of Reinmar into Dr Christoph's ear. I asked him if Channell knew.

'A flicker of a smile crossed his face.

' "Indeed no. And I will exact from you a promise never to breathe to him what I have told you. He is my patient, and I must first consider his case. At present he thinks that Reinmar is a wicked and beautiful lady whom he may some day meet. That is romance, and it is good for him to think so . . . If he were told the truth, he would be pitiful, and in Herr Channell's condition it is important that he should not be vexed with such emotions as pity." '

Ship to Tarshish

Ralph Collat's story 'Ship to Tarshish' in *The Runagates Club* (1928) first appeared as 'Ships to Tarshish' in *Pall Mall Magazine* in November 1927 and was subsequently sold to several papers during the 1930s. It is an ironic updating of the Old Testament story of Jonah.

Now the word of the Lord came unto Jonah the son of Amittai, saying, Arise, go to Nineveh... But Jonah... found a ship going to Tarshish: so he paid the fare thereof, and went down into it, to go with them unto Tarshish from the presence of the Lord.

Jonah I. i-iii

THE TALK ONE evening turned on the metaphysics of courage. It is a subject which most men are a little shy of discussing. They will heartily applaud a friend's pluck, but it is curious how rarely they will label a man a coward. Perhaps the reason is that we are all odd mixtures of strength and weakness, brave in certain things, timid in others; and since each is apt to remember his private funks more vividly than the things about which he is bold, we are chary about dogmatising.

Lamancha propounded the thesis that everybody had a yellow streak in them. We all, he said, at times shirk unpleasant duties, and invent an honourable explanation, which we know to be a lie.

Sandy Arbuthnot observed that the most temerarious deeds were often done by people who had begun by funking, and then, in the shame of the rebound, did a good deal more than those who had no qualms. 'The man who says I go not, and afterwards repents and goes, generally travels the devil of a long way.'

'Like Jonah,' said Lamancha, 'who didn't like the job allotted him, and took ship to Tarshish to get away from it, and then repented and went like a raging lion to Nineveh.'

Collatt, who had been a sailor and one of the Q-boat heroes in the war, demurred. 'I wonder if Nineveh was as unpleasant as the whale's belly,' he said. Then he told us a story in illustration, not as one would have expected, out of his wild sea memories, but from his experience in the City, where he was now a bill-broker.

I got to know Jim Hallward first when he had just come down from the University. He was a tall, slim, fair-haired lad, with a soft voice and the kind of manners which make the ordinary man feel a lout. Eton and Christ Church had polished him till he fairly glistened. His clothes were sober works of art, and he was the cleanest thing you ever saw – always seemed to have just shaved and bathed after a couple of hours' hard exercise. We all liked him, for he was a companionable soul and had no frills, but in the City he was about as useless as a lily in a quickset hedge. Somebody called him an 'apolaustic epicene', which sounded accurate, though I don't know what the words mean. He used to come down to business about eleven o'clock and leave at four – earlier in summer, when he played polo at Hurlingham.

This lotus-eating existence lasted for two years. His father was the head of Hallwards, the merchant-bankers who had been in existence since before the Napoleonic wars. It was an old-fashioned private firm with a tremendous reputation, but for some years it had been dropping a little out of the front rank. It had very few of the big issues, and, though reckoned as solid as the Bank of England, it had hardly kept pace with new developments. But just about the time Jim came down from Oxford his father seemed to get a new lease of life. Hallwards suddenly became ultra-progressive, took in a new manager from one of the big joint-stock banks, and launched out into business which before it would not have touched with the end of a barge-pole. I fancy the old man wanted to pull up the firm before he died, so as to leave a good thing to his only child.

In this new activity Jim can't have been of much use. His other engagements did not leave him a great deal of time to master the complicated affairs of a house like Hallwards. He spoke of his City connection with a certain distaste. The set he had got into were mostly eldest sons with political ambitions, and if Jim had any serious inclination it was towards Parliament, which he proposed to enter in a year or two. For the rest he played polo, and hunted, and did a little steeplechasing, and danced assiduously. Dancing was about the only thing he did really well, for he was only a moderate horseman and his politics were not to be taken seriously. So he was the complete *flâneur*, agreeable, popular, beautifully mannered, highly ornamental, and the most useless creature on earth. You see, he had slacked at school, and had just scraped through college, and had never done a real piece of work in his life.

In the autumn of 192–, whispers began to circulate about Hallwards. It seemed that they were doing a very risky class of business, and people shrugged their shoulders. But no one was prepared for the almighty crash which came at the beginning of the New Year. The firm had been trying to get control of a colonial railway, and for this purpose was quietly buying up the ordinary stock. But an American group, with unlimited capital, was out on the same tack, and the result was that the price was forced up, and Hallwards were foolish enough to go on buying. They borrowed up to the limit of their capacity, and called a halt too late. If the thing had been known in time the City might have made an effort to keep the famous old firm on its legs, but it all came like a thunderclap. Hallwards went down, the American group got their railway stock at a knockout price, and old Mr Hallward, who had been ailing for some months, had a stroke of paralysis and died.

I was desperately sorry for Jim. The foundations of his world were upset, and he hadn't a notion what to do about it. You see, he didn't know the rudiments of the business, and couldn't be made to understand it. He went about in a dream, with staring, unseeing eyes, like a puzzled child. At first he screwed himself up to a sort of effort. He had many friends who would help, he thought, and he made various suggestions, all of a bottomless futility. Very soon he found that his Mayfair popularity was no sort of asset to him. He must have realised that people were beginning to turn a colder eye on a pauper than on an eligible young man, and his overtures were probably met with curt refusals. Anyhow, in a week he had given up hope. He felt himself a criminal and behaved as such. He saw nobody but his solicitors, and when he met a friend in the street he turned and ran. A perfectly unreasonable sense of disgrace took possession of him, and there was a moment when I was afraid he might put an end to himself.

This went on for the better part of a month, while I and one or two others were trying to save something from the smash. We put up a fund and bought some of the wreckage, with the idea of getting

together a little company to nurse it. It was important to do something, for though Jim was an only child and his mother was dead,
there were various elderly female relatives who had their incomes from
Hallwards. The firm had been much respected and old Hallward had
been popular, and Jim had no enemies. There is a good deal of
camaraderie in the City, and a lot of us were willing to combine and
keep Jim going. We were all ready to help him, if he would only sit
down and put his back into the job.

But that was just what Jim would not do. He had got a horror of
the City, and felt a pariah whenever he met anybody who knew about
the crash. He had eyes like a hunted hare's, and one couldn't get any
sense out of him. I don't think he minded the change in his comforts —
the end of polo and hunting and politics, and the prospect of cheap
lodgings and long office hours. I believe he welcomed all that as a kind
of atonement. It was the disgrace of the thing that came between him
and his sleep. He knew only enough of the City to have picked up a
wrong notion of its standards, and imagined that everybody was
pointing a finger at him as a fool, and possibly a crook.

It was very little use reasoning with him. I pointed out that the
right thing for him to do was to shoulder the burden and retrieve his
father's credit. He laughed bitterly.

'Much good I'd be at that,' he said. 'You know I'm a baby in
business, though you're too polite to tell me so.'

'You can have a try,' I said. 'We'll all lend you a hand.'

It was no use. References to his father and the firm's ancient
prestige and his old great-aunts only made him shiver. You could see
that his misery made him blind to argument. Then I began to lose my
temper. I told him that it was his duty as a man to face the music. I
asked him what else he proposed to do.

He said he meant to go to Canada and start life anew. He would
probably change his name. I got out of patience with his silliness.

'You're offered a chance here to make good,' I told him. 'In Canada
you'll have to find your chance, and how in God's name are you going
to do it? You haven't been bred the right way to succeed in the
Dominions. You'll probably starve.'

'Quite likely,' was his dismal answer. 'I'll make my book for that. I
don't mind anything so long as I'm in a place where nobody knows
me.'

'Remember, you are running away,' I said, 'running away from what I consider your plain duty. You can't expect to win out if you begin by funking.'

'I know – I know,' he wailed. 'I am a coward.'

I said no more, for when a man is willing to admit that he is a coward his nerves have got the better of his reason.

Well, the upshot was that Jim sailed for Canada with a little short of two hundred pounds in his pocket – what was left of his last allowance. He could have had plenty of introductions, but he wouldn't take them. He seemed to be determined to bury himself, and I daresay, too, he got a morbid satisfaction out of discomfort. He had still the absurd notion of disgrace, and felt that any handicap he laid on himself was a kind of atonement.

He reached Montreal in the filthy weeks when the spring thaw begins – the worst sample of weather to be found on the globe. Jim had not procured any special outfit, and he landed with a kit consisting of two smart tweed suits, a suit of flannels, riding breeches and knickerbockers – the remnants of his London wardrobe. It wasn't quite the rig for a poor man to go looking for a job in. He had travelled steerage, and, as might have been expected from one in his condition, had not made friends, but he had struck up a tepid acquaintanceship with an Irishman who was employed in a lumber business. The fellow was friendly, and was struck by Jim's obvious air of education and good-breeding, so, when he heard that he wanted work, he suggested that a clerkship might be got in his firm.

Jim applied, and was taken on as the clerk in charge of timber-cutting rights in Eastern Quebec. The work was purely mechanical, and simply meant keeping a record of numbered lots, checking them off on the map, and filling in the details in the register as they came to hand. But it required accuracy and strict attention, and Jim had little of either. Besides, he wrote the vile fist which is the special privilege of our public schools. He held down the job for a fortnight and then was fired.

He had found cheap lodgings in a boarding-house down east, and trudged the two miles in the slush to his office. His fellow-lodgers were willing enough to be friendly – clerks and shop-boys and typists and newspaper reporters most of them. Jim wasn't a snob, but he was rapidly becoming a hermit, for all his nerves were exposed and he shrank from his fellows. His shyness was considered English swank, and the others invented nicknames for him and sniggered when he appeared. Luckily he was too miserable to pay much attention. He had no interest in their games, their visits to the movies and to cheap dance-halls, and their precocious sweethearting. He could not get the hang of their knowing commercial jargon. They set him down as a snob, and he shrank from them as barbarians.

But there was one lodger, a sub-editor on a paper which I shall call the *Evening Hawk*, who saw a little farther than the rest. He realised that Jim was an educated man – a 'scholar' he called it, and he managed to get part of his confidence. So when Jim lost his lumber job he was offered a billet on the *Hawk*. There was no superfluity of men of his type in local journalism, and the editor thought it might give tone to his paper to have someone on the staff who could write decent English and keep them from making howlers about Europe. The *Hawk* was a lively, up-to-date production, very much Americanised in its traditions and its literary style, but it had just acquired some political influence and it hankered after more.

But Jim was no sort of success in journalism. He was tried out in a variety of jobs – as reporter, special correspondent, sub-editor – but he failed to give satisfaction in any. To begin with he had no news-sense. Not many things interested him in his present frame of mind, and he had no notion what would interest the *Hawk*'s readers. He couldn't compose snappy headlines, and it made him sick to try. His writing was no doubt a great deal more correct than that of his colleagues, but it was dull as ditch-water. To add to everything else he was desperately casual. It was not that he meant to be slack, but that he had no stimulus to make him concentrate his attention, and he was about the worst sub-editor, I fancy, in the history of the press.

Summer came, and sleet and icy winds gave place to dust and heat. Jim tramped the grilling streets, one vast ache of homesickness. He had to stick to his tweeds, for his flannel suit had got lost in his journeys between boarding-houses, and, as he mopped his brow in the airless newspaper rooms smelling of printers' ink and shaken by the great presses, he thought of green lawns at Hurlingham, and cool backwaters of the Isis, and clipped yew hedges in old gardens, and a pleasant club window overlooking St James's Street. He hungered for fresh air, but when on a Sunday morning he went for a long walk, he found no pleasure in the adjacent countryside. It all seemed dusty and tousled and unhomely. He wasn't complaining, for it seemed to him part of a rightful expiation, but he was very lonely and miserable.

I have said that he had landed with a couple of hundred pounds, and this he had managed to keep pretty well intact. One day at a quick-luncheon counter he got into talk with a man called McNee, a Manitoban who had fought in the war, and knew something about horses. McNee, like Jim, did not take happily to town life, and was very sick of his job with an automobile company, and looking about for a better. There was not much in common between the two men, except a dislike of Montreal, for I picture McNee as a rough diamond, an active enterprising fellow meant by Providence for a backwoodsman. He had heard of a big dam somewhere down in the Gaspé district, which was being constructed in connection with a pulp scheme. He knew one of the foremen, and believed that money might be made by anyone who could put up a little capital and run a store in the construction camp. He told Jim that it was a fine wild country with plenty of game in the woods, and that, besides making money easily, a storekeeper could have a white man's life. But every bit of a thousand dollars capital would be needed, and he could only lay his hands on a couple of hundred. To Jim in his stuffy lodging-house the scheme offered a blessed escape. He wanted to make money, he wanted fresh air and trees and running water, for your Englishman, though town-bred, always hankers after the country. So he gave up his job on the *Hawk*, just when it was about to give him up, and started out with McNee.

The place was his first disappointment. It was an ugly clearing in an interminable forest of dull spruces, which ran without a break to New Brunswick. However far you walked there was nothing to see except the low muffled hills and the monotonous green of the firs. The partners were given a big shack for their store, and made their sleeping quarters in one end of it. For stock they had laid in a quantity of tinned goods, tobacco, shirts and socks and boots, and a variety of musical instruments. But they found that most of their stuff was unmarketable, since the men were well fed and clothed by the company, and after a week their store had become a rough kind of café, selling hotdogs, and icecream and soft drinks. McNee was immensely proud of it and ornamented the walls with 'ideal faces' from the American magazines. He was a born restaurant keeper, if he had got his chance, but unfortunately there was not much profit in coco-cola and gingerade.

In about a fortnight the place became half eating-house, half club, where the workmen gathered of an evening to play cards. McNee was in his element, but Jim was no more use than a sick pup. He didn't understand the lingo, and his shyness and absorption made him as unpopular as in the Montreal boarding-houses. He saw his little capital slipping away, and there was no compensation in the way of a pleasant life. He tried to imitate McNee's air of hearty bonhomie, and miserably failed. His partner was a good fellow, and stood up for him when an irate navvy consigned him to perdition as a 'God-darned London dude', and Jim's own good temper and sense of only getting what he deserved did something to protect him. But he soon realised that he was a ghastly failure, and this knowledge prevented him expostulating with the other for his obvious shortcomings. For McNee soon became too much of a social success. Gaspé was not 'dry', and there was more than soft drinks consumed in the store, especially by the joint proprietor and his friend the foreman. Also McNee was a bit of a gambler and was perpetually borrowing small sums from capital to meet his losses.

Now and then Jim took a holiday, and tramped all of a long summer day. The country around being only partially surveyed, there was no map to be had, and he repeatedly lost himself. Once he struck a lumber camp and was given pork and beans by cheerful French-Canadians whose *patois* he could not follow. Once he had almost a happy day, when he saw his first moose. But generally he came back from stifling encounters with cedar swamps and *bois brûlé*, weary but unrefreshed. He was not in the frame of mind to get much comfort out of the Canadian wilds, for he was always sore with longing for a different kind of landscape.

The river on which the camp lay was the famous Maouchi, and twelve miles down on the St Lawrence shore was a big fishing-lodge owned by a rich New Yorker. Jim used to see members of the party – young men in marvellous knickerbockers and young women in jumpers like Joseph's coat, and he hid himself at the sight of them. Occasionally a big roadster would pass the store, conveying fishermen to some of the upper lakes. Once, when he was feeling specially dispirited after a long hot day, a car stopped at the door, and two people descended. They came into the store, and the young man asked for lemonade, declaring that their tongues were hanging out of their mouths. Happily McNee was there to serve them, while Jim sheltered behind the curtain of the sleeping-room. He knew them both. One

[129]

was a subaltern in the cavalry with whom he had played bridge in the club, the other was a girl whom he had danced with. Their workmanlike English clothes, their quiet clear English voices gave him a bad dose of homesickness. They were returning, he reflected, to hot baths and cool clean clothes and delicate food and civilised talk . . . For a moment he sickened at the sour stale effluvia of the eating-house, and the rank smell of the pork which McNee had been frying. Then he cursed himself for a fool and a child.

In the fall the work on the dam was shut down, and the store was closed. The partners couldn't remove their unsaleable goods, so the whole stock was sold at junk prices among the nearest villages. Jim found himself with about three hundred dollars in the world, and the long Canadian winter to get through. The fall on the other side of the Atlantic is the pick of the year, and the beauty of the flaming hillsides did a little to revive his spirits. McNee wanted to get back to Manitoba, where he had heard of a job, and Jim decided that he would try Toronto, which was supposed to be rather more healthy for Englishmen than the other cities. So the two travelled west together, and Jim insisted on paying McNee's fare to Winnipeg, thereby leaving himself a hundred and fifty dollars or so on which to face the world.

Toronto is the friendliest place on earth for the man who knows how to make himself at home there. There were plenty to help him if he had looked for them, for nowhere will you find more warm-hearted people to the square mile. But Jim's shyness and prickliness put him outside the pale. He made no effort to advertise the few assets he had, he was desperately uncommunicative, and his self-absorption was not unnaturally taken for 'side'. Also he made the mistake of letting himself get a little too far down in the social scale. His clothes had become very shabby, and his boots were bad; when the first snows came in November he bought himself a thick overcoat, and that left him no money to supplement the rest of his wardrobe, so that by Christmas he was a very good imitation of a tramp.

He tried journalism first, but as he gave no information about himself except that he had been for a few weeks on the Montreal *Hawk*, he had some difficulty in getting a job. At last he got work on a weekly rag simply because he had some notion of grammar. It lasted exactly a fortnight. Then he tried tutoring, and spent some of his last dollars on advertising; he had several nibbles, but always fell down at the interviews. One kind of parent jibbed at his superior manners, another at his inferior clothes. After that he jolted from one temporary job to another – a book-canvasser, an extra hand in a dry-goods-store in the Christmas week, where the counter hid the deficiencies of his raiment, a temporary clerk during a municipal election, a packer in a fancy-stationery business, and finally a porter in a third-class hotel. His employment was not continuous, and between jobs he must have nearly starved. He had begun in the ordinary cheap boarding-house, but, before he found quarters in the attic of the hotel he worked at, he had sunk to a pretty squalid kind of doss-house.

The physical discomfort was bad enough. He tramped the streets ill-clad and half-fed, and saw prosperous people in furs, and cheerful young parties, and fire-lit, book-lined rooms. But the spiritual trouble was worse. Sometimes, when things were very bad, he was fortunate enough to have his thoughts narrowed down to the obtaining of food and warmth. But at other times he would be tormented by a feeling that his misfortunes were deserved, and that Fate with a heavy hand was belabouring him because he was a coward. His trouble was no longer the idiotic sense of guilt about his father's bankruptcy; it was a much more rational penitence, for he was beginning to realise that I had been right, and that he had behaved badly in running away from a plain duty. At first he choked down the thought, but all that miserable winter it grew upon him. His disasters were a direct visitation of the Almighty on one who had shown the white feather. He came to have an almost mystical feeling about it. He felt that he was branded like Cain, so that everybody knew that he had funked, and yet he realised that a rotten morbid pride ironly prevented him from retracing his steps.

The second spring found him thin from bad feeding and with a nasty cough. He had the sense to see that a summer in that hotel would be the end of him, so, although he was in the depths of hopelessness, the instinct of self-preservation drove him to make a move. He wanted to get into the country, but it was impossible to get work on a farm from Toronto, and he had no money to pay for railway fares. In the end he was taken on as a navvy on a bit of railway construction work in the wilds of northern Ontario. He was given the price of his ticket and ten dollars advance on his wages to get an outfit, and one day late in April he found himself dumped at a railhead on a blue lake, with firs, firs, as far as the eye could reach. But it was springtime, the mating wildfowl were calling, the land was greening, and

Jim drew long breaths of sweet air and felt that he was not going to die just yet.

But the camp was a roughish place, and he had no McNee to protect him. There was every kind of roughneck and deadbeat there, and Jim was a bad mixer. He was an obvious softy and new chum and a natural butt, and, since he was being tortured all the time by his conscience, his good nature and humble-mindedness were not so proof as they had been in Gaspé. His poor physical condition made him a bad workman, and he came in for a good deal of abuse as a slacker from the huskies who wrought beside him. The section boss was an Irishman called Malone with a tongue like a whiplash, and he found plenty of opportunities for practising his gift on Jim. But he was a just man, and after a bit of rough-tonguing he saw that Jim was very white about the gills and told him to show his hands. Not being accustomed to the pick, these were one mass of sores. Malone cross-examined him, found that he had been at college, and took him off construction and put him in charge of stores.

There he had an easier life, but he was more than ever the butt of the mess shack and the sleeping quarters. His crime was not only speaking with an English accent and looking like Little Willie, but being supposed to be a favourite of the boss. By and by the ragging became unbearable, and after his mug of coffee had been three times struck out of his hand at one meal, Jim lost his temper and hit out. In the fight which followed he was ridiculously outclassed. He had been fairly good at games, but he had never boxed since his private school, and it is well for Jim's kind of man to think twice before he takes on a fellow who has all his life earned his living by his muscles. But he stood up pluckily, and took a good deal of punishment before he was knocked out, and he showed no ill-will afterwards. The incident considerably improved his position. Malone, who heard of it, asked him where in God's name he had been brought up that he couldn't use his hands better, but didn't appear ill-pleased. The fight had another consequence. It gave him just a suspicion of self-confidence, and helped him on his way to the decision to which he was slowly being compelled.

A week later he was sent a hundred miles into the forest to take supplies to an advance survey party. It was something of a compliment that Malone should have picked him for the job, but Jim did not realise that. His brain was beating like a pendulum on his private trouble – that he had run away, that all his misfortunes were the punishment for his cowardice, and that, though he confessed his fault, he could not make his shrinking flesh go back. He saw England as an Eden indeed, but with angels and flaming swords at every gate. He pictured the lifted eyebrows and the shrugged shoulders as he crept into a clerk's job, with not only his father's shame on his head, but the added disgrace of his own flight. It had seemed impossible a year ago to stay on in London, but now it was a thousandfold more impossible to go home.

Yet the thought gave him no peace by day or night. He had six men in his outfit, two of them half-breeds, and the journey was partly by canoe – with heavy portages – and partly on foot with the stores in pack loads. It rained in torrents, the river was in flood, and the first day they made a bare twenty miles. The half-breeds were tough old customers, but the other four were not much to bank on, and on the third day, when they had to hump their packs and foot it on a bad trail through swampy woods in a cloud of flies, they decided that they had had enough. There was a new gold area just opened not so far away, and they announced that they intended to help themselves to what they wanted from the stores and then make a bee-line for the mines. They were an ugly type of tough, and had physically the upper hand of Jim and his half-breeds.

It was a nasty situation, and it shook Jim out of his private vexations. He spoke them fair, and proposed to make camp and rest for a day to talk it out. Privately he sent one of the half-breeds ahead to the survey-party for help, while he kept his ruffians in play. Happily he had some whisky with him and he had them drinking and playing cards, which took him well into the afternoon. Then they discovered the half-breed's absence, and wouldn't believe Jim's yarn that he had gone off to find fresh meat. His only chance was to bluff high, and, since he didn't much care what happened to him, he succeeded. He went to bed that night with a tough beside him who had announced his intention of putting a bullet through his head if there was any dirty work. Sometime after midnight his messenger arrived with help, and fortunately his bedside-companion's bullet went wide. The stores, a bit depleted, were safely delivered, and when Jim got back to his base he received a solid cursing from his boss for his defective stewardship. But Malone concluded with one of his rare compliments. 'You'll train on, sonny,' he said. 'There's guts in you for all your goo-goo face.'

That episode put an end to Jim's indecision. His time in Canada had been one long chapter of black disasters, and he was confident that they were sent to him as a punishment. His last adventure had somehow screwed up his manhood. He hated Canada like poison, but the thought of going back to England made him green with apprehension. Yet he was clear that he must do it or never have a moment's peace. So he wrote to me and told me that for a year he had been considering things, and had come to the conclusion that he had behaved like a cad. He was coming back to get into any kind of harness I directed, and would I advance him thirty pounds for his journey?

Now the little company we had put together to nurse the wreckage of Hallwards had been doing rather well. One or two things had unexpectedly turned up trumps. There was enough money to keep the maiden aunts going, and it looked as if there would be a good deal presently for Jim. He had gone off leaving no address, so I had had no means of communicating with him. I cabled him a hundred pounds, and told him to come along.

One afternoon near the end of June he turned up in my office. He had crossed the Atlantic steerage, and his clothes were those of a docker who has been months out of work. The first thing he did was to plank eighty pounds on my desk. 'You sent me too much,' he said. 'I don't want to owe more than is necessary. You can stop the twenty quid out of my wages.'

At first sight I thought him very little changed in face. He was incredibly lean and tanned and his hair wanted cutting, but he had the same shy, hunted eyes as the boy who had bolted a year before. He did not seem to have won any self-confidence, except that the set of his mouth was a little firmer.

'I want to start work at once,' he said. 'I've come home to make atonement.'

It took me a long time to make him understand the position of affairs – that he could count even now on a respectable income, and that, if he put his back into it, Hallwards might once again become a power in the City. 'I was only waiting for you to come back,' I said, 'to revive the old name. Hallwards has a better sound than the Anglo-Orient Company.'

'But I can't touch a penny,' he said. 'What about the people who suffered through the bankruptcy?'

'There were very few,' I told him. 'None of the widow-and-orphan business. The banks were amply secured. The chief sufferers were your aunts and yourself, and that's going to be all right now.'

He listened with wide eyes, and slowly bewilderment gave place to relief, and relief to rapture. 'The first thing you've got to do,' I said, 'is to go to your tailor and get some clothes. You'd better put up at an hotel till you can find a flat. I'll see about your club membership. If you want to play polo I'll lend you a couple of ponies. Come and dine with me tonight and tell me your story.'

'My God!' he murmured. 'Do you realise that for a year I've been on my uppers? That's my story.'

The rest of that summer Jim walked about in a happy mystification. Once he was decently dressed, I could see that Canada had improved him. He was better-looking, tougher, manlier; his shyness was now wariness and he had got a new and sounder code of values. He worked like a beaver in the office, and, though he was curiously slow and obtuse about some things, I began to see that he had his father's brains, and something, too, that old Hallward had never had, a sensitive, subtle imagination. For the rest he enjoyed himself. He came in for the end of the polo season, and he was welcomed back to his old set as if nothing had happened.

Then I ceased to see much of him. I had been overworking badly and needed a long holiday, so I went off to a Scotch deer-forest in the middle of August and did not return till the beginning of October. Jim stuck tight to the office; he said that he had had all the holidays he wanted for a year or two.

On the second day after my return he came into my room and said that he wanted to speak to me privately. He wished, he said, that nothing should be done about the restoring the name of Hallwards. He would like the Anglo-Orient to go on just as it was before he returned, and he did not want the directorship which had been arranged.

'Why in the world?' I asked in amazement.

'Because I am going away. And I may be away for quite a time.'

When I found words, and that took some time, I asked if he had grown tired of England.

'Bless you, no! I love it better than any place on earth. The autumn scents are beginning, and London is snugging down for its blessed cosy winter, and the hunting will soon be starting, and last Sunday I heard the old cock pheasants shouting—'

'Where are you going? Canada?'

He nodded.

'Have you fallen in love with it?'

'I hate it worse than hell,' he said solemnly, and proceeded to say things which in the interest of Imperial good feeling I refrain from repeating.

'Then you must be mad!'

'No,' he said, 'I'm quite sane. It's very simple, and I've thought it all out. You know I ran away from my duty eighteen months ago. Well, I was punished for it. I was a howling failure in Canada . . . I haven't told you half . . . I pretty well starved . . . I couldn't hold down any job . . . I was simply a waif and a laughing stock. And I loathed it – my God, how I loathed it! But I couldn't come back – the very thought of facing London gave me a sick pain. It took me a year to screw up my courage to do what I knew was my manifest duty. Well, I turned up, as you know.'

'Then that's all right, isn't it?' I observed obtusely. 'You find London better than you thought?'

'I find it Paradise,' and he smiled sadly. 'But it's a Paradise I haven't deserved. You see, I made a failure in Canada and I can't let it go at that. I hate the very name of the place and most of the people in it . . . Oh, I daresay there is nothing wrong with it, but one always hates a place where one has been a fool . . . I have got to go back and make good. I shall take two hundred pounds, just what I had when I first started out.'

I only stared, and he went on: 'I funked once, and that may be forgiven. But a man who funks twice is a coward. I funk Canada like the devil, and that is why I am going back. There was a man there – only one man – who said I had guts. I'm going to prove to that whole damned Dominion that I have guts, but principally I've got to prove it to myself . . . After that I'll come back to you, and we'll talk business.'

I could say nothing: indeed I didn't want to say anything. Jim was showing a kind of courage several grades ahead of old Jonah's. He had returned to Nineveh and found that it had no terrors, and was now going back to Tarshish, whales and all.

Tendebant Manus

Sir Arthur Warcliff's story in *The Runagates Club* (1928) appeared first in *Pall Mall Magazine* in December 1927. George Souldern shares many characteristics with Buchan's Oxford friend, Raymond Asquith, who was killed during the First World War, but the possible inspiration may have come from his friends the Grenfell twins, Rivy and Francis, both killed during the war and the subject of one of Buchan's first post-war books, *Francis and Riversdale Grenfell* (1920). Buchan's youngest brother, Alastair, was killed at Arras in 1917, but the unconscious reworkings of his feelings about a dead brother are more likely to relate to his brother William, much closer in age and temperament, who died in 1912.

Send not on your soul before
To dive from that beguiling shore,
And let not yet the swimmer leave
His clothes upon the sands of eve.
                    A.E. HOUSMAN

ONE NIGHT WE were discussing Souldern, who had died a week before and whose memorial service had been held that morning in St Margaret's. He had come on amazingly in Parliament, one of those sudden rises which were common in the immediate post-war years, when the older reputations were being questioned and the younger men were too busy making a livelihood to have time for hobbies. His speeches, his membership of a commission where he had shown both originality and courage, and his reputed refusal, on very honourable grounds, of a place in the Cabinet, had given him in the popular mind a flavour of mystery and distinction. The papers had devoted a good deal of space to him, and there was a general feeling that his death – the result of a

[137]

motor smash – was a bigger loss to the country than his actual achievement warranted.

'I never met him,' Palliser-Yates said. 'But I was at school with his minor. You remember Reggie Souldern, Charles? An uncommon good fellow – makings of a fine soldier, too – disappeared with most of his battalion in March '18, and was never heard of again. Body committed to the pleasant land of France but exact spot unknown – rather like a burial at sea.'

'I knew George Souldern well enough,' said Lamancha, whom he addressed. 'I sat in the House with him for two years before the war. That is to say, I knew as much of him as anybody did, but there was very little you could lay hold of. He used to be a fussy, ineffective chap, very fertile in ideas which he never thought out, and always starting hares that he wouldn't hunt. But just lately he seems to have had a call, and he looked as if he might have a career. Rotten luck that a sharp corner and a lout of a motor-cyclist should have put an end to it.'

He turned to his neighbour. 'Wasn't he a relation of yours, Sir Arthur?'

The man addressed was the oldest member of the Club and by far the most distinguished. Sir Arthur Warcliff had been a figure of note when most of us were in our cradles. He began life in the Sappers, and before he was thirty had been in command of a troublesome little Somaliland expedition; then he had governed a variety of places with such success that he was seriously spoken of for India. In the war he would have liked to have returned back to soldiering, but they used him as the Cabinet handy-man, and he had all the worst diplomatic and administrative jobs to tackle. You see, he was a master of detail and had to translate the generalities of policy into action. He had never, as the jargon goes, got his personality over the footlights, so he was only a name to the public – but a tremendous name, of which every party spoke respectfully. He had retired now, and lived alone with his motherless boy. Usually, for all his sixty-five years, he seemed a contemporary, for he was curiously young at heart, but every now and then we looked at his wise, worn face, realised what he had been and was, and sat at his feet.

'Yes,' he said in reply to Lamancha. 'George Souldern was my wife's cousin, and I knew him well for the last twenty years. Since the war I knew him better, and in the past eighteen months I was, I think, his only intimate friend.'

'Was he a really big man?' Sandy Arbuthnot asked. 'I don't take much stock in his profession – but I thought – just for a moment – in that Irish row – that I got a glimpse of something rather out of the ordinary.'

'He had first-class brains.'

Sandy laughed. 'That doesn't get you very far,' he said. The phrase 'first-class brains' had acquired at the time a flavour of comedy.

'No. It doesn't. If you had asked me the question six years ago I should have said that George was a brilliant failure. Immensely clever in his way, really well educated – which very few of us are – laborious as a beaver, but futile. The hare that is always being passed by every kind of tortoise. He had everything in his favour, but nothing ever came out as he wanted it. I only knew him after he came down from Oxford, but I believe that at the University he was a nonpareil.'

'I was up with him,' said Peckwether, the historian. 'Oh, yes, he was a big enough figure there. He was head of Winchester, and senior scholar of Balliol, and took two Firsts and several University prizes in his stride. He must have sat up all night, for he never appeared to work – you see, it was his pose to do things easily – a variety of the Grand Manner. He was a most disquieting undergraduate. In his political speeches he had the air of having just left a Cabinet meeting.'

'Was he popular?' someone asked.

'Not a bit,' said Peckwether. 'And for all his successes we didn't believe in him. He was too worldly-wise – what we used to call 'banausic' – too bent on getting on. We felt that he had all his goods in the shop window, and that there was no margin to him.'

Sir Arthur smiled. 'A young man's contemporaries are pretty shrewd judges. When I met him first I felt the same thing. He wasn't a prig, and he had a sense of humour, and he had plenty of ordinary decent feeling. But he was the kind of man who could never forget himself and throw his cap over the moon. One couldn't warm to him ... But, unlike you, I thought he would succeed. The one thing lacking was money, and within two years he had remedied that. He married a rich wife; the lady died, but the fortune remained. I believe it was an honest love match, and for a long time he was heart-broken, and when he recovered he buried himself in work. You would have said that something was bound to happen. Young, rich, healthy, incredibly industrious, able, presentable – you would have said that any constituency would have welcomed him, that his party would have jumped at him, that he would have been a prodigious success.

'But he wasn't. He made a bad candidate, and had to stand three times before he got into the House. And there he made no kind of impression, though he spoke conscientiously and always on matters he knew about. He wrote a book on the meaning of colonial nationalism – fluent, well expressed, sensible, even in parts eloquent, but somehow it wasn't read. He was always making speeches at public dinners and at the annual meetings of different kinds of associations, but it didn't seem to signify what he said, and he was scarcely reported. There was no conspiracy of silence to keep him down, for people rather liked him. He simply seemed to have no clear boundary lines and to be imperfectly detached from the surrounding atmosphere. I could never understand why.'

'Lack of personality,' said Lamancha. 'I remember, feeling that.'

'Yes, but what is personality? He had the things that make it – brains and purpose. One liked him – was impressed by his attainments, but, if you understand me, one wasn't impressed by the man ... It wasn't ordinary lack of confidence, for on occasion he could be aggressive. It was the lack of a continuity of confidence – in himself and in other things. He didn't *believe* enough. That was why, as you said, he was always starting hares that he wouldn't hunt. Some excellent and unanswerable reason would occur to him why he should slack off. He was what I believe you call a good party man and always voted orthodoxly, but, after four years in the House, instead of being a leader he was rapidly becoming a mere cog in the machine. He didn't seem to be able to make himself count.

'That was his position eight years ago, and it was not far from a tragedy. He was as able as any man in the Cabinet, but he lacked the dæmonic force which even stupid people sometimes possess. I can only describe him in paradoxes. He was at once conceited and shy, inordinately ambitious and miserably conscious that he never got the value of his abilities out of life ... Then came the war.'

'He served, didn't he?' Leithen asked. 'I remember running across him at GHQ.'

'You may call it serving, if you mean that he was never out of uniform for four years. But he didn't fight. I wanted him to. I thought a line battalion might make a man of him, but he shrank from the notion. It wasn't lack of courage – I satisfied myself of that. But he hadn't the nerve to sink himself into the ranks of ordinary men. You understand why? It would have meant the realisation of what was the inmost fear of his heart. He had to keep up the delusion that he was some sort of a swell – had to have authority to buttress his tottering vanity.

'So he had a selection of footling staff jobs – *liaison* with this and that, deputy-assistant to Tom, Dick and Harry, quite futile, but able to command special passes and staff cars. He ranked, I think, as a full colonel, but an Army Service Corps private was more useful than ten of him. And he was as miserable as a man could be. He liked people to think that his trouble was the strain of the war, but the real strain was that there was no strain. He knew that he simply didn't matter. At least he was candid with himself, and he was sometimes candid with me. He rather hoped, I think, that I would inspan him into something worth doing, but in common honesty I couldn't, for you see I too had come to disbelieve in him utterly.

'Well, that went on till March 1918, when his brother Reggie was killed in the German push. Ninth Division, wasn't it?'

Palliser-Yeates nodded. 'Ninth. South African Brigade. He went down at Marrières Wood, but he and his lot stuck up the enemy for the best part of a Sunday, and I solemnly believe, saved our whole front. They were at the critical point, you see, the junction of Gough and Byng. His body was never found.'

'I know,' said Sir Arthur, 'and that is just the point of my story.'

He stopped. 'I suppose I'm right to tell you this. He left instructions that if anything happened to him I was to have his diary. He can't have meant me to keep it secret ... No, I think he would have liked one or two people to know.'

He looked towards Palliser-Yeates. 'You knew Reggie Souldern? How would you describe him?'

'The very best stamp of British regimental officer,' was the emphatic reply.

'Clever?'

'Not a bit. Only average brains, but every ounce of them useful. Always cheery and competent, and a born leader of men. He was due for a brigade when he fell, and if the war had lasted another couple of years he might have had a corps. I never met the other Souldern, but from what you say he must have been the plumb opposite of Reggie.'

'Just so. George had a great opinion of his brother – in addition to the ordinary brotherly love, for there were only the two of them. I thought the news of his death would break him altogether. But it didn't. He took it with extraordinary calm, and presently it looked as if he were actually more cheerful ... You see, they never found the body. He never saw him lying dead, or even the grave where he was buried, and he never met anybody who had. Reggie had been translated mysteriously out of the world, but the melancholy indisputable signs of death were lacking.'

'You mean he thought he was only missing and might turn up some day?'

'No. He *knew* he was dead – the proof was too strong, the presumption was too heavy ... But while there was enough to convince his reason, there was too little for his imagination – no white face and stiff body, no wooden cross in the cemetery. He could *picture* him as still alive, and George had a queer sensitive imagination about which most people knew nothing.'

Sir Arthur looked round the table and saw that we were puzzled.

'It is a little difficult to explain ... Do you remember a story of the French at Verdun making an attack over ground they had been fighting on for months? They shouted "*En avant, les morts*," and they believed that the spirits of the dead responded and redressed the balance. I think it was the last action at Vaux ... I don't suppose the *poilu* thought the dead came back to help him, but he pretended they were still combatants, and got a moral support from the fancy ... That was something like George Souldern's case. If you had asked him, you would have found that he had no doubt that what was left of Reggie was somewhere in the churned-up wilderness north of Péronne. And there was never any nonsense about visitations or messages from the dead ... But the lack of *visible* proofs enabled his imagination to picture Reggie as still alive, and going from strength to strength. He nursed the fancy till it became as real to him as anything in his ordinary life ... Reggie was becoming a great man and would soon be the most famous man in the world, and something of Reggie went into him and he shared in Reggie's glory. In March '18 a partnership began for George Souldern with his dead brother, and the dead, who in his imagination was alive and triumphant, lifted him out of the sticky furrow which he had been ploughing since he left Oxford.'

We were all silent except Pugh, who said that he had come across the same thing in the East – some Rajput prince, I think.

'How did you know this?' Lamancha asked.

'From the diary. George set down very fully every stage of his new career. But I very nearly guessed the truth for myself. You see, knowing him as I did, I had to admit a sudden and staggering change.'

'How soon?'

'The week after the news came. I had been in Paris, and on my return ran across George in the Travellers' and said the ordinary banal words of sympathy. He looked at me queerly, as he thanked me, and if I had not known how deeply attached the brothers were, I would have said that he was exhilarated by his loss. It was almost as if he had been given a drug to strengthen his arteries. He seemed to me suddenly a more substantial fellow, calmer, more at peace with himself. He said an odd thing too. "Old Reggie has got his chance," he said, and then, as if pulling himself up, "I mean, he had the chance he wanted."

'In June it was clear that something had happened to George Souldern. Do you remember how about that time a wave of dejection passed over all the Allied countries? It was partly the mess in Russia, partly in this country a slight loss of confidence in the Government, which seemed to have got to loggerheads with the soldiers, but mainly the "drag" that comes in all wars. It was the same in the American Civil War before Gettysburg. Foch was marking time, but he was doing it by retreating pretty fast on the Aisne. Well, our people needed a little cheering up, and our politicians tried their hand at it. There was a debate in Parliament, and far the best speech was George's. The rest was mere platitude and rhetoric, but he came down on the point like a steam-hammer.'

'I know,' said Lamancha. 'I read it in the *Times* in a field hospital in Palestine.'

'In his old days nobody would have paid much attention. He would have been clever and epigrammatic – sound enough, but "precious". His speech would have read well, if it had been reported, but it wouldn't have mattered a penn'orth to anybody ... Instead he said just the wise, simple, stalwart thing that every honest man had at the back of his head, and he said it with an air which made everybody sit up. For the first time in his life he spoke as one having authority. The press reported him nearly verbatim, for the journalists in the Gallery have a very acute sense of popular values.

'The speech put George, as the phrase goes, on the political map. The Prime Minister spoke to me about him, and there was some talk of employing him on a mission which never materialised. I met him one day in the street and congratulated him, and I remember that I was struck by the new vigour in his personality. He made me come home with him to tea, and to talk to him was like breathing ozone. He asked me one or two questions about numbers, and then he gave me his views on the war. At the time it was fashionable to think that no decision would be reached till the next summer, but George maintained that, if we played our cards right, victory was a mathematical certainty before Christmas. He showed a knowledge of the military situation which would have done credit to any soldier, and he could express himself, which few soldiers can do. His arguments stuck in my head, and I believe I used them in the War Cabinet. I left with a very real respect for one whom I had written off as a failure.

'Well, then came the last battle of the Marne, and Haig's great advance, and all the drama and confusion of the autumn months. I lost sight of George, for I was busy with the peace overtures, and I don't think I even heard of him again till the new year ... But the diary tells all about those months. I am giving you the bones of the story, but I am going to burn the diary, for it is too intimate for other eyes ... According to it Reggie finished the war as a blazing hero. It was all worked out in detail with maps and diagrams. He had become a corps commander by August, and in October he was the chief fighting figure on the British front, the conduit pipe of Foch's ideas, for he could work out in practice what the great man saw as a vision. It sounds crazy, but it was so convincingly done that I had to rub my eyes and make myself remember that Reggie was lying in a nameless grave on the Somme and not a household word in two hemispheres ... George, too, shared in his glory, but just how was not very clear. Anyway, the brothers were in the front of the stage, Reggie the bigger man and George his civilian adviser and opposite number. I can see now how he got his confidence. He was no longer a struggler, but a made man; he had arrived, he was proved, the world required him. Whatever he said or did must be attended to, and, because he believed this, it was.'

Lamancha whistled long and low. 'But how could his mind work, if he lived among fairy tales?' he asked.

'He didn't,' said Sir Arthur. 'He lived very much in the real world. But he had all the time his private imaginative preserve, into which his normal mind did not penetrate. He drew his confidence from this preserve, and, having once got it, could carry it also into the real world.'

'Wasn't he intolerably conceited?' someone asked.

'No, for the great man was Reggie and he was only a satellite. He was Reggie's prophet, and assured enough on that side, but there was no personal arrogance. His dead brother had become, so to speak, his familiar spirit, his *dæmon*. The fact is that George was less of an egotist than he had ever been before. His vanity was burned up in a passion of service.

'I saw him frequently during the first half of '19, and had many talks with him. He had been returned to Parliament by a big majority, but he wasn't much in the public eye. He didn't like the way things were going, but at the same time as a good citizen he declined to make things more difficult for the Government. The diary gives his thoughts at that time. He considered that the soldiers should have had the chief share in the settlement of the world – Foch and Haig and Hindenburg – and Reggie. He held that they would have made a cleaner and fairer job of it than the kind of circus that appeared at Versailles. Perhaps he was right – I can't be dogmatic, for I was a performer in the circus.

'That, of course, I didn't know till the other day. But the change in George Souldern was soon manifest to the whole world. There was the Irish business, when he went down to the worst parts of the South and West, and seemed to be simply asking for a bullet in his head. He was half Irish, you know. He wrote and said quite frankly that he didn't care a straw whether Ireland was inside or outside the British Empire, that the only thing which mattered was that she should find a soul, and that she had a long road to travel before she got one. He told her that at present she was one vast perambulating humbug, and that till she got a little discipline and sense of realities she would remain on the level of Hayti. Why some gunman didn't have a shot at him I can't imagine, except that such naked candour and courage was a new thing and had to be respected... Then there was the Unemployment Commission. You remember the majority report – pious generalities and futile compromises, George's dissenting report made him for a month the best abused man in Britain, for he was impartially contemptuous of all sides. To-day – well, I fancy most of us would agree with George, and I observe that he is frequently quoted by the Labour people.

'What struck me about his line of country was that it was like that of a good soldier's. He had the same power of seeing simple facts and of making simple syllogisms, which the clever intellectual – such as George used to be – invariably misses. And there was the soldier's fidelity and sense of service. George plainly had no axe to grind. He had intellectual courage and would back his views as a general backs his strategy, but he kept always a curious personal modesty. I tell you it seemed nothing short of a miracle to one who had known him in the old days.

'I accepted it as the act of God and didn't look for any further explanation. I think that what first set me questioning was his behaviour about Reggie's memorial. The family wanted a stone put up in the churchyard of the family place in Gloucestershire. George absolutely declined. He stuck his toes into the ground and gave nothing but a flat refusal. One might have thought that the brothers had been estranged, but it was common knowledge that they had been like twins and had written to each other every day.

'Then there was the business about a memoir of Reggie. The regiment wanted one, and his Staff College contemporaries. Tollett – you remember him, the man on the Third Army Staff – volunteered to write it, of course with George's assistance. George refused bluntly and said that he felt the strongest distaste for the proposal. Tollett came to me about it, and I had George to luncheon and thrashed it out with him. I found his reasons very difficult to follow, for he objected even to a regimental history being compiled. He admitted that Tollett was as good a man as could be found for the job, but he said he hated the idea. Nobody understood Reggie but himself. Someday, he suggested, he might try to do justice to him in print – but not yet. I put forward all the arguments I could think of, but George was adamant.

'Walking home, I puzzled a good deal about the affair. It couldn't be merely the jealousy of a writer who wanted to reserve a good subject for himself – that wasn't George's character, and he had no literary vanity. Besides, that wouldn't explain his aversion to a prosaic regimental chronicle, and still less his objection to the cenotaph in the Gloucestershire churchyard. I wondered if there was not some quirk in George, some odd obsession about his brother. For a moment I thought that he might have been dabbling in spiritualism and have got some message from Reggie, till I remembered that I had heard him a week before declare his unbridled contempt for such mumbo-jumbo.

'I thought a good deal about it, and the guess I made was that George was living a double life – that in his subconsciousness Reggie was still alive for him. It was only a guess, but it was fairly near the truth, and last year I had it from his own lips.

'We were duck-shooting together on Croftsmoor, the big marsh near his home. That had been Reggie's pet game; he used to be out at all hours in the winter dawns and dusks stalking wildfowl. George never cared for it, or indeed for any field sport. He would take his place at a covert shoot or a grouse drive and was useful enough with a gun, but he would have been the first to disclaim the title of sportsman. But now he was as keen and tireless as Reggie. He kept me out for eight hours in a filthy day of rain wading in trench boots in Gloucestershire mud.

'We did fairly well, and just before sunset the weather improved. The wind had gone into the north, and promised frost, and as we sat on an old broken-backed stone bridge over one of the dykes, waiting for the birds to be collected from the different stands, the western sky was one broad band of palest gold. We were both tired, and the sudden change from blustering rain to a cold stillness, and from grey mist to colour and light, had a strange effect upon my spirits. I felt peaceful and solemnised. I lit a pipe, but let it go out, for my attention was held by the shoreless ocean in the west, against which the scarp of the Welsh hills showed in a dim silhouette. The sharp air, the wild marsh scents, the faint odour of tobacco awoke in me a thousand half-sad and half-sweet recollections.

'I couldn't help it. I said something about Reggie.

'George was sitting on the bridge with his eyes fixed on the sky. I thought he hadn't heard me, till suddenly he repeated "Reggie. Yes, old Reggie."

' "This was what he loved," I said.

' "He still loves it," was the answer, spoken very low. And then he repeated – to himself as it were:

> " 'Fight on, fight on,' said Sir Andrew Barton.
>   'Though I be wounded I am not slain.
> I'll lay me down and bleed awhile
>   And then I'll rise and fight again.' "

'He turned his fine-drawn face to me.

' "You think Reggie is dead?"

[147]

'I didn't know what to say. "Yes," I stammered, 'I suppose—"

' "What do you mean by death?" His voice was almost shrill. "We know nothing about it. What does it matter if the body is buried in a shell-hole—?"

'He stopped suddenly, as a lamp goes out when you press the switch. I had the impression that those queer shrill words came not from George but from some other who had joined us.

' "I believe that the spirit is immortal," I began.

' "The spirit—" again the shrill impersonal voice – "I tell you the whole man lives . . . He is nearer to me than he ever was . . . we are never parted . . ."

'Again the light went out. He seemed to gulp, and when he spoke it was in his natural tones.

' "I apologise," he said, "I must seem to you to be talking nonsense . . . You don't understand. *You* would understand, if anyone could, but I can't explain – yet – someday . . ."

'The head-keeper, the beaters and the dogs came out of the reed beds, and at the same time the uncanny glow in the west was shrouded with the film of the coming night. It was almost dark when we turned to walk home, and I was glad of it, for neither of us wished to look at the other's face.

'I felt at once embarrassed and enlightened. I had been given a glimpse into the cloudy places of a man's soul, and had surprised his secret. My guess had been right. In George's subconscious mind Reggie was still alive – nay more, was progressing in achievement as if he had never disappeared in the March battle. It was no question of a disembodied spirit establishing communication with the living – that was a business I knew nothing about, nor George either. It was a question of life, complete life, in a peculiar world, companionship in some spiritual fourth dimension, and from that companionship he was drawing sustenance. He had learned Reggie's forthrightness and his happy simplicity . . . I wondered and I trembled. There is a story of an early Victorian statesman who in his leisure moments played at being Emperor of Byzantium. The old Whig kept the two things strictly separate – he was a pious humanitarian in his English life, though he was a ruthless conqueror in the other. But in George's case the two were mingling. He was going about his daily duties with the power acquired from his secret world; that secret world, in which, with Reggie, he had become a master, was giving him a mastery over our common life . . . I did not believe it would last. It was against nature that a man could continue to live as a parasite on the dead.

'I am almost at the end of my story. Two months later, George became a figure of national importance. It was he who chiefly broke up the Coalition at the Grafton House meeting, and thereby, I suppose, saved his party. His speech, you remember, clove through subtleties and irrelevances with the simple declaration that he could not work with what he could not trust, and unless things changed, must go out of public life. That was Reggie's manner, you know – pure Reggie. Then came the general election and the new Government, and George, very much to people's surprise, refused Cabinet office. The reason he gave was that on grounds of principle he had taken a chief part in wrecking the late Ministry, and he felt he could not allow himself to benefit personally by his action. We all thought him high-minded, if finical and quixotic, but the ordinary man liked it – it was a welcome change from the old gang of *arrivistes*. But it was not the real reason. I found that in the diary.'

Sir Arthur stopped, and there was a silence while he seemed to be fumbling for words.

'Here we are walking on the edge of great mysteries,' he continued. 'The reason why he refused the Prime Minister's offer was Reggie . . . Somehow the vital force in that subconscious world of his was ebbing . . . I cannot explain how, but Reggie was moving away from what we call realities and was beckoning him to follow . . . The Grafton House speech was George's last public utterance. Few people saw him after that, for he rarely attended the House. I saw him several times in Gloucestershire . . . Was he happy? Yes, I should say utterly happy, but too detached, too peaceful, as if he had done with the cares of his world . . . I think I guessed what was happening, when he told me that he had consented to the cenotaph in the churchyard. He took a good deal of pains about it, too, and chose an inscription, which his maiden aunts thought irreligious. It was Virgil's *"Tendebant manus ripoe ulterioris amore"* . . . He withdrew his objection to the memoir, too, and Tollett got to work, but he gave him no help – it was as if he had lost interest . . . It is an odd thing to say, but I have been waiting for the news which was in last week's paper.'

'You don't mean that he engineered the motor smash?' Lamancha asked.

'Oh no,' said Sir Arthur gently. 'As I said, we are treading on the brink of great mysteries. Say that it was predestined, fore-ordained, decreed by the Master of Assembly . . . I know that it had to be. If you join hands with the dead they will pull you over the stream.'

The Last Crusade

'The Last Crusade' is Francis Martendale's story from *The Runagates Club* (1928). It was serialised in *Pall Mall Magazine* (January 1928), where it appeared alongside stories from Leslie Charteris and Edgar Wallace. It is prefaced by a quotation from Edmund Burke, a writer Buchan much admired. He had produced a selection of Burke's writings for the Nelson Sevenpennies in 1925 and uses figures from Burke in several stories like Charles Townshend in 'The Company of the Marjolaine' and the Marquis de la Tour in *The Three Hostages* (1924).

It is often impossible, in these political inquiries, to find any proportion between the apparent force of any moral causes we may assign, and their known operation. We are therefore obliged to deliver up that operation to mere chance; or, more piously (perhaps more rationally), to the occasional interposition and the irresistible hand of the Great Disposer.

BURKE

ONE EVENING THE talk at dinner turned on the Press. Lamancha was of opinion that the performances of certain popular newspapers in recent years had killed the old power of the anonymous printed word. 'They bluffed too high,' he said, 'and they had their bluff called. All the delphic oracle business has gone from them. You haven't today what you used to have – papers from which the ordinary man docilely imbibes all his views. There may be one or two still, but not more.'

Sandy Arbuthnot, who disliked journalism as much as he liked journalists, agreed, but there was a good deal of difference of opinion among the others. Palliser-Yeates thought that the Press had more influence than ever, though it might not be much liked; a man, he said, no longer felt the kind of loyalty towards his newspaper that he felt towards his club and his special brand of cigar, but he was mightily influenced by it all the same. He might read it only for its news, but in the selection of news a paper could wield an uncanny power.

Francis Martendale was the only journalist among us, and he listened with half-closed sleepy eyes. He had been a war correspondent as far back as the days of the South African War, and since then had seen every serious row on the face of the globe. In France he had risen to command a territorial battalion, and that seemed to have satisfied his military interest, for since 1919 he had turned his mind to business. He was part-owner of several provincial papers, and was connected in some way with the great Ladas news agency. He had several characters which he kept rigidly separate. One was a philosopher, for he had translated Henri Poincaré, and published an acute little study of Bergson; another was a yachtsman, and he used to race regularly in the twelve-metre class at Cowes. But these were his relaxations, and five days in the week he spent in an office in the Fleet Street neighbourhood. He was an enthusiast about his hobbies and a cynic about his profession, a not uncommon mixture; so we were surprised when he differed from Lamancha and Sandy and agreed with Palliser-Yeates.

'No doubt the power of the leader-writer has waned,' he said. 'A paper cannot set a Cabinet trembling because it doesn't like its policy. But it can colour the public mind most damnably by a steady drip of tendentious news.'

'Lies?' Sandy asked.

'Not lies – truths judiciously selected – half-truths with no context. Facts – facts all the time. In these days the Press is obliged to stick to facts. But it can make facts into *news*, which is a very different class of goods. And it can interpret facts – don't forget that. It can report that Burminster fell asleep at a public dinner – which he did – in such a way as to make everybody think that he was drunk – which he wasn't.'

'Rather a dirty game?' someone put in.

'Sometimes – often perhaps. But now and then it works out on the side of the angels. Do any of you know Roper Willinck?'

There was a general confession of ignorance.

'Pity. He would scarcely fit in here, but he is rather a great man and superbly good company. There was a little thing that Willinck once did – or rather helped to do, with about a million other people who hadn't a notion what was happening. That's the fun of journalism. You light a match and fling it away, and the fire goes smouldering round the globe, and ten thousand miles off burns down a city. I'll tell you about it if you like, for it rather proves my point.'

It all began – said Martendale – with an old Wesleyan parson of the name of Tubb, who lived at a place called Rhenosterspruit on the east side of Karroo. He had been a missionary, but the place had grown from a small native reserve to an ordinary up-country dorp; the natives were all Christians now, and he had a congregation of store-keepers, and one or two English farmers, and the landlady of the hotel, and the workmen from an adjacent irrigation dam. Mr Tubb was a man of over seventy, a devoted pastor with a gift of revivalist eloquence, but not generally considered very strong in the head. He was also a bachelor. He had caught a chill and had been a week in bed, but he rose on the Sunday morning to conduct service as usual.

Now about that time the Russian Government had been rather distinguishing themselves. They had had a great function at Easter, run by what they called the Living Church, which had taken the shape of a blasphemous parody of the Christian rites and a procession of howling dervishes who proclaimed that God was dead and Heaven and Hell wound up. Also they had got hold of a Patriarch, a most respected Patriarch, put him on trial for high treason, and condemned him to death. They had postponed the execution, partly by way of a refinement of cruelty, and partly, I suppose, to see just how the world would react; but there seemed not the slightest reason to doubt that they meant to have the old man's blood. There was a great outcry, and the Archbishop of Canterbury and the Pope had something to say, and various Governments made official representations, but the Bolshies didn't give a hoot. They felt that they needed to indulge in some little bit of extra blackguardism just to show what stout fellows they were.

Well, all this was in the cables from Riga and Warsaw and Helsingfors, and it got into the weekly edition of the *Cape Times*. There Mr Tubb read it, as he lay sick in bed, and, having nothing else to worry about, it fretted him terribly. He could not bear to think of those obscene orgies in Moscow, and the story of the Patriarch made him frantic. This, it seemed to him, was a worse persecution than Nero's or Diocletian's, and the Patriarch was a nobler figure than any martyr of

[153]

the Roman amphitheatre; and all the while the Christian peoples of the world were doing nothing. So Mr Tubb got out of bed on that Sunday morning, and, having had no time to prepare a sermon, delivered his soul from the pulpit about the Bolshies and their doings. He said that what was needed was a new crusade, and he called on every Christian man and woman to devote their prayers, their money, and, if necessary, their blood to this supreme cause. Old as he was, he said, he would gladly set off for Moscow that instant and die beside the Patriarch, and count his life well lost in such a testimony of his faith.

I am sure that Mr Tubb meant every word he said, but he had an unsympathetic audience, who were not interested in Patriarchs; and the hotel-lady slumbered, and the store-keepers fidgeted and the girls giggled and whispered just as usual. There the matter would have dropped, had not a young journalist from Cape Town been spending his holidays at Rhenosterspruit and out of some caprice been present at the service. He was an ambitious lad, and next morning despatched to his paper a brightly written account of Mr Tubb's challenge. He wrote it with his tongue in his cheek, and headed it, 'Peter the Hermit at Rhenosterspruit' with, as a sub-title, 'The Last Crusade'. His editor cut it savagely, and left out all his satirical touches, so that it read rather bald and crude. Still it got about a quarter of a column.

That week the Ladas representative at Cape Town was rather short of material, and just to fill up his budget of outgoing news put in a short message about Rhenosterspruit. It ran: 'On Sunday Tubb Wesleyan Minister Rhenosterspruit summoned congregation in name Christianity release Patriarch and announced intention personally lead crusade Moscow.' That was the result of the cutting of the bright young correspondent's article. What he had meant as fantasy and farce was so summarised as to appear naked facts. Ladas in London were none too well pleased with the message. They did not issue it to the British Press, and they cabled to the Cape Town people that, while they welcomed 'human interest' stories, they drew the line at that sort of thing. What could it matter to the world what a Wesleyan parson in the Karroo thought about Zinovieff? They wanted news, not nonsense.

Now behold the mysterious workings of the Comic Spirit. Ladas, besides their general service to the Canadian Press, made special services to several Canadian papers. One of these was called, shall we say?

the *Toronto Watchman*. The member of the Ladas staff who had the compiling of the *Watchman* budget was often hard-pressed, for he had to send news which was not included in the general service. That week he was peculiarly up against it, so he went through the files of the messages that had come in lately and had not already been transmitted to Canada, and in the Cape Town section he found the Rhenosterspruit yarn. He seized on it joyfully, for he did not know of the disfavour with which his chief had regarded it, and he dressed it up nicely for Toronto. The *Watchman* he knew was a family paper, with a strong religious connection, and this would be meat and drink to it. So he made the story still more matter-of-fact. Mr Tubb had sounded a call to the Christian Church, and was himself on the eve of setting out against Trotsky like David against Goliath. He left the captions to the Toronto sub-editors, but of his own initiative he mentioned John Knox. That, he reflected comfortably, as he closed up and went off to play golf, would fetch the Presbyterian-minded *Watchman*.

It did. The Editor of the *Watchman*, who was an elder of the Kirk and Liberal Member of Parliament, had been getting very anxious about the ongoings in Russia. He was not very clear what a Patriarch was, but he remembered that various Anglican ecclesiastics had wanted to affiliate the English and Greek Churches, so he concluded that he was some kind of Protestant. He had, like most people, an intense dislike of Moscow and its ways, and he had been deeply shocked by the Easter sacrilege. So he went large on the Ladas message. It was displayed on his chief page, side by side with all the news he could collect about the Patriarch, and he had no less than two leaders on the subject. The first, which he wrote himself, was headed 'The Weak Things of the World and the Strong'. He said that Mr Tubb's clarion-call, 'the voice of a simple man of God echoing from the lonely veld', might yet prove a turning-point in history, and he quoted Burke about a child and a girl at an inn changing the fate of nations. It might – it should – arouse the conscience of the Christian world, and inaugurate a new crusade, which would lift mankind out of the rut of materialism and open its eyes to the eternal verities. Christianity had been challenged by the miscreants in Russia, and the challenge must be met. I don't think he had any very clear idea what he meant, for he was strongly opposed to anything that suggested war, but it was a fine chance for 'uplift' writing. The second leader was called 'The Deeper Obligations of Empire', and, with a side glance at

Mr Tubb, declared that unless the British Empire was a spiritual and moral unity it was not worth talking about.

The rest of the Canadian Press did not touch the subject. They had not had the Rhenosterspruit message, and were not going to lift it. But the *Watchman* had a big circulation, and Mr Tubb began to have a high, if strictly local, repute. Several prominent clergymen preached sermons on him, and a weekly paper printed a poem in which he was compared to St Theresa and Joan of Arc.

The thing would have been forgotten in a fortnight, if McGurks had not chosen to take a hand. McGurks, as you probably know, is the biggest newspaper property in the world directed by a single hand. It owns outright well over a hundred papers, and has a controlling interest in perhaps a thousand. Its tone is strictly national, not to say chauvinistic; its young men in Europe at that time were all hundred-per-cent Americans, and returned to the States a hundred and twenty per cent, to allow for the difference in the exchange. McGurks does not love England, for it began with strong Irish connections, and it has done good work in pointing out to its immense public the predatory character of British Imperialism and the atrocities that fill the shining hours in India and Egypt. As a matter of fact, however, its politics are not very serious. What it likes is a story that can be told in thick black headlines, so that the stupidest of its free-born readers, glancing in his shirt-sleeves at the first page of his Sunday paper, can extract nourishment. Murders, rapes, fires and drownings are its daily bread, and it fairly revels in details – measurements and plans, names and addresses of witnesses, and appalling half-tone blocks. Most unfairly it is called sensational, for the stuff is as dull as a directory.

With regard to Russia, McGurks had steered a wavy course. It had begun in 1917 by flaunting the banner of freedom, for it disliked monarchies on principle. In 1919 it wanted America to recognise the Russian Government, and take hold of Russian trade. But a series of rebuffs to its special correspondents changed its view, and by 1922 it had made a speciality of Bolshevik horrors. The year 1923 saw it again on the fence, from which in six months it had tumbled off in a state of anti-Bolshevik hysteria. It was out now to save God's country from foreign microbes, and it ran a good special line of experts who proved that what America needed was a *cordon sanitaire* to protect her purity from a diseased world. At the time of which I speak it had worked itself up into a fine religious enthusiasm, and had pretty well captured

the 'hick' public. McGurks was first and foremost a business proposition, and it had decided that crime and piety were the horses to back.
I should add that, besides its papers, it ran a news agency, the PU,
which stood for Press Union, but which was commonly and affectionately known as Punk.

McGurks seized upon the story in the *Toronto Watchman* as a gift
from the gods, and its headlines were a joy for ever. All over the States
men read 'Aged Saint Defies Demoniacs – Says That In God's Name
He Will Move Mountains' – 'Vengeance From The Veld' – 'The First
Trumpet Blast' – 'Who Is On The Lord's Side – WHO?' I daresay
that in the East and beyond the Rockies people were only mildly
interested, but in the Middle West and in the South the thing caught
like measles. McGurks did not leave its stunts to perish of inanition.
As soon as it saw that the public was intrigued it started out to
organise that interest. It circularised every parson over big areas, it
arranged meetings of protest and sympathy, it opened subscription
lists, and, though it refrained from suggesting Government action, it
made it clear that it wanted to create such a popular feeling that the
Government would be bound to bestir itself. The home towns caught
fire, the Bible Belt was moved to its foundations, every Methodist
minister rallied to his co-religionist of Rhenosterspruit, the Sunday
Schools uplifted their voice, and even the red-blooded he-men of the
Rotary Clubs got going. The Holiness Tabernacle of Sarcophagus,
Neb., produced twenty volunteers who were ready to join Mr Tubb in
Moscow, and the women started knitting socks for them, just as they
did in the war. The First Consecration Church of Jumpersville, Tenn.,
followed suit, and McGurks made the most of the doings of every
chapel in every one-horse township. Punk, too, was busy, and cabled
wonderful stories of the new crusade up and down the earth. Old-
established papers did not as a rule take the Punk service, so only a
part of it was printed, but it all helped to create an atmosphere.

Presently Concord had to take notice. This, as you know, is the
foremost American press agency – we call it the C.C. – and it had no
more dealings with Punk than the Jews with the Samaritans. It was in
close alliance with Ladas, so it cabled testily wanting to know why it
had not received the Rhenosterspruit message. Ladas replied that they
had considered the story too absurd to waste tolls on, but, since the
C.C. was now carrying a lot of stuff about the new crusade, they felt
obliged to cable to Cape Town to clear things up. Punk had already

got on to that job, and was asking its correspondents for pictures of Rhenosterspruit, interviews with the Reverend Tubb, details about what he wore and ate and drank, news of his mother and his childhood, and his premonitions of future greatness. Half a dozen anxious journalists converged upon Rhenosterspruit.

But they were too late. For Mr Tubb was dead – choked on a chicken-bone at his last Sunday dinner. They were only in time to attend the funeral in the little, dusty, sun-baked cemetery. Very little was to be had from his congregation, which, as I have said, had been mostly asleep during the famous sermon; but a store-keeper remembered that the minister had not been quite like himself on that occasion and that he had judged from his eyes that he had still a bad cold. McGurks made a great fuss with this scrap of news. The death of Mr Tubb was featured like the demise of a President or a film star, and there was a moving picture of the old man, conscious that he was near his end (the chicken-bone was never mentioned), summoning his failing strength to one supreme appeal – 'his eyes,' said McGurks, 'now wet with tears for the world's sins, now shining with the reflected radiance of the Better Country'.

I fancy that the thing would have suddenly died away, for there was a big prize-fight coming on, and there seemed to be the risk of the acquittal of a nigger who had knifed a bootlegger in Chicago, and an Anti-Kink Queen was on the point of engaging herself to a Dentifrice King, and similar stirring public events were in the offing. But the death of Mr Tubb kept up the excitement, for it brought in the big guns of the Fundamentalists. It seemed to them that the old man had not died but had been miraculously translated, just like Elijah or William Jenings Bryan after the Dayton trial. It was a Sign, and they were bound to consider what it signified.

This was much heavier metal than the faithful of Sarcophagus and Jumpersville. The agitation was now of national importance; it had attained 'normalcy', as you might say, the 'normalcy' of the periodic American movement. Conventions were summoned and addressed by divines whose names were known even in New York. Senators and congressmen took a hand, and J. Constantine Buttrick, the silver trumpet of Wisconsin, gave tongue, and was heard by several million wireless outfits. Articles even appeared about it in the intellectual weeklies. Congress wasn't in session, which was fortunate, but Washington began to be uneasy, for volunteers for the crusade were enrolling fast. The C.C. was compelled to carry long despatches, and Ladas had to issue them to the English Press, which usually printed them in obscure corners with the names misspelt. England is always apathetic about American news, and, besides, she had a big strike on her hands at the time. Those of us who get American press-clippings realised that quite a drive was starting to do something to make Moscow respectful to religion, but we believed that it would be dropped before any serious action could be taken. Meanwhile Zinovieff and Trotsky carried on as usual, and we expected any day to hear that the Patriarch had been shot and buried in the prison yard.

Suddenly Fate sent Roper Willinck mooning round to my office. I suppose Willinck is the least known of our great men, for you fellows have never even heard his name. But he *is* a great man in his queer way, and I believe his voice carries farther than any living journalist's, though most people do not know who is speaking. He doesn't write much in the Press here, only now and then a paper in the heavy monthlies, but he is the prince of special correspondents, and his 'London Letters' in every known tongue are printed from Auckland to Seattle. He seems to have found the common denominator of style which is calculated to interest the whole human family. On the Continent he is the only English journalist whose name is known to the ordinary reader – rather like Maximilian Harden before the war. In America they reckon him a sort of Pope, and his stuff is syndicated in all the country papers. His enthusiasms make a funny hotch-potch – the League of Nations and the British Empire, racial purism and a sentimental socialism; but he is a devout Catholic, and Russia had become altogether too much for him. That was why I thought he would be interested in McGurks' stunt, of which he had scarcely heard; so he sat down in an armchair and, during the consumption of five caporal cigarettes, studied my clippings.

I have never seen a man so roused. 'I see light,' he cried, pushing his double glasses up on his forehead. 'Martendale, this is a revelation. Out of the mouths of babes and sucklings ... Master Ridley, Master Ridley, we shall this day kindle a fire which will never be extinguished...'

'Nonsense,' I said. 'The thing will fizzle out in a solemn protest from Washington to Moscow with which old Trotsky will light his pipe. It has got into the hands of highbrows, and in a week will be clothed in the jargon of the State Department, and the home towns will wonder what has been biting them.'

'We must retrieve it,' he said softly. 'Get it back to the village green and the prayer-meeting. It was the prayer-meeting, remember, which brought America into the war.'

'But how? McGurks has worked that beat to death.'

'McGurks!' he cried contemptuously. 'The time is past for slobber, my son. What they want is the prophetic, the apocalyptic, and by the bones of Habbakuk they shall have it. I am going to solemnise the remotest parts of the great Republic, and then,' he smiled serenely, 'I shall interpret that solemnity to the world. First the fact and then the moral – that's the lay-out.'

He stuffed my clippings into his pocket and took himself off, and there was that in his eye which foreboded trouble. Someone was going to have to sit up when Willinck looked like that. My hope was that it would be Moscow, but the time was getting terribly short. Any day might bring the news that the Patriarch had gone to his reward.

I heard nothing for several weeks, and then Punk suddenly became active, and carried some extraordinary stuff. It was mostly extracts from respectable papers in the Middle West and the South, reports of meetings which seemed to have worked themselves into hysteria, and rumours of secret gatherings of young men which suggested the Ku-Klux-Klan. Moscow had a Press agency of its own in London, and it began to worry Ladas for more American news. Ladas in turn worried the C.C., but the C.C. was reticent. There was a Movement, we were told, but the Government had it well in hand, and we might disregard the scare-stuff Punk was sending; everything that was important and reliable would be in its own service. I thought I detected Willinck somewhere behind the scenes, and tried to get hold of him, but learned that he was out of town.

One afternoon, however, he dropped in, and I noticed that his high-boned face was leaner than ever, but that his cavernous eyes were happy. ' "The good work goes cannily on",' he said – he was always quoting – and he flung at me a bundle of green clippings.

They were articles of his own in the American Press, chiefly the Sunday editions, and I noticed that he had selected the really influential country papers – one in Tennessee, one in Kentucky, and a batch from the Corn States.

I was staggered by the power of his stuff – Willinck had never to

my knowledge written like this before. He didn't rave about Bolshevik
crimes – people were sick of that – and he didn't bang the religious
drum or thump the harmonium. McGurks had already done that to
satiety. He quietly took it for granted that the crusade had begun and
that plain men all over the earth, who weren't looking for trouble, felt
obliged to start out and abolish an infamy or never sleep peacefully in
their beds again. He assumed that presently from all corners of the
Christian world there would be an invading army moving towards
Moscow, a thing that Governments could not check, a people's rising
as irresistible as the change of the seasons. Assuming this, he told
them just exactly what they would see.

I can't do justice to Willinck by merely describing these articles; I
ought to have them here to read to you. Noble English they were, and
as simple as the Psalms ... He pictured the constitution of the army,
every kind of tongue and dialect and class, with the same kind of
discipline as Cromwell's New Model – Ironsides every one of them,
rational, moderate-minded fanatics, the most dangerous kind. It was
like *Paradise Lost* – Michael going out against Belial ... And then the
description of Russia – a wide grey world, all pale colours and watery
lights, broken villages, tattered little towns ruled by a few miscreants
with rifles, railway tracks red with rust, ruinous great palaces plastered
over with obscene posters, starving hopeless people, children with old
vicious faces ... God knows where he got the stuff from – mainly his
macabre imagination, but I daresay there was a lot of truth in the
details, for he had his own ways of acquiring knowledge.

But the end was the masterpiece. He said that the true rulers were
not those whose names appeared in the papers, but one or two secret
madmen who sat behind the screen and spun their bloody webs. He
described the crusaders breaking through shell after shell, like one of
those Chinese boxes which you open only to find another inside till
you end with a thing like a pea. There were layers of Jew officials and
Lett mercenaries and camouflaging journalists, and always as you
went deeper the thing became more inhuman and the air more fetid.
At the end you had the demented Mongol – that was a good touch for
the Middle West – the incarnation of the backworld of the Orient.
Willinck only hinted at this ultimate camarilla, but his hints were
gruesome. To one of them he gave the name of Uriel – a kind of
worm-eaten archangel of the Pit, but the worst he called Glubet. He
must have got the word out of a passage in Catullus which is not read

in schools, and he made a shuddering thing of it – the rancid toad-man, living among the half-lights and blood, adroit and sleepless as sin, but cracking now and then into idiot laughter.

You may imagine how this took hold of the Bible Belt. I never made out what exactly happened, but I have no doubt that there were the rudiments of one of those mass movements, before which Governments and newspapers, combines and Press agencies, Wall Street and Lombard Street and common prudence are helpless. You could see it in the messages C.C. sent and its agitated service cables to its people. The Moscow Agency sat on our doorstep and bleated for more news, and all the while Punk was ladling out fire-water to every paper that would take it.

'So much for the facts,' Willinck said calmly. 'Now I proceed to point the moral in the proper quarters!'

If he was good at kindling a fire he was better at explaining just how hot it was and how fast it would spread. I have told you that he was about the only English journalist with a Continental reputation. Well, he proceeded to exploit that reputation in selected papers which he knew would cross the Russian frontier. He was busy in the Finnish and Latvian and Lithuanian Press, he appeared in the chief Polish daily, and in Germany his stuff was printed in the one big Berlin paper and – curiously enough – in the whole financial chain. Willinck knew just how and where to strike. The line he took was very simple. He quietly explained what was happening in America and the British Dominions – that the outraged conscience of Christiandom had awakened among simple folk, and that nothing on earth could hold it. It was a Puritan crusade, the most deadly kind. From every corner of the globe believers were about to assemble, ready to sacrifice themselves to root out an infamy. This was none of your Denikins and Koltchaks and Czarist *émigré* affairs; it was the world's Christian democracy, and a business democracy. No flag-waving or shouting, just a cold steady determination to get the job done, with ample money and men and an utter carelessness of what they spent on both. Cautious Governments might try to obstruct, but the people would compel them to toe the line. It was a militant League of Nations, with the Bible in one hand and the latest brand of munition in the other.

We had a feverish time at Ladas in those days. The British Press was too much occupied with the strike to pay full attention, but the Press of every other country was on its hind legs. Presently things began to happen. The extracts from *Pravda* and *Izvestia*, which we got from Riga and Warsaw, became every day more like the howling of epileptic wolves: Then came the news that Moscow had ordered a very substantial addition to the Red Army. I telephoned this item to Willinck, and he came round to see me.

'The wind is rising,' he said. 'The fear of the Lord is descending on the tribes, and that we know is the beginning of wisdom.'

I observed that Moscow had certainly got the wind up, but that I didn't see why. 'You don't mean to say that you have got them to believe in your precious crusade.'

He nodded cheerfully. 'Why not? My dear Martendale, you haven't studied the mentality of these gentry as I have. Do you realise that the favourite reading of the Russian peasant used to be Milton? Before the war you could buy a translation of *Paradise Lost* at every book kiosk in every country fair. These rootless intellectuals have cast off all they could, but at the back of their heads the peasant superstition remains. They are afraid in their bones of a spirit that they think is in Puritanism. That's why this American business worries them so. They think they are a match for Rome, and they wouldn't have minded if the racket had been started by the Knights of Columbus or that kind of show. But they think it comes from the meeting-house, and that scares them cold.'

'Hang it all,' I said, 'they must know the soft thing modern Puritanism is – all slushy hymns and inspirational advertising.'

'Happily they don't. And I'm not sure that their ignorance is not wiser than your knowledge, my emancipated friend. I'm inclined to think that something may yet come out of the Bible Christian that will surprise the world . . . But not this time. I fancy the trick has been done. You might let me know as soon as you hear anything.' And he moved off, whistling contentedly through his teeth.

He was right. Three days later we got the news from Warsaw, and the Moscow Agency confirmed it. The Patriarch had been released and sent across the frontier, and was now being coddled and fêted in Poland. I rang up Willinck, and listened to his modest *Nunc dimittis* over the telephone.

He said he was going to take a holiday and go into the country to sleep. He pointed out for my edification that the weak things of the world – meaning himself – could still confound the strong, and he advised me to reconsider the foundations of my creed in the light of this surprising miracle.

Well, that is my story. We heard no more of the crusade in America, except that the Fundamentalists seemed to have got a second wind from it and started a large-scale heresy hunt. Several English bishops said that the release of the Patriarch was an answer to prayer; our Press pointed out how civilisation, if it spoke with one voice, would be listened to even in Russia; and Labour papers took occasion to enlarge on the fundamental reasonableness and urbanity of the Moscow Government.

Personally I think that Willinck drew the right moral. But the main credit really belonged to something a great deal weaker than he – the aged Tubb, now sleeping under a painted cast-iron gravestone among the dust-devils and meerkats of Rhenosterspruit.

Sing a Song of Sixpence

One of Buchan's best-known stories, 'Sing a Song of Sixpence' first appeared in *Pall Mall Magazine* (February 1928), during the 1930s in *The Golden Book, The Scholastic* and *Argosy*, and in July 1954 in the American *Ellery Queen Magazine*. Edward Leithen's story in *The Runagates Club* (1928), it was also included in a 1935 Hodder compilation of novels and stories featuring the same character.

The effect of night, of any flowing water, of lighted cities, of the peep of day, of ships, of the open ocean, calls up in the mind an army of anonymous desires and pleasures. Something, we feel, should happen; we know not what, yet we proceed in quest of it.

R.L. STEVENSON

LEITHEN'S FACE HAD that sharp chiselling of the jaw and that compression of the lips which seem to follow upon high legal success. Also an overdose of German gas in 1918 had given his skin a habitual pallor, so that he looked not unhealthy, but notably urban. As a matter of fact he was one of the hardest men I have ever known, but a chance observer might have guessed from his complexion that he rarely left the pavements.

Burminster, who had come back from a month in the grass countries with a face like a deep-sea mariner's, commented on this one evening.

'How do you manage always to look the complete Cit, Ned?' he asked. 'You're as much a Londoner as a Parisian is a Parisian, if you know what I mean.'

Leithen said that he was not ashamed of it, and he embarked on a eulogy of the metropolis. In London you met sooner or later everybody you had ever known; you could lay your hand on any knowledge you wanted; you could pull strings that controlled the innermost Sahara and the topmost Pamirs. Romance lay in wait for you at every street corner. It was the true City of the Caliphs.

'That is what they say,' said Sandy Arbuthnot sadly, 'but I never found it so. I yawn my head off in London. Nothing amusing ever finds me out – I have to go and search for it, and it usually costs the deuce of a lot.'

'I once stumbled upon a pretty generous allowance of romance,' said Leithen, 'and it cost me precisely sixpence.'

Then he told us this story.

It happened a good many years ago, just when I was beginning to get on at the Bar. I spent busy days in court and chambers, but I was young and had a young man's appetite for society, so I used to dine out most nights and go to more balls than were good for me. It was pleasant after a heavy day to dive into a different kind of life. My rooms at the time were in Down Street, the same house as my present one, only two floors higher up.

On a certain night in February I was dining in Bryanston Square with the Nantleys. Mollie Nantley was an old friend, and used to fit me as an unattached bachelor into her big dinners. She was a young hostess and full of ambition, and one met an odd assortment of people at her house. Mostly political, of course, but a sprinkling of art and letters, and any visiting lion that happened to be passing through. Mollie was a very innocent lion-hunter, but she had a partiality for the breed.

I don't remember much about the dinner, except that the principal guest had failed her. Mollie was loud in her lamentations. He was a South American President who had engineered a very pretty *coup d'état* the year before, and was now in England on some business concerning the finances of his State. You may remember his name – Ramon Pelem – he made rather a stir in the world for a year or two. I had read about him in the papers, and had looked forward to meeting him, for he had won his way to power by extraordinary boldness and courage, and he was quite young. There was a story that he was partly English and that his grandfather's name had been Pelham. I don't know what truth there was in that, but he knew England well and Englishmen liked him.

Well, he had cried off on the telephone an hour before, and Mollie was grievously disappointed. Her other guests bore the loss with more fortitude, for I expect they thought he was a brand of cigar.

In those days dinners began earlier and dances later than they do to-day. I meant to leave soon, go back to my rooms and read briefs, and then look in at Lady Samplar's dance between eleven and twelve. So at nine-thirty I took my leave.

Jervis, the old butler, who had been my ally from boyhood, was standing on the threshold, and in the square there was a considerable crowd now thinning away. I asked what the trouble was.

'There's been an arrest, Mr Edward,' he said in an awestruck voice. 'It 'appened when I was serving coffee in the dining-room, but our Albert saw it all. Two foreigners, he said – proper rascals by their look – were took away by the police just outside this very door. The constables was very nippy and collared them before they could use their pistols – but they 'ad pistols on them and no mistake. Albert says he saw the weapons.'

'Did they propose to burgle you?' I asked.

'I cannot say, Mr Edward. But I shall give instructions for a very careful lock-up to-night.'

There were no cabs about, so I decided to walk on and pick one up. When I got into Great Cumberland Place it began to rain sharply, and I was just about to call a prowling hansom, when I put my hand into my pocket. I found that I had no more than one solitary sixpence.

I could of course have paid when I got to my flat. But as the rain seemed to be slacking off, I preferred to walk. Mollie's dining-room had been stuffy, I had been in court all day, and I wanted some fresh air.

You know how in little things, when you have decided on a course, you are curiously reluctant to change it. Before I got to the Marble Arch it had begun to pour in downright earnest. But I still stumped on. Only I entered the Park, for even in February there is a certain amount of cover from the trees.

I passed one or two hurried pedestrians, but the place was almost empty. The occasional lamps made only spots of light in a dripping darkness, and it struck me that this was a curious patch of gloom and loneliness to be so near to crowded streets, for with the rain had come a fine mist. I pitied the poor devils to whom it was the only home. There was one of them on a seat which I passed. The collar of his thin shabby overcoat was turned up, and his shameful old felt hat was turned down, so that only a few square inches of pale face were visible. His toes stuck out of his boots, and he seemed sunk in a sodden misery.

I passed him and then turned back. Casual charity is an easy dope for the conscience, and I indulge in it too often. When I approached him he seemed to stiffen, and his hands moved in his pockets.

'A rotten night,' I said. 'Is sixpence any good to you?' And I held out my solitary coin.

He lifted his face, and I started. For the eyes that looked at me were not those of a waster. They were bright, penetrating, authoritative – and they were young. I was conscious that they took in more of me than mine did of him.

'Thank you very much,' he said, as he took the coin, and the voice was that of a cultivated man. 'But I'm afraid I need rather more than sixpence.'

'How much?' I asked. This was clearly an original.

'To be accurate, five million pounds.'

He was certainly mad, but I was fascinated by this wisp of humanity. I wished that he would show more of his face.

'Till your ship comes home,' I said, 'you want a bed, and you'd be the better of a change. Sixpence is all I have on me. But if you come to my rooms I'll give you the price of a night's lodging, and I think I might find you some old clothes.'

'Where do you live?' he asked.

'Close by – in Down Street.' I gave the number.

He seemed to reflect, and then he shot a glance on either side into the gloom behind the road. It may have been fancy, but I thought that I saw something stir in the darkness.

'What are you?' he asked.

I was getting abominably wet, and yet I submitted to be cross-examined by this waif.

'I am a lawyer,' I said.

He looked at me again, very intently.

'Have you a telephone?' he asked.

I nodded.

'Right,' he said. 'You seem a good fellow, and I'll take you at your word. I'll follow you . . . Don't look back, please. It's important . . . I'll be in Down Street as soon as you . . . *Marchons.*'

It sounds preposterous, but I did exactly as I was bid. I never looked back, but I kept my ears open for the sound of following footsteps. I thought I heard them, and then they seemed to die away. I turned out of the Park at Grosvenor Gate and went down Park Lane. When I reached the house which contained my flat, I looked up and down the street, but it was empty except for a waiting four-wheeler. But just as I turned in I caught a glimpse of some one running at the Hertford Street end. The runner came to a sudden halt, and I saw that it was not the man I had left.

To my surprise I found the waif on the landing outside my flat. I was about to tell him to stop outside, but as soon as I unlocked the door he brushed past me and entered. My man, who did not sleep on the premises, had left the light burning in the little hall.

'Lock the door,' he said in a tone of authority. 'Forgive me taking charge, but I assure you it is important.'

Then to my amazement he peeled off the sopping overcoat, and kicked off his disreputable shoes. They were odd shoes, for what looked like his toes sticking out was really part of the make-up. He stood up before me in underclothes and socks, and I noticed that his underclothing seemed to be of the finest material.

'Now for your telephone,' he said.

I was getting angry at these liberties.

'Who the devil are you?' I demanded.

'I am President Pelem,' he said, with all the dignity in the world. 'And you?'

'I? – oh, I am the German Emperor.'

He laughed. 'You know you invited me here,' he said. 'You've brought this on yourself.' Then he stared at me. 'Hullo, I've seen you before. You're Leithen. I saw you play at Lord's. I was twelfth man for Harrow that year... Now for the telephone.'

There was something about the fellow, something defiant and debonair and young, that stopped all further protest on my part. He might or might not be President Pelem, but he was certainly not a wastrel. Besides, he seemed curiously keyed up, as if the occasion were desperately important, and he infected me with the same feeling. I said no more, but led the way into my sitting-room. He flung himself on the telephone, gave a number, was instantly connected, and began a conversation in monosyllables.

It was a queer jumble that I overheard. Bryanston Square was mentioned, and the Park, and the number of my house was given – to somebody. There was a string of foreign names – Pedro and Alejandro and Manuel and Alcaza – and short breathless inquiries. Then I heard – 'a good fellow – looks as if he might be useful in a row,' and I wondered if he was referring to me. Some rapid Spanish followed, and then, 'Come round at once – they will be here before you. Have policemen below, but don't let them come up. We should be able to manage alone. Oh, and tell Burton to ring up here as soon as he has news.' And he gave my telephone number.

I put some coals on the fire, changed into a tweed jacket, and lit a pipe. I fetched a dressing-gown from my bedroom and flung it on the sofa. 'You'd better put that on,' I said when he had finished.

He shook his head.

'I would rather be unencumbered,' he said. 'But I should dearly love a cigarette ... and a liqueur brandy, if you have such a thing. That Park of yours is infernally chilly.'

I supplied his needs, and he stretched himself in an armchair, with his stockinged feet to the fire.

'You have been very good-humoured, Leithen,' he said. 'Valdez – that's my aide-de-camp – will be here presently, and he will probably be preceded by other guests. But I think I have time for the short explanation which is your due. You believe what I told you?'

I nodded.

'Good. Well, I came to London three weeks ago to raise a loan. That was a matter of life or death for my big stupid country. I have succeeded. This afternoon the agreement was signed. I think I mentioned the amount to you – five million sterling.'

He smiled happily and blew a smoke-ring into the air.

'I must tell you that I have enemies. Among my happy people there are many rascals, and I had to deal harshly with them. "So foul a sky clears not without a storm" – that's Shakespeare, isn't it? I learned it at school. You see, I had Holy Church behind me, and therefore I had against me all the gentry who call themselves liberators. Red Masons, anarchists, communists, that sort of crew. A good many are now reposing beneath the sod, but some of the worst remain. In particular, six followed me to England with instructions that I must not return.

'I don't mind telling you, Leithen, that I have had a peculiarly rotten time the last three weeks. It was most important that nothing should happen to me till the loan was settled, so I had to lead the sheltered life. It went against the grain, I assure you, for I prefer the offensive to the defensive. The English police were very amiable, and I never stirred without a cordon, your people and my own. The Six wanted to kill me, and as it is pretty easy to kill anybody if you don't mind being killed yourself, we had to take rather elaborate precautions. As it was, I was twice nearly done in. Once my carriage broke down mysteriously, and a crowd collected, and if I hadn't had the luck to board a passing cab, I should have had a knife in my ribs. The second was at a public dinner – something not quite right about the cayenne pepper served with the oysters. One of my staff is still seriously ill.'

He stretched his arms.

'Well, that first stage is over. They can't wreck the loan, whatever happens to me. Now I am free to adopt different tactics and take the offensive. I have no fear of the Six in my own country. There I can take precautions, and they will find it difficult to cross the frontier or to live for six hours thereafter if they succeed. But here you are a free people, and protection is not so easy. I do not wish to leave England just yet – I have done my work and have earned a little play. I know your land and love it, and I look forward to seeing something of my friends. Also I want to attend the Grand National. Therefore, it is necessary that my enemies should be confined for a little, while I take my holiday. So for this evening I made a plan. I took the offensive. I deliberately put myself in their danger.'

He turned his dancing eyes towards me, and I have rarely had such an impression of wild and mirthful audacity.

'We have an excellent intelligence system,' he went on, 'and the Six have been assiduously shadowed. But as I have told you, no precautions avail against the fanatic, and I do not wish to be killed on my little holiday. So I resolved to draw their fire – to expose myself as ground bait, so to speak, that I might have the chance of netting them. The Six usually hunt in couples, so it was necessary to have three separate acts in the play, if all were to be gathered in. The first—'

'Was in Bryanston Square,' I put in, 'outside Lady Nantley's house?'

'True. How did you know?'

'I have just been dining there, and heard that you were expected. I saw the crowd in the square as I came away.'

'It seems to have gone off quite nicely. We took pains to let it be known where I was dining. The Six, who mistrust me, delegated only two of their number for the job. They never put all their eggs in one basket. The two gentlemen were induced to make a scene, and, since they proved to be heavily armed, were taken into custody and may get a six months' sentence. Very prettily managed, but unfortunately it was the two that matter least – the ones we call Little Pedro and Alejandro the Scholar. Impatient, blundering children, both of them. That leaves four.'

The telephone bell rang, and he made a long arm for the receiver. The news he got seemed to be good, for he turned a smiling face to me.

'I should have said two. My little enterprise in the Park has proved a brilliant success . . . But I must explain. I was to be the bait for my enemies, so I showed myself to the remaining four. That was really rather a clever piece of business. They lost me at the Marble Arch and they did not recognise me as the scarecrow sitting on the seat in the rain. But they knew I had gone to earth there, and they stuck to the scent like terriers. Presently they would have found me, and there would have been shooting. Some of my own people were in the shadow between the road and the railings.'

'When I saw you, were your enemies near?' I asked.

'Two were on the opposite side of the road. One was standing under the lamp-post at the gate. I don't know where the fourth was at that moment. But all had passed me more than once . . . By the way, you very nearly got yourself shot, you know. When you asked me if sixpence was any good to me . . . That happens to be their password. I take great credit to myself for seeing instantly that you were harmless.'

'Why did you leave the Park if you had your trap so well laid?' I asked.

'Because it meant dealing with all four together at once, and I do them the honour of being rather nervous about them. They are very quick with their guns. I wanted a chance to break up the covey, and your arrival gave it me. When I went off two followed, as I thought they would. My car was in Park Lane, and gave me a lift; and one of them saw me in it. I puzzled them a little, but by now they must be certain. You see, my car has been waiting for some minutes outside this house.'

'What about the other two?' I asked.

'Burton has just telephoned that they have been gathered in. Quite an exciting little scrap. To your police it must have seemed a bad case of highway robbery – two ruffianly looking fellows hold up a peaceful elderly gentleman returning from dinner. The odds were not quite like that, but the men I had on the job are old soldiers of the Indian wars and can move softly... I only wish I knew which two they have got. Burton was not sure. Alcaza is one, but I can't be certain about the other. I hope it is not the Irishman.'

My bell rang very loud and steadily.

'In a few seconds I shall have solved that problem,' he said gaily. 'I am afraid I must trouble you to open the door, Leithen.'

'Is it your aide-de-camp?'

'No. I instructed Valdez to knock. It is the residuum of the Six. Now listen to me, my friend. These two, whoever they are, have come here to kill me, and I don't mean to be killed... My first plan was to have Valdez here – and others – so that my two enemies should walk into a trap. But I changed my mind before I telephoned. They are very clever men, and by this time they will be very wary. So I have thought of something else.'

The bell rang again, and a third time insistently.

'Take these,' and he held out a pair of cruel little bluish revolvers. 'When you open the door, you will say that the President is at home and, in token of his confidence, offers them these. *'Une espèce d'Irlandais, Messieurs. Vous commencez trop tard, et vous finissez trop tôt.'* Then bring them here. Quick now. I hope Corbally is one of them.'

I did exactly as I was told. I cannot say that I had any liking for the task, but I was a good deal under the spell of that calm young man, and I was resigned to my flat being made a rendezvous for desperadoes. I had locked and chained and bolted the door, so it took me a few moments to open it.

I found myself looking at emptiness.

'Who is it?' I called. 'Who rang?'

I was answered from behind me. It was the quickest thing I have ever seen, for they must have slipped through in the moment when my eyes were dazzled by the change from the dim light of the hall to the glare of the landing. That gave me some notion of the men we had to deal with.

'Here,' said the voice. I turned and saw two men in waterproofs and felt hats, who kept their hands in their pockets and had a fraction of an eye on the two pistols I swung by the muzzles.

'M. le Président will be glad to see you, gentlemen,' I said. I held out the revolvers, which they seemed to grasp and flick into their pockets with a single movement. Then I repeated slowly the piece of rudeness in French.

One of the men laughed. 'Ramon does not forget,' he said. He was a young man with sandy hair and hot blue eyes and an odd break in his long drooping nose. The other was a wiry little fellow, with a grizzled beard and what looked like a stiff leg.

I had no guess at my friend's plan, and was concerned to do precisely as I was told. I opened the door of my sitting-room, and noticed that the President was stretched on my sofa facing the door. He was smoking and was still in his underclothes. When the two men behind me saw that he was patently unarmed they slipped into the room with a quick cat-like movement, and took their stand with their backs against the door.

'Hullo, Corbally,' said the President pleasantly. 'And you, Manuel. You're looking younger than when I saw you last. Have a cigarette?' and he nodded towards my box on the table behind him. Both shook their heads.

'I'm glad you have come. You have probably seen the news of the loan in the evening papers. That should give you a holiday, as it gives me one. No further need for the hectic oversight of each other, which is so wearing and takes up so much time.'

'No,' said the man called Manuel, and there was something very grim about his quiet tones. 'We shall take steps to prevent any need for that in the future.'

'Tut, tut – that is your old self, Manuel. You are too fond of melodrama to be an artist. You are a priest at heart.'

The man snarled. 'There will be no priest at your deathbed.' Then to his companion. 'Let us get this farce over.'

The President paid not the slightest attention but looked steadily at the Irishman. 'You used to be a sportsman, Mike. Have you come to share Manuel's taste for potting the sitting rabbit?'

'We are not sportsmen, we are executioners of justice,' said Manuel.

The President laughed merrily. 'Superb! The best Roman manner.' He still kept his eyes on Corbally.

'Damn you, what's your game, Ramon?' the Irishman asked. His freckled face had become very red.

'Simply to propose a short armistice. I want a holiday. If you must know, I want to go to the National.'

'So do I.'

'Well, let's call a truce. Say for two months or till I leave England – whichever period shall be the shorter. After that you can get busy again.'

The one he had named Manuel broke into a spluttering torrent of Spanish, and for a little they all talked that language. It sounded like a commination service on the President, to which he good-humouredly replied. I had never seen this class of ruffian before, to whom murder was as simple as shooting a partridge, and I noted curiously the lean hands, the restless wary eyes, and the ugly lips of the type. So far as I could make out, the President seemed to be getting on well with the Irishman but to be having trouble with Manuel.

'Have ye really and truly nothing on ye?' Corbally asked.

The President stretched his arms and revealed his slim figure in its close-fitting pants and vest.

'Nor him there?' and he nodded towards me.

'He is a lawyer; he doesn't use guns.'

'Then I'm damned if I touch ye. Two months it is. What's your fancy for Liverpool?'

This was too much for Manuel. I saw in what seemed to be one movement his hand slip from his pocket, Corbally's arm swing in a circle, and a plaster bust of Julius Cæsar tumble off the top of my bookcase. Then I heard the report.

'Ye nasty little man,' said Corbally, as he pressed him to his bosom in a bear's hug.

'You are a traitor,' Manuel shouted. 'How will we face the others? What will Alejandro say and Alcaza—'

'I think I can explain,' said the President pleasantly. 'They won't know for quite a time, and then only if you tell them. You two gentlemen are all that remain for the moment of your patriotic company. The other four have been the victims of the English police – two in Bryanston Square, and two in the Park close to the Marble Arch.'

'Ye don't say!' said Corbally with admiration in his voice. 'Faith, that's smart work!'

'They too will have a little holiday. A few months to meditate on politics, while you and I go to the Grand National.'

Suddenly there was a sharp rat-tat at my door. It was like the knocking in *Macbeth* for dramatic effect. Corbally had one pistol at my ear in an instant, while a second covered the President.

'It's all right,' said the latter, never moving a muscle. 'It's General Valdez, whom I think you know. That was another argument which I was coming to if I hadn't had the good fortune to appeal to Mr Corbally's higher nature. I know you have sworn to kill me, but I take it that the killer wants to have a sporting chance of escape. Well, there wouldn't have been the faintest shadow of a chance here. Valdez is at the door, and the English police are below. You are brave men, I know, but even brave men dislike the cold gallows.'

The knocker fell again. 'Let him in, Leithen,' I was told, 'or he will be damaging your valuable door. He has not the northern phlegm of you and me and Mr Corbally.'

A tall man in an ulster, which looked as if it covered a uniform, stood on the threshold. Some one had obscured the lights on the landing so that the staircase was dark, but I could see in the gloom other figures. 'President Pelem . . .' he began.

'The President is here,' I said. 'Quite well and in great form. He is entertaining two other guests.'

The General marched to my sitting-room. I was behind him and did not see his face, but I can believe that it showed surprise when he recognised the guests. Manuel stood sulkily defiant, his hands in his waterproof pockets, but Corbally's light eyes were laughing.

'I think you know each other,' said the President graciously.

'My God!' Valdez seemed to choke at the sight. 'These swine! . . . Excellency, I have . . .'

'You have nothing of the kind. These are friends of mine for the next two months, and Mr Corbally and I are going to the Grand National together. Will you have the goodness to conduct them downstairs and explain to the inspector of police below that all has gone well and that I am perfectly satisfied, and that he will hear from me in the morning? . . . One moment. What about a stirrup-cup? Leithen, does your establishment run to a whisky and soda all round?'

It did. We all had a drink, and I believe I clinked glasses with Manuel.

I looked in at Lady Samplar's dance as I had meant to. Presently I saw a resplendent figure arrive – the President, with the ribbon of the Gold

Star of Bolivar across his chest. He was no more the larky under-graduate, but the responsible statesman, the father of his country. There was a considerable crowd in his vicinity when I got near him, and he was making his apologies to Mollie Nantley. She saw me and insisted on introducing me. 'I so much wanted you two to meet. I had hoped it would be at my dinner – but anyhow I have managed it.' I think she was a little surprised when the President took my hand in both of his. 'I saw Mr Leithen play at Lord's in '97,' he said. 'I was twelfth man for Harrow that year. It is delightful to make his acquaintance; I shall never forget this meeting.'

'How English he is!' Mollie whispered to me as we made our way out of the crowd.

They got him next year. They were bound to, for in that kind of business you can have no real protection. But he managed to set his country on its feet before he went down . . . No, it was neither Manuel nor Corbally. I think it was Alejandro the Scholar.

The Wind in the Portico

'The Wind in the Portico', Henry Nightingale's story in *The Runagates Club* (1928), first appeared in *Pall Mall Magazine* in March 1928. Nightingale, who had first appeared in *The Three Hostages* (1924), bears certain resemblances to a close friend of Buchan at the time, T.E. Lawrence.

A dry wind of the high places ... not to fan nor to cleanse, even a full wind from those places shall come unto me.

Jeremiah IV. xi–xii

NIGHTINGALE WAS A hard man to draw. His doings with the Bedawin had become a legend, but he would as soon have talked about them as claimed to have won the war. He was a slim dark fellow about thirty-five years of age, very short-sighted, and wearing such high-powered double glasses that it was impossible to tell the colour of his eyes. This weakness made him stoop a little and peer, so that he was the strangest figure to picture in a burnous leading an army of desert tribesmen. I fancy his power came partly from his oddness, for his followers thought that the hand of Allah had been laid on him, and partly from his quick imagination and his flawless courage. After the war he had gone back to his Cambridge fellowship, declaring that, thank God, that chapter in his life was over.

As I say, he never mentioned the deeds which had made him famous. He knew his own business, and probably realised that to keep his mental balance he had to drop the curtain on what must have been the most nerve-racking four years ever spent by man. We respected his decision and kept off Arabia. It was a remark of Hannay's that drew from him the following story. Hannay was talking about his Cotswold house, which was on the Fosse Way, and saying that it always puzzled him how so elaborate a civilisation as Roman Britain could have been destroyed utterly and left no mark on the national history beyond a few roads and ruins and place-names. Peckwether, the historian, demurred, and had a good deal to say about how much the Roman tradition was woven into the Saxon culture. 'Rome only sleeps,' he said; 'she never dies.'

Nightingale nodded. 'Sometimes she dreams in her sleep and talks. Once she scared me out of my senses.'

After a good deal of pressing he produced this story. He was not much of a talker, so he wrote it out and read it to us.

There is a place in Shropshire which I do not propose to visit again. It lies between Ludlow and the hills, in a shallow valley full of woods. Its name is St Sant, a village with a big house and park adjoining, on a stream called the Vaun, about five miles from the little town of Faxeter. They have queer names in those parts, and other things queerer than the names.

I was motoring from Wales to Cambridge at the close of the long vacation. All this happened before the war, when I had just got my fellowship and was settling down to academic work. It was a fine night in early October, with a full moon, and I intended to push on to Ludlow for supper and bed. The time was about half-past eight, the road was empty and good going, and I was trundling pleasantly along when something went wrong with my headlights. It was a small thing, and I stopped to remedy it beyond a village and just at the lodge-gates of a house.

On the opposite side of the road a carrier's cart had drawn up, and two men, who looked like indoor servants, were lifting some packages from it on to a big barrow. The moon was up, so I didn't need the feeble light of the carrier's lamp to see what they were doing. I suppose I wanted to stretch my legs for a moment, for when I had finished my job I strolled over to them. They did not hear me coming, and the carrier on his perch seemed to be asleep.

The packages were the ordinary consignments from some big shop in town. But I noticed that the two men handled them very gingerly, and that, as each was laid in the barrow, they clipped off the shop label and affixed one of their own. The new labels were odd things, large and square, with some address written on them in very black capital letters. There was nothing in that, but the men's faces puzzled me. For they seemed to do their job in a fever, longing to get it over and yet in a sweat lest they should make some mistake. Their commonplace task seemed to be for them a matter of tremendous importance. I moved so as to get a view of their faces, and I saw that they were white and strained. The two were of the butler or valet class, both elderly, and I could have sworn that they were labouring under something like fear.

I shuffled my feet to let them know of my presence and remarked that it was a fine night. They started as if they had been robbing a corpse. One of them mumbled something in reply, but the other caught a package which was slipping, and in a tone of violent alarm growled to his mate to be careful. I had a notion that they were handling explosives.

I had no time to waste, so I pushed on. That night, in my room at Ludlow, I had the curiosity to look up my map and identify the place where I had seen the men. The village was St Sant, and it appeared that the gate I had stopped at belonged to a considerable demesne called Vauncastle. That was my first visit.

At that time I was busy on a critical edition of Theocritus, for which I was making a new collation of the manuscripts. There was a variant of the Medicean Codex in England, which nobody had seen since Gaisford, and after a good deal of trouble I found that it was in the library of a man called Dubellay. I wrote to him at his London club, and got a reply to my surprise from Vauncastle Hall, Faxeter. It was an odd letter, for you could see that he longed to tell me to go to the devil, but couldn't quite reconcile it with his conscience. We exchanged several letters, and the upshot was that he gave me permission to examine his manuscript. He did not ask me to stay, but mentioned that there was a comfortable little inn in St Sant.

My second visit began on the 27th of December, after I had been home for Christmas. We had had a week of severe frost, and then it had thawed a little; but it remained bitterly cold, with leaden skies that threatened snow. I drove from Faxeter, and as we ascended the valley I remember thinking that it was a curiously sad country. The hills were too low to be impressive, and their outlines were mostly blurred with woods; but the tops showed clear, funny little knolls of grey bent that suggested a volcanic origin. It might have been one of those backgrounds you find in Italian primitives, with all the light and colour left out. When I got a glimpse of the Vaun in the bleached meadows it looked like the 'wan water' of the Border ballads. The woods, too, had not the friendly bareness of English copses in winter-time. They remained dark and cloudy, as if they were hiding secrets. Before I reached St Sant, I decided that the landscape was not only sad, but ominous.

I was fortunate in my inn. In the single street of one-storied cottages it rose like a lighthouse, with a cheery glow from behind the red curtains of the bar parlour. The inside proved as good as the outside. I found a bedroom with a bright fire, and I dined in a wainscoted room full of preposterous old pictures of lanky hounds and hollow-backed horses. I had been rather depressed on my journey, but my spirits were raised by this comfort, and when the house produced a most respectable bottle of port I had the landlord in to drink a glass. He was an ancient man who had been a gamekeeper, with a much younger wife, who was responsible for the management. I was curious to hear something about the owner of my manuscript, but I got little from the landlord. He had been with the old squire, and had never served the present one. I heard of Dubellays in plenty – the landlord's master, who had hunted his own hounds for forty years, the Major his brother, who had fallen at Abu Klea; Parson Jack, who had had the living till he died, and of all kinds of collaterals. The 'Deblays' had been a high-spirited, open-handed stock, and much liked in the place. But of the present master of the Hall he could or would tell me nothing. The Squire was a 'great scholard', but I gathered that he followed no sport and was not a convivial soul like his predecessors. He had spent a mint of money on the house, but not many people went there. He, the landlord, had never been inside the grounds in the new master's time, though in the old days there had been hunt breakfasts on the lawn for the whole countryside, and mighty tenantry dinners. I went to bed with a clear picture in my mind of the man I was to interview on the morrow. A scholarly and autocratic recluse, who collected treasures and beautified his dwelling and probably lived in his library. I rather looked forward to meeting him, for the bonhomous sporting squire was not much in my line.

After breakfast next morning I made my way to the Hall. It was the same leaden weather, and when I entered the gates the air seemed to grow bitterer and the skies darker. The place was muffled in great trees which even in their winter bareness made a pall about it. There was a long avenue of ancient sycamores, through which one caught only rare glimpses of the frozen park. I took my bearings, and realised that I was walking nearly due south, and was gradually descending.

The house must be in a hollow. Presently the trees thinned, I passed through an iron gate, came out on a big untended lawn, untidily studded with laurels and rhododendrons, and there before me was the house front.

I had expected something beautiful – an old Tudor or Queen Anne façade or a dignified Georgian portico. I was disappointed, for the front was simply mean. It was low and irregular, more like the back parts of a house, and I guessed that at some time or another the building had been turned round, and the old kitchen door made the chief entrance. I was confirmed in my conclusion by observing that the roofs rose in tiers, like one of those recessed New York skyscrapers, so that the present back parts of the building were of an impressive height.

The oddity of the place interested me, and still more its dilapidation. What on earth could the owner have spent his money on? Everything – lawn, flower-beds, paths – was neglected. There was a new stone doorway, but the walls badly needed pointing, the window woodwork had not been painted for ages, and there were several broken panes. The bell did not ring, so I was reduced to hammering on the knocker, and it must have been ten minutes before the door opened. A pale butler, one of the men I had seen at the carrier's cart the October before, stood blinking in the entrance.

He led me in without question, when I gave my name, so I was evidently expected. The hall was my second surprise. What had become of my picture of the collector? The place was small and poky, and furnished as barely as the lobby of a farmhouse. The only thing I approved was its warmth. Unlike most English country houses there seemed to be excellent heating arrangements.

I was taken into a little dark room with one window that looked out on a shrubbery, while the man went to fetch his master. My chief feeling was of gratitude that I had not been asked to stay, for the inn was paradise compared with this sepulchre. I was examining the prints on the wall, when I heard my name spoken and turned round to greet Mr Dubellay.

He was my third surprise. I had made a portrait in my mind of a fastidious old scholar, with eye-glasses on a black chord, and a finical *weltkind*-ish manner. Instead I found a man still in early middle age, a heavy fellow dressed in the roughest country tweeds. He was as untidy as his demesne, for he had not shaved that morning, his flannel collar was badly frayed, and his fingernails would have been the better for a scrubbing brush. His face was hard to describe. It was high-coloured, but the colour was not healthy; it was friendly, but it was also wary; above all, it was *unquiet*. He gave me the impression of a man whose nerves were all wrong, and who was perpetually on his guard.

He said a few civil words, and thrust a badly tied brown paper parcel at me.

'That's your manuscript,' he said jauntily.

I was staggered. I had expected to be permitted to collate the codex in his library, and in the last few minutes had realised that the prospect was distasteful. But here was this casual owner offering me the priceless thing to take away.

I stammered my thanks, and added that it was very good of him to trust a stranger with such a treasure.

'Only as far as the inn,' he said. 'I wouldn't like to send it by post. But there's no harm in your working at it at the inn. There should be confidence among scholars.' And he gave an odd cackle of a laugh.

'I greatly prefer your plan,' I said. 'But I thought you would insist on my working at it here.'

'No, indeed,' he said earnestly. 'I shouldn't think of such a thing. . . Wouldn't do at all . . . An insult to our freemasonry . . . That's how I should regard it.'

We had a few minutes' further talk. I learned that he had inherited under the entail from a cousin, and had been just over ten years at Vauncastle. Before that he had been a London solicitor. He asked me a question or two about Cambridge – wished he had been at the University – much hampered in his work by a defective education. I was a Greek scholar? – Latin, too, he presumed. Wonderful people the Romans . . . He spoke quite freely, but all the time his queer restless eyes were darting about, and I had a strong impression that he would have liked to say something to me very different from these commonplaces – that he was longing to broach some subject but was held back by shyness or fear. He had such an odd appraising way of looking at me.

I left without his having asked me to a meal, for which I was not sorry, for I did not like the atmosphere of the place. I took a short cut over the ragged lawn, and turned at the top of the slope to look back. The house was in reality a huge pile, and I saw that I had been right and that the main building was all at the back. Was it, I wondered, like the Alhambra, which behind a front like a factory concealed a treasure-house? I saw, too, that the woodland hollow was more spacious than I had fancied. The house, as at present arranged, faced due north, and behind the south front was an open space in which I guessed that a lake might lie. Far beyond I could see in the December dimness the lift of high dark hills.

That evening the snow came in earnest, and fell continuously for the better part of two days. I banked up the fire in my bedroom and spent a happy time with the codex. I had brought only my working boots with me and the inn boasted no library, so when I wanted to relax I went down to the tap-room, or gossiped with the landlady in the bar parlour. The yokels who congregated in the former were pleasant fellows, but, like all the folk on the Marches, they did not talk readily to a stranger and I heard little from them of the Hall. The old squire had reared every year three thousand pheasants, but the present squire would not allow a gun to be fired on his land and there were only a few wild birds left. For the same reason the woods were thick with vermin. This they told me when I professed an interest in shooting. But of Mr Dubellay they would not speak, declaring that they never saw him. I daresay they gossiped wildly about him, and their public reticence struck me as having in it a touch of fear.

The landlady who came from a different part of the shire, was more communicative. She had not known the former Dubellays and so had no standard of comparison, but she was inclined to regard the present squire as not quite right in the head. 'They do say,' she would begin, but she, too, suffered from some inhibition, and what promised to be sensational would tail off into the commonplace. One thing apparently puzzled the neighbourhood above others, and that was his rearrangement of the house. 'They do say,' she said in an awed voice, 'that he have built a great church.' She had never visited it – no one in the parish had, for Squire Dubellay did not allow intruders – but from Lyne Hill you could see it through a gap in the woods. 'He's no good Christian,' she told me, 'and him and Vicar has quarrelled this many a day. But they do say as he worships summat there.' I learned that there were no women servants in the house, only the men he had brought from London. 'Poor benighted souls, they must live in a sad hobble,' and the buxom lady shrugged her shoulders and giggled.

On the last day of December I decided that I needed exercise and must go for a long stride. The snow had ceased that morning, and the dull skies had changed to a clear blue. It was still very cold, but the sun was shining, the snow was firm and crisp underfoot, and I proposed to survey the country. So after luncheon I put on thick boots and gaiters, and made for Lyne Hill. This meant a considerable circuit, for the place lay south of the Vauncastle park. From it I hoped to get a view of the other side of the house.

I was not disappointed. There was a rift in the thick woodlands, and below me, two miles off, I suddenly saw a strange building, like a classical temple. Only the entablature and the tops of the pillars showed above the trees, but they stood out vivid and dark against the background of snow. The spectacle in that lonely place was so startling that for a little I could only stare. I remember that I glanced behind me to the snowy line of the Welsh mountains, and felt that I might have been looking at a winter view of the Apennines two thousand years ago.

My curiosity was now alert, and I determined to get a nearer view of this marvel. I left the track and ploughed through the snowy fields down to the skirts of the woods. After that my troubles began. I found myself in a very good imitation of a primeval forest, where the undergrowth had been unchecked and the rides uncut for years. I sank into deep pits, I was savagely torn by briars and brambles, but I struggled on, keeping a line as best I could. At last the trees stopped. Before me was a flat expanse which I knew must be a lake, and beyond rose the temple.

It ran the whole length of the house, and from where I stood it was hard to believe that there were buildings at its back where men dwelt. It was a fine piece of work – the first glance told me that – admirably proportioned, classical, yet not following exactly any of the classical models. One could imagine a great echoing interior dim with the smoke of sacrifice, and it was only by reflecting that I realised that the peristyle could not be continued down the two sides, that there was no interior, and that what I was looking at was only a portico.

The thing was at once impressive and preposterous. What madness had been in Dubellay when he embellished his house with such a grandiose garden front? The sun was setting and the shadow of the wooded hills darkened the interior, so I could not even make out the back wall of the porch. I wanted a nearer view, so I embarked on the frozen lake.

Then I had an odd experience. I was not tired, the snow lay level and firm, but I was conscious of extreme weariness. The biting air had become warm and oppressive. I had to drag boots that seemed to weigh tons across that lake. The place was utterly silent in the stricture of the frost, and from the pile in front no sign of life came.

I reached the other side at last and found myself in a frozen shallow of bulrushes and skeleton willow-herbs. They were taller than my head, and to see the house I had to look upward through their snowy traceries. It was perhaps eighty feet above me and a hundred yards distant, and, since I was below it, the delicate pillars seemed to spring to a great height. But it was still dusky, and the only detail I could see was on the ceiling, which seemed either to be carved or painted with deeply-shaded monochrome figures.

Suddenly the dying sun came slanting through the gap in the hills, and for an instant the whole portico to its farthest recesses was washed in clear gold and scarlet. That was wonderful enough, but there was something more. The air was utterly still with not the faintest breath of wind – so still that when I had lit a cigarette half an hour before the flame of the match had burned steadily upward like a candle in a room. As I stood among the sedges not a single frost crystal stirred . . . But there was a wind blowing in the portico.

I could see it lifting feathers of snow from the base of the pillars and fluffing the cornices. The floor had already been swept clean, but tiny flakes drifted on to it from the exposed edges. The interior was filled with a furious movement, though a yard from it was frozen peace. I felt nothing of the action of the wind, but I knew that it was hot, hot as the breath of a furnace.

I had only one thought, dread of being overtaken by night near that place. I turned and ran. Ran with labouring steps across the lake, panting and stifling with a deadly hot oppression, ran blindly by a sort of instinct in the direction of the village. I did not stop till I had wrestled through the big wood, and come out on some rough pasture above the highway. Then I dropped on the ground, and felt again the comforting chill of the December air.

The adventure left me in an uncomfortable mood. I was ashamed of myself for playing the fool, and at the same time hopelessly puzzled, for the oftener I went over in my mind the incidents of that afternoon the more I was at a loss for an explanation. One feeling was uppermost, that I did not like this place and wanted to be out of it. I had already broken the back of my task, and by shutting myself up for two days I completed it; that is to say, I made my collation as far as I had advanced myself in my commentary on the text. I did not want to go back to the Hall, so I wrote a civil note to Dubellay, expressing my gratitude and saying that I was sending up the manuscript by the landlord's son, as I scrupled to trouble him with another visit.

I got a reply at once, saying that Mr Dubellay would like to give himself the pleasure of dining with me at the inn before I went, and would receive the manuscript in person.

It was the last night of my stay in St Sant, so I ordered the best dinner the place could provide, and a magnum of claret, of which I discovered a bin in the cellar. Dubellay appeared promptly at eight o'clock, arriving to my surprise in a car. He had tidied himself up and put on a dinner jacket, and he looked exactly like the city solicitors you see dining in the Junior Carlton.

He was in excellent spirits, and his eyes had lost their air of being on guard. He seemed to have reached some conclusion about me, or decided that I was harmless. More, he seemed to be burning to talk to me. After my adventure I was prepared to find fear in him, the fear I had seen in the faces of the men-servants. But there was none; instead there was excitement, overpowering excitement.

He neglected the courses in his verbosity. His coming to dinner had considerably startled the inn, and instead of a maid the landlady herself waited on us. She seemed to want to get the meal over, and hustled the biscuits and the port on to the table as soon as she decently could. Then Dubellay became confidential.

He was an enthusiast, it appeared, an enthusiast with a single hobby. All his life he had pottered among antiquities, and when he succeeded to Vauncastle he had the leisure and money to indulge himself. The place, it seemed, had been famous in Roman Britain – Vauni Castra – and Faxeter was a corruption of the same. 'Who was Vaunus?' I asked. He grinned, and told me to wait.

There had been an old temple up in the high woods. There had always been a local legend about it, and the place was supposed to be haunted. Well, he had had the site excavated and he had found— Here he became the cautious solicitor, and explained to me the law of treasure trove. As long as the objects found were not intrinsically valuable, not gold or jewels, the finder was entitled to keep them. He had done so – had not published the results of his excavations in the proceedings of any learned society – did not want to be bothered by tourists. I was different, for I was a scholar.

What had he found? It was really rather hard to follow his babbling talk, but I gathered that he had found certain carvings and sacrificial implements. And – he sunk his voice – most important of all, an altar, an altar of Vaunus, the tutelary deity of the vale.

When he mentioned this word his face took on a new look – not of fear but of secrecy, a kind of secret excitement. I have seen the same look on the face of a street-preaching Salvationist.

Vaunus had been a British god of the hills, whom the Romans in their liberal way appear to have identified with Appolo. He gave me a long confused account of him, from which it appeared that Mr Dubellay was not an exact scholar. Some of his derivations of place-names were absurd – like St Sant from Sancta Sanctorum – and in quoting a line of Ausonius he made two false quantities. He seemed to hope that I could tell him something more about Vaunus, but I said that my subject was Greek, and that I was deeply ignorant about Roman Britain. I mentioned several books, and found that he had never heard of Haverfield.

One word he used, 'hypocaust', which suddenly gave me a clue. He must have heated the temple, as he heated his house, by some very efficient system of hot air. I know little about science, but I imagined that the artificial heat of the portico, as contrasted with the cold outside, might create an air current. At any rate that explanation satisfied me, and my afternoon's adventure lost its uncanniness. The reaction made me feel friendly towards him, and I listened to his talk with sympathy, but I decided not to mention that I had visited his temple.

He told me about it himself in the most open way. 'I couldn't leave the altar on the hillside,' he said, 'I had to make a place for it, so I turned the old front of the house into a sort of temple. I got the best advice, but architects are ignorant people, and I often wished I had been a better scholar. Still the place satisfies me.'

'I hope it satisfies Vaunus,' I said jocularly.

'I think so,' he replied quite seriously, and then his thoughts seemed to go wandering, and for a minute or so he looked through me with a queer abstraction in his eyes.

'What do you do with it now you've got it?' I asked.

He didn't reply, but smiled to himself.

'I don't know if you remember a passage in Sidonius Apollinaris,' I said, 'a formula for consecrating pagan altars to Christian uses. You begin by sacrificing a white cock or something suitable, and tell Apollo with all friendliness that the old dedication is off for the present. Then you have a Christian invocation—'

He nearly jumped out of his chair.

'That wouldn't do – wouldn't do at all! ... Oh Lord, no! ... Couldn't think of it for one moment!'

It was as if I had offended his ears by some horrid blasphemy, and the odd thing was that he never recovered his composure. He tried, for he had good manners, but his ease and friendliness had gone. We talked stiffly for another half-hour about trifles, and then he rose to leave. I returned him his manuscript neatly parcelled up, and expanded in thanks, but he scarcely seemed to heed me. He stuck the thing in his pocket, and departed with the same air of shocked absorption.

After he had gone I sat before the fire and reviewed the situation. I was satisfied with my hypocaust theory, and had no more perturbation in my memory about my afternoon's adventure. Yet a slight flavour of unpleasantness hung about it, and I felt that I did not quite like Dubellay. I set him down as a crank who had tangled himself up with a half-witted hobby, like an old maid with her cats, and I was not sorry to be leaving the place.

My third and last visit to St Sant was in the following June – the midsummer of 1914. I had all but finished my Theocritus, but I needed another day or two with the Vauncastle manuscript, and, as I wanted to clear the whole thing off before I went to Italy in July, I wrote to Dubellay and asked if I might have another sight of it. The thing was a bore, but it had to be faced, and I fancied that the valley would be a pleasant place in that hot summer.

I got a reply at once, inviting, almost begging me to come, and insisting that I should stay at the Hall. I couldn't very well refuse, though I would have preferred the inn. He wired about my train, and wired again saying he would meet me. This time I seemed to be a particularly welcome guest.

I reached Faxeter in the evening, and was met by a car from a Faxeter garage. The driver was a talkative young man, and, as the car was a closed one, I sat beside him for the sake of fresh air. The term had tired me, and I was glad to get out of stuffy Cambridge, but I cannot say that I found it much cooler as we ascended the Vaun valley. The woods were in their summer magnificence but a little dulled and tarnished by the heat, the river was shrunk to a trickle, and the curious hill-tops were so scorched by the sun that they seemed almost yellow above the green of the trees. Once again I had the feeling of a landscape fantastically un-English.

'Squire Dubellay's been in a great way about your coming, sir,' the driver informed me. 'Sent down three times to the boss to make sure it was all right. He's got a car of his own, too, a nice little Daimler, but he don't seem to use it much. Haven't seen him about in it for a month of Sundays.'

As we turned in at the Hall gates he looked curiously about him. 'Never been here before, though I've been in most gentlemen's parks for fifty miles round. Rum old-fashioned spot, isn't it, sir?'

If it had seemed a shuttered sanctuary in midwinter, in that June twilight it was more than ever a place enclosed and guarded. There was almost an autumn smell of decay, a dry decay like touchwood. We seemed to be descending through layers of ever-thickening woods. When at last we turned through the iron gate I saw that the lawns had reached a further stage of neglect, for they were as shaggy as a hay-field.

The white-faced butler let me in, and there, waiting at his back, was Dubellay. But he was not the man whom I had seen in December. He was dressed in an old baggy suit of flannels, and his unwholesome red face was painfully drawn and sunken. There were dark pouches under his eyes, and these eyes were no longer excited, but dull and pained. Yes, and there was more than pain in them – there was fear. I wondered if his hobby were becoming too much for him.

He greeted me like a long-lost brother. Considering that I scarcely knew him, I was a little embarrassed by his warmth. 'Bless you for coming, my dear fellow,' he cried. 'You want a wash and then we'll have dinner. Don't bother to change, unless you want to. I never do.' He led me to my bedroom, which was clean enough but small and shabby like a servant's room. I guessed that he had gutted the house to build his absurd temple.

We dined in a fair-sized room which was a kind of library. It was lined with old books, but they did not look as if they had been there long; rather it seemed like a lumber room in which a fine collection had been stored. Once no doubt they had lived in a dignified Georgian chamber. There was nothing else, none of the antiques which I had expected.

'You have come just in time,' he told me. 'I fairly jumped when I got your letter, for I had been thinking of running up to Cambridge to insist on your coming down here. I hope you're in no hurry to leave.'

'As it happens,' I said, 'I *am* rather pressed for time, for I hope to go abroad next week. I ought to finish my work here in a couple of days. I can't tell you how much I'm in your debt for your kindness.'

'Two days,' he said. 'That will get us over midsummer. That should be enough.' I hadn't a notion what he meant.

I told him that I was looking forward to examining his collection. He opened his eyes. 'Your discoveries, I mean,' I said, 'the altar of Vaunus . . .'

As I spoke the words his face suddenly contorted in a spasm of what looked like terror. He choked and then recovered himself. 'Yes, yes,' he said rapidly. 'You shall see it – you shall see everything – but not now – not tonight. Tomorrow – in broad daylight – that's the time.'

After that the evening became a bad dream. Small talk deserted him, and he could only reply with an effort to my commonplaces. I caught him often looking at me furtively, as if he were sizing me up and wondering how far he could go with me. The thing fairly got on my nerves, and to crown all it was abominably stuffy. The windows of the room gave on a little paved court with a background of laurels, and I might have been in Seven Dials for all the air there was.

When coffee was served I could stand it no longer. 'What about smoking in the temple?' I said. 'It should be cool there with the air from the lake.'

I might have been proposing the assassination of his mother. He simply gibbered at me. 'No, no,' he stammered. 'My God, no!' It was half an hour before he could properly collect himself. A servant lit two oil lamps, and we sat on in the frowsty room.

'You said something when we last met,' he ventured at last, after many a sidelong glance at me. 'Something about a ritual for re-dedicating an altar.'

I remembered my remark about Sidonius Apollinaris.

'Could you show me the passage? There is a good classical library here, collected by my great-grandfather. Unfortunately my scholar-ship is not equal to using it properly.'

I got up and hunted along the shelves, and presently found a copy of Sidonius, the Plantin edition of 1609. I turned up the passage, and roughly translated it for him. He listened hungrily and made me repeat it twice.

'He says a cock,' he hesitated. 'Is that essential?'

'I don't think so. I fancy any of the recognised ritual stuff would do.'

'I am glad,' he said simply. 'I am afraid of blood.'

'Good God, man,' I cried out, 'are you taking my nonsense seriously? I was only chaffing. Let old Vaunus stick to his altar!'

He looked at me like a puzzled and rather offended dog.

'Sidonius was in earnest ...'

'Well, I'm not,' I said rudely. 'We're in the twentieth century and not in the third. Isn't it about time we went to bed?'

He made no objection, and found me a candle in the hall. As I undressed I wondered into what kind of lunatic asylum I had strayed. I felt the strongest distaste for the place, and longed to go straight off to the inn; only I couldn't make use of a man's manuscripts and insult his hospitality. It was fairly clear to me that Dubellay was mad. He had ridden his hobby to the death of his wits and was now in its bondage. Good Lord! he had talked of his precious Vaunus as a votary talks of a god. I believed he had come to worship some figment of his half-educated fancy.

I think I must have slept for a couple of hours. Then I woke dripping with perspiration, for the place was simply an oven. My window was as wide open as it would go, and, though it was a warm night, when I stuck my head out the air was fresh. The heat came from indoors. The room was on the first floor near the entrance and I was looking on to the overgrown lawns. The night was very dark and utterly still, but I could have sworn that I heard wind. The trees were as motionless as marble, but somewhere close at hand I heard a strong gust blowing. Also, though there was no moon, there was somewhere near me a steady glow of light; I could see the reflection of it round the end of the house. That meant that it came from the temple. What kind of saturnalia was Dubellay conducting at such an hour?

When I drew in my head I felt that if I was to get any sleep something must be done. There could be no question about it; some fool had turned on the steam heat, for the room was a furnace. My temper was rising. There was no bell to be found, so I lit my candle and set out to find a servant.

[192]

I tried a cast downstairs and discovered the room where we had dined. Then I explored a passage at right angles, which brought me up against a great oak door. The light showed me that it was a new door, and that there was no apparent way of opening it. I guessed that it led into the temple, and, though it fitted close and there seemed to be no keyhole, I could hear through it a sound like a rushing wind . . . Next I opened a door on my right and found myself in a big store cupboard. It had a funny, exotic, spicy smell, and, arranged very neatly on the floor and shelves, was a number of small sacks and coffers. Each bore a label, a square of stout paper with very black lettering. I read '*Pro servitio Vauni*'.

I had seen them before, for my memory betrayed me if they were not the very labels that Dubellay's servants had been attaching to the packages from the carrier's cart that evening in the past autumn. The discovery made my suspicions an unpleasant certainty. Dubellay evidently meant the labels to read 'For the service of Vaunus'. He was no scholar, for it was an impossible use of the word 'servitium', but he was very patently a madman.

However, it was my immediate business to find some way to sleep, so I continued my quest for a servant. I followed another corridor, and discovered a second staircase. At the top of it I saw an open door and looked in. It must have been Dubellay's, for his flannels were tumbled untidily on a chair, but Dubellay himself was not there and the bed had not been slept in.

I suppose my irritation was greater than my alarm – though I must say I was getting a little scared – for I still pursued the evasive servant. There was another stair which apparently led to attics, and in going up it I slipped and made a great clatter. When I looked up the butler in his nightgown was staring down at me, and if ever a mortal face held fear it was his. When he saw who it was he seemed to recover a little.

'Look here,' I said, 'for God's sake turn off that infernal hot air. I can't get a wink of sleep. What idiot set it going?'

He looked at me owlishly, but he managed to find his tongue.

'I beg your pardon, sir,' he said, 'but there is no heating apparatus in this house.'

There was nothing more to be said. I returned to my bedroom and it seemed to me that it had grown cooler. As I leaned out of the window, too, the mysterious wind seemed to have died away, and the glow no longer showed from beyond the corner of the house. I got into bed and slept heavily till I was roused by the appearance of my shaving water about half-past nine. There was no bathroom, so I bathed in a tin pannikin.

It was a hazy morning which promised a day of blistering heat. When I went down to breakfast I found Dubellay in the dining-room. In the daylight he looked a very sick man, but he seemed to have taken a pull on himself, for his manner was considerably less nervy than the night before. Indeed, he appeared almost normal, and I might have reconsidered my view but for the look in his eyes.

I told him that I proposed to sit tight all day over the manuscript, and get the thing finished. He nodded. 'That's all right. I've a lot to do myself, and I won't disturb you.'

'But first,' I said, 'you promised to show me your discoveries.'

He looked at the window where the sun was shining on the laurels and on a segment of the paved court.

'The light is good,' he said – an odd remark. 'Let us go there now. There are times and seasons for the temple.'

He led me down the passage I had explored the previous night. The door opened not by a key but by some lever in the wall. I found myself looking suddenly at a bath of sunshine with the lake below as blue as a turquoise.

It is not easy to describe my impressions of that place. It was unbelievably light and airy, as brilliant as an Indian colonnade in midsummer. The proportions must have been good, for the columns soared and swam, and the roof (which looked like cedar) floated as delicately as a flower on its stalk. The stone was some local limestone, which on the floor took a polish like marble. All around was a vista of sparkling water and summer woods and far blue mountains. It should have been as wholesome as the top of a hill.

And yet I had scarcely entered before I knew that it was a prison. I am not an imaginative man, and I believe my nerves are fairly good, but I could scarcely put one foot before the other, so strong was my distaste. I felt shut off from the world, as if I were in a dungeon or on an ice-floe. And I felt, too, that though far enough from humanity, we were not alone.

On the inner wall there were three carvings. Two were imperfect friezes sculptured in low-relief, dealing apparently with the same subject. It was a ritual procession, priests bearing branches, the ordinary *dendrophori* business. The faces were only half-human, and that was from no lack of skill, for the artist had been a master. The striking thing was that the branches and the hair of the hierophants were being tossed by a violent wind, and the expression of each was of a being in the last stage of endurance, shaken to the core by terror and pain.

Between the friezes was a great roundel of a Gorgon's head. It was not a female head, such as you commonly find, but a male head, with the viperous hair sprouting from chin and lip. It had once been coloured, and fragments of a green pigment remained in the locks. It was an awful thing, the ultimate horror of fear, the last dementia of cruelty made manifest in stone. I hurriedly averted my eyes and looked at the altar.

That stood at the west end on a pediment with three steps. It was a beautiful piece of work, scarcely harmed by the centuries, with two words inscribed on its face – APOLL. VAUN. It was made of some foreign marble, and the hollow top was dark with ancient sacrifices. Not so ancient either, for I could have sworn that I saw there the mark of recent flame.

I do not suppose I was more than five minutes in the place. I wanted to get out, and Dubellay wanted to get me out. We did not speak a word till we were back in the library.

'For God's sake give it up!' I said. 'You're playing with fire, Mr Dubellay. You're driving yourself into Bedlam. Send these damned things to a museum and leave this place. Now, now, I tell you. You have no time to lose. Come down with me to the inn straight off and shut up this house.'

He looked at me with his lip quivering like a child about to cry.

'I will. I promise you I will... But not yet... After tonight.... Tomorrow I'll do whatever you tell me... You won't leave me?'

'I won't leave you, but what earthly good am I to you if you won't take my advice?'

'Sidonius ...' he began.

'Oh, damn Sidonius! I wish I had never mentioned him. The whole thing is arrant nonsense, but it's killing you. You've got it on the brain. Don't you know you're a sick man?'

'I'm not feeling very grand. It's so warm today. I think I'll lie down.'

It was no good arguing with him, for he had the appalling obstinacy of very weak things. I went off to my work in a shocking bad temper.

The day was what it had promised to be, blisteringly hot. Before midday the sun was hidden by a coppery haze, and there was not the faintest stirring of wind. Dubellay did not appear at luncheon – it was not a meal he ever ate, the butler told me. I slogged away all the afternoon, and had pretty well finished my job by six o'clock. That would enable me to leave next morning, and I hoped to be able to persuade my host to come with me.

The conclusion of my task put me into a better humour, and I went for a walk before dinner. It was a very close evening, for the heat haze had not lifted; the woods were as silent as a grave, not a bird spoke, and when I came out of the cover to the burnt pastures the sheep seemed too languid to graze. During my walk I prospected the environs of the house, and saw that it would be very hard to get access to the temple except by a long circuit. On one side was a mass of outbuildings, and then a high wall, and on the other the very closest and highest quickset hedge I have ever seen, which ended in a wood with savage spikes on its containing wall. I returned to my room, had a cold bath in the exiguous tub, and changed.

Dubellay was not at dinner. The butler said that his master was feeling unwell and had gone to bed. The news pleased me, for bed was the best place for him. After that I settled myself down to a lonely evening in the library. I browsed among the shelves and found a number of rare editions which served to pass the time. I noticed that the copy of Sidonius was absent from its place.

I think it was about ten o'clock when I went to bed, for I was unaccountably tired. I remember wondering whether I oughtn't to go and visit Dubellay, but decided that it was better to leave him alone. I still reproach myself for that decision. I know now I ought to have taken him by force and haled him to the inn.

Suddenly I came out of heavy sleep with a start. A human cry seemed to be ringing in the corridors of my brain. I held my breath and listened. It came again, a horrid scream of panic and torture.

I was out of bed in a second, and only stopped to get my feet into slippers. The cry must have come from the temple. I tore downstairs expecting to hear the noise of an alarmed household. But there was no sound, and the awful cry was not repeated.

The door in the corridor was shut, as I expected. Behind it pandemonium seemed to be loose, for there was a howling like a tempest – and something more, a crackling like fire. I made for the front door, slipped off the chain, and found myself in the still, moonless night. Still, except for the rending gale that seemed to be raging in the house I had left.

From what I had seen on my evening's walk I knew that my one chance to get to the temple was by way of the quickset hedge. I thought I might manage to force a way between the end of it and the wall. I did it, at the cost of much of my raiment and my skin. Beyond was another rough lawn set with tangled shrubberies, and then a precipitous slope to the level of the lake. I scrambled along the sedgy margin, not daring to lift my eyes till I was on the temple steps.

The place was brighter than day with a roaring blast of fire. The very air seemed to be incandescent and to have become a flaming ether. And yet there were no flames – only a burning brightness. I could not enter, for the waft from it struck my face like a scorching hand and I felt my hair singe . . .

I am short-sighted, as you know, and I may have been mistaken, but this is what I think I saw. From the altar a great tongue of flame seemed to shoot upwards and lick the roof, and from its pediment ran flaming streams. In front of it lay a body – Dubellay's – a naked body, already charred and black. There was nothing else, except that the Gorgon's head in the wall seemed to glow like a sun in hell.

I suppose I must have tried to enter. All I know is that I found myself staggering back, rather badly burned. I covered my eyes, and as I looked through my fingers I seemed to see the flames flowing under the wall, where there may have been lockers, or possibly another entrance. Then the great oak door suddenly shrivelled like gauze, and with a roar the fiery river poured into the house.

I ducked myself in the lake to ease the pain, and then ran back as hard as I could by the way I had come. Dubellay, poor devil, was beyond my aid. After that I am not very clear what happened. I know that the house burned like a haystack. I found one of the men-servants on the lawn, and I think I helped to get the other down from his room by one of the rainpipes. By the time the neighbours arrived the house was ashes, and I was pretty well mother-naked. They took me to the inn and put me to bed, and I remained there till after the inquest. The coroner's jury were puzzled, but they found it simply death by mis-adventure; a lot of country houses were burned that summer. There was nothing found of Dubellay; nothing remained of the house except a few blackened pillars; the altar and the sculptures were so cracked and scarred that no museum wanted them. The place has not been rebuilt, and for all I know they are there today. I am not going back to look for them.

Nightingale finished his story and looked round his audience.

'Don't ask me for an explanation,' he said, 'for I haven't any. You may believe if you like that the god Vaunus inhabited the temple which Dubellay built for him, and, when his votary grew scared and tried Sidonius's receipt for shifting the dedication, became angry and slew him with his flaming wind. That wind seems to have been a perquisite of Vaunus. We know more about him now, for last year they dug up a temple of his in Wales.'

'Lightning,' some one suggested.

'It was a quiet night, with no thunderstorm,' said Nightingale.

'Isn't the countryside volcanic?' Peckwether asked. 'What about pockets of natural gas or something of the kind?'

'Possibly. You may please yourself in your explanation. I'm afraid I can't help you. All I know is that I don't propose to visit that valley again!'

'What became of your Theocritus?'

'Burned, like everything else. However, that didn't worry me much. Six weeks later came the war, and I had other things to think about.'

The Frying-pan and the Fire

Originally published as 'Human Quarry' in the April 1928 issue of *Pall Mall Magazine*, 'The Frying-pan and the Fire' was included as The Duke of Burminster's story in *The Runagates Club* (1928) and in a 1934 anthology, *Modern Stories*. It reintroduces the character Tommy Deloraine from *The Power House* (1916).

From the Bath, in its most exotic form, degenerate patrician youth passed to the coarse delights of the Circus, and thence to that parody of public duties which it was still the fashion of their class to patronise.

VON LETTERBECK: Imperial Rome

Part I
The Frying-pan

LAMANCHA HAD BEEN staying for the week-end at some country house, and had returned full of wrath at the way he had been made to spend his evenings. 'I thought I hated bridge,' he said, 'but I almost longed for it as a change from cracking my brain and my memory to find lines from poets I had forgotten to describe people I didn't know. I don't like games that make me feel a congenital idiot. But there was one that rather amused me. You invented a preposterous situation and the point was to explain naturally how it came about. Drink, lunacy and practical joking were barred as explanations. One problem given was the Bishop of London on a camel, with a string of sea-trout round his neck, playing on a penny whistle on the Hoe at Plymouth. There was a fellow there, a Chancery K.C., who provided a perfectly sensible explanation.'

'I have heard of stranger things,' said Sandy Arbuthnot, and he winked at Burminster, who flushed and looked uncomfortable. As the rest of our eyes took the same direction the flush deepened on that round cheerful face.

'It's no good, Mike,' said Arbuthnot. 'We've been waiting months for that story of yours, and this is the place and the hour for it. We'll take no denial.'

'Confound you, Sandy, I can't tell it. It's too dashed silly.'

'Not a bit of it. It's full of profound philosophical lessons, and it's sheer romance, as somebody has defined the thing – strangeness flowering from the commonplace. So pull up your socks and get going.'

'I don't know how to begin,' said Burminster.

'Well, I'll start it for you ... The scene is the railway station of Langshiels on the Scottish Borders on a certain day last summer. On the platform are various gentlemen in their best clothes with rosettes in their buttonholes – all strictly sober, it being but the third hour of the afternoon. There are also the rudiments of a brass band. Clearly a distinguished visitor is expected. The train enters the station, and from a third-class carriage descends our only Mike with a muddy face and a scratched nose. He is habited in dirty white cord breeches, shocking old butcher boots, a purple knitted waistcoat, and what I believe is called a morning coat; over all this splendour a ticky ulster – clearly not his own since it does not meet – and on his head an unspeakable bowler hat. He is welcomed by the deputation and departs, attended by the band, to a political meeting in the Town Hall. But first – I quote from the local paper – 'The Duke, who had arrived in sporting costume, proceeded to the Station Hotel, where he rapidly changed.' We want to know the reason of these cantrips.'

Burminster took a long pull at his tankard, and looked round the company with more composure.

'It isn't much of a story, but it's true, and, like nearly every scrape I ever got into, Archie Roylance was at the bottom of it. It all started from a discussion I had with Archie. He was staying with me at Larristane, and we got talking about the old Border raiders and the way the face of the countryside had changed and that sort of thing. Archie said that, now the land was as bare as a marble-topped table and there was no cover on the hills to hide a tomtit, a man couldn't ride five miles anywhere between the Cheviots and the Clyde without being seen by a dozen people. I said that there was still plenty of cover if you knew how to use it – that you could hide yourself as well on bent and heather as in a thick wood if you studied the shadows and the lie of the land, same as an aeroplane can hide itself in an empty sky. Well, we argued and argued, and the upshot was that I backed myself to ride an agreed course, without Archie spotting me. There wasn't much money on it – only an even sovereign – but we both worked ourselves up into considerable keenness. That was where I fell down. I might have known that anything Archie was keen about would end in the soup.

'The course we fixed was about fifteen miles long, from Gledfoot bridge over the hills between Gled and Aller and the Blae Moor to the Mains of Blae. That was close to Kirk Aller, and we agreed, if we didn't meet before, to foregather at the Cross Keys and have tea and motor home. Archie was to start from a point about four miles north-east of Gledfoot and cut in on my road at a tangent. I could shape any course I liked, but I couldn't win unless I got to the Mains of Blae before five o'clock without being spotted. The rule about that was that he must get within speaking distance of me – say three hundred yards – before he held me up. All the Larristane horses were at grass, so we couldn't look for pace. I chose an old hunter of mine that was very leery about bogs; Archie picked a young mare that I had hunted the season before and that he had wanted to buy from me. He said that by rights he ought to have the speedier steed, since, if he spotted me, he had more or less to ride me down.

'We thought it was only a pleasant summer day's diversion. I didn't want to give more than a day to it, for I had guests arriving that evening, and on the Wednesday – this was a Monday – I had to take the chair for Deloraine at a big Conservative meeting at Langshiels, and I meant to give a lot of time to preparing a speech. I ought to say that neither of us knew the bit of country beyond its general lines, and we were forbidden to carry maps. The horses were sent on, and at 9.30 A.M. I was at Gledfoot bridge ready to start. I was wearing khaki riding breeches, polo boots, an old shooting coat and a pretty old felt hat. I mention my costume, for later it became important.

'I may as well finish with Archie, for he doesn't come any more into this tale. He hadn't been half an hour in the saddle when he wandered into a bog, and it took him till three in the afternoon to get his horse out. Consequently he chucked in his hand, and went back to Larristane. So all the time I was riding cunning and watching out of my right eye to see him on the skyline he was sweating and blaspheming in a peat moss.

'I started from Gledfoot up the Rinks burn in very good spirits, for I had been studying the big Ordnance map and I believed I had a soft thing. Beyond the Rinks Hope I would cross the ridge to the top of the Skyre burn, which at its head is all split up into deep grassy gullies. I had guessed this from the map, and the people at Gledfoot had confirmed it. By one or other of these gullies I could ride in good cover till I reached a big wood of firs that stretched for a mile down the left bank of the burn. Archie, to cut in on me, had a pretty steep hill to cross, and I calculated that by the time he got on the skyline I would be in the shelter of one of the gullies or even behind the wood. Not seeing me on the upper Skyre, he would think that I had bustled a bit and would look for me lower down the glen. I would lie doggo and watch for him, and when I saw him properly started I meant to slip up a side burn and get into the parallel glen of the Hollin. Once there I would ride like blazes, and either get to the Blae Moor before him – in which case I would simply canter at ease up to the Mains of Blae – or, if I saw him ahead of me, fetch a circuit among the plantings and come in on the farm from the other side. That was the general layout, but I had other dodges in hand in case Archie tried to be clever.

'So I tittuped along the hill turf beside the Rinks burn, feeling happy and pretty certain I would win. My horse, considering he was fresh from the grass, behaved very well, and we travelled in good style. My head was full of what I was going to say at Langshiels, and I thought of some rather fine things – "Our opponents would wreck the old world in order to build a new, but you cannot found any system on chaos, not even Communism" – I rather fancied that. Well, to make a long story short, I got to the Rinks Hope in thirty minutes, and there I found the herd gathering his black-faced lambs.

'Curiously enough I knew the man – Prentice they called him – for he had been one of the young shepherds at Larristane. So I stopped to have a word with him, and watched him at work. He was short-handed for the job, and he had a young collie only half-trained, so I offered to give him a hand and show my form as a mounted stockman. The top of that glen was splendid going, and I volunteered to round up the west hirsel. I considered that I had plenty of time and could spare ten minutes to help a pal.

'It was a dashed difficult job, and it took me a good half-hour, and it was a mercy my horse didn't get an over-reach among the mossy well-heads. However, I did it, and when I started off again both I and my beast were in a lather of sweat. That must have confused me, and the way I had been making circles round the sheep, for I struck the wrong feeder, and instead of following the one that led to the top of the Skyre burn I kept too much to my left. When I got to the watershed I looked down on a country utterly different from what I had expected. There was no delta of deep gullies, but a broad green cup seamed with stone walls, and below it a short glen which presently ran out into the broader vale of the Aller.

'The visibility was none too good, so I could not make out the further prospect. I ought to have realised that this was not the Skyre burn. But I only concluded that I had misread the map, and besides, there was a big wood lower down which I thought was the one I had remarked. There was no sign of Archie as yet on the high hills to my right, so I decided I had better get off the skyline and make my best speed across that bare green cup.

'It took me a long time, for I had a lot of trouble with the stone dykes. The few gates were all fastened up with wire, and I couldn't manage to undo them. So I had to scramble over the first dyke, and half pull down the next, and what with one thing and another I wasted a shocking amount of time. When I got to the bottom I found that the burn was the merest trickle, not the strong stream of the Skyre, which is a famous water for trout. But there, just ahead of me, was the big wood, so I decided I must be right after all.

'I had kept my eye lifting to the ridge on the right, and suddenly I saw Archie. I know now that it wasn't he, but it was a man on a horse and it looked his living image. He was well down the hillside and he was moving fast. He didn't appear to have seen me, but I realised that he would in a minute, unless I found cover.

'I jogged my beast with the spur, and in three seconds was under cover of the fir-wood. But here I found a track, and it struck me that it was this track which Archie was following, and that he would soon be up with me. The only thing to do seemed to be to get inside the wood. But this was easier said than done, for a great wall with broken bottles on the top ran round that blessed place. I had to do something pretty quick, for I could hear the sound of hoofs behind me, and on the left there was nothing but the benty side of a hill.

'Just then I saw a gate, a massive thing of close-set oak splints, and for a mercy it was open. I pushed through it and slammed it behind me. It shut with a sharp click as if it was a patent self-locking arrangement. A second later I heard the noise of a horse outside and hands trying the gate. Plainly they couldn't open it. The man I thought was Archie said "Damn" and moved away.

'I had found sanctuary, but the question now was how to get out of it. I dismounted and wrestled with the gate, but it was as firm as a rock. About this time I began to realise that something was wrong, for I couldn't think why Archie should have wanted to get through the gate if he hadn't seen me, and, if he had seen me, why he hadn't shouted, according to our rules. Besides, this wasn't a wood, it was the grounds of some house, and the map had shown no house in the Skyre glen . . . The only thing to do was to find someone to let me out. I didn't like the notion of riding about in a stranger's policies, so I knotted my bridle and let my beast graze, while I proceeded on foot to prospect.

'The ground shelved steeply, and almost at once my feet went from under me and I slithered down a bank of raw earth. You see there was no grip in the smooth soles of my polo boots. The next I knew I had banged hard into the back of a little wooden shelter which stood on a sunny mantelpiece of turf above the stream. I picked myself up and limped round the erection, rubbing the dirt from my eyes, and came face to face with a group of people.

'They were all women, except one man, who was reading aloud to them, and they were all lying in long chairs. Pretty girls they seemed to be from the glimpse I had of them, but rather pale, and they all wore bright-coloured cloaks.

'I daresay I looked a bit of a ruffian, for I was very warm and had got rather dirty in slithering down, and had a rent in my breeches. At the sight of me the women gave one collective bleat like a snipe, and gathered up their skirts and ran. I could see their cloaks glimmering as they dodged like woodcock among the rhododendrons.

'The man dropped his book and got up and faced me. He was a young fellow with a cadaverous face and side-whiskers, and he seemed to be in a funk of something, for his lips twitched and his hands shook as if he had fever. I could see that he was struggling to keep calm.

'"So you've come back, Mr Brumby," he said. "I hope you had a g-good time?"

'For a moment I had a horrid suspicion that he knew me, for they used to call me "Brummy" at school. A second look convinced me that we had never met, and I realised that the word he had used was

Brumby. I hadn't a notion what he meant, but the only thing seemed to be to brazen it out. That was where I played the fool. I ought to have explained my mistake there and then, but I still had the notion that Archie was hanging about, and I wanted to dodge him. I dropped into a long chair, and said that I had come back and that it was a pleasant day. Then I got out my pipe.

'"Here, you mustn't do that," he said. "It isn't allowed."

'I put my pipe away, and wondered what lunatic asylum I had wandered into. I wasn't permitted to wonder long, for up the path from the rhododendrons came two people in a mighty hurry. One was an anxious-faced oldish man dressed like a valet, and the other a middle-aged woman in nurse's uniform. Both seemed to be excited, and both to be trying to preserve an air of coolness.

'"Ah, Schwester," said the fellow with the whiskers. "Here is Mr Brumby back again and none the worse."

'The woman, who had kind eyes and a nice gurgling voice, looked at me reproachfully.

'"I hope you haven't taken any harm, sir," she said. "We had better go back to the house, and Mr Grimpus will give you a nice bath and a change, and you'll lie down a bit before luncheon. You must be very tired, sir. You'd better take Mr Grimpus's arm."

'My head seemed to be spinning, but I thought it best to lie low and do what I was told till I got some light. Silly ass that I was, I was still on the tack of dodging Archie. I could easily have floored Grimpus, and the man with the whiskers wouldn't have troubled me much, but there was still the glass-topped wall to get over, and there might be heftier people about, grooms and gardeners and the like. Above all, I didn't want to make any more scenes, for I had already scared a lot of sick ladies into the rhododendrons.

'So I went off quite peaceably with Grimpus and the sister, and presently we came to a house like a small hydropathic, hideously ugly but beautifully placed, with a view south to the Aller Valley. There were more nurses in the hall and a porter with a jaw like a prize-fighter. Well, I went up in a lift to the second floor, and there was a bedroom and a balcony, and several trunks, and brushes on the dressing-table lettered H.B. They made me strip and get into a dressing-gown, and then a doctor arrived, a grim fellow with gold spectacles and a soft, bedside manner. He spoke to me soothingly about the beauty of the weather and how the heather would soon be in bloom on the hill; he also felt my pulse and took my blood pressure, and talked for a long time in a corner with the sister. If he said there was anything wrong with me he lied, for I had never felt fitter in my life except for the bewilderment of my brain.

'Then I was taken down in a lift to the basement, and Grimpus started out to give me a bath. My hat! That was a bath! I lay in six inches of scalding water, while a boiling cataract beat on my stomach; then it changed to hot hail and then to gouts that hit like a pickaxe; and then it all turned to ice. But it made me feel uncommonly frisky. After that they took me back to my bedroom and I had a gruelling massage, and what I believe they call violet rays. By this time I was fairly bursting with vim, but I thought it best to be quite passive, and when they told me I must try to sleep before luncheon, I only grinned and put my head on the pillow like a child. When they left me I badly wanted to smoke, but my pipe had gone with my clothes, and I found laid out for me a complete suit of the man Brumby's flannels.

'As I lay and reflected I began to get my bearings. I knew where I was. It was a place called Craigiedean, about six miles from Kirk Aller, which had been used as a shell-shock hospital during the war and had been kept on as a home for nervous cases. It wasn't a private asylum, as I had thought at first; it called itself a Kurhaus, and was supposed to be the last thing in science outside Germany. Now and then, however, it got some baddish cases, people who were almost off their rocker, and I fancied that Brumby was one. He was apparently my double, but I didn't believe in exact doubles, so I guessed that he had just arrived, and hadn't given the staff time to know him well before he went off on the bend. The horseman whom I had taken for Archie must have been out scouring the hills for him.

'Well, I had dished Archie all right, but I had also dished myself. At any moment the real Brumby might wander back, and then there would be a nice show up. The one thing that terrified me was that my identity should be discovered, for this was more or less my own countryside, and I should look a proper ass if it got about that I had been breaking into a nerve-cure place, frightening women, and getting myself treated like a gentle loony. Then I remembered that my horse was in the wood and might be trusted to keep on grazing along the inside of the wall where nobody went. My best plan seemed to be to wait my chance, slip out of the house, recover my beast and find some way out of the infernal park. The wall couldn't be everywhere, for after all the place wasn't an asylum.

'A gong sounded for luncheon, so I nipped up, and got into Brumby's flannels. They were all right for length, but a bit roomy. My money and the odds and ends from my own pockets were laid out on the dressing-table, but not my pipe and pouch, which I judged had been confiscated.

'I wandered downstairs to a big dining-room, full of little tables, with the most melancholy outfit seated at them that you ever saw in all your days. The usual thing was to have a table to oneself, but sometimes two people shared one – husband and wife, no doubt, or mother and daughter. There were eight males including me, and the rest were females of every age from flappers to grandmothers. Some looked pretty sick, some quite blooming, but all had a watchful air, as if they were holding themselves in and pursuing some strict regime. There was no conversation, and everybody had brought a book or a magazine which they diligently studied. In the centre of each table, beside the salt and pepper, stood a little fleet of medicine bottles. The sister who led me to my place planted down two beside me.

'I soon saw the reason of the literary absorption. The food was simply bestial. I was hungry and thirsty enough to have eaten two beefsteaks and drunk a quart of beer, and all I got was three rusks, a plate of thin soup, a purée of vegetables and a milk pudding in a teacup. I envied the real Brumby, who at that moment, if he had any sense, was doing himself well in a public-house. I didn't dare to ask for more in case of inviting awkward questions, so I had plenty of leisure to observe the company. Nobody looked at anybody else, for it seemed to be the fashion to pretend you were alone in a wilderness, and even the couples did not talk to each other. I made a cautious preliminary survey to see if there was anyone I knew, but they were all strangers. After a time I felt so lonely that I wanted to howl.

'At last the company began to get up and straggle out. The sister whom I had seen first – the others called her Schwester and she seemed to be rather a boss – appeared with a bright smile and gave me my medicine. I had to take two pills and some horrid drops out of a brown bottle. I pretended to be very docile, and I thought that I'd take the chance to pave the way to getting to my horse. So I said that I felt completely rested, and would like a walk that afternoon. She shook her head.

' "No, Mr Brumby. Dr Miggle's orders are positive that you rest today."

' "But I'm feeling really very fit," I protested. "I'm the kind of man who needs a lot of exercise."

' "Not yet," she said with a patient smile. "At present your energy is morbid. It comes from an irregular nervous complex, and we must first cure that before you can lead a normal life. Soon you'll be having nice long walks. You promised your wife, you know, to do everything that you were told, and it was very wrong of you to slip out last night and make us all so anxious. Dr Miggle says that must *never* happen again.' And she wagged a reproving finger.

'So I had a wife to add to my troubles. I began now to be really worried, for not only might Brumby turn up any moment, but his precious spouse, and I didn't see how I was to explain to her what I was doing in her husband's trousers. Also the last sentence disquieted me. Dr Miggle was determined that I should not bolt again, and he looked a resolute lad. That meant that I would be always under observation, and that at night my bedroom door would be locked.

'I made an errand to go up to my room, while Grimpus waited for me in the hall, and had a look at the window. There was a fine thick Virginia creeper which would make it easy to get to the floor beneath, but it was perfectly impossible to reach the ground, for below was a great chasm of a basement. There was nothing doing that way, unless I went through the room beneath, and that meant another outrage and probably an appalling row.

'I felt very dispirited as I descended the stairs, till I saw a woman coming out of that identical room ... Blessed if it wasn't my Aunt Letitia!

'I needn't have been surprised, for she gave herself out as a martyr to nerves, and was always racing about the world looking for a cure. She saw me, took me for Brumby, and hurried away. Evidently Brumby's doings had got about, and there were suspicions of his sanity. The moment was not propitious for following her, since Grimpus was looking at me.'

'I was escorted to the terrace by Grimpus, tucked up in a long chair, and told to stay there and bask in the sun. I must not read, but I could sleep if I liked. I never felt less like slumber, for I was getting to be a very good imitation of a mental case. I must get hold of Aunt Letitia. I could see her in her chair at the other end of the terrace, but if I got up

and went to her she would take me for that loony Brumby and have a
fit.

'I lay cogitating and baking in the sun for about two hours. Then I
observed that sisters were bringing out tea or medicines to some of the
patients and I thought I saw a chance of a move. I called one of them
to me, and in a nice invalidish voice complained that the sun was too
hot for me and that I wanted to be moved to the other end where there
was more shade. The sister went off to find Grimpus and presently
that sportsman appeared.

'"I've had enough of this sun-bath," I told him, "and I feel a
headache coming. I want you to shift me to the shade of the beeches
over there."

'"Very good, sir," he said, and helped me to rise, while he picked
up chair and rugs. I tottered delicately after him, and indicated a
vacant space next to Aunt Letitia. She was dozing, and mercifully did
not see me. The chair on my other side was occupied by an old
gentleman who was sound asleep.

'I waited for a few minutes and began to wriggle my chair a bit
nearer. Then I made a pellet of earth from a crack in the paving stones
and jerked it neatly on to her face.

'"Hist!" I whispered. "Wake up, Aunt Letty."

'She opened one indignant eye, and turned it on me, and I thought
she was going to swoon.

'"Aunt Letty," I said in an agonised voice. "For Heaven's sake don't
shout. I'm not Brumby. I'm your nephew Michael."

'Her nerves were better than I thought, for she managed to take a
pull on herself and listen to me while I muttered my tale. I could see
that she hated the whole affair, and had some kind of grievance
against me for outraging the sanctity of her pet cure. However, after a
bit of parleying, she behaved like a brick.

'"You are the head of our family, Michael," she said, "and I am
bound to help you out of the position in which your own rashness has
placed you. I agree with you that it is essential to have no disclosure of
identity. It is the custom here for patients to retire to their rooms at
eight-thirty. At nine o'clock I shall have my window open, and if you
enter by it you can leave by the door. That is the most I can do for you.
Now please be silent, for I am ordered to be very still for an hour
before tea."

'You can imagine that after that the time went slowly. Grimpus brought me a cup of tea and a rusk, and I fell asleep and only woke when he came at half-past six to escort me indoors. I would have given pounds for a pipe. Dinner was at seven, and I said that I would not trouble to change, though Brumby's dress-clothes were laid out on the bed. I had the needle badly, for I had a horrid fear that Brumby might turn up before I got away.

'Presently the doctor arrived, and after cooing over me a bit and feeling my pulse, he started out to cross-examine me about my past life. I suppose that was to find out the subconscious complexes which were upsetting my wits. I decided to go jolly carefully, for I suspected that he had either given Brumby the once-over or had got some sort of report about his case. I was right, for the first thing he asked me was about striking my sister at the age of five. Well, I haven't got a sister, but I had to admit to beating Brumby's, and I said the horrible affair still came between me and my sleep. That seemed to puzzle him, for apparently I oughtn't to have been thinking about it; it should have been buried deep in my unconscious self, and worrying me like a thorn in your finger which you can't find. He asked me a lot about my nurse, and I said that she had a brother who went to gaol for sheep stealing. He liked that, and said it was a fruitful line of inquiry. Also he wanted to know about my dreams, and said I should write them down. I said I had dreamed that a mare called Nursemaid won the Oaks, but found there was no such animal running. That cheered him up a bit, and he said that he thought my nurse might be the clue. At that I very nearly gave the show away by laughing, for my nurse was old Alison Hyslop, who is now the housekeeper at Larristane, and if anybody called her a clue she'd have their blood.

'Dinner was no better than luncheon – the same soup and rusks and vegetables, with a bit of ill-nourished chicken added. This time I had to take three kinds of medicine instead of two. I told the sister that I was very tired, and Grimpus took me upstairs at eight o'clock. He said that Dr Miggle proposed to give me another go of violet rays, but I protested so strongly that I was too sleepy for his ministrations that Grimpus, after going off to consult him, announced that for that evening the rays would be omitted. You see I was afraid that they would put me to bed and remove my clothes, and I didn't see myself trapesing about the country in Brumby's pyjamas.

'As Grimpus left me I heard the key turn in the lock. It was as well that I had made a plan with Aunt Letitia.

'At nine o'clock I got out of my window. It was a fine night, with the sun just setting and a young moon. The Virginia creeper was sound, and in less than a minute I was outside Aunt Letitia's window. She was waiting in a dressing-gown to let me in, and I believe the old soul really enjoyed the escapade. She wanted to give me money for my travels, but I told her that I had plenty. I poked my nose out, saw that the staircase and hall were empty, and quietly closed the door behind me.

'The big hall door was shut, and I could hear the prize-fighting porter moving in his adjacent cubby hole. There was no road that way, so I turned to the drawing-room, which opened on the terrace. But that was all in darkness, and I guessed that the windows were shuttered. There was nothing for it but to try downstairs. I judged that the servants would be at supper, so I went through a green-baize swing-door and down a long flight of stone steps.

'Suddenly I blundered into a brightly lit kitchen. There was no one in it, and beyond was a door which looked as if it might lead to the open air. It actually led to a scullery, where a maid was busy at a tap. She was singing to herself a song called "When the kye come hame", so I knew she belonged to the countryside. So did I, and I resolved to play the bold game.

' "Hey, lassie," I said. "Whaur's the road out o' this hoose? I maun be back in Kirk Aller afore ten."

'The girl stopped her singing and stared at me. Then in response to my grin she laughed.

' "Are ye frae Kirk Aller?" she asked.

' "I've gotten a job there," I said. "I'm in the Cally station, and I cam' up about a parcel for ane o' the leddies here. But I come frae further up the water, Larristane way."

' "D'ye say sae? I'm frae Gledside mysel'. What gars ye be in sic a hurry? It's a fine nicht and there's a mune."

'She was a flirtatious damsel, but I had no time for dalliance.

' "There's a lassie in Kirk Aller will take the heid off me if I keep her waitin'."

'She tossed her head and laughed. "Haste ye then, my mannie. Is it Shanks' powny?"

' "Na, na, I've a bicycle ootbye."

' "Well, through the wash-hoose and up the steps and roond by the roddydendrums and ye're in the yaird. Guid nicht to ye."

[211]

'I went up the steps like a lamplighter and dived into the rhodo-dendrons, coming out on the main avenue. It ran long and straight to the lodge gates, and I didn't like the look of it. My first business was to find my horse, and I had thought out more or less the direction. The house stood on the right bank of the burn, and if I kept to my left I would cross the said burn lower down and could then walk up the other side. I did this without trouble. I forded the burn in the meadow, and was soon climbing the pine-wood which clothed the gorge. In less than twenty minutes I had reached the gate in the wall by which I had entered.

'There was no sign of my horse anywhere. I followed the wall on my left till it curved round and crossed the burn, but the beast was not there, and it was too dark to look for hoof-marks. I tried to my right and got back to the level of the park, but had no better luck. If I had had any sense I would have given up the quest, and trusted to getting as far as Gledsfoot on my own feet. The horse might be trusted to turn up in his own time. Instead I went blundering on in the half-light of the park, and presently blundered into trouble.

'Grimpus must have paid another visit to my room, found me gone, seen the open window, and started a hue-and-cry. They would not suspect my Aunt Letitia, and must have thought that I had dropped like a cat into the basement. The pursuit was coming down the avenue, thinking I had made for the lodge gates, and as ill-luck would have it, I had selected that moment to cross the drive, and they spotted me. I remember that out of a corner of one eye I saw the lights of a fly coming up the drive, and I wondered if Brumby had selected this inauspicious moment to return.

'I fled into the park with three fellows after me. Providence never meant me for a long-distance runner, and, besides, I was feeling weak from lack of nourishment. But I was so scared of what would happen if I was caught that I legged it like a miler, and the blighters certainly didn't gain on me.

'But what I came to was the same weary old wall with the bottle glass on the top of it. I was pretty desperate, and I thought I saw a way. A young horse-chestnut tree grew near the wall and one bough overhung it. I made a jump at the first branch, caught it, and with a bit of trouble swung myself up into the crutch. This took time, and one of the fellows came up and made a grab at my leg, but I let him have Brumby's rubber-soled heel in the jaw.

'I caught the bigger branch and wriggled along it till I was above and beyond the wall. Then the dashed thing broke with my twelve stone, and I descended on what looked like a highroad.

'There was no time to spare, though I was a bit shaken, for the pursuit would not take long to follow me. I started off down that road looking for shelter, and I found it almost at once. There was a big covered horse-van moving ahead of me, with a light showing from the interior. I sprinted after it, mounted the step and stuck my head inside.

' "Can I come in?" I panted. "Hide me for ten minutes and I'll explain."

'I saw an old, spectacled, whiskered face. It was portentously solemn, but I thought I saw a twinkle in the eye.

' "Ay," said a toothless mouth, "ye can come in." A hand grabbed my collar, and I was hauled inside. That must have been just when the first of my pursuers dropped over the wall.'

Part II
The Fire

'I had got into a caravan which was a sort of bedroom, and behind the driver's seat was a double curtain. There I made myself inconspicuous while the old man parleyed with the pursuit.

' "Hae ye seen a gentleman?" I could hear a panting voice. "Him that drappit ower the wa'? He was rinnin' hard."

' "What kind of a gentleman?"

' "He had on grey claithes – aboot the same height as mysel'." The speaker was not Grimpus.

' "Naebody passed me," was the strictly truthful answer. "Ye'd better seek the ither side o' the road among the bracken. There's plenty hidy-holes there. Wha's the man?"

' "Ane o' the doctor's folk." I knew, though I could not see, that the man had tapped his forehead significantly. "Aweel, I'll try back. Guid nicht to ye."

'I crept out of my refuge and found the old man regarding me solemnly under the swinging lamp.

' "I'm one of the auld-fashioned Radicals," he announced, "and I'm for the liberty o' the individual. I dinna hold wi' lockin' folks up because a pernicketty doctor says they're no wise. But I'd be glad to be assured, sir, that ye're not a dangerous lunattic. If ye are, Miggle has nae business to be workin' wi' lunattics. His hoose is no an asylum."

'"I'm as sane as you are," I said, and as shortly as I could I told him my story. I said I was a laird on Gledwater-side – which was true, and that my name was Brown – which wasn't. I told him about my bet with Archie and my ride and its disastrous ending. His face never moved a muscle; probably he didn't believe me, but because of his political principles he wasn't going to give me away.

'"Ye can bide the night with me," he said. "The morn we'll be busy and ye can gang wherever ye like. It's a free country in spite o' our God-forsaken Government."

'I blessed him, and asked to whom I was indebted for this hospitality.

'"I'm the Great McGowan," he said. "The feck o' the pawraphernalia is on ahead. We open the morn in Kirk Aller."

'He had spoken his name as if it were Mussolini or Dempsey, one which all the world should know. I knew it too, for it had been familiar to me from childhood. You could have seen it any time in the last twenty years flaming upon hoardings up and down the Lowlands – The Great McGowan's Marvellous Multitudinous Menagerie – McGowan's Colossal Circassian Circus – The Only Original McGowan.

'We rumbled on for another half-mile, and then turned from the road into a field. As we bumped over the grass I looked out of the door and saw about twenty big caravans and wagons at anchor. There was a strong smell of horses and of cooking food, and above it I seemed to detect the odour of unclean beasts. We took up our station apart from the rest, and after the proprietor had satisfied himself by a brief inspection that the whole outfit was there, he announced that it was time to retire. Mr McGowan had apparently dined, and he did not offer me food, which I would have welcomed, but he mixed me a rummer of hot toddy. I wondered if it would disagree with the various medicines I had been compelled to take, and make me very sick in the night. Then he pointed out my bunk, undressed himself as far as his shirt, pulled a nightcap over his venerable head, and in five minutes was asleep. I had had a wearing day, and in spite of the stuffiness of the place it wasn't long before I dropped off also.

'I awoke next morning to find myself alone in the caravan. I opened the window and saw that a fine old racket was going on. The show had started to move, and as the caravan bumped over the turf various specimens inside were beginning to give tongue. It was going to be a gorgeous day and very hot. I was a little bit anxious about my next move, for Kirk Aller was unpleasantly near Craigiedean and Dr Miggle. In the end I decided that my best plan would be to take the train to Langshiels and there hire a car to Larristane, after sending a telegram to say I was all right, in case my riderless steed should turn up before me. I hadn't any headgear, but I thought I could buy something in Kirk Aller, and trust to luck that nobody from the Kurhaus spotted me in the street. I wanted a bath and a shave and breakfast, but I concluded I had better postpone them till I reached the hotel at Langshiels.

'Presently Mr McGowan appeared, and I could see by his face that something had upset him. He was wearing an old check dressing-gown, and he had been padding about in his bare feet on the dewy grass.

' "Ye telled me a story last night, Mr Brown," he began solemnly, "which I didna altogether believe. I apologise for being a doubting Thomas. I believe every word o't, for I've just had confirmation."

'I mumbled something about being obliged to him, and he went on.

' "Ay, for the pollis were here this morning – seeking you. Yon man at Craigiedean is terrible ill-set against ye, Mr Brown. The pollisman – his name's Tam Doig, I ken him fine – says they're looking for a man that personated an inmate, and went off wi' some o' the inmate's belongings. I'm quotin' Tam Doig. I gave Tam an evasive answer, and he's off on his bicycle the other road, but – I ask ye as a freend, Mr Brown – what is precisely the facts o' the case?"

' "Good God!" I said. "It's perfectly true. These clothes I'm wearing belong to the man Brumby, though they've got my own duds in exchange. He must have come back after I left. What an absolutely infernal mess! I suppose they could have me up for theft."

' "Mair like obtaining goods on false pretences, though I think ye have a sound answer. But that's no the point, Mr Brown. The doctor is set on payin' off scores. Ye've entered his sawnatorium and gone through a' the cantrips he provides, and ye've made a gowk o' him. He wants to make an example o' *you*. Tam Doig was sayin' that he's been bleezin' half the night on the telephone, an' he'll no rest till ye're grippit. Now ye tell me that ye're a laird and a man o' some poseetion, and I believe ye. It wad be an ill job for you and your freends if ye was to appear before the Shirra."

'I did some rapid thinking. So far I was safe, for there was nothing about the clothes I had left behind to identify me. I was pretty certain that my horse had long ago made a bee-line for the Larristane stables. If I could only get home without being detected, I might regard the episode as closed.

' "Supposing I slip off now," I said. "I have a general notion of the land, and I might get over the hills without anybody seeing me."

'He shook his head. "Ye wouldn't travel a mile. Your description has been circulated and a' body's lookin' for ye – a man in a grey flannel suit and soft shoes wi' a red face and nae hat. Guid kens what the doctor has said about ye, but the countryside is on the look-out for a dangerous, and maybe lunattic, criminal. There's a reward offered of nae less than twenty pound."

' "Can you not take me with you to Kirk Aller?" I asked despairingly.

' "Aye, ye can stop wi' me. But what better wad ye be in Kirk Aller? That's where the Procurator Fiscal bides."

'Then he put on his spectacles and looked at me solemnly.

' "I've taken a fancy to ye, Mr Brown, and ye can tell the world that. I ask you, are ye acquaint wi' horses?"

'I answered that I had lived among them all my life, and had been in the cavalry before I went into the Air Force.

' "I guessed it by your face. Horses have a queer trick o' leavin' their mark on a body. Now, because I like ye, I'll make a proposeetion to ye that I would make to no other man ... I'm without a ring-master. Joseph Japp, who for ten years has had the job with me, is lyin' wi' the influenzy at Berwick. I could make shift with Dublin Davie, but Davie has no more presence than a messan dog, and forbye Joseph's clothes wouldna fit him. When I cast my eyes on ye this mornin' after hearin' Tam Doig's news, I says to mysel', 'Thou art the man.' "

'Of course I jumped at the offer. I was as safe in Kirk Aller, as Joseph Japp's understudy, as I was in my own house. Besides, I liked the notion; it would be a good story to tell Archie. But I said it could only be for one night, and that I must leave tomorrow, and he agreed. "I want to make a good show for a start in Kirk Aller – forbye, Joseph will be ready to join me at Langshiels."

'I borrowed the old boy's razor and had a shave and a wash, while

he was cooking breakfast. After we had fed he fetched my pre-
decessor's kit. It fitted me well enough, but Lord! I looked a proper
blackguard. The cord breeches had been recently cleaned, but the
boots were like a pair of dilapidated buckets, and the coat would have
made my tailor weep. Mr McGowan himself put on a frock-coat and a
high collar and spruced himself up till he looked exactly like one of
those high-up Irish dealers you see at the Horse Show – a cross
between a Cabinet Minister and a Methodist parson. He said the ring-
master should ride beside the chief exhibit, so we bustled out and I
climbed up in front of a wagon which bore a cage containing two very
low-spirited lions. I was given a long whip, and told to make myself
conspicuous.

'I didn't know Kirk Aller well, so I had no fear of being recognised
either as myself or as the pseudo-Brumby. The last time I had been
there was when I had motored over from Larristane to dine with the
Aller Shooting Club. My present entry was of a more sensational kind.
I decided to enjoy myself and to attract all the notice I could, and I
certainly succeeded. Indeed, you might say I received an ovation. As it
happened it was a public holiday, and the streets were pretty full. We
rumbled up the cobbled Westgate, and down the long High Street,
with the pavements on both sides lined with people and an attendant
mob of several hundred children. The driver was a wizened little fellow
in a jockey cap, but I was the principal figure on the box. I gave a fine
exhibition with my whip, and when we slowed down I picked out
conspicuous figures in the crowd and chaffed them. I thought I had
better use Cockney patter, as being more in keeping with my job, and
I made a happy blend of the table-talk of my stud-groom and my old
batman in the regiment. It was rather a high-class performance and
you'd be surprised how it went down. There was one young chap with
a tremendous head of hair that I invited to join his friends in the cage,
and just then one of the dejected lions let out a growl, and I said that
Mamma was calling to her little Percy. And there was an old herd
from the hills, who had been looking upon the wine-cup, and who, in
a voice like a fog-horn, wanted to know what we fed the beasts on.
Him I could not refrain from answering in his own tongue. "Braxy,
my man," I cried, "The yowes ye lost when we were fou last Boswell's
Fair." I must have got home somehow, for the crowd roared, and his
friends thumped the old chap on the back and shouted: "That's a guid
ane! He had you there, Tam."

'My triumphant procession came to an end on the Aller Green, where the show was to be held. A canvas palisade had been set up round a big stretch of ground, and the mob of children tailed off at the gate. Inside most of our truck had already arrived. The stadium for the circus had been marked off, and tiers of wooden seats were being hammered together. A big tent had been set up, which was to house the menagerie, and several smaller tents were in process of erection. I noticed that the members of the troupe looked at me curiously till Mr McGowan arrived and introduced me. "This is Mr Brown, a friend of mine," he said, "who will take on Joe Japp's job for the night." And, aside to me, "Man, I heard ye comin' down the High Street. Ye did fine. Ye're a great natural talent for the profession." After that we were all very friendly, and the whole company had a snack together in one of the tents – bread and cheese and bottled beer.

'The first thing I did was to make a bundle of Brumby's clothes, which Mr McGowan promised to send back to Craigiedean when the coast was clear. Then I bribed a small boy to take a telegram to the Post Office – to Archie at Larristane, saying I had been detained and hoped to return next day. After that I took off my coat and worked like a beaver. It was nearly six o'clock before we had everything straight, and the show opened at seven, so we were all a bit the worse for wear when we sat down to high tea. It's a hard job an artiste's, as old McGowan observed.

'I never met a queerer, friendlier, more innocent company, for the proprietor seemed to have set out to collect originals, and most of them had been with him for years. The boss of the menagerie was an ex-sailor, who had a remarkable way with beasts; he rarely spoke a word, but just grinned and whistled through broken teeth. The clown, who said his name was Sammle Dreep, came from Paisley, and was fat enough not to need the conventional bolster. Dublin Davie, my second in command, was a small Irishman who had been an ostler, and limped owing to having been with the Dublin Fusiliers at Gallipoli. The clown had a wife who ran the commissariat, when she wasn't appearing in the ring as Zenobia, the Pride of the Sahara. Then there were the Sisters Wido – a young married couple with two children; and the wife of a man who played the clarionet – figured in the bill as Elise the Equestrienne. I had a look at the horses, which were the ordinary skinny, broad-backed, circus ponies. I found out later that they were so well trained that I daresay they could have done their turns in the dark.

'At a quarter to seven we lit the naphtha flares and our orchestra started in. McGowan told me to get inside Japp's dress-clothes, and rather unwillingly I obeyed him, for I had got rather to fancy my morning's kit. I found there was only a coat and waistcoat, for I was allowed to retain the top-boots and cords. Happily the shirt was clean, but I had a solitaire with a sham diamond as big as a shilling, and the cut of the coat would have been considered out-of-date by a self-respecting waiter in Soho. I had also a scarlet silk handkerchief to stuff in my bosom, a pair of dirty white kid gloves, and an immense coach whip.

'The menagerie was open, but that night the chief attraction was the circus, and I don't mind saying that about the best bit of the circus was myself. In one of the intervals McGowan insisted on shaking hands and telling me that I was wasted in any other profession than a showman's. The fact is I was rather above myself, and entered into what you might call the spirit of the thing. We had the usual Dick Turpin's ride to York, and an escape of Dakota Dan (one of the Sisters Wido) from Red Indians (the other Wido, Zenobia and Elise, with about a ton of feathers on their heads). The Equestrienne equestered, and the Widos hopped through hoops, and all the while I kept up my patter and spouted all the rot I could remember.

'The clown was magnificent. He had a Paisley accent you could have cut like a knife, but he prided himself on talking aristocratic English. He had a lot of badinage with Zenobia about her life in the desert. One bit I remember. She kept on referring to bulbuls, and asked him if he had ever seen a bull-bull. He said he had, for he supposed it was a male coo-coo. But he was happiest at my expense. I never heard a chap with such a flow of back-chat. A funny thing – but when he wasn't calling me "Little Pansy-face", he addressed me as "Your Grace" and "Me Lord Dook", and hoped that the audience would forgive my négligé attire, seeing my coronet hadn't come back from the wash.

'Altogether the thing went down with a snap from beginning to end, and when old McGowan, all dressed up with a white waistcoat, made a speech at the end and explained about the next performances he got a perfect hurricane of applause. After that we had to tidy up. There was the usual trouble with several procrastinating drunks, who wanted to make a night of it. One of them got into the ring and tried to have a row with me. He was a big loutish fellow with small eyes and red hair, and had the look of a betting tout. He stuck his face close to mine and bellowed at me:

' "I ken ye fine, ye—! I seen ye at Lanerick last back-end . . . Ye ca'd yoursel' Gentleman Geordie, and ye went off wi' my siller. By God, I'll get it out o' ye, ye—welsher."

'I told him that he was barking up the wrong tree, and that I was not a bookie and had never been near Lanerick, but he refused to be convinced. The upshot was that Davie and I had to chuck him out, blaspheming like a navvy and swearing that he was coming back with his pals to do me in.

'We were a very contented lot of mountebanks at supper that night. The takings were good and the menagerie also had been popular, and we all felt that we had been rather above our form. McGowan, for whom I was acquiring a profound affection, beamed on us, and produced a couple of bottles of blackstrap to drink the health of the Colossal Circassian Circus. That old fellow was a nonesuch. He kept me up late – for I stopped with him in his caravan – expounding his philosophy of life. It seemed he had been intended for the kirk, but had had too much *joie de vivre* for the pulpit. He was a born tramp, and liked waking up most days in a new place, and he loved his queer outfit and saw the comedy of it. "For three and thirty years I've travelled the country," he said, "and I've been a public benefactor, Mr Brown. I've put colour into many a dowie life, and I've been a godsend to the bairns. There's no vulgarity in my performances – they're a' as halesome as spring water." He quoted Burns a bit, and then he got on to politics, for he was a great Radical, and maintained that Scotland was about the only true democracy, because a man was valued precisely for what he was and no more. "Ye're a laird, Mr Brown, but ye're a guid fellow, and this night ye've shown yourself to be a man and a brither. What do you and me care for mawgnates? We take no stock in your Andra Carnegies and your Dukes o' Burminster." And as I dropped off to sleep he was obliging with a verse of "A man's a man for a' that".

'I woke in excellent spirits, thinking what a good story I should have to tell when I returned to Larristane. My plan was to get off as soon as possible, take the train to Langshiels, and then hire. I could see that McGowan was sorry to part with me, but he agreed that it was too unhealthy a countryside for me to dally in. There was to be an afternoon performance, so everybody had to hustle, and there was no reason for me to linger. After breakfast I borrowed an old ulster from him, for I had to cover up my finery, and a still older brown bowler to replace the topper I had worn on the preceding day.

'Suddenly we heard a fracas, and the drunk appeared who had worried me the night before. He had forced his way in and was pushing on through an expostulating crowd. When he saw me he made for me with a trail of blasphemy. He was perfectly sober now and looked very ugly.

' "Gie me back my siller," he roared. "Gie me back the five-pound note I won at Lanerick when I backed Kettle o' Fish." If I hadn't warded him off he would have taken me by the throat.

'I protested again that he was mistaken, but I might as well have appealed to a post. He swore with every variety of oath that I was Gentleman Geordie, and that I had levanted with his winnings. As he raved I began to see a possible explanation of his madness. Some bookmaker, sporting my sort of kit, had swindled him. I had ridden several times in steeplechases at Lanerick and he had seen me and got my face in his head, and mixed me up with the fraudulent bookie.

'It was a confounded nuisance, and but for the principle of the thing I would have been inclined to pay up. As it was we had to fling him out, and he went unwillingly, doing all the damage he could. His parting words were that he and his pals weren't done with me, and that though he had to wait fifty years he would wring my neck.

'After that I thought I had better waste no time, so I said good-bye to McGowan and left the show-ground by the back entrance close to the Aller. I had a general notion of the place, and knew that if I kept down the river I could turn up a lane called the Water Wynd, and get to the station without traversing any of the main streets. I had ascertained that there was a train at 10.30 which would get me to Langshiels at 11.15, so that I could be at Larristane for luncheon.

'I had underrated the persistence of my enemy. He and his pals had picketed all the approaches to the show, and when I turned into the Water Wynd I found a fellow there, who at the sight of me blew a whistle. In a second or two he was joined by three others, among them my persecutor.

' "We've gotten ye noo," he shouted, and made to collar me.

' "If you touch me," I said. "it's assault, and a case for the police."

' "That's your game, is it?" he cried. "Na, na, we'll no trouble the pollis. They tell me the Law winna help me to recover a bet, so I'll just trust to my nieves. Will ye pay up, ye—, or take the bloodiest bashin' ye ever seen?"

'I was in an uncommon nasty predicament. There was nobody in the Wynd but some children playing, and the odds were four to one. If I fought I'd get licked. The obvious course of safety was to run up the Wynd towards the High Street, where I might find help. But that would mean a street row and the intervention of the police, a case in court, and the disclosure of who I was. If I broke through and ran back to McGowan I would be no farther forward. What was perfectly clear was that I couldn't make the railway station without landing myself in the worst kind of mess.

'There wasn't much time to think, for the four men were upon me. I hit out at the nearest, saw him go down, and then doubled up the Wynd and into a side alley on the right.

'By the mercy of Providence this wasn't a cul-de-sac, but twisted below the old walls of the burgh, and then became a lane between gardens. The pursuit was fairly hot, and my accursed boots kept slipping on the cobbles and cramped my form. They were almost upon me before I reached the lane, but then I put on a spurt, and was twenty yards ahead when it ended in a wall with a gate. The gate was locked, but the wall was low, and I scrambled over it, and dropped into the rubbish heap of a garden.

'There was no going back, so I barged through some gooseberry bushes, skirted a lawn, squattered over a big square of gravel, and charged through the entrance gates of a suburban villa. My enemies plainly knew a better road, for when I passed the entrance they were only a dozen yards off on my left. That compelled me to turn to the right, the direction away from Kirk Aller. I was now on a highway where I could stretch myself, and it was not long before I shook off the pursuit. They were whiskyfied ruffians and not much good in a hunt. It was a warm morning, but I did not slacken till I had put a good quarter of a mile between us. I saw them come round a turn, lumbering along, cooked to the world, so I judged I could slow down to an easy trot.

'I was cut off from my lines of communication, and the only thing to do was to rejoin them by a detour. The Aller valley, which the railway to Langshiels followed, gave me a general direction. I remembered that about six miles off there was a station called Rubersdean, and that there was an afternoon train which got to

Langshiels about three o'clock. I preferred to pick it up there, for I didn't mean to risk showing my face inside Kirk Aller again.

'By this time I had got heartily sick of my adventures. Being chased like a fox is amusing enough for an hour or two, but it soon palls. I was becoming a regular outlaw – wanted by the police for breaking into a nursing-home and stealing a suit, and very much wanted by various private gentlemen on the charge of bilking. Everybody's hand seemed to be against me, except old McGowan's, and I had had quite enough of it. I wanted nothing so much as to be back at Larristane, and I didn't believe I would tell Archie the story, for I was fed up with the whole business.

'I didn't dare go near a public-house, and the best I could do for luncheon was a bottle of ginger-beer and some biscuits which I bought at a sweetie-shop. To make a long story short, I reached Rubersdean in time, and as there were several people on the platform I waited till the train arrived before showing myself. I got into a third-class carriage at the very end of it.

'The only occupants were a woman and a child, and my appearance must have been pretty bad, for the woman looked as if she wanted to get out when she saw me. But I said it was a fine day and "guid for the crops", and I suppose she was reassured by my Scotch tongue, for she quieted down. The child was very inquisitive, and they discussed me in whispers. "What's that man, Mamaw?" it asked. "Never mind, Jimmie." "But I want to ken, Mamaw." "Wheesht, dearie. He's a crool man. He kills the wee mawpies." At that the child set up a howl, but I felt rather flattered, for a rabbit-trapper was a respectable profession compared to those with which I had recently been credited.

'At the station before Langshiels they collect the tickets. I had none, so when the man came round I could only offer a Bank of England five-pound note. He looked at it very suspiciously, asked me rudely if I had nothing smaller, consulted the station-master, and finally with a very ill grace got me change out of the latter's office. This hung up the train for a good five minutes, and you could see by their looks that they thought I was a thief. The thing had got so badly on my nerves that I could have wept. I counted the minutes till we reached Langshiels, and I was not cheered by the behaviour of my travelling companion. She was clearly convinced of the worst, and when we came out of a tunnel she was jammed into the farthest corner, clutching her child and her bag, and looking as if she had escaped from death. I can tell you it was a thankful man that shot out on to the platform at Langshiels . . .

'I found myself looking into the absolutely bewildered eyes of Tommy Deloraine . . . I saw a lot of fellows behind him with rosettes and scared faces, and I saw what looked like a band . . .

'It took me about a hundredth part of a second to realise that I had dropped out of the frying-pan into the fire. You will scarcely believe it, but since I had rehearsed my speech going up the Rinks burn, the political meeting at Langshiels had gone clean out of my head. I suppose I had tumbled into such an utterly new world that no link remained with the old one. And as my foul luck would have it, I had hit on the very train by which I had told Deloraine I would travel.

' "For heaven's sake, Tommy, tell me where I can change," I hissed. "Lend me some clothes or I'll murder you."

'Well, that was the end of it. I got into a suit of Tommy's at the Station Hotel – luckily he was about my size – and we proceeded with the brass band and the rosetted committee to the Town Hall. I made a dashed good speech, though I say it who shouldn't, simply because I was past caring what I did. Life had been rather too much for me the last two days.'

Burminster finished his tankard, and a light of reminiscence came into his eye.

'Last week,' he said, 'I was passing Buckingham Palace. One of the mallards from St James's Park had laid away, and had hatched out a brood somewhere up Constitution Hill. The time had come when she wanted to get the ducklings back to the water. There was a big crowd, and through the midst of it marched two bobbies with the mother-duck between them, while the young ones waddled behind. I caught the look in her eye, and, if you believe me, it was the comicalest mixture of relief and embarrassment, shyness, self-consciousness and desperation.

'I would like to have shaken hands with that bird. I knew exactly how she felt.'

Skule Skerry

Anthony Hurrell's story from *The Runagates Club* (1928),
'Skule Skerry' was serialised in *Pall Mall Magazine* (May
1928). Apart from appearing in a privately published collection, *The Far Islands* (*c*.1984), it has not been reprinted
since first publication.

———————

Who's there, besides foul weather?
King Lear

MR ANTHONY HURRELL was a small man, thin to the point of emaciation,
but erect as a ramrod and wiry as a cairn terrier. There was no grey in
his hair, and his pale far-sighted eyes had the alertness of youth, but his
lean face was so wrinkled by weather that in certain lights it looked
almost venerable, and young men, who at first sight had imagined him
their contemporary, presently dropped into the 'sir' reserved for
indisputable seniors. His actual age was, I believe, somewhere in the
forties. He had inherited a small property in Northumberland, where
he had accumulated a collection of the rarer wildfowl; but much of his
life had been spent in places so remote that his friends could with
difficulty find them on the map. He had written a dozen ornithological
monographs, was joint editor of the chief modern treatise on British
birds, and had been the first man to visit the *tundras* of the Yenisei. He
spoke little and that with an agreeable hesitation, but his ready smile,
his quick interest, and the impression he gave of having a fathomless
knowledge of strange modes of life, made him a popular and intriguing
figure among his friends. Of his doings in the War he told us nothing;
what we knew of them – and they were sensational enough in all
conscience – we learned elsewhere. It was Nightingale's story which
drew him from his customary silence. At the dinner following that
event he made certain comments on current explanations of the super-

normal. 'I remember once,' he began, and before we knew he had surprised us by embarking on a tale.

He had scarcely begun before he stopped. 'I'm boring you,' he said deprecatingly. 'There's nothing much in the story . . . You see, it all happened, so to speak, inside my head . . . I don't want to seem an egotist . . .'

'Don't be an ass, Tony,' said Lamancha. 'Every adventure takes place chiefly inside the head of somebody. Go on. We're all attention.'

'It happened a good many years ago,' Hurrell continued, 'when I was quite a young man. I wasn't the cold scientist then that I fancy I am to-day. I took up birds in the first instance chiefly because they fired what imagination I possess. They fascinated me, for they seemed of all created things the nearest to pure spirit – those little beings with a normal temperature of 125°. Think of it. The goldcrest, with a stomach no bigger than a bean, flies across the North Sea! The curlew sandpiper, which breeds so far north that only about three people have ever seen its nest, goes to Tasmania for its holidays! So I always went bird-hunting with a queer sense of expectation and a bit of a tremor, as if I were walking very near the boundaries of the things we are not allowed to know. I felt this especially in the migration season. The small atoms, coming God knows whence and going God knows whither, were sheer mystery – they belonged to a world built in different dimensions from ours. I don't know what I expected, but I was always waiting for something, as much in a flutter as a girl at her first ball. You must realise that mood of mine to understand what follows.

'One year I went to the Norland Islands for the spring migration. Plenty of people do the same, but I had the notion to do something a little different. I had a theory that migrants go north and south on a fairly narrow road. They have their corridors in the air as clearly defined as a highway, and keep an inherited memory of these corridors, like the stout conservatives they are. So I didn't go to the Blue Banks or to Noop or to Hermaness or any of the obvious places, where birds might be expected to make their first landfall.

'At that time I was pretty well read in the sagas, and had taught myself Icelandic for the purpose. Now it is written in the Saga of Earl Skuli, which is part of the Jarla Saga or Saga of the Earls, that Skuli, when he was carving out his earldom in the Scots islands, had much to do with a place called the Isle of the Birds. It is mentioned repeatedly, and the saga-man has a lot to say about the amazing multitude of birds there. It couldn't have been an ordinary gullery, for the Northmen saw too many of these to think them worth mentioning. I got it into my head that it must have been one of the alighting places of the migrants, and was probably as busy a spot to-day as in the eleventh century. The saga said it was near Halmarsness, and that is on the west side of the island of Una, so to Una I decided to go. I fairly got that Isle of Birds on the brain. From the map it might be any one of a dozen skerries under the shadow of Halmarsness.

'I remember that I spent a good many hours in the British Museum before I started, hunting up the scanty records of those parts. I found – I think it was in Adam of Bremen – that a succession of holy men had lived on the isle, and that a chapel had been built there and endowed by Earl Rognvald, which came to an end in the time of Malise of Strathearn. There was a bare mention of the place, but the chronicler had one curious note. 'Insula Avium,' ran the text, 'quæ est ultima insula et proxima Abysso.' I wondered what on earth he meant. The place was not ultimate in any geographical sense, neither the farthest north nor the farthest west of the Norlands. And what was the 'abyss'? In monkish Latin the word generally means Hell – Bunyan's Bottomless Pit – and sometimes the grave; but neither meaning seemed to have much to do with an ordinary sea skerry.

'I arrived at Una about eight o'clock in a May evening, having been put across from Voss in a flit-boat. It was a quiet evening, the sky without clouds but so pale as to be almost grey, the sea grey also but with a certain iridescence in it, and the low lines of the land a combination of hard greys and umbers, cut into by the harder white of the lighthouse. I can never find words to describe that curious quality of light that you get up in the North. Sometimes it is like looking at the world out of deep water – Farquharson used to call it 'milky', and one saw what he meant. Generally it is a sort of essence of light, cold and pure and distilled, as if it were reflected from snow. There is no colour in it, and it makes thin shadows. Some people find it horribly depressing – Farquharson said it reminded him of a churchyard in the early morning where all his friends were buried – but personally I found it tonic and comforting. But it made me feel very near the edge of the world.

'There was no inn, so I put up at the post office, which was on a causeway between a fresh-water loch and a sea voe, so that from the doorstep you could catch brown trout on one side and sea-trout on the other. Next morning I set off for Halmarsness, which lay five miles to the west over a flat moorland all puddled with tiny lochans. There seemed to be nearly as much water as land. Presently I came to a bigger loch under the lift of ground which was Halmarsness. There was a gap in the ridge through which I looked straight out to the Atlantic, and there in the middle distance was what I knew instinctively to be my island.

'It was perhaps a quarter of a mile long, low for the most part, but rising in the north to a grassy knoll beyond the reach of any tides. In parts it narrowed to a few yards width, and the lower levels must often have been awash. But it was an island, not a reef, and I thought I could make out the remains of the monkish cell. I climbed Halmarsness, and there, with nesting skuas swooping angrily about my head, I got a better view. It was certainly my island, for the rest of the archipelago were inconsiderable skerries, and I realised that it might well be a resting-place for migrants, for the mainland cliffs were too thronged with piratical skuas and other jealous fowl to be comfortable for weary travellers.

'I sat for a long time on the headland looking down from the three hundred feet of basalt to the island half a mile off – the last bit of solid earth between me and Greenland. The sea was calm for Norland waters, but there was a snowy edging of surf to the skerries which told of a tide rip. Two miles farther south I could see the entrance to the famous Roost of Una, where, when tide and wind collide, there is a wall like a house, so that a small steamer cannot pass it. The only sign of human habitation was a little grey farm in the lowlands toward the Roost, but the place was full of the evidence of man – a herd of Norland ponies, each tagged with its owner's name – grazing sheep of the piebald Norland breed – a broken barbed-wire fence that drooped over the edge of the cliff. I was only an hour's walk from a telegraph office, and a village which got its newspapers not more than three days late. It was a fine spring noon, and in the empty bright land there was scarcely a shadow . . . All the same, as I looked down at the island I did not wonder that it had been selected for attention by the saga-man and had been reputed holy. For it had an air of concealing something, though it was as bare as a billiard-table. It was an intruder, an irrelevance in the picture, planted there by some celestial caprice. I decided forthwith to make my camp on it, and the decision, inconsequently enough, seemed to me to be something of a venture.

'That was the view taken by John Ronaldson, when I talked to him after dinner. John was the post-mistress's son, more fisherman than crofter, like all Norlanders, a skilful sailor and an adept at the dipping lug, and noted for his knowledge of the western coast. He had difficulty in understanding my plan, and when he identified my island he protested.

'"Not Skule Skerry!" he cried. "What would take ye there, man? Ye'll get a' the birds ye want on Halmarsness and a far better bield. Ye'll be blawn away on the skerry, if the wund rises."

'I explained to him my reasons as well as I could, and I answered his fears about a gale by pointing out that the island was sheltered by the cliffs from the prevailing winds, and could be scourged only from the south, south-west, or west, quarters from which the wind rarely blew in May. "It'll be cauld," he said, "and wat." I pointed out that I had a tent and was accustomed to camping. "Ye'll starve" – I expounded my proposed methods of commissariat. "It'll be an ill job getting ye on and off" – but after cross-examination he admitted that ordinarily the tides were not difficult, and that I could get a rowboat to a beach below the farm I had seen – its name was Sgurravoe. Yet when I had said all this he still raised objections, till I asked him flatly what was the matter with Skule Skerry.

'"Naebody gangs there," he said gruffly.

'"Why should they?" I asked. "I'm only going to watch the birds."

'But the fact that it was never visited seemed to stick in his throat, and he grumbled out something that surprised me. "It has an ill name," he said. But when I pressed him he admitted that there was no record of shipwreck or disaster to account for the ill name. He repeated the words "Skule Skerry" as if they displeased him. "Folk dinna gang near it. It has aye had an ill name. My grandfather used to say that the place wasna canny."

'Now your Norlander has nothing of the Celt in him, and is as different from the Hebridean as a Northumbrian from a Cornishman. They are a fine, upstanding, hard-headed race, almost pure Scandinavian in blood, but they have as little poetry in them as a Manchester Radical. I should have put them down as utterly free from superstition, and, in all my many visits to the islands, I have never yet come across a folk-tale – hardly even a historical legend. Yet here was John Ronaldson, with his weather-beaten face and stiff chin and shrewd blue eyes, declaring that an innocent-looking island "wasna

[229]

canny", and showing the most remarkable disinclination to go near it.

'Of course all this only made me keener. Besides, it was called Skule Skerry, and the name could only come from Earl Skuli; so it was linked up authentically with the oddments of information I had collected in the British Museum – the Jarla Saga and Adam of Bremen and all the rest of it. John finally agreed to take me over next morning in his boat, and I spent the rest of the day in collecting my kit. I had a small tent, and a Wolseley valise and half a dozen rugs, and, since I had brought a big box of tinned stuffs from the Stores, all I needed was flour and meal and some simple groceries. I learned that there was a well on the island, and that I could count on sufficient driftwood for my fire, but to make certain I took a sack of coals and another of peats. So I set off next day in John's boat, ran with the wind through the Roost of Una when the tide was right, tacked up the coast, and came to the skerry early in the afternoon.

'You could see that John hated the place. We ran into a cove on the east side, and he splashed ashore as if he expected to have his landing opposed, looking all the time sharply about him. When he carried my stuff to a hollow under the knoll, which gave a certain amount of shelter, his head was always twisting round. To me the place seemed to be the last word in forgotten peace. The swell lipped gently on the reefs and the little pebbled beaches, and only the babble of gulls from Halmarsness broke the stillness.

'John was clearly anxious to get away, but he did his duty by me. He helped me to get the tent up, found a convenient place for my boxes, pointed out the well and filled my water bucket, and made a zareba of stones to protect my camp on the Atlantic side. We had brought a small dinghy along with us, and this was to be left with me, so that when I wanted I could row across to the beach at Sgurravoe. As his last service he fixed an old pail between two boulders on the summit of the knoll, and filled it with oily waste, so that it could be turned into a beacon.

' "Ye'll maybe want to come off," he said, "and the boat will maybe no be there. Kindle your flare, and they'll see it at Sgurravoe and get the word to me, and I'll come for ye though the Muckle Black Silkie himsel' was hunkerin' on the skerry."

'Then he looked up and sniffed the air. "I dinna like the set of the sky," he declared. "It's a bad weatherhead. There'll be mair wund than I like in the next four-and-twenty hours."

'So saying, he hoisted his sail, and presently was a speck on the waters towards the Roost. There was no need for him to hurry, for the tide was now wrong, and before he could pass the Roost he would have three hours to wait on this side of the Mull. But the man, usually so deliberate and imperturbable, had been in a fever to be gone.

'His departure left me in a curious mood of happy loneliness and pleasurable expectation. I was left solitary with the seas and the birds. I laughed to think that I had found a streak of superstition in the granite John. He and his Muckle Black Silkie! I knew the old legend of the North which tells how the Finns, the ghouls that live in the deeps of the ocean, can on occasion don a seal's skin and come to land to play havoc with mortals. But *diablerie* and this isle of mine were worlds apart. I looked at it as the sun dropped, drowsing in the opal-coloured tides, under a sky in which pale clouds made streamers like a spectral *aurora borealis*, and I thought that I had stumbled upon one of those places where Nature seems to invite one to her secrets. As the light died the sky was flecked as with the roots and branches of some great nebular tree. That would be the "weatherhead" of which John Ronaldson had spoken.

'I set my fire going, cooked my supper, and made everything snug for the night. I had been right in my guess about the migrants. It must have been about ten o'clock when they began to arrive – after my fire had died out and I was smoking my last pipe before getting into my sleeping-bag. A host of fieldfares settled gently on the south part of the skerry. A faint light lingered till after midnight, but it was not easy to distinguish the little creatures, for they were aware of my presence and did not alight within a dozen yards of me. But I made out bramblings and buntings and what I thought was the Greenland wheatear; also jack snipe and sanderling; and I believed from their cries that the curlew sandpiper and the whimbrel were there. I went to sleep in a state of high excitement, promising myself a fruitful time on the morrow.

'I slept badly, as one often does one's first night in the open. Several times I woke with a start, under the impression that I was in a boat rowing swiftly with the tide. And every time I woke I heard the flutter of myriad birds, as if a velvet curtain were being slowly switched along an oak floor. At last I fell into deeper sleep, and when I opened my eyes it was full day.

'The first thing that struck me was that it had got suddenly colder.

The sky was stormily red in the east, and masses of woolly clouds were banking in the north. I lit my fire with numbed fingers and hastily made tea. I could see the nimbus of seafowl over Halmarsness, but there was only one bird left on my skerry. I was certain from its forked tail that it was a Sabine's gull, but before I got my glass out it was disappearing into the haze towards the north. The sight cheered and excited me, and I cooked my breakfast in pretty good spirits.

'That was literally the last bird that came near me, barring the ordinary shearwaters and gulls and cormorants that nested round about Halmarsness. (There was not one single nest of any sort on the island. I had heard of that happening before in places which were regular halting-grounds for migrants.) The travellers must have had an inkling of the coming weather and were waiting somewhere well to the south. For about nine o'clock it began to blow. Great God, how it blew! You must go to the Norlands if you want to know what wind can be. It is like being on a mountain-top, for there is no high ground to act as a wind-break. There was no rain, but the surf broke in showers and every foot of the skerry was drenched with it. In a trice Halmarsness was hidden, and I seemed to be in the centre of a maelstrom, choked with scud and buffeted on every side by swirling waters.

'Down came my tent at once. I wrestled with the crazy canvas and got a black eye from the pole, but I managed to drag the ruins into the shelter of the zareba which John had built, and tumble some of the bigger boulders on it. There it lay, flapping like a sick albatross. The water got into my food boxes, and soaked my fuel, as well as every inch of my clothing ... I had looked forward to a peaceful day of watching and meditation, when I could write up my notes; and instead I spent a morning like a Rugger scrum. I might have enjoyed it, if I hadn't been so wet and cold, and could have got a better lunch than some clammy mouthfuls out of a tin. One talks glibly about being "blown off" a place, generally an idle exaggeration – but that day I came very near the reality. There were times when I had to hang on for dear life to one of the bigger stones to avoid being trundled into the yeasty seas.

'About two o'clock the volume of the storm began to decline, and then for the first time I thought about the boat. With a horrid sinking of the heart I scrambled to the cove where we had beached it. It had been drawn up high and dry, and its painter secured to a substantial boulder. But now there was not a sign of it except a ragged rope-end round the stone. The tide had mounted to its level, and tide and wind had smashed the rotten painter. By this time what was left of it would be tossing in the Roost.

'This was a pretty state of affairs. John was due to visit me next day, but I had a cold twenty-four hours ahead of me. There was of course the flare he had left me, but I was not inclined to use this. It looked like throwing up the sponge and confessing that my expedition had been a farce. I felt miserable, but obstinate, and, since the weather was clearly mending, I determined to put the best face on the business, so I went back to the wreckage of my camp, and tried to tidy up. There was still far too much wind to do anything with the tent, but the worst of the spindrift had ceased, and I was able to put out my bedding and some of my provender to dry. I got a dry jersey out of my pack, and, as I was wearing fisherman's boots and oilskins, I managed to get some slight return of comfort. Also at last I succeeded in lighting a pipe. I found a corner under the knoll which gave me a modicum of shelter, and I settled myself to pass the time with tobacco and my own thoughts.

'About three o'clock the wind died away completely. That I did not like, for a dead lull in the Norlands is often the precursor of a new gale. Indeed, I never remembered a time when some wind did not blow, and I had heard that when such a thing happened people came out of their houses to ask what the matter was. But now we had the deadest sort of calm. The sea was still wild and broken, the tides raced by like a mill-stream, and a brume was gathering which shut out Halmarsness – shut out every prospect except a narrow circuit of grey water. The cessation of the racket of the gale made the place seem uncannily quiet. The present tumult of the sea, in comparison with the noise of the morning, seemed no more than a mutter and an echo.

'As I sat there I became conscious of an odd sensation. I seemed to be more alone, more cut off, not only from my fellows but from the habitable earth, than I had ever been before. It was like being in a small boat in mid-Atlantic – but worse, if you understand me, for that would have been loneliness in the midst of a waste which was nevertheless surrounded and traversed by the works of man, whereas now I felt that I was clean outside man's ken. I had come somehow to the edge of that world where life is, and was very close to the world which has only death in it.

'At first I do not think there was much fear in the sensation –

chiefly strangeness, but the kind of strangeness which awes without exciting. I tried to shake off the mood, and got up to stretch myself. There was not much room for exercise, and as I moved with stiff legs along the reefs I slipped into the water, so that I got my arms wet. It was cold beyond belief – the very quintessence of deathly Arctic ice, so cold that it seemed to sear and bleach the skin.

'From that moment I date the most unpleasant experience of my life. I became suddenly the prey of a black depression, shot with the red lights of terror. But it was not a numb terror, for my brain was acutely alive... I had the sense to try to make tea, but my fuel was still too damp, and the best I could do was to pour half the contents of my brandy flask into a cup and swallow the stuff. That did not properly warm my chilled body, but – since I am a very temperate man – it speeded up my thoughts instead of calming them. I felt myself on the brink of a childish panic.

'One thing I thought I saw clearly – the meaning of Skule Skerry. By some alchemy of nature, at which I could only guess, it was on the track by which the North exercised its spell, a cableway for the magnetism of that cruel frozen Uttermost, which man might penetrate but could never subdue or understand. Though the latitude was only 61°, there were folds and tucks in space, and this isle was the edge of the world. Birds knew it, and the old Northmen, who were primitive beings like the birds, knew it. That was why an inconsiderable skerry had been given the name of a conquering Jarl. The old Church knew it, and had planted a chapel to exorcise the demons of darkness. I wondered what sights the hermit, whose cell had been on the very spot where I was cowering, had seen in the winter dusks.

'It may have been partly the brandy acting on an empty stomach, and partly the extreme cold, but my brain, in spite of my efforts to think rationally, began to run like a dynamo. It is difficult to explain my mood, but I seemed to be two persons – one a reasonable modern man trying to keep sane and scornfully rejecting the fancies which the other, a cast-back to something elemental, was furiously spinning. But it was the second that had the upper hand... I felt myself loosed from my moorings, a mere waif on uncharted seas. What is the German phrase? *Urdummheit* – Primal Idiocy? That was what was the matter with me. I had fallen out of civilisation into the Outlands and was feeling their spell... I could not think, but I could remember, and what I had read of the Norse voyagers came back to me with horrid persistence. They had known the outland terrors – the Sea Walls at the world's end, the Curdled Ocean with its strange beasts. Those men did not sail north as we did, in steamers, with modern food and modern instruments, huddled into crews and expeditions. They had gone out almost alone, in brittle galleys, and they had known what we could never know.

'And then, I had a shattering revelation. I had been groping for a word and I suddenly got it. It was Adam of Bremen's *"proxima Abysso"*. This island was next door to the Abyss, and the Abyss was that blanched world of the North which was the negation of life.

'That unfortunate recollection was the last straw. I remember that I forced myself to get up and try again to kindle a fire. But the wood was still too damp, and I realised with consternation that I had very few matches left, several boxes having been ruined that morning. As I staggered about I saw the flare which John had left for me, and had almost lit it. But some dregs of manhood prevented me – I could not own defeat in that babyish way – I must wait till John Ronaldson came for me next morning. Instead I had another mouthful of brandy, and tried to eat some of my sodden biscuits. But I could scarcely swallow; the infernal cold, instead of rousing hunger, had given me only a raging thirst.

'I forced myself to sit down again with my face to the land. You see, every moment I was becoming more childish. I had the notion – I cannot call it a thought – that down the avenue from the North something terrible and strange might come. My nervous state must have been pretty bad, for though I was cold and empty and weary I was scarcely conscious of physical discomfort. My heart was fluttering like a scared boy's; and all the time the other part of me was standing aside and telling me not to be a damned fool . . . I think that if I had heard the rustle of a flock of migrants I might have pulled myself together, but not a blessed bird had come near me all day. I had fallen into a world that killed life, a sort of Valley of the Shadow of Death.

'The brume spoiled the long northern twilight, and presently it was almost dark. At first I thought that this was going to help me, and I got hold of several of my half-dry rugs, and made a sleeping-place. But I could not sleep, even if my teeth had stopped chattering, for a new and perfectly idiotic idea possessed me. It came from a recollection of John Ronaldson's parting words. What had he said about the Black Silkie – the Finn who came out of the deep and hunkered on this skerry? Raving mania! But on this lost island in the darkening night, with icy tides lapping about me, was any horror beyond belief?

'Still, the sheer idiocy of the idea compelled a reaction. I took hold of my wits with both hands and cursed myself for a fool. I could even reason about my folly. I knew what was wrong with me. I was suffering from *panic* – a physical affection produced by natural causes, explicable, though as yet not fully explained. Two friends of mine had once been afflicted with it: one in a lonely glen in the Jotunheim, so that he ran for ten miles over stony hills till he found a sæter and human companionship; the other in a Bavarian forest, where both he and his guide tore for hours through the thicket till they dropped like logs beside a highroad. This reflection enabled me to take a pull on myself and to think a little ahead. If my troubles were physical then there would be no shame in looking for the speediest cure. Without further delay I must leave this God-forgotten place.

'The flare was all right, for it had been set on the highest point of the island, and John had covered it with a peat. With one of my few remaining matches I lit the oily waste, and a great smoky flame leapt to heaven.

'If the half-dark had been eerie, this sudden brightness was eerier. For a moment the glare gave me confidence, but as I looked at the circle of moving waters evilly lit up all my terrors returned ... How long would it take John to reach me? They would see it at once at Sgurravoe – they would be on the look-out for it – John would not waste time, for he had tried to dissuade me from coming – an hour – two hours at the most ...

'I found I could not take my eyes from the waters. They seemed to flow from the north in a strong stream, black as the heart of the elder ice, irresistible as fate, cruel as hell. There seemed to be uncouth shapes swimming in them, which were more than the flickering shadows from the flare ... Something portentous might at any moment come down that river of death ... Someone ...

'And then my knees gave under me and my heart shrank like a pea, for I saw that the someone had come.

'He drew himself heavily out of the sea, wallowed for a second, and then raised his head and, from a distance of five yards, looked me blindly in the face. The flare was fast dying down, but even so at that short range it cast a strong light, and the eyes of the awful being seemed to be dazed by it. I saw a great dark head like a bull's – an old face wrinkled as if in pain – a gleam of enormous broken teeth – a dripping beard – all formed on other lines than God has made mortal creatures. And on the right of the throat was a huge scarlet gash. The thing seemed to be moaning, and then from it came a sound – whether of anguish or wrath I cannot tell – but it seemed to be the cry of a tortured fiend.

'That was enough for me. I pitched forward in a swoon, hitting my head on a stone, and in that condition three hours later John Ronaldson found me.

'They put me to bed at Sgurravoe with hot earthenware bottles, and the doctor from Voss next day patched up my head and gave me a sleeping draught. He declared that there was little the matter with me except shock from exposure, and promised to set me on my feet in a week.

'For three days I was as miserable as a man could be, and did my best to work myself into a fever. I had said not a word about my experience, and left my rescuers to believe that my only troubles were cold and hunger, and that I had lit the flare because I had lost the boat. But during these days I was in a critical state. I knew that there was nothing wrong with my body, but I was gravely concerned about my mind.

'For this was my difficulty. If that awful thing was a mere figment of my brain, then I had better be certified at once as a lunatic. No sane man could get into such a state as to see such portents with the certainty with which I had seen that creature come out of the night. If, on the other hand, the thing was a real presence, then I had looked on something outside natural law, and my intellectual world was broken in pieces. I was a scientist, and a scientist cannot admit the supernatural. If with my eyes I had beheld the monster in which Adam of Bremen believed, which holy men had exorcised, which even the shrewd Norlanders shuddered at as the Black Silkie, then I must burn my books and revise my creed. I might take to poetry or theosophy, but I would never be much good again at science.

'On the third afternoon I was trying to doze, and with shut eyes fighting off the pictures which tormented my brain. John Ronaldson and the farmer of Sgurravoe were talking at the kitchen door. The latter asked some question, and John replied:

' "Aye, it was a wall-ross and nae mistake. It came ashore at Gloop Ness and Sandy Fraser has gotten the skin of it. It was deid when he found it, but no long deid. The puir beast would drift south on some floe, and it was sair hurt, for Sandy said it had a hole in its throat ye could put your nieve in. There hasna been a wall-ross come to Una since my grandfather's day."

'I turned my face to the wall and composed myself to sleep. For now I knew that I was sane, and need not forswear science.'

Dr Lartius

'Dr Lartius' was John Palliser-Yeates's story in *The Runagates Club* (1928) and has not been reprinted in book form for almost seventy years. The story is supposedly based on an official propaganda plan that Buchan vetoed.

The idols have spoken vanity, and the diviners have seen a lie, and have told false dreams; they comfort in vain; therefore they went their way as a flock.

Zechariah X. ii

IN THE EARLY spring Palliser-Yeates had 'flu, and had it so badly that he was sent to recruit for a fortnight on the Riviera. There, being profoundly bored, he wrote out and sent to us this story. He would not give the name of the chief figure, because he said he was still a serving soldier, and his usefulness, he hoped, was not exhausted. The manuscript arrived opportunely, for some of us had just been trying, without success, to extract from Sandy Arbuthnot the truth of certain of his doings about which rumour had been busy.

I

In the second week of January 1917, a modest brass plate appeared on a certain door in Regent Street, among modistes and hat-makers and vendors of cosmetics. It bore the name of Dr S. Lartius. On the third floor were the rooms to which the plate was the signpost, a pleasant set, newly decorated with powder-blue wallpapers, curtains of orange velveteen, and sham marqueterie. The milliners' girls who frequented that staircase might have observed, about eleven in the morning, the figure of Dr Lartius arriving. They did not see him leave, for they had flown to their suburban homes long before the key turned of an evening in the doctor's door.

He was a slim young man of the middle height, who held himself straighter than the usual run of sedentary folk. His face was very pale, and his mop of hair and fluffy beard were black as jet. He wore large tortoise-shell spectacles, and, when he removed them, revealed slightly protuberant and very bright hazel eyes, which contrasted oddly with his pallor. Had such a figure appeared on the stage, the gallery experts, familiar with stage villains, would have unhesitatingly set him down as the anarchist from Moscow about to assassinate the oppressive nobleman and thereby give the hero his chance. But his clothes were far too good for that part. He wore a shiny top-hat and an expensive fur coat, and his neat morning coat, fine linen, unobtrusive black tie, and pearl pin suggested the high finance rather than the backstairs of revolution.

It appeared that Dr Lartius did a flourishing business. Suddenly London had begun to talk about him. First there were the people that matter, the people who are ever on the hunt for a new sensation and must always be in the first flight of any fad. Lady A told the Duchess of B about a wonderful new man who really had Power – no ordinary vulgar spiritualist, but a true Seeker and Thinker. Mr D, that elderly gossip, carried the story through many circles, and it grew with the telling. The curious began to cultivate Dr Lartius, and soon the fame of him came to the ears of those who were not curious, only anxious or broken-hearted; and because the last were a great multitude, and were ready to give their all for consolation, there was a busy coming and going on Dr Lartius's staircase.

His way with his clients was interesting. He had no single method of treatment, and varied his manner according to the motives of the inquirer. The merely inquisitive he entertained with toys. 'I am no professor of an art,' he told them laughingly. 'I am a student, grop-ing on the skirts of great mysteries.' And to the more intelligent he would propound an illustration. 'Take the mathematics of the Fourth Dimension,' he would say. 'I can show you a few simple mechanical puzzles, which cannot be explained except by the aid of abstruse mathematics, and not always then. But these puzzles tell you nothing about the Fourth Dimension, except that there is a world about us inexplicable on the rule of three dimensions. It is the same with my toys – my crystal ball, my pool of ink, my star-maps, even those superinduced moods of abstraction in which we seem to hear the noise of wings and strange voices. They only tell me that there is more in earth and heaven than is dreamed of in man's philosophy.'

But his toys were wonderful. The idle ladies who went there for a thrill were not disappointed. In the dusky room, among the strange rosy lights, their hearts seemed to be always fluttering on the brink of a revelation, and they came away excited and comforted, for Dr Lartius was an adept at delicate flattery. Fortune-telling in the ordinary sense there was none, but this young man seemed to have an uncanny knowledge of private affairs, which he used so discreetly that even those who had most reason to desire secrecy were never disquieted. For such entertainments he charged fees – high fees, as the fur coat and the pearl pin required. 'You wish to be amused,' he would say, 'and it is right that you should pay me for it.'

Even among the idle clients there was a sprinkling of the earnest. With these he had the air of a master towards initiates; they were fellow-pilgrims with him on the Great Road. He would talk to them by the hour, very beautifully, in a soft musical voice. He would warn them against charlatans, those who sought to prostitute a solemn ritual to purposes of vulgar gain. He would unroll for them the history of the great mystics and tell of that secret science known to the old adepts, which had been lost for ages, and was now being recovered piecemeal. These were the most thrilling hours of all, and the fame of Dr Lartius grew great in the drawing-rooms of the Elect. 'And he's such a gentleman, my dear – so well-bred and sympathetic and unworldly and absolutely honest!'

But from others he took no fees. The sad-faced women, mostly in black, who sat in his great velvet chair and asked broken questions, found a very different Dr Lartius. He was no longer fluent and silver-tongued; sometimes he seemed almost embarrassed. He would repeat most earnestly that he was a disciple, a seeker, not a master of hidden things. On such occasions the toys were absent, and if some distracted mother sought knowledge that way she was refused. He rarely had anything definite to impart. When Lady H's only son was about to exchange from the cavalry to the Foot Guards and his mother wanted to know how the step would affect his chances of survival, she got nothing beyond the obvious remark that this was an infantry war and he would have a better prospect of seeing fighting. Very rarely, he spoke out. Once to Mrs K, whose boy was a prisoner, he gave a full account of life in a German prison-camp, so that, in the absence of letters, her imagination had henceforth something to bite on. Usually his visitors were too embarrassed to be observant, but one or two noted that he was uncommonly well informed about the British Army. He never made a mistake about units, and seemed to know a man's battalion before he was told it. And when mothers poured out details to him – for from the talk of soldiers on leave and epistolary indiscretions a good deal of information circulated about London – he now and then took notes.

Yet, though they got little from him that was explicit, these visitors, as a rule, went away comforted. Perhaps it was his gentle soothing manner. Perhaps, as poor Lady M said, it was that he seemed so assured of the spiritual life that they felt that their anxieties were only tiny eddies on the edge of a great sea of peace. At any rate, it was the afflicted even more than the idly curious who spoke well of Dr Lartius.

Sometimes he had masculine clients – fathers of fighting sons, who said they came on their wives' behalf, elderly retired Generals who preferred spiritualism to golf, boys whose nerves were in tatters and wanted the solace which in other ages and lands would have been found in the confessional. With these last Dr. Lartius became a new man. He would take off his spectacles and look them in the face with his prominent lustrous eyes, and talk to them with a ring in his pleasant voice. It was not what he said so much, perhaps, as his manner of saying it, but he seemed to have a singular power over boys just a little bit loose from their moorings. 'Queer thing,' said one of these, 'but one would almost think you had been a soldier yourself.' Dr Lartius had smiled and resumed his spectacles. 'I am a soldier, but in a different war. I fight with the sword of the spirit against the hidden things of darkness.'

Towards the end of March the brass plate suddenly disappeared. There was a great fluttering in the dovecotes of the Elect when the news went round that there had been trouble with the police. It had been over the toys, of course, and the taking of fees. The matter never came into court, but Dr Lartius had been warned to clear out, and he obeyed. Many ladies wrote indignant letters to the Home Secretary about persecution, letters which cited ominous precedents from the early history of the Christian Church.

But in April came consolation. The rumour spread that the Seekers were not to lose their guide. Mr Greatheart would still be available for the comforting of pilgrims. A plate with the name of Dr S. Lartius reappeared in a quiet street in Mayfair. But for the future there would be no question of fees. It was generally assumed that a few devout women had provided a fund for the sustenance of the prophet.

In May his fame was greater than ever. One evening Lady Samplar, the most ardent of his devotees, spoke of him to a certain General who was a power in the land. The General was popular among the women of her set, but a notorious scoffer. Perhaps this was the secret of his popularity, for each hoped to convert him.

'I want you to see him yourself,' she said. 'Only once. I believe in him so firmly that I am willing to stake everything on one interview. Promise me you will let me take you. I only want you to see him and talk to him for ten minutes. I want you to realise his unique personality, for if you once *feel* him you will scoff no more.'

The General laughed, shrugged his shoulders, but allowed himself to be persuaded. So it came about that one afternoon in early June he accompanied Lady Samplar to the flat in Mayfair. 'You must go in alone,' she told him in the ante-room. 'I have spoken about you to him, and he is expecting you. I will wait for you here.'

For half an hour the General was closeted with Dr Lartius. When he returned to the lady his face was red and wrathful.

'That's the most dangerous fellow in London,' he declared. 'Look here, Mollie, you and your friends have been playing the fool about that man. He's a German spy, if there ever was one. I caught him out, for I trapped him into speaking German. You say he's a Swiss, but I swear no Swiss ever spoke German just as he speaks it. The man's a Bavarian. I'll take my oath he is!'

It was a very depressed and rather frightened lady who gave him tea a little later in her drawing-room.

'That kind of sweep is far too clever for you innocents,' she was told. 'There he has been for months pumping you all without your guessing it. You say he's a great comfort to the mourners. I daresay he is, but the poor devils tell him everything that's in their heads. That man has a unique chance of knowing the inside of the British Army. And how has he used his knowledge? That's what I want to know.'

'What are you going to do about it?' she quavered.

'I'm going to have him laid by the heels,' he said grimly, as he took his departure. 'Interned – or put up against a wall, if we can get the evidence. I tell you he's a Boche pure and simple – not that there's much purity and simplicity about him.'

The General was as good as his word, but in one matter he was wrong. The credentials of the prophet's Swiss nationality were good enough. There was nothing for it but to deport him as an undesirable, so one fine morning Dr S. Lartius got his marching orders. He made no complaint, and took a dignified farewell of his friends. But the Faithful were not silent, and the friendship between Lady Samplar and the General died a violent death. The thing got into the papers. Dr Lartius figured in many unrecognisable portraits in the press, and a bishop preached a sermon in a City church about the worship of false gods.

II

As Dr Lartius, closely supervised by the French police, pursued his slow and comfortless journey to the Swiss frontier, he was cheered by several proofs that his fame had gone abroad and that he was not forgotten. At Paris there were flowers in his dingy hotel bedroom, the gift of an unknown admirer, and a little note of encouragement in odd French. At Dijon he received from a strange lady another note telling him that his friends were awaiting him in Berne. When he crossed the border at Pontarlier there were more flowers and letters. The young man paid little attention to such tributes. He spent the journey in quiet reading and meditation, and when he reached Berne did not seem to expect any one to greet him, but collected his luggage and drove off unobtrusively to an hotel.

He had not been there an hour when a card was brought to him bearing the name of Ernst Ulrici, Doctor of Philosophy in the University of Bonn.

'Dr Lartius,' said the visitor, a middle-aged man with a peaked grey beard and hair cut *en brosse*. 'It is an honour to make your acquaintance. We have heard of your fine work and your world-moulding discoveries.'

The young man bowed gravely. 'I am only a seeker,' he said. 'I make no claim to be a master – yet. I am only a little way on the road to enlightenment.'

'We have also heard,' said the other, 'of how shamelessly the British Government has persecuted learning in your person.'

The reply was a smile and a shrug. 'I make no complaint. It is natural that my studies should seem foolishness to the children of this world.'

Dr Ulrici pressed him further on the matter of Britain, but could wake no bitterness.

'There is war to-day,' he said at last. 'You are of German race. Your sympathies are with us?'

'I have no nationality,' was the answer. 'All men are my brothers. But I would fain see this bloodshed at an end.'

'How will it end?' came the question.

'I am no prophet,' said Dr Lartius. 'Yet I can tell that Germany will win, but how I can tell I cannot tell.'

The conversation lasted long and explored many subjects. The German led it cunningly to small matters, and showed a wide acquaintance with the young man's science. He learned that much of his work had been done with soldiers and soldiers' kin, and that in the process of it he had heard many things not published in the news-papers. But when he hinted, ever so delicately, that he would be glad to buy the knowledge, a flush passed over the other's pale face and his voice sharpened.

'I am no spy,' he said. 'I do not prostitute my art for hire. It matters nothing to me which side wins, but it matters much that I keep my soul clean.'

So Dr Ulrici tried another tack. He spoke of the mysteries of the craft, and lured the young man into the confession of hopes and ideals. There could be no communion with the dead, he was told, until communion had first been perfected with the spirits of the living. 'Let the time come,' said Dr Lartius, 'when an unbroken fellowship can be created between souls separated by great tracts of space, and the key has been found. Death is an irrelevant accident. The spirit is untouched by it. Find the *trait d'union* between spirits still in their fleshly envelope, and it can be continued when that envelope is shed.'

'And you have progressed in this affair?' asked Ulrici, with scepti-cism in his tone.

'A few stages,' said the other, and in the ardour of exposition he gave proofs. He had clients, he said, with whom he had established the mystic *catena*. He could read their thoughts even now, though they were far away, share in their mental changes, absorb the knowledge which they acquired.

'Soldiers?' asked the German.

'Some are soldiers. All are the kin of soldiers.'

But Ulrici was still cold. 'That is a great marvel,' he said, 'and not easy to believe.'

Dr Lartius was fired. 'I will give you proofs,' he said, with unwonted passion in his voice. 'You can it test them at your leisure. I know things which have not yet come to pass, though no man has spoken to me of them. How do I know them? Because they have come within the cognisance of minds attuned to my own.'

For a moment he seemed to hesitate. Then he spoke of certain matters − a little change in the method of artillery barrages, a re-adjustment in the organisation of the British Air Force, an alteration in certain British commands.

'These may be trivial things,' he said. 'I do not know. I have no technical skill. But they are still in the future. I offer them to you as proofs of my knowledge.'

'So?' said the other. 'They are indeed small things, but they will do for a test . . .'

Then he spoke kindly, considerately, of Dr Lartius's future.

'I think I will go to Munich,' said the young man. 'Once I studied at the University there, and I love the bright city. They are a sympathetic people and respect knowledge.'

Dr Ulrici rose to take his leave. 'It may be I am able to further your plans, my friend,' he said.

Late that night in a big sitting-room in another hotel, furnished somewhat in the style of an official bureau, Ulrici talked earnestly with another man, a heavy, bearded man, who wore the air of a prosperous bagman, but who was addressed with every token of respect.

'This Lartius fellow puzzles me. He is a transparent fanatic, with some odd power in him that sets him above others of his kidney. I fear he will not be as useful to us as we had hoped. If only we had known of him sooner and could have kept him in England.'

'He can't go back, I suppose?'

'Impossible, sir. But there is still a chance. He has some wild theory that he has established a link with various people, and so acquires automatically whatever new knowledge they gain. Some of these people are soldiers. He has told me things − little things − that I may test this power of his. I am no believer in the spiritualist mumbo-jumbo, but I have lived long enough not to reject a thing because it is new and strange. About that we shall see. If there is anything in it there will be much. Meantime I keep closely in touch with him.'

'What is he going to do?'

'He wants to go to Munich. I am in favour of permitting it, sir. Our good Bavarians are somewhat light in the head, and are always seeking a new thing. They want a little ghostly consolation at present, and this man will give it them. He believes most firmly in our German victory.'

The other yawned and flung away the end of his cigar. 'The mountebank seems to have some glimmerings of sense,' he said.

III

So it came about that in August of the year 1917 Dr Lartius was settled in comfortable rooms off the Garmischstrasse in the Bavarian capital, and a new plate of gun-metal and oxidised silver, lettered in the best style of *art nouveau*, advertised his name to the citizens of Munich.

Fortune still attended the young man, for, as in London, he seemed to spring at once into fame. Within a week of his arrival people were talking about him, and in a month his chambers were crowded. Perhaps his friend Ulrici had spoken a word in the right place. It was the great season before Caporetto, and Dr Lartius spoke heartening things to his clients. Victory was near and the days of glory; but when asked about the date of peace he was coy. Peace would come, but not yet; for the world there was another winter of war.

His methods were the same as those which had captured Lady Samplar and her friends. To the idly curious he showed toys; to the emotional he spoke nobly of the life of the spirit and the locked doors of hidden knowledge which were now almost ajar. Rich ladies, bored with the dullness of the opera season and the scarcity of men, found in him a new interest in life. To the sorrowful he gave the comfort which he had given to his London circle – no more. His personality seemed to exhale hope and sympathy, and mourners, remembering his pleasant voice and compelling eyes, departed with a consolation which they could not define.

That was for the ordinary run of clients; but there were others – fellow-students they professed themselves – to whom he gave stronger meat. He preached his doctrine of the mystic community of thought and knowledge between souls far apart, and now and then he gave proofs such as he had given to Ulrici. It would appear that these proofs stood the test, for his reputation grew prodigiously. He told them little things about forthcoming changes in the Allied armies, and the event always proved him right. They were not things that mattered greatly; but if he could disclose trivialities, some day his method might enable him to reveal a mighty secret. So more than one *Generalstabschef* came to sit with him in his twilit room.

About once a month he used to go back to Berne, and was invariably met at the station by Ulrici. He had been given a very special passport, which took him easily and expeditiously over the frontier, and he had no trouble with station commandants. In these visits he would be closeted with Ulrici for hours. Occasionally he would slip out of his hotel at night for a little, and when Ulrici heard of it he shrugged his shoulders and laughed. 'He is young,' he would say with a leer. 'Even a prophet must have his amusements.' But he was wrong, for Dr Lartius had not the foibles he suspected.

The winter passed slowly, and the faces in the Munich streets grew daily more pinched and wan, clothing more shabby, and boots more down at heel. But there was always comfort for seekers in the room in the Garmischstrasse. Whoever lost faith it was not Dr Lartius. Peace was coming, and his hearers judged that he had forgotten his scientific detachment from all patriotisms and was becoming a good German.

Then in February of the New Year came the rumour of the great advance preparing in the West. The High Command had promised speedy and final victory in return for a little more endurance. Dr Lartius seemed to have the first news of it. 'It is Peace,' he said, 'Peace before winter;' and his phrase was repeated everywhere and became a popular watchword. So, when the news came at the end of March of the retreat of the French and English to the gates of Amiens, the hungry people smiled to each other and said, 'He is right, as always. It is Peace.' Few now cared much about victory, except the high officers and the very rich, but on Peace all were determined.

April passed into May, and ere the month was out came glorious tidings. Ludendorff had reached the Marne, and was within range of Paris. About this time his closest disciples marked a change in Dr Lartius. He seemed to retire into himself, and to be struggling with some vast revelation. His language was less intelligible, but far more impressive. Ulrici came up from Berne to see him, for he had stopped for some months his visits to Switzerland. There were those who said his health was breaking, others that he was now, in very truth, looking inside the veil. This latter was the general view, and the fame of the young man became a superstition.

'You tell us little now about our enemies,' Ulrici complained.

'*Mystica catena rupta est*,' Dr Lartius quoted sadly. 'My friends are your enemies, and they are suffering. Their hearts and nerves are breaking. Therefore the link is thin and I cannot feel their thoughts. That is why I am so sad, for against my will the sorrow of my friends clouds me.'

Ulrici laughed in his gross way. 'Then the best omen for us is that you fall into melancholia? When you cut your throat we shall know that we have won.'

Yet Ulrici was not quite happy. The young prophet was in danger of becoming a Frankenstein's monster, which he could not control. For his popular fame was now a thing to marvel at. It had gone abroad through Germany, and to all the fighting fronts, and the phrase linked to it was that of 'Peace before winter'. Peace had become a conviction, an obsession. Ulrici and his friends would have preferred the word to be 'Victory'.

In the early days of July a distinguished visitor came from Berlin to the Garmischstrasse. He was an *Erster Generalstabsoffizier*, high in the confidence of the Supreme Command. He sat in the shaded room and asked an urgent question.

'I am not a Delphian oracle,' said Dr Lartius, 'and I do not prophesy. But this much I can tell you. The hearts of your enemies have become like water, and they have few reserves left. I am not a soldier, so you can judge better than I. You say you are ready to strike with a crushing force. If you leave your enemies leisure they will increase and their hearts may recover.'

'That is my view,' said the soldier. 'You have done much for the German people in the past, sir. Have you no word now to encourage them?'

'There will be peace before winter. This much I can tell, but how I know I cannot tell.'

'But on what terms?'

'That depends upon your armies,' was the oracular reply.

The staff officer had been gazing intently at the speaker. Now he rose and switched on the electric light.

'Will you oblige me by taking off your glasses, sir?' he asked, and there was the sharpness of command in his voice.

Dr Lartius removed his spectacles, and for some seconds the two men looked at each other.

'I thank you,' said the soldier at last. 'For a moment I thought we had met before. You reminded me of a man I knew long ago. I was mistaken.'

After that it was noted by all that the melancholy of Dr Lartius increased. His voice was saddened, and dejection wrapped him like a cloud. Those of the inner circle affected to see in this a good omen. 'He is *en rapport* with his English friends,' they said. 'He cannot help himself, and their despair is revealed in him. The poor Lartius! He is suffering for the sins of our enemies.' But the great public saw only the depression, and as August matured, and bad news filtered through the land, it gave their spirits an extra push downhill.

In those weeks only one word came from the Garmischstrasse. It was 'Peace – peace before winter.' The phrase became the universal formula whispered wherever people spoke their minds. It ran like lightning through the camps and along the fronts, and in every workshop and tavern. It became a passion, a battle-cry. The Wise Doctor of Munich had said it. Peace before winter – Peace at all costs – only Peace.

In September Ulrici was in communication with a certain bureau in Berlin. 'The man is honest enough, but he is mad. He has served his purpose. It is time to suppress him.' Berlin agreed, and one morning Ulrici departed from Berne.

But when he reached the Garmischstrasse he found the flamboyant plate unscrewed from the door and the pleasant rooms deserted.

For a day or two before Dr Lartius had been behaving oddly. He gave out that he was ill, and could not receive; but he was very busy indoors with his papers. Then late one evening, after a conversation on the telephone with the railway people, he left his rooms, with no luggage but a small dressing-case, and took the night train for Innsbruck. His admirable passport franked him anywhere. From Innsbruck he travelled to the Swiss frontier, and when he crossed it, in the darkness of the September evening and in an empty carriage, he made a toilet which included the shaving of his silky black beard. He was whistling softly and seemed to have recovered his spirits. At Berne he did not seek his usual hotel, but went to an unfrequented place in a back street, where, apparently, he was well known. There he met during the course of the day various people, and their conversation was not in the German tongue.

That night he again took train, but it was westward to Lausanne and the French border.

IV

In the early days of November, when the Allies were approaching Maubeuge and Sedan, and the German plenipotentiaries were trying to dodge the barrage and get speech with Foch, two British officers were sitting in a little room at Versailles. One was the General we have already met, the quondam friend of Lady Samplar. The other was a slim young man who wore the badges of a lieutenant-colonel and the gorget patches of the staff. He had a pale face shaven clean, black hair cut very short, and curious, bright, protuberant hazel eyes. He must have seen some service, for he had two rows of medal ribbons on his breast.

'Unarm, Eros,' quoted the General, looking at the last slip on a pile of telegrams. '"The long day's task is done." It has been a grim business, and, Tommy, my lad, I think you had the most difficult patch of the lot to hoe... It was largely due to you that the Boche made his blunder on 15th July, and stretched his neck far enough to let Foch hit him.'

The young man grinned. 'I wouldn't like to go through it again, sir. But it didn't seem so bad when I was at it, though it is horrible to look back on. The worst part was the loneliness.'

'You must have often had bad moments.'

'Not so many. I only remember two as particularly gruesome. One was when I heard you slanging me to Lady Samplar, and I suddenly felt hopelessly cut off from my kind... The other was in July, when von Mudra came down from Berlin to see me. He dashed nearly spotted me, for he was at the Embassy when I was in Constantinople.'

The General lifted a flamboyant plate whereon the name of Dr S. Lartius was inscribed in letters of oxidised silver. 'You've brought away your souvenir all right. I suppose you'll have it framed as a trophy for your ancestral hall. By the way, what did the letter S stand for?'

'When I was asked,' said the young man, 'I said "Sigismund". But I really meant it for "Spurius" – the chap, you remember, who held the bridge with Horatius.'

The Magic Walking Stick

Buchan's children's story, 'The Magic Walking Stick', first appeared in *Sails of Gold* (1927), an anthology edited by Cynthia Asquith, whom he had known since his time at Oxford and whose son Michael was friendly with Buchan's own children. The story was published by Hodder in an expanded book version in 1932 and serialised, first in *Windsor Magazine* in January 1932 and then subsequently in *Strand Magazine, Pearson Magazine, Woman's Journal* and the *Daily Express*.

WHEN BILL CAME back for long-leave that autumn half he had before him a complex programme of entertainment. Thomas, the Keeper, whom he revered more than anyone else in the world, was to take him in the afternoon to try for a duck in the big marsh called Alemoor. In the evening Hallowe'en would be celebrated in the nursery with his small brother Peter, and he would be permitted to sit up after dinner till ten o'clock. Next day, which was Sunday, would be devoted to wandering about with Peter, hearing from him all the appetising home news, and pouring into his greedy ears the gossip of the foreign world of school. On Monday morning, after a walk with the dogs, he was to motor to London, lunch with Aunt Alice, go to a conjuring show, and then, after a noble tea, return to school in time for lock-up.

It seemed to Bill all that could be desired in the way of excitement. But he did not know just how exciting that long leave was destined to be.

The first shadow of a cloud appeared after luncheon, when he had changed into knickerbockers, and Peter and the dogs were waiting at the gun-room door. Bill could not find his own proper stick. It was a long hazel staff, given him by the second stalker in a Scotch deer-forest the year before – a staff rather taller than Bill, of glossy hazel, with a shapely polished crook, and without a ferrule, like all stalking sticks.

He hunted for it high and low, but it could not be found. Without it in his hand Bill felt that an expedition lacked something vital, and he was not prepared to take instead one of his father's shooting sticks, as Groves, the butler, recommended. Nor would he accept a knubbly cane proffered by Peter. Feeling a little aggrieved and imperfectly equipped, he rushed out to join Thomas. He would cut himself an ashplant in the first hedge.

But as the two ambled down the lane which led to Alemoor, they came on an old man sitting under a hornbeam. He was a funny little wizened old man, in a shabby long green overcoat, which had once been black, and he wore on his head the oldest and tallest and greenest bowler hat that ever graced a human head. Thomas walked on as if he did not see him, and Gyp, the spaniel, and Shawn, the Irish setter, at the sight of him dropped their tails between their legs, and remembered an engagement a long way off. But Bill stopped, for he saw that the old man had a bundle under his arm, a bundle of ancient umbrellas and queer ragged sticks.

The old man smiled at him, and he had very bright eyes. He seemed to know what was wanted, for he at once took from his bundle a stick. You would not have said that it was the kind of stick Bill was looking for. It was short, and heavy, and made of some dark foreign wood, and instead of a crook it had a handle shaped like a crescent, cut out of some white substance which was neither bone nor ivory. Yet Bill, as soon as he saw it, felt that it was the one stick in the world for him.

'How much?' he asked.

'One farthing,' said the old man, and his voice squeaked like a winter wind in a chimney.

Now a farthing is not a common coin, but Bill happened to have one – a gift from Peter on his arrival that day, along with a brass cannon, five empty cartridges, a broken microscope, and a badly-printed, brightly-illustrated narrative called 'Two Villains Foiled'. But a farthing sounded too little, so Bill proffered one of his scanty shillings.

'I said one farthing,' said the old man rather snappily.

The small coin changed hands, and the little old wizened face seemed to light up with an elfish glee. ''Tis a fine stick, young sir,' he squeaked, 'a noble stick, when you gets used to the ways of it.'

Bill had to run to catch up Thomas, who was plodding along with the dogs, now returned from their engagement.

'That's a queer chap – the old stick-man, I mean,' he said.

'I ain't seen no old man, Maaster Bill,' said Thomas. 'What be 'ee talkin' about?'

'The fellow back there. I bought this stick of him.'

Thomas cast a puzzled glance at the stick. 'That be a craafty stick, Maaster Bill—' but he said no more, for Bill had shaken it playfully at the dogs. As soon as they saw it they set off to keep another engagement – this time, apparently, with a hare – and Thomas was yelling and whistling for ten minutes before he brought them to heel.

It was a soft grey afternoon, and Bill was stationed beside one of the deep dykes in the moor, well in cover of a thorn bush, while Thomas and the dogs went off on a long circuit to show themselves beyond the big mere, so that the duck might move in Bill's direction. It was rather cold, and very wet underfoot, for a lot of rain had fallen in the past week, and the mere, which was usually only a sedgy pond, had now grown to a great expanse of shallow flood-water. Bill began his vigil in high excitement. He drove his new stick into the ground, and used the handle as a seat, while he rested his gun in the orthodox way in the crook of his arm. It was a double-barrelled, sixteen bore, and Bill knew that he would be lucky if he got a duck with it; but a duck was to him a bird of mystery, true wild game, and he preferred the chance of one to the certainty of many rabbits.

The minutes passed, the grey afternoon sky darkened towards twilight, but no duck came. Bill saw a wedge of geese high up in the sky and longed to salute them; also he heard snipe, but could not locate them in the dim weather. Far away he thought he detected the purring noise which Thomas made to stir the duck, but no overhead beat of wings followed. Soon the mood of eager anticipation died away, and he grew bored and rather despondent. He scrambled up the bank of the dyke and strained his eyes over the moor between the bare boughs of the thorn. He thought he saw duck moving – yes, he was certain of it – they were coming from the direction of Thomas and the dogs. It was perfectly clear what was happening. There was far too much water on the moor, and the birds, instead of flighting across the mere to the boundary slopes, were simply settling on the flood. From the misty grey water came the rumour of many wildfowl.

Bill came back to his wet stand grievously disappointed. He did not dare to leave it in case a flight did appear, but he had lost all hope. He tried to warm his feet by moving them up and down in the squelchy turf. His gun was now under his arm, and he was fiddling idly with the handle of the stick which was still embedded in earth. He made it revolve, and as it turned he said aloud: 'I wish I was in the middle of the big flood.'

Then a remarkable thing happened. Bill was not conscious of any movement, but suddenly his surroundings were completely changed. He had still his gun under his left arm and the stick in his right hand, but instead of standing on wet turf he was up to the waist in water ... And all around him were duck – shovellers, pintail, mallard, teal, widgeon, pochard, tufted – and bigger things that might be geese – swimming or diving or just alighting from the air. In a second Bill realised that his wish had been granted. He was in the very middle of the flood-water.

He got a right and left at mallards, missing with his first barrel. Then the birds rose in alarm, and he shoved in fresh cartridges and fired wildly into the brown. His next two shots were at longer range, but he was certain that he had hit something. And then the duck vanished in the brume, and he was left alone with the grey waters running out to the dimness.

He lifted up his voice and shouted wildly for Thomas and the dogs, and looked about him to retrieve what he had shot. He had got two anyhow – a mallard drake and a young teal, and he collected them. Presently he heard whistling and splashing, and Gyp the spaniel appeared half swimming, half wading. Gyp picked up a second mallard, and Bill left it at that. He thought he knew roughly where the deeper mere lay so as to avoid it, and with his three duck he started for where he believed Thomas to be. The water was often up to his armpits and once he was soused over his head, and it was a very wet, breathless and excited boy that presently confronted the astounded keeper.

'Where in goodness ha' ye been, Maaster Bill? Them ducks was tigglin' out to the deep water and I was feared ye wouldn't get a shot. Three on 'em, no less! My word, ye 'ave poonished 'em.'

'I was in the deep water,' said Bill, but he explained no more, for it had just occurred to him that he couldn't. It was a boy not less puzzled than triumphant that returned to show his bag to his family, and at dinner he was so abstracted that his mother thought he was ill and sent him early to bed. Bill made no complaint, for he wanted to be alone to think things out.

It was plain that a miracle had happened, and it must be connected with the stick. He had wished himself in the middle of the flood-water – he remembered that clearly – and at the time he had been doing something to the stick. What was it? It had been stuck in the ground, and he had been playing with the handle. Yes, he had it. He had been turning it round when he uttered the wish. Bill's mind was better stored with fairy tales than with Latin and Greek, and he remembered many precedents. The stick was in the rack in the hall, and he had half a mind to slip downstairs and see if he could repeat the performance. But he reflected that he might be observed, and that this was a business demanding profound secrecy. So he resolutely composed himself to sleep. He had been allowed for a treat to have his old bed in the night-nursery, next to Peter, and he realised that he must be up bright and early to frustrate that alert young inquirer.

He woke before dawn, and at once put on socks and fives-shoes and a dressing-gown, and tiptoed downstairs. He heard a housemaid moving in the direction of the dining-room, and Groves opening the library shutters, but the hall was deserted. He groped in the rack and found the stick, struggled with the key of the garden door, and emerged into the foggy winter half-light. It was very cold, as he padded down the lawn to a retired half-moon of shrubbery beside the pond, and his shoes were soon soaked with hoar-frost. He shivered and drew his dressing-gown around him, but he had decided what to do. In this kind of weather he wished to be warm. He planted his stick in the turf.

'I want to be on the beach in the Solomon Islands,' said Bill, and three times twisted the handle.

In a second his eyes seemed to dazzle with excess of light and something beat on his body like a blast from on open furnace . . . He was standing on an expanse of blinding white sand at which a lazy blue sea was licking. Behind him at a distance of perhaps two hundred yards was a belt of high green forest, out of which stuck a tall crest of palms. A hot wind was blowing and tossing the tree-tops, but it only crisped the sea.

Bill gasped with joy to find his dream realised. He was in the far Pacific where he had always longed to be . . . But he was very hot, and could not endure the weight of winter pyjamas and winter dressing-gown. Also he longed to bathe in those inviting waters. So he shed everything and hopped gaily down to the tide's edge, leaving the stick still upright in the sand.

The sea was as delicious as it looked, but Bill, though a good swimmer, kept near the edge for fear of sharks. He wallowed and splashed, with the fresh salt smell which he loved in his nostrils. Minutes passed rapidly, and he was just on the point of striking out for a little reef, when he cast a glance towards the shore . . .

At the edge of the forest stood men – dark-skinned men, armed with spears.

Bill scrambled to his feet with a fluttering heart, and as he rose the men moved forward. He was, perhaps, fifty yards from the stick, which cast its long morning shadow on the sand, and they were two hundred yards on the farther side. At all costs he must get there first. He sprang out of the sea, and as he ran he saw to his horror that the men ran also – ran in great bounds – shouting and brandishing their spears.

Those fifty yards seemed miles, but Bill won the race. No time to put on his clothes. He seized his dressing-gown with one hand and the stick with the other, and as he twirled the handle a spear whizzed by his ear. 'I want to be home,' he gasped, and the next second he stood naked between the shrubbery and the pond, clutching his dressing-gown. The Solomon Islands had got his fives-shoes and his pyjamas.

The cold of a November morning brought him quickly to his senses. He clothed his shivering body in his dressing-gown and ran by devious paths to the house. Happily the gun-room door was unlocked, and he was able to ascend by way of empty passages and back-stairs to the nursery floor. He did not, however, escape the eagle eye of Elsie, the nurse, who read a commination service over a boy who went out of doors imperfectly clad on such a morning. She prophesied pneumonia, and plumped him into a hot bath.

Bill applied his tongue to the back of his hand. Yes. It tasted salt, and the salt smell was still in his nose. It had not been a dream . . . He hugged himself in the bath and made strange gurgling sounds of joy. Life had suddenly opened up for him in dazzling vistas of adventure.

His conduct in church that morning was exemplary, for while Peter at his side had his usual Sunday attack of St Vitus's Dance, Bill sat motionless as a mummy. On the way home his mother commented on it and observed that Lower Chapel seemed to have taught him how to behave. But his thoughts during the service had not been devotional. The stick lay beside him on the floor, and for a moment he had a wild notion of twisting it during the Litany and disappearing for a few minutes to Kamschatka. Then prudence supervened. He must go very cautiously in this business, and court no questions. That afternoon he and Peter would seek a secluded spot and make experiments. He would take the stick back to school and hide it in his room – he had a qualm when he thought what a 'floater' it would be if a lower boy appeared with it in public! For him no more hours of boredom. School would no longer be a place of exile, but a rapturous holiday. He would slip home now and then and see what was happening – he would go often to Glenmore – he would visit any spot in the globe which took his fancy. His imagination reeled at the prospect, and he cloaked his chortles of delight in a fervent Amen.

At luncheon it was decided that Peter and he should go for a walk together, and should join the others at a place called the Roman Camp. 'Let the boys have a chance of being alone,' his father had said. This exactly suited Bill's book, and as they left the dining-room he clutched his small brother. 'Shrimp,' he said in his ear, 'You're going to have the afternoon of your life.'

It was a mild, grey day, with the leafless woods and the brown ploughlands lit by a pale November sun. Peter, as he trotted beside him, jerked out breathless inquiries about what Bill proposed to do, and was told to wait and see.

Arrived at a clump of beeches which promised privacy, Bill first swore his brother to secrecy by the most awful oaths which he could imagine.

'Put your arm round my waist and hang on to my belt,' he told him. 'I'm going to take you to have a look at Glenmore.'

'Don't be silly,' said Peter. 'That only happens in Summer, and we haven't packed yet.'

'Shut up and hold tight,' said Bill as he twirled the stick and spoke the necessary words...

The boys were looking not at the smooth boles of beeches, but at a little coppice of rowans and birches above the narrow glen of the hill burn. It was Glenmore in very truth. There was the strip of mossy lawn, the white-washed gable end of the lodge; there to the left beside the walled garden was the smoking chimney of the keeper's cottage;

there beyond the trees was the long lift of brown moorland and the blue top of Stob Ghabhar. To the boys Glenmore was the true home of the soul, but they had seen it only in the glory of late summer and early autumn. In its winter dress it seemed for a moment strange. Then the sight of an old collie waddling across the lawn gave the connecting link.

'There's Wattie,' Peter gasped, and lifted up his voice in an excited summons. His brother promptly scragged him.

'Don't be an ass, Shrimp,' he said fiercely. 'This is a secret, you fathead. This is magic. Nobody must know we are here. Come on and explore.'

For an hour – it must have been an hour, Bill calculated afterwards, but it seemed like ten minutes – the two visited their favourite haunts. They found the robbers' cave in the glen where a raven nested, and the pool where Bill had caught his first pound trout, and the stretch in the river where their father that year had had the thirty pound salmon. There were no blaeberries or crowberries in the woods, but there were many woodcock, and Bill had a shot with his catapult at a wicked old blackcock on a peat-stack. Also they waylaid Wattie, the collie, and induced him to make a third in the party. All their motions were as stealthy as an Indian's, and the climax of the adventure was reached when they climbed the garden wall and looked in at the window of the keeper's cottage.

Tea was laid before a bright peat fire in the parlour, so Mrs Macrae must be expecting company. It looked a very good tea, for there were scones and pancakes, and shortbread and currant-loaf and heather honey. Both boys felt suddenly famished at the sight.

'Mrs Macrae always gives me a scone and honey,' Peter bleated. 'I'm hungry. I want one.'

So did Bill. His soul longed for food, but he kept hold of his prudence.

'We daren't show ourselves,' he whispered. 'But, perhaps, we might pinch a scone. It wouldn't be stealing, for if Mrs Macrae saw us she would say "Come awa in, laddies, and get a jeely piece." I'll give you a back, Shrimp, and in you get.'

The window was open, and Peter was hoisted through, falling with a bang on a patch-work rug. But he never reached the table, for at that moment the parlour door opened and someone entered. After that things happened fast. Peter, urged by Bill's anguished whisper, turned

[259]

back to the window, and was hauled through by the scruff of the neck. A woman's voice was heard crying, 'Mercy on us, it's the bairns,' as the culprits darted to the shelter of the gooseberry bushes.

Bill realised that there was no safety in the garden, so he dragged Peter over the wall by the way they had come, thereby seriously damaging a pear tree. But they had been observed, and as they scrambled out of a rose-bed, they heard cries and saw Mrs Macrae appearing round the end of the wall, having come through the stable yard. Also a figure, which looked like Angus, the river gillie, was running from the same direction.

There was nothing for it but to go. Bill seized Peter with one hand and the stick with the other, and spoke the words, with Angus not six yards away ... As he looked once more at the familiar beech boles, his ears were still full of the cries of an excited woman and the frenzied howling of Wattie, the dog.

The two boys, very warm and flustered and rather scratched about the hands and legs, confronted their father and mother and their sister, Barbara, who was sixteen and very proud.

'Hullo, hullo,' they heard their father say. 'I thought you'd be hiding somewhere hereabouts. You young rascals know how to take cover, for you seemed to spring out of the ground. You look as if you'd been playing football. Better walk home with us and cool down ... Bless my soul, Peter, what's that you've got? It's bog myrtle! Where on earth did you find it? I've never seen it before in Oxfordshire.'

Then Barbara raised a ladylike voice. 'Oh, Mummy, look at the mess they've made of themselves. They've been among the brambles, for Peter has two holes in his stockings. Just look at Bill's hands!' And she wrinkled her finical nose, and sniffed.

Bill kept a diplomatic silence, and Peter, usually garrulous, did the same, for his small wrist was in his brother's savage clutch.

That night, before Peter went to bed, he was compelled once more to swear solemn oaths, and Bill was so abstracted that his mother thought that he was sickening for some fell disease. He lay long awake, planning out the best way to use his marvellous new possession. His thoughts were still on the subject next morning, and to his family's amazement he made no protest when, to suit his mother's convenience, it was decided to start for London soon after breakfast, and the walk with the dogs was cancelled. He departed in high spirits, most unlike his usual leave-takings, and his last words to Peter were fierce exhortations to secrecy.

All the way to London he was in a happy dream, and at luncheon he was so urbane that Aunt Alice, who had strong and unorthodox views about education, announced that in Bill's case, at any rate, the public school system seemed to answer, and gave him double her customary tip.

Then came the conjuring show at the Grafton Hall. Bill in the past had had an inordinate appetite for such entertainments, and even in his new ecstasy he looked forward to this one. But at the door of the hall he had a shock. Hitherto he had kept close to his stick, but it was now necessary to give it up and receive a metal check for it. To his mother's surprise he protested hotly. 'It won't do any harm,' he pleaded. 'It will stay beside me under the seat.' But the rule was inexorable and he had to surrender it. 'Don't be afraid, darling,' his mother told him. 'That funny new stick of yours won't be lost. The check is a receipt for it, and they are very careful.'

The show was not up to his expectations. What were all these disappearing donkeys and vanishing ladies compared to the performances he had lately staged? Bill was puffed up with a great pride. With the help of his stick he could make rings round this trumpery cleverness. He was the true magician . . . He wished that the thing would end that he might feel the precious stick again in his hand.

At the counter there was no sign of the man who had given him the check. Instead there was a youth who seemed to be new to the business, and who was very slow in returning the sticks and umbrellas. When it came to Bill's turn he was extra slow, and presently announced that he could find no Number 229.

Bill's mother, seeing his distress, intervened, and sent the wretched youth to look again, while other people were kept waiting, but he came back with the same story. There was no duplicate Number 229, or any article to correspond to the check. After that he had to be allowed to attend to the others, and Bill, almost in tears, waited hysterically till the crowd had gone. Then there was a thorough search, and Bill and his mother were allowed to go behind the counter. But no Number 229 could be found, and there were no sticks left, only three umbrellas.

Bill was now patently in tears.

'Never mind, darling,' his mother said, 'we must be off now, or you will be late for lock-up. I promise that your father will come here to-morrow and clear up the whole business. Never fear – the stick will be found.'

But it is still lost.

When Bill's father went there next day, and cross-examined the wretched youth – for he had once been a barrister – he extracted a curious story. If the walking-stick was lost, so also was the keeper of the walking-sticks, for the youth was only an assistant. The keeper – his name was Jukes and he lived in Hammersmith – had not been seen since yesterday afternoon during the performance, and Mrs Jukes had come round and made a scene last night, and that morning the police had been informed. Mr Jukes, it appeared, was not a very pleasant character, and he had had too much beer at luncheon. When the audience had all gone in, he had expressed to his assistant his satiety of life. The youth's testimony ran as follows: 'Mr Jukes, 'e was wavin' his arm something chronic and carryin' on about 'ow this was no billet for a man like 'im. He picks up a stick, and I thought he was goin' to 'it me. "Percy, me lad," says 'e, "I'm fed up – fed up to the back teeth." He starts twisting the stick, and says 'e "I wish to 'eaven I was out of 'ere." After that I must 'ave come over faint, for when I looks again, 'e 'ad 'opped it.'

Mr Jukes' case is still a puzzle to Mrs Jukes and the police, but Bill understands only too clearly what happened. Mr Jukes and the stick have gone 'out of 'ere', and where that may be neither Bill nor I can guess.

But he still lives in hope, and he wants me to broadcast this story in case the stick may have come back to earth. So let every boy and girl keep a sharp eye on shops where sticks are sold. The magic walking-stick is not quite four feet long, and about one inch and a quarter thick. It is made of a heavy dark-red wood, rather like the West Indian purpleheart. Its handle is in the shape of a crescent with the horns uppermost, made of some white substance which is neither bone nor ivory. If anyone sees such a stick, then Bill will give all his worldly wealth for news of it.

Failing that, he would like information about the man who sold it to him. He is very old, small and wizened, but his eyes are the brightest you ever saw in a human head. He wears a shabby, greeny-black overcoat which reaches down to his heels, and a tall, greeny-black bowler hat. It is possible that the stick may have returned to him. So if you meet anyone like him, look sharply at his bundle, and if it is there and he is willing to sell, *buy it – buy it – buy it*, or you will regret it all your days. For this purpose it is wiser always to have a farthing in your pocket, for he won't give change.

The Strange Adventures of
Mr Andrew Hawthorn

Another of Buchan's children's stories anthologised by Cynthia Asquith, this time in *The Silver Ship* (1932), 'The Strange Adventures of Mr Andrew Hawthorn' is about a young Scotsman's adventures abroad after he mysteriously disappears one day.

———————

ANY DISAPPEARANCE IS a romantic thing, especially if it be unexpected and inexplicable. To vanish from the common world and leave no trace, and to return with the same suddenness and mystery, satisfies the eternal human sense of wonder. That is why the old stories make so much of it. Tamlane and Kilmeny and Ogier the Dane retired to Fairyland, and Oisin to the Land of the Ever Living, and no man knows the manner of their going or their return. The common world goes on, but they are far away in a magic universe of their own.

But even ordinary folk can disappear. Sometimes they never come back and leave only blank mystery behind them. But sometimes they return and can explain what happened. Here is a true tale of what befell a most prosaic Scots gentleman rather less than two centuries ago.

Let us call him Andrew Hawthorn. He was thirty-two years of age and had no wife, but lived with his sister, Barbara, in a steep-roofed, stone house a dozen miles from Edinburgh. The house stood above a narrow wooded glen, what is called in Scotland a 'dean', at the bottom of which ran a brawling stream.

Mr Hawthorn was a stiff gentleman, very set in his ways. His wig was always carefully powdered, his clothes were trim, and his buckles bright. He enjoyed a modest competence, which enabled him to devote his life to his hobbies. These were principally antiquities, and he had been busy for some years on a great work on the Antonines.

He was in the habit of breakfasting at seven with his sister, and being particular in his habits, he liked to have his meal served punctually at that hour. He was always in the little dining-room as the clock struck, while his sister was usually a few minutes late. His custom was to take a walk after breakfast and be at his books at eight o'clock. Therefore he liked to finish his meal by a quarter after seven, and this meant punctilious service. In especial he disliked having his porridge so hot that he had to delay some minutes before he could begin on it.

On a fine May morning Mr Hawthorn appeared in the breakfast room at the exact hour. His sister was not down, but two steaming bowls of porridge stood on the table. Mr Hawthorn was annoyed. He strode into the little hall and shouted upstairs.

'Babbie,' he cried, 'how often have I told you the porridge should be dished up earlier? They are scalding hot again. I am going out of doors until they cool.'

He walked out into the garden. He also walked out of the world for five years and seven months.

There was a great hue and cry in the countryside. The Procurator Fiscal made his precognitions, and even the capital city was stirred by the mystery, but no trace could be found of Mr Andrew Hawthorn. His footsteps were followed on the coarse dewy turf which ran along the edge of the dean, and there they disappeared. In the dean itself there were signs of an old fire on a little shelf of ground, and a good deal of trampled grass and broken underwood; but the latter might have been due to the cattle-beasts that were always straying in from the neighbouring hillside.

Mr Hawthorn had no near kin besides his sister, but his lawyers offered a considerable reward for news of him. None came, and most people assumed that he was dead. His sister, who was his heir-at-law, would have succeeded to his estate had his death been presumed, but she resolutely refused to admit the presumption. Andrew, she said, would come back, though she would give no grounds for her belief. She conducted the household as usual, and every morning she had a plate of porridge set for him at breakfast, as if at any moment he might appear from the garden. She even remembered his wishes and saw to it that the porridge was dished up a little earlier.

Mr Hawthorn went out into the bright sunshine and impatiently sniffed the morning freshness. He walked to the edge of the dean, and

there, on the well trodden path among the fir trees, he saw one Bauldy
Grieve, a packman, whose rounds took him up and down the Lowlands. Bauldy was an old friend who had often provided him with
minor antiquities. It appeared that he had something important to
communicate, for he was sitting there to intercept the laird on his
morning walk.

'I've some michty wonders to show your honour,' he announced.
'The pleughman at the Back o' the Buss turned up an auld kist in the
field. He didna let on to his master, but he telled me. I bocht what was
in it, a wheen auld siller coins and some muckle flaigons. The
pleughman – Tam Dod is his name – thocht the flaigons were brass,
so I got them cheap, though he haggled sair over the siller. But they
are no brass, your honour – they're gowd, as sure as I'm a living man.
Nae doot they were buried by the ancient Romans. So I cam off post
haste to see ye, and have gotten them in my pack. Will your honour
step doun wi' me and hae a look at them?'

Mr Hawthorn was excited and forgot all about breakfast. He followed the packman down through the bracken to a shelf above the
burn, where Bauldy had spent the night. At the first sight of the
flagons his eyes opened wide. They were amphorae of exquisite design,
probably vessels used for some ceremonial rite. He scraped off a little
of the encrusted dirt, and saw the gleam of bright metal.

Now, as ill-luck would have it, news of the find had got abroad,
perhaps because Bauldy had gossiped in his cups. Anyhow, three
tinkler ruffians of the Baillie clan were on the trail, and had followed
Bauldy to his camp for the night. They had seen him speak to the laird
and were now lurking in the undergrowth.

'Guid save us, Bauldy,' said Mr Hawthorn. 'This is a most
remarkable discovery. The like has not been seen in Scotland.'

'Are they gowd, your honour?' the packman asked.

'I have little doubt of it,' said Mr Hawthorn. 'Things so beautiful
could be made of no baser metal.'

This was enough for the tinklers. They leaped out upon the two,
and one, with his big staff, or 'kent', struck the packman a savage
blow on the back of his head. Mr Hawthorn, though taken by surprise, put up a stout fight, for the passion of the antiquarian put fire
into his manhood. But he was soon overpowered and knocked sense-
less by a blow from behind.

After that Mr Hawthorn's memory became confused. The tinklers were men of caution and foresight. It was not enough to annex the contents of the pedlar's pack, they must get rid of compromising evidence. The pedlar looked pretty bad, and the gentleman not much better. It would never do to leave them on the scene of the assault, for they had seen too much of their assailants.

Now, on the highway on the other side of the dean, the tinklers had a covered cart, which they were accustomed to use for nefarious business. They swung their two victims on their shoulders and cautiously made their way to the cart, and some time that evening were safe in a hovel near the water-front in Leith.

The pedlar never recovered, for his neck had been broken. Mr Hawthorn came back to consciousness with an intolerable headache and a raging thirst; he was given a drink, which must have been hocussed, for he lost his senses again. The body of the pedlar was secretly buried, a ceremony for which the tinklers had their own contrivances, and it was not likely that a wandering packman would be missed.

But Mr Hawthorn was a different matter. The hue and cry over his loss alarmed them, and they saw no other course but to get rid of him too. Murder was their first idea, but presently a better presented itself. They had already done some traffic in kidnapping and exporting the able-bodied to the American plantations, and they had a shipmaster who was in their secret. One dark night Mr. Hawthorn, still hocussed, was smuggled aboard a vessel, and when his wits fully returned to him he was a prisoner on the broad Atlantic.

It would take a long time to tell the full story of Mr Hawthorn's life in the Carolinas. He was sold under an indenture to a tobacco planter, which meant that till the period of his indenture expired he was virtually a slave. His ill-treatment at the hands of the tinklers had affected both his memory and his wits, and it was a long time before his head cleared. Bit by bit, however, recollection came back to him, but the last scene he remembered clearly was leaving his steaming porridge in the little dining-room of his house. All that had happened in the dean remained in a misty confusion.

He was strong in body and of careful habits, and this stood him well in the hard toil of the plantation. Also he was a prudent soul, and, having decided that there was nothing for it but to submit, he did his work and kept his thoughts to himself. His companions were mostly the scum of British prisons, and he might have endured a good deal of rough usage at their hands. But Mr Hawthorn had a stiff temper of his own, and his fellows realised that there was a point when he would show fight and defend himself. So slowly he won a position of some respect among the others, while his industry and docility secured him reasonable treatment from the overseer.

His master was a man of pleasure who spent his days chiefly in horse-racing and card-playing. Several times Mr Hawthorn, after his memory returned to him, tried to approach him to state his case, but it was long before he got an opportunity. When it came he found that he was not believed. Such yarns had often been heard before from redemptioners. But the superior breeding of Mr Hawthorn impressed his master. Here was one who in deportment and speech appeared to be a gentleman, though he looked a dull dog and spoke with a strong Scots accent. The upshot was that when the butler broke his neck one dark night Mr Hawthorn was promoted to fill his place. Among his other gifts it appeared that he had a very fair knowledge of wine.

Now it happened some months later, when the household under Mr Hawthorn's sway had acquired a new precision, that a neighbouring squire came to dinner. The guest was of a very different type from the master of the house, for he was something of a politician and something of a scholar. During the meal he quoted a tag from Horace, but could not remember its conclusion. His host could not help him out, but, to his surprise, the butler volunteered the missing line.

The result was that the guest had some speech with Mr Hawthorn before he left, heard his story, and believed it. He was a man of a philanthropic spirit, and his first aim was to remove this unhappy scholar to more congenial surroundings. So after various negotiations, which had something to do with a young thoroughbred filly, Mr Hawthorn was transferred to the establishment of his new-found friend.

There he dwelt not unhappily for a considerable time. At his request his new master wrote to a Scottish correspondent, and, without revealing Mr Hawthorn's existence, secured the full details of the events which had mystified all Lothian. He learned that Miss Barbara was living in the house, confident that her brother would some day return. Mr Hawthorn would not let him proceed further. Somewhere in his sober bosom was a spark of romance; as he had departed mysteriously, so he would return. His new life interested him, he had formed an attachment to his new master, and he had almost forgotten about his great work on the Antonines. Also, Mr Hawthorn was proud. He was determined to be beholden to no man for the cost of his return, and he was waiting until he had saved sufficient money from his wages.

At last the day arrived when he was ready and willing to leave. But in those days of continuous war with France it was no slight business to cross the Atlantic, and there were many adventures in store for him before he reached his native land.

He embarked on a ship which was taken off Land's End by a French privateer. He was carried to Havre and found himself a prisoner in the enemy's hands. This misfortune achieved what none of his sufferings in Carolina had achieved – it broke Mr Hawthorn's temper. He managed to escape, and for several months was a fugitive on the French roads. Having some command of the French tongue, and dwelling much upon his Scottish nationality and the old friendship between Scotland and France, he managed to secure the good offices of a priest, who facilitated his journey to the capital.

In Paris Mr Hawthorn had a friend, a fellow antiquarian, to whom he appealed for help. This was willingly given, but it was not easy at the moment to leave France, and Mr Hawthorn had to spend several months in Paris, where, after his proud fashion, he insisted on supporting himself by teaching. He had to pass as a Scottish Jacobite, a disguise which gave him intense annoyance, for he was a zealous supporter of the Hanoverian Government.

It was April when he found it possible to depart from French soil. A smuggler's sloop landed him by night on the Sussex coast, and he was free once more to assume the character of a law-abiding Scotsman. He had enough money for the journey to the North, but, having acquired frugal habits during his wanderings, he insisted on making that journey in the most inexpensive fashion. Late on the evening of a day in early May, a timber barque from Hull deposited him at the pier at Leith.

He slept the night in a waterside inn, and before dawn next morning he was well on the road for his home. It was a fresh, bright day, very much the same weather as when he had left. He ascended the dean and crossed the strip of rough lawn. As he entered the dining-room the clock was striking seven.

There were two plates of smoking porridge on the table, much too hot to eat.

He strode into the hall. 'Babbie!' he cried, 'how often have I told you that the porridge should be dished up earlier?'

But he did not go out into the garden again to wait until it cooled.

Ho! The Merry Masons

Although little known today, 'Ho! The Merry Masons' was one of Buchan's most successful stories, appearing during the spring and summer of 1933 in some half a dozen American magazines and at the end of that year in *Nelson's Help Yourself Annual*. The story, which features many of Buchan's best-known characters and a successor to the Runagates Club, was rediscovered by Kate Macdonald in 1989. In it Burminster has become Burmester and there is reference back to Hollond, the central figure in his 1910 story 'Space'.

THE THURSDAY CLUB — the successor of the old Runagates Club of which I have compiled a few chronicles — is not quite the same home of wild tales as its progenitor. Its newer members are too pre-occupied with the cares of life, and are apt to engage in grave discussions of current problems. But now and then the conversation strays into fantastic paths, and sometimes a story emerges.

One April night, when the street corners were scented with wall-flowers, and oysters were no longer on the dinner menu, the company was small, for half a dozen members had gone after salmon to the Dee, the Whye, and the Blackwater. Burmester, who was in the chair, brought the news of the death of one who had often been a guest, Sir Alwyn Thomasson, the retired diplomat, who had recently settled in Gloucestershire. 'Rotten bad luck,' he said. 'He was only in his early seventies, and as healthy as a blood-horse. I'd have given him another ten or fifteen years. You had heard about it, Ned?' and he turned to Leithen. 'Wasn't he a near neighbour?'

Leithen nodded. 'I went over to Scaip yesterday. It's a melancholy business, and that poor girl of his has a lonely future.'

Some man asked what he had died of.

'Heart failure, they say,' Burmester replied, 'though he didn't look like a man with a heart. But you never know with a fellow that has lived in hot countries and led a pretty gruelling life. Had you any suspicions, Ned?'

'No. And I don't believe he had himself.' Leithen's fine-drawn sallow face was curiously grave, as if this death meant more to him than that of an ordinary country neighbour, and Burmester discreetly passed from the subject.

That evening, I remember, was like one of the old Runagates sederunts. It was a soft spring night, the windows were left open and the curtains undrawn, and the only light came from the unshaded candles which burned without a flicker. The talk wandered discursively from the dangers of yellow fever spreading to East Africa, through the latest pronouncements of Mussolini, to certain speculations in the physics of hyper-space which a Cambridge professor had just made public. Peckwether, who was scientist as well as historian, had something to say about the last, and he stirred up Anthony Hurrell, the ornithologist.

'Have you ever considered,' Hurrell asked, 'that physics may provide a scientific explanation of certain ghost stories? There are some, you know, which are perfectly authenticated as facts, but are wholly inexplicable. Ordinary causality simply doesn't apply. But our new physics may provide the missing link.'

Leithen, who had spoken little at dinner, now found his voice. 'That was what Hollond used to say. Did any of you ever know Hollond? He perished years ago on the Chamonix Aiguilles. A genius in his way, and, though he is superseded now, he was the forerunner of Einstein and Planck and all that lot. He used to say that he could not see why some event should not have left an indelible mark on the ether, and that under certain conditions that mark might become audible or visible or present in some way to the human consciousness. There are places, you know, where you can wake an echo only by striking a particular note; to any other note in the scale the place is dumb.'

Burmester observed that the ether was a dashed queer thing. Someone had been telling him that every sound made since the beginning of time was still tucked away in the ether, and that some day scientific instruments might be devised which would be capable of eliciting them. He had been told that it might even be possible to dig out the actual Sermon on the Mount and Caesar's *Et tu, Brute*, if Caesar ever said it, and Philip Sidney's dying words, and the notion had solemnised him.

But Hurrell was not to be diverted by Burmester's fantasies. He said that he agreed with Hollond, whom he had known a little. 'Suppose you have some great crisis of human emotion – panic, lust, hate, self-sacrifice – a murder, a great renunciation – anything which strains the nerves to the extreme limit. We talk about an atmosphere being tense, and the tenseness may be not merely subjective. Why shouldn't human passion create some subtle physical dislocation which abides in the air of a particular place, and which may be recalled if somehow the *trait d'union* appears again? That would explain certain ghost stories – or, at least, it would point the way to their explanation.'

I do not know if Hurrell was serious – possibly not – but to our surprise Leithen was serious enough. This shrewd, matter-of-fact lawyer, who rejoiced to prick most speculative bubbles, suddenly revealed an unexpected credulity.

'It needn't be only in the air,' he said. 'Why should it not be in the whole physical environment – stones, trees, a glen, a hillside? We do not know what queer intricate effects the human soul may have on inanimate things. A physical environment may be charged with psychical stuff as a battery is charged with electricity, and, when the right conductor appears there may be the deuce to pay.'

He stopped.

'Go on,' said Hurrell. 'Explain yourself.'

'I can't,' said Leithen. 'It's only a whimsy, and won't bear explanation.'

Then Burmester showed his acumen.

'There's a story here,' he said. 'Let's have it, Ned.'

Leithen looked embarrassed.

'There is a story. It's about Scaip – where Thomasson died. But I'm not sure that I should tell it.' He hesitated. 'Yet, I don't know. We were all friends of his – and I've rather got it on my mind . . . I think I should like to tell it you. I can trust your discretion, for, as you'll see, it's not a thing that should be talked about.'

It all happened years ago, he said, just after I acquired Borrowby. Borrowby was rather a ruin, and I had to do a good deal to make it habitable, besides putting in bathrooms and lighting and that sort of thing. I employed a young architect who understood what I wanted, but I was so desperately keen that I couldn't keep away from the place, and was always running down to see how the builders were getting on. So that year, when the courts rose before Easter, I decided to spend my vacation in the Cotswolds. I meant to put up at a local pub, but suddenly out of the blue came an invitation from Barnes Lacey to stay with him at Scaip. Scaip is only five miles from Borrowby, so I gladly accepted.

You remember old Lacey? Bankers often dabble in scholarship, but he was the only stockbroker I have ever known who cultivated the Muses. Pretty arid Muses they were, for his hobby was the backstairs of the Middle Ages – all the dustiest backstairs, too, for he didn't care a rush for poetry and art, but only for conundrums in law and custom. He has been dead for some time, and I gather that his reputation is growing – constantly quoted by the pundits, for apparently he had some original theories which Maitland pooh-poohed, but which people nowadays are inclined to accept. He was the genuine antiquary and never so happy as when he was up to the neck in grubby charters. How he was so successful in the City I can't explain, but he was. He made a pot of money, and was just about to retire and look for a country house, when he inherited the family place from a distant cousin.

Scaip was the right kind of house for him. It is in one of those steep little valleys that cut into the west side of the Cotswold escarpment. Coming from the east, you cross the upland plateau with its stone walls and beech clumps and wild thorny meadows, and come suddenly to an edge and look over the Severn to the Welsh hills forty miles off. The glen drops straight from your feet, with a stream in it that lower down is dammed into a string of ponds. Near the top on a shelf is the village of Greenbourton, one of the prettiest in England – thirteenth-century church, green, cross, well spreading into watercress beds, and twenty grey stone-roofed cottages that look as ancient as hillside boulders – the most delicious place on earth, especially in April when it is smothered in a foam of cherry-blossom. Half a mile down on the next shelf stands the manor-house of Scaip, to which all the glen and about ten square miles of the uplands belong.

Have you ever seen Scaip? Well, go and look at it, for you won't forget the first sight of it. It has all the gloom and mystery of the back-world of England. Seen from the hill above it appears to be a little town, with all manner of tiny quadrangles and falling terraces, but if you look up at it from below it is more like some Tyrolese Schloss, a dark, craggy, impenetrable fortress. Or it is like a Border keep built to protect the gates of the Marches. There is Norman work in it, but the tower dates from just before the Wars of the Roses, and tacked on to it is the main block built about the time of Henry VII. It is the austerest kind of early Tudor, a grim façade broken up by a few shallow rectangular bow windows. The remarkable thing about it is that it has not been altered, except for a classical Jacobean porch at the main entrance, and a kitchen built out in the eighteenth century. Below it, dropping to the stream and the ponds, are funny little stone curtains, and terraces flanked with things like dovecots, and twisting stone stairways. All the purlieus are a maze of fantastic stonework, but the house itself rises above them as solid and self-contained as a mountain.

Inside it was the last word in discomfort, for it had been scarcely lived in for a century, the Laceys having another place in Norfolk which was not entailed and so had not descended to Barnes. The staircases ran at impossible angles, and to find your way about was a perpetual game of hide-and-seek. A good deal of the furniture was three centuries old and I have never seen such a museum of day-beds and settles and chairs in which ease was impossible. Barnes, who liked his comforts, had done his best, and he had excellent servants, but we had to bathe in hip-baths, and all the water had to be fetched from the courtyard well, and the food was apt to be cold, since it had to be brought about a quarter of a mile from the kitchen. His antiquarian conscience would not allow him to alter much, so he himself roosted in a medieval bed-chamber which smelt of mould, and put up with tepid meals. But he had introduced some reasonable armchairs and had the chimneys altered so that they did not smoke, and he knocked two rooms on the terrace together so as to make one decent guest-chamber. I, being a disconsidered bachelor, had a medieval cubby hole next to his own.

The weather when I arrived was the quiet, hazy, early April kind before the riot of spring begins. I arrived late and saw nothing of Scaip till the next morning, and then it seemed to me the last word in perfection, so that I fell sadly out of conceit with my own Borrowby. I looked from my window over the falling courts and gardens to the shining waters of a little lake, and beyond to a green shoulder of hill where sheep were feeding. I couldn't lie in bed, so I went for a walk before breakfast and looked into the terrace guest-room. It had not been spoiled by the reconstruction, and the small dark panels, the stone fireplace, the exquisite plaster mouldings of the ceiling, and the tapestry of the bed hangings and the curtains, were as they might have been three or four centuries ago. The view outside, too, had nothing modern in it, and I had a pleasant feeling of having cheated time as I paced the terrace. There was a far-off sound of bleating sheep, and a great cawing of rooks from the hillside beeches, and somewhere very distant the slow sweet chiming of bells. I thought what a kind and habitable land our England was, and how Scaip had an extra share of its graciousness. No harshness, I told myself, could ever have broken the peace of this happy vale.

On the second afternoon of my visit Barnes took me for a walk along the slopes of the hills in brisk shiny weather. A south wind was blowing that made the buds swell visibly. He wanted to show me the church at Fanways, which I had never seen, and which contained several Lacey tombs. We came to it about four o'clock, which I have always considered the cheerfullest hour in the day. I won't try to describe Fanways, for I daresay most of you have been there, for it is the show place of that bit of country. The village straggles on both sides of a narrow road and the cottages are perched high up on the banks with, below them, rock-gardens which were blazing with aubrietia and arabis. The church is at the foot, rising out of the water meadows like a baron's keep, and dwarfing the village, dwarfing even the hills. You cannot imagine anything more snug and comfortable than that string of ancient homesteads, each sending up its drift of smoke from its stone chimneys. But not so the famous church. Even in the clear April sunshine it threatened and commanded, pulled the mind out of its ease and warned it of the mystery of life and the terrors of death. Seen under a wild December sunset, it must be a solemnising spectacle.

I had this impression strong on me as we passed through the churchyard yews to the main porch. Barnes didn't seem to share it. He became the pitiless antiquarian, calling my attention to all kinds of architectural tit-bits, and talking a language I imperfectly understood. In the interior gloom, heavy with incense, for the vicar was an extreme Anglo-Catholic, he scarcely showed decent reverence, for he was eager to point out a dozen things in the carved woodwork and stonework which he pronounced to be grotesque and obscene. Other people had discoursed to me of the traces of diabolism in the holy places of our ancestors, and I did not pay much attention to Barnes.

But as we were leaving, and stood under the great eastern buttress, he suddenly revealed a sensitiveness with which I had not credited him. 'A noble house of God,' he said. 'Yes, but I swear that the Devil had a good deal to do with the building of it.'

He held the point of his stick at my breast in a way he had when he wanted to be emphatic.

'There's no greater nonsense,' he said, 'than the stuff the modern medieval sentimentalist talks about simple piety flowering into stone and lime and craftsmen working solely to the glory of God. There was a little of that, no doubt, but there was a pretty ugly other side. A great church often had its origin in the vulgarest rivalry. One magnate wanted to score off another, and that was the best way he could do it in public. "As sure as God's in Gloucestershire," the proverb says. Well, I've unearthed some pretty queer tales which show that the Almighty can't have been very happy about some of the houses built for him.'

'Not only that,' he went on. 'Someone ought to tell the truth about the medieval craftsmen. They had their gilds as you know, close corporations which were often guilty of the bloodiest tyranny. Our innocent trade unions today don't know the first thing about their jobs. Some of them – the masons especially – had secret societies with a fairly devilish side to them. They were under the special protection of the Church, you see, in their work, and made sure of Heaven at their death, so in their lives they could dabble with impunity in Hell. They might be building a shrine for the Virgin or St Peter, but it was Priapus or Nodens or Vaunus, or some other old Pagan miscreant that often inspired their work. You can find it here and in many other places – there's a spirit in the stone, a spirit of black malice and blood and cynical mockery. They were queer lads, some of those old masons, and they have left behind them something which is not quite dead. Often their work speaks to me, and what it says scares me. So when I read rhapsodies about the Ages of Faith, and the consecration of the old builders, and their gentle ribaldry which belongs only to people who are assured in their faith, I'm inclined to laugh. I know too much about the merry masons.'

That night, I remember, Barnes buried himself in family papers which he was trying to put into some order, for the Lacey muniment room had been neglected. It was a chilly evening and we sat in two new armchairs before a blazing fire, in what I suppose had once been the withdrawing-room behind the dining-hall and was now the library. I was re-reading *Guy Mannering* for the tenth time, and he had a pile of documents beside him on the floor from which he was making notes. He had another pile on an adjacent table, which he would often get up to consult, and he had a vast family tree opened out on another table to which he added pencil jottings. His occupation made him a restless companion, especially as he kept frowning and muttering to himself as if he were being constantly puzzled.

'What's shortness of breath?' he suddenly asked me.

'The thing we all die of,' I said.

'I know. But why should anyone want to set down that as the cause of death? It's foolish tautology – like saying a man died because he ceased to live.'

'Not worse than heart failure,' I said, 'and that's a common finding of the doctors.'

'No. Heart failure is a specific thing. It means that there is something organically wrong with the heart. But shortness of breath! Unless something like asthma is meant. But I don't see . . .'

'What have you got there?' I asked.

'I've been trying to find out what my forebears died of, the few who happened to die in their beds. And "shortness of bryth" spelled in twenty different ways, seems to have been their favourite affliction. It must mean some definite disease, like asthma or lung trouble. But I don't see how it could have been that either, for apparently it took them suddenly. Here is Giles Lacey, who was one of the strongest men of his time, and Henry VIII's favourite boon companion. He carries all before him in the tilt-yard in London, comes back here, and forthwith dies of shortness of breath. Don't tell me that a fellow who could clear the lists in plate armour that must have weighed a ton was a consumptive. His nephew Christopher was one of Raleigh's men, and a sun-dried, whipcord mariner. Same thing happened to him after he had ridden from Plymouth in thirty hours, which must have been a fairish achievement. Sir John Lacey came here after Naseby to hide, and was dead in two days of the same ailment. There's a funny sentence in his brother's letter about him. "Poor Jack," he says, "hath scaped the sword of the godly and the stranger to be the prey of his familiar devils." Now, what on earth did he mean by that?'

'It looks like some disease in the blood,' I said.

'It does,' he replied. 'But what could it be that carried off strong men without warning in the prime of their strength?'

I told him that there were very odd ailments in older days. 'Could it have been some pestilence that lingered in this valley?' I suggested. 'Or in this house?'

He was clear that it could not have been in the valley. The place, he said, was about the healthiest in England; he had made inquiries and there was never any legend of maladies in the village. He thought much the same about the house. 'It's stuffy, of course,' he said, 'like all very old buildings, but I had it carefully vetted, and there's not a hint of dry rot, and the water is perfectly pure. I daresay that in old days the absence of drains was appalling, but bad plumbing wouldn't kill a strong man in twenty-four hours. Besides, that would have meant a fever, and fever is never mentioned. Only shortness of breath.'

I asked what the later record had been, and was told that the Laceys had left Scaip shortly after the Restoration for Bartleham, in Norfolk, which had come to them by marriage. 'And that's also a queer thing,' he said. 'They were great sportsmen and mad about hunting and fowling. Bartleham was quite a little place till it was added to in the time of George III, and it lies in a dull unsporting county, whereas Scaip had everything that a sportsman could wish. But once they migrated they never returned here, except on a short visit, though they saw that it didn't fall into disrepair. They never let it, either – perhaps they couldn't find a tenant. Another thing – at Bartleham there seems to have been no more shortness of breath. They took to perishing of surfeits and apoplexies and paralytic strokes and such-like Christian diseases. I'd give a good deal to know what ailed them at Scaip.'

As I went to bed in my powdering-closet I puzzled a little over Barnes' tale and concluded that his ancestors had probably suffered from some form of congenital epilepsy. But what stuck in my memory were his words that afternoon at Fanways, and I wondered in what kind of spirit my beloved Borrowby had been built. I had a sort of nightmare about it, for I saw myself on Borrowby lawn surrounded by a host of little men with trowels and mallets, horrid red-eyed fellows, who leered at me and sang 'Ho, the merry masons'.

Next day we motored over to Coldbrook to the local point-to-point. I had been keeping horses there and hunting regularly that winter, and had entered a mare for the Hunt Cup. I am not much of a performer over the sticks, and had ridden in few races except in the Bar Point-to-Point, but since I was settling in the neighbourhood I thought I might as well do the thing thoroughly. The course was an easy one, in good condition, and I was getting on nicely, till the second time round, at the second fence from the finish, I was cannoned into by a half-witted undergraduate. The consequence was a bad take-off, and a most hearty spill. I didn't quite roll clean, and got kicked by the mare just above my left eye.

As is usual in a concussion, I remembered nothing after the moment we lined up for the start. I was unconscious for about half an hour and came to myself in the kitchen of an adjacent farmhouse, where the local doctor was preparing to sew up the cut. It was deep, right down to the bone, but the skull was unharmed, and he promised me a good recovery if I would lie up for a week. Barnes was in a great fuss and wanted to get a nurse, but the doctor told him that the case was simple and that all I needed was quiet. 'Scaip's the very place for him,' he said. 'Thick walls and not a railway whistle or a motor-horn within hearing. He'll probably have a headache for twenty-four hours and then feel as fit as a fiddle. No. There's no dope for that kind of headache. He must grin and bear it.'

Barnes took me home at a snail's pace, and decided that I must have the new guest-room on the terrace, so as to avoid the steep stairs. So about six o'clock I found myself in a great four-post bed, with a fire crackling on the hearth, and the windows filled with the green April twilight. I was given a light dinner and told to go to sleep as soon as possible, since I must neither read nor talk. Barnes's butler, a man called Thistle, attended to me and, since there was no electric light at Scaip, he put matches and a couple of candlesticks on the bedside table. There was also an electric bell with its own battery. He informed me that he slept two storeys above me, but that Mr Lacey had experimented and that the bell could easily be heard in his room. The doctor was coming first thing in the morning, and his chief injunction was that I was to keep perfectly still.

My feeling, I remember, when he left me was one of great comfort and peace. I did not regret my accident, for I would have a few quiet days for reflection, and I had too few of such spells in my life. I lay for a little with both candles burning, watching a small corner of the ceiling, which was all I could see because of the bed curtains. The plastering was new and an admirable piece of work, but everything else in the room was hoar-ancient. The walls with their dark panelling were in gloom, broken only at one point by the glow of the fire. I had the fancy that the tiny bit of plaster moulding I could see was my one link with the familiar world, and that for the rest I had been snatched back into the deep comforting shadows of the past. It was what I hoped to achieve at Borrowby, and I blew out the light with a pleasant sense of bodily and spiritual well-being.

The doctor was wrong. I had no headache, but I had the most devastating dreams. I fell asleep at once, but it was not proper sleep for I seemed to remain half-conscious of my environment. I was having a long argument with a solicitor, one of my best clients, who insisted on keeping his face hidden. That I remember, for I had heard that he had shaved his beard and wanted to see what he looked like, but he obstinately evaded me. The place seemed to be my Temple chambers, but it was also Scaip, and at one end was the choir of the Fanways church. Presently I woke feeling outraged, for the solicitor was cocking snooks at me – I saw his hands and was exasperated because I could not see more of him.

I lay awake for a little, telling myself that this was the kind of thing I might expect after a concussion. My bodily comfort had gone, and I felt restless and rather hot. The fire had sunk to one red coal.

In my second dream there could be no doubt about the place. I was in the Scaip guest-room, and, though there was no light anywhere and the windows were shuttered, I could see it clearly. The bed had gone and also the furniture; the chamber was perfectly bare, and, what is more, it did not seem to be quite finished. There was a hole where the fireplace should have been, and above it, instead of panelling, a patch of wet mortar. I disliked the place intensely, disliked it and dreaded it in the irrational way one has in dreams. But at the same time I knew I was dreaming. Though I could not see myself I was aware that I was lying somewhere in the room. I was even aware that I had had an accident and must not move – otherwise I wanted to get up and go away.

And then, suddenly, I was aware of something else in the room, which I could feel, but could not see. It was somewhere near the hole which should have been the fireplace. My eyes, in the dream, saw nothing; but my mind received the impression of something menacing and horrible. I saw no movement, but all the same I was certain that the presence was advancing towards me. Terror awoke me, and I found my bandaged forehead damp with sweat.

I lit a candle with shaking fingers, and there was the corner of new plaster-work on the ceiling and all around the silent shadows. I was having an abominable night, and I had a childish longing to ring the bell merely for the sight of Thistle's honest features. But I resisted the impulse and forced myself to lie still on my back, while I repeated all the cheerful poetry I remembered. I went over the details of the library I was fitting up at Borrowby, and by and by I fell asleep again.

This time I had the worst nightmare of all. I was still in the room, but now I could see nothing whatsoever. Darkness, like thick black velvet, muffled the air. But I could hear, and what I heard was a faint tapping, like the sound of a mason's mallet. Steadily, rhythmically, it continued, and sometimes it was accompanied by a hollow sound, as if the worker was beating on the rim of some cavity. I had the impression that the space round me was becoming constricted; that if I stretched out my hands I might touch raw stone and wet mortar. This time I had no subconscious awareness that it was a dream. It seemed to me an awful reality, and I did not dare to put out an arm to make the test, for I believed that in a minute I should want all my strength to fight off a burden that would suffocate me ...

And then, in the dark, the lineaments of a face slowly took shape. I remember nothing about it except that it was the face of a human being in the last agonies. The mouth was open, the eyes protruding, the cheeks livid, the veins on the forehead black and swollen. It did not menace me, but it made me suffer with it. I felt a clutch at my throat and a ton's weight on my chest, and I awoke gasping.

I was terrified – I freely admit it – but I think my discomfort was more of body than of mind. For my difficulty in breathing did not end with the nightmare. I was lying broad awake, and I had the same horrible constriction of breath that I had had in my dreams. I lit a candle and decided that the trouble was the curtains of the four-poster and the heavy windows. Yet the bed-curtains had been looped up high, and I remembered that Thistle at my request had opened the upper part of the windows.

I had a struggle not to ring the bell. What prevented me was the thought that all this might be the result of my accident. I had never had a concussion before, and this one might be behaving according to form. That reflection did a good deal to lessen my fright, but it did not make my breath more comfortable. I seemed to be shut up in a chest, and was gasping like a fish out of water. The air I inhaled did not fill my lungs, and my heart was fluttering wildly, just like a man suffering from claustrophobia. But I took a pull on myself and managed to keep quiet till I became a little easier. I was resolved not to fall asleep, for I was in terror of seeing that livid, tortured face again.

But the upshot was that towards morning I did fall asleep and had no further dreams. I woke to find the candles burned down to their sockets, and Thistle undoing the curtains and letting in the light of the spring morning. He expressed the hope that I had had a good night, as he set my early tea beside me.

The doctor came after breakfast and was very displeased with me. He re-did my bandages and informed me that my temperature was up. 'What have you been doing with yourself?' he asked. 'No headache, you say? But you have got quite a lot of fever. How did you sleep?'

I told him that I had had the most infernal nightmares.

'That's odd,' he said. 'You're a strong man, suffering from nothing but a clean hole in your head and a slight concussion. Last night you were the perfect patient, and this morning you are all to bits. You haven't anything to worry you by any chance?'

When I told him that my conscience was clear, he answered that he would call in in the evening and, if necessary, give me a sedative. The temperature, he expected, would go down during the day.

It did, but I had a very disturbed time for all that. It was glorious weather, and through the open window came the spring scents and the sun, and the sound of birds and sheep. Barnes sat with me for most of the morning, and read me the newspaper. Thistle brought me admirable meals, at which I only pecked. The trouble was that I was wrestling with cowardice. I was in a blind funk of another night in that room, and longed to ask Barnes to move me back to my old powdering-closet, and at the same time I was heartily ashamed of myself.

I never spent a more miserable day. I was certain that I had no fever, and after luncheon I had a couple of hours of quiet sleep. Barnes had tea with me and complimented me on my obedience to doctor's orders. The doctor came about six and was better pleased with me. He was willing to give me some sort of mild dope, but I refused, for I had a notion that I mustn't sleep soundly, for if I did I might be caught by the gaping, agonised face.

The weather all day had been still and fine, but about twilight there came a brisk April shower. It stirred up all sorts of echoes in the old house. The wind sang in the chimney, and the raindrops pattered on the terrace and drifted against the window panes. To my ear there was a tune in the place, a jigging dance tune with an odd wild catch in it. Now, as you know, I am the most unmusical creature on God's earth, but I have a good memory for airs – the rudiments of them, for I get the details all wrong. You remember Summerfield, who was the great authority on old folk music and published several collections. Well, Summerfield used to play some of his discoveries to me on a flute or a penny whistle, and one took my fancy. When I asked about it he looked wise. 'That's witch music,' he said. 'I had the devil of a job to find it, and there are places in England and Wales even today where the old folk wouldn't let you even hum it. If you started it in a public-house, the tap-room would empty. Heaven knows what antique devilry was at the making of it.'

Well, it seemed to me that I was hearing Summerfield's tune somewhere in the joists and the panelling. It had a good effect on me, for it made me ashamed of my babyishness. I told myself angrily that I was behaving like a fool, and the result was that I screwed up my resolution. Once for all I would put this nonsense outside my mind. When Thistle brought me my dinner I was quite cheerful, and told him that I was feeling better. But before he tucked me up for the night I bade him leave the curtains undrawn and open the windows at the bottom, though he protested that it was early April and the night might be chilly. I also bade him leave the door ajar which opened on to the terrace. The room was in a projecting buttress of the house, and the terrace door opened at the side into an alcove which was shielded from the wind, so there was no question of draughts. I gave these orders – at least, so I told myself – not because I was any longer nervous, but because I believed that somehow the place got unbearably stuffy during the night.

I lay for some time in a fairly comfortable mood, watching the fire which flickered in the light airs that blew from the windows, and the gently shaken curtains, and the window squares which were ebony dark before moonrise. Slowly, I must have drifted into sleep, and the first hour or two must have been peaceful. I know that from the timing of what happened later, for the moon did not rise till nearly midnight.

When I began to dream I was conscious only of a deep unhappiness. There was no fright in it, but the bottom seemed to have dropped out of everything and left an aching emptiness. I knew where I was – with my mind, for I saw nothing with my eyes. I was in Scaip, and Scaip was a shrine of the uttermost sorrow. I felt, so acutely that it seemed like ice in my veins, the misery of life. I am a cheerful being and never in my days had I known anything like it. Wave upon wave of abysmal distress seemed to flow over me and paralyse me.

And then a form of words began to run in my brain. I traced them afterwards – they were from one of Lord Rosebery's perorations about the Empire. 'Cemented with men's blood and tears' – a harmless platitude you will say. But, as they came to me out of the void, they were like a dreadful incantation. They sharpened my consciousness of my environment, for they were the voice of the walls that surrounded me. I knew I was in a place which had been built out of the heart of darkness. The mortar had been wet with tears and blood, and death had plied the mallets.

Suddenly, I seemed to be looking into a gulf of unimaginable evil. I say 'unimaginable', for it bore no relation to the world I knew. It was something that had rotted in the hoary past and on which God had mercifully shut the door. It was only an impression you understand – I remember no details, only the blank, heavy cloud of horror. Things had been wrought here – in these walls and in this room – which came from the nether Pit, things aeons removed from the common trivial wickedness of mankind. The weight of them suffocated my mind and senses, and, though my soul shuddered at them, my body and will were atrophied and I could only sink – sink.

I woke to find myself stifling. Not my mind, but my body. There was no weight on my chest, no clutch at my throat, but I simply could not breathe. Honest fear galvanised my impotence. I fumbled for the electric bell, and tried to press the button, but there was no strength in my fingers. I put my knuckles on it, but my fist seemed to have become as frail as gossamer.

I was now in the uttermost panic. Somehow or other I rolled out of bed, and lay gasping on the floor. The moon was up, and I saw the windows as squares of light. If I could reach them I might breathe free air.

I crawled towards an open sash – reached it – and found no comfort. Outside was the quiet moonlit night and a green hill with sheep on it. If I could clamber over the sill I knew I could breathe, but I was too weak for that. The terrible room had me in its clutches. It made a curtain of suffocation beyond which I could not penetrate, though only an inch or two separated me from freedom.

I felt that I was dying, that in a few seconds more I should be a corpse on the floor... There was a thin streak of moonlight at the terrace door which Thistle had left ajar. I struggled towards that, as a drowning man struggles towards a life-belt. Of that awful moment I have no clear memory, but I must have reached the door, for when Thistle opened it he found me at the threshold.

Yes, the bell had rung somehow, and Thistle says he skipped down at once. There cannot have been more than a few minutes between my waking and his finding me ... They took me to the cottage hospital, for I couldn't have stayed in that house another hour. As it was, I was a sick man for most of the summer, not the concussion, which never troubled me, but an odd kind of low fever which puzzled the doctors.

'Explanation?' Leithen said, when he had finished his tale. 'You may take any you like, for I have none. You may say that it was the result of a crack on the head combined with a peculiar nervous system, though I've never considered myself neurotic. You may take Hurrell's view, that I was chosen by Providence to be the spark that fired some old devilry that was built into the walls of Scaip.'

'What became of Lacey?' Peckwether asked.

'Dead. He gave up Scaip in the same year as my story – said the place did not suit his health – and went to live in Cornwall. Scaip had no tenant till poor Thomasson leased it last autumn. If I could prevent it, it wouldn't have another.'

Leithen answered the unspoken question in Hurrell's eye.

'Yes. I mean that. I went over there yesterday, as I've told you. Thomasson occupied the terrace room, the one I had. He died in it. The doctor called it heart failure, which no doubt it was in the end. But something came before – shortness of breath.'